Blood Influence

I C Lawrance

Copyright © I C Lawrance 2021
Published: 2021 by The Book Reality Experience

**

ISBN: 978-1-922670-04-5 - Paperback Edition
ISBN: 978-1-922670-05-2 - eBook Edition

All rights reserved.

The right of I C Lawrance to be identified as author of this Work has been asserted by him in accordance with sections 77 and 78 of the
Copyright, Designs and Patents Act 1988.

This book is a work of fiction and any resemblance to actual persons, living or dead, is purely coincidental.

No part of this publication may be reproduced, stored in a retrieval system, copied in any form or by any means, electronic, mechanical, photocopying, recording or otherwise transmitted without written permission from the publisher. You must not circulate this book in any format.

Cover Design by Luke Buxton | www.lukebuxton.com

To Mark

Without whom I would never have started and whose insight took us to places I didn't expect.

Chapter 1

It really was a beautiful view. The sun, low in the western sky, created long shadows that stretched from the Western Slopes, putting the Bowl into a relief that allowed for a better appreciation of the land. The fading light highlighted its beauty and showed off the sheer, snow-capped mountains that encircled a country of fertile fields and rich pastures. She granted the scene a moment of contemplation before *it* had to be done.

How long she had been here, she did not know, but it was much longer than anyone could want. It had not been a choice to come. No-one would choose to come here. There never was a choice – once you had been selected it was inevitable. You weren't even aware that you were being selected until it was done, and you were brought here to the Tower. Left here in this dark and lonely place, to find a way to endure or fail.

Confined to the dark. In this place, and in the dark. A darkness that subtly shifted between a cold, lifeless grey, and the inky blackness of a tomb. The sun, light, wind, and sky were removed and replaced by a still, breathless air that was chilled by the smooth black stone that surrounded her. Days were no longer marked by the dawn or the moon. The passage of time was noted only by the appearance of meagre rations of food and water, further punctuated by the requirements of bodily functions and the necessity of sleep – such as it was, filled with shapes and dreams that were as vivid as the torments of the waking hours.

What she remembered was fading. She knew that there had to be so much more where those memories used to be, but now all she knew was the darkness of the Tower. As everything about her and who she had been became less distinct, less clear, like the impressions left of a dream after waking, the Tower became firmer and stronger. The Tower was becoming more present. Who she was, and who she would be.

She remembered being collected and brought to the Tower. She alone had been taken. She could remember voices crying and pleading for her but could no longer see their faces. She assumed they were her family. Her mother, perhaps, or a sister, although she had no memory of either. In the dark she could still remember the sun and the feeling of freedom from having the wind on her face. And now, here at the window, she could once again feel the wind. It was a comfort to her when comfort was all but forgotten. She did not mourn – how could she mourn people she no longer remembered or a life that no longer left its mark? Her world now consisted of the Tower and nothing more.

Once up the stairs and through the great entrance, the door had closed, removing the outside world and leaving her alone with the dark and what it held. Throughout her time here there had only been contact with one other being. One that she feared, although it appeared infrequently. Each time it came, things got worse; but still, she longed for it to come so that she would not have to be alone. To know that there was someone or something else, even if it caused her harm.

It came to test her. If she failed, she would lose a bit more of herself to the Tower. To succeed was to gain some of that back. Time and again it came, and time and again she had to endure the suffering.

She knew that she was failing more often now and that eventually she would fade completely. What it was that made her *her* would no longer exist and she would be fully part of the Tower. To never again have a thought of her own. Never more to feel or hope or wish. In a place like this, that could be a comfort. Still, right now, enough of herself remained to hope for a way out, a way to avoid losing herself completely to the Tower. To hope for freedom.

In the dark she had stayed for so long, wandering circular halls and winding passages. Only now had she found the stairs which wound up and up, such a long way up. In almost complete darkness she had climbed, resting at intervals until she arrived. Here, in a circular chamber halfway up the Tower, there was a single window looking out to the west. Looking out, out of the Tower. Why had she not found this before? Perhaps she had but could not remember. Here she had a way to reclaim herself. This, she felt, was her last chance. One more visit from the being and she would lose herself completely, trapped forever by the Tower. There may be more time to do this, or perhaps not; she could not tell.

It was time.

Seated on the windowsill, feet hanging freely over the space between her and the land below, she fixed her eyes on the sun as it gradually set behind the

Western Slopes. She felt the wind on her face and embraced it as a friend. Feeling more herself than she had since she began to forget, she leant forward and looked down. At least for the briefest of moments she could be free. Free of the darkness and free of the Tower before it would not matter anymore. That was freedom, that was hope, and that would be her victory.

Raising her head to the last of the light, she pushed forward with her arms and felt the air encompass her. Enfolded in the rushing wind, she fell.

***

Angus just remembered that he had to deliver the tonic tonight. Maima had been preparing it all day and had been insistent that it must be taken while it was still fresh.

"It works best if taken as soon as it is complete. Delays will just make things worse for her, so take it tonight and make sure that she drinks it all. Tell her that then she must fast till morning. It will be ready by the time you get back."

And so, despite being tired after finishing the rest of the deliveries, he still had to make one last trip before supper. There was no use complaining as it had to be done. Maima was attending a difficult birth in one of the poorer areas of Town and so it was up to him. After putting on his cap he carefully wrapped up the small, lidded bowl, making sure that none of the liquid could escape. This delivery would take him a bit out of his normal paths. He had to make his way into the "better" parts of Town where the important families lived.

The sun was heading behind the Western Slopes by the time he set out. Looking ahead, he saw Town creeping up the lower parts of the Eastern Slopes. It contracted more and more as it climbed the slopes until it stopped at the foot of the Tower. The last of the sun's rays illuminated both the slopes and the Tower. But, while the mountains glowed with a rosy tinge, the Tower stood as a black silhouette, seemingly absorbing the light, reflecting nothing.

Heading off, Angus hoped that Maima would be back before him, as he would like a hot supper. He knew that if she was not then it was going to be reasonably poor fare. He would have to muddle something together that didn't require cooking. He might have to get Maima to teach him to cook. He had to prepare his own meals more frequently now and, although he would never admit it to his friends, cooking was a skill that he thought all should learn, not just the women.

At fifteen, Angus was not yet sure what it was that he wanted to do. Maima was insistent on book learning. It did not come naturally to him, but he persisted. None of his friends could read. They never had the chance. There were none, apart from Maima — and now, of course, him — who could in their area of Town. Reading had been, and remained, the domain of the well-to-do. It was the province of the powerful and was not something that they were likely to relinquish.

"Books," Maima said, "are the foundation of what I do. Without them I would be as helpless as all the rest. What help I can provide comes from my books. It is the lack of understanding that keeps the lowly low and those without hope hopeless."

And this was true as far as Angus could see. Maima's learning was able to give some ease to those who were sick. It prevented injury in difficult situations and limited further damage when things went wrong. She was the one person always called upon. At any hour, day or night, she could be relied upon to provide help. Those she helped would use what wealth they had as payment. There was bread from the baker or fruits from the grocer. Where there was less to spare, goodwill was even more bountiful. Maima and Angus were, therefore, continually cradled by a multitude in a sea of gratitude and love. There were certainly worse ways of living and so Angus had persisted. By learning to read he gained a deeper understanding of the world that surrounded them.

Walking up into the better parts of Town revealed the benefits that wealth provided. These become more marked the further he went. The roads become wider, paved with cobblestones instead of being bare, compacted soil, allowing easy travel regardless of the weather. Here, the dwellings were sturdier, more permanent, with private land separated from public areas by walls. Further on the dwellings become larger and more elaborate, in proportion to the ever-higher walls surrounding them. Eventually, only the wall was visible, and one could merely assume that there was a house somewhere beyond the barricade. It was to one of these estates that Angus made his way.

Arriving at a small gate, way off to the side from the ornate main entrance, Angus gave several quick taps. A face appeared through the open panel. Explaining the purpose of his visit, Angus was quickly escorted to the kitchens, where he was expected. Cook had been ill for a week, suffering severe stomach cramps and nausea. For Cook this was unpleasant. However, if she did not provide sufficient numbers of quality dishes on a daily basis then things could get so much worse. Not only for her but all her staff. The family did not care who prepared their food, or at what cost; only that the food was to their taste and ready when wanted.

If Cook was unable to cook the ire of the family would hit them all. Not only those in the kitchen, but all the servants, from the highest to the lowest.

Such was the urgency that the chief steward himself had visited Maima that morning pleading for something to cure Cook. After he had related her symptoms as best he could, Maima had prepared a tonic in the hope it would aid recovery. Presenting the tonic, Angus repeated Maima's instructions, making sure Cook drank it all before reclaiming the bowl. He was then quickly ushered out of the house and grounds by those anxious for the family to remain oblivious to his visit.

Once again outside in the street, Angus looked about. The sky was almost dark as he started his way home. The area was unfamiliar, and in the low light he mistook where he was and made a wrong turn. He found himself reaching the very edge of Town where the houses ceased and the rough, rocky ground of the Eastern Slopes had yet to be tamed. He had no cause for concern. As long as he headed down the slope he would reach the lower parts of Town, and from there he was certain that he would easily recognise where he was and make it home without incident. It was then that he felt something. A gnawing in his stomach that told him that there was something not right. From experience he knew not to ignore the feeling, so he stopped and listened.

***

She fell, out of the Tower and free. A million thoughts and sensations surrounded her: all competing, and all important. Foremost, however, was a feeling of hope, something she had almost lost in the Tower. She felt hope that there could be something, anything, apart from the Tower. She now had a wish to live, knowing that the Tower could be escaped.

Time slowed.

She could see the sun almost hidden by the western mountains. She could hear the wind rushing by her ears like a roar, cheering her freedom. She could feel the air as it cascaded over her skin, bringing it to life with desire. Air was her element. It was life and now it could save her.

Concentrate. Feel. Weave. I can do this. I can create. The Tower was wrong, I am not destined to fail. There's so much to do and now is the time to do it. I am not going to end here. I can be more.

Looking into herself and accepting who she truly was, that was the key. Not to fight her central essence, but to be at home with who she was and not be in conflict. She had tried so hard but failed, again and again. Now she knew her hurts and desires and, also, her strengths. Now was the time to acknowledge and accept them and then be who she needed to be. This time, she had to. She still had time. To fall took only moments, but to be truly herself, as time stood still, could take an eternity. In this space she must accept. Letting her mind go blank she opened herself to just *feel*. Not to think. Just to feel, and create.

Slowly, carefully, she started to weave, taking parts of the air about her, folding it, compressing it. She could feel it respond. Like water it flowed. It was erratic but she needed it to be controlled, to answer her and her need. Taking the air from around her, she placed parts on top of others, holding them together and constricting the way they moved. She compressed them into a blanket beneath her. More and more sections were placed with the others, held together by energy. Energy that came from her, from the very core of who she was. Any fear and any doubt could now cause it all to come apart.

Feel, don't think. Just do.

Time crept forward and she could feel herself slowing in the fall. It took great effort and was severely taxing her strength. Slowing was good, but she was still falling too fast. She knew that she would not be able to slow her fall sufficiently in time. Below her was the gravel and craggy rocks of the Eastern Slopes in front of the Tower and just out of Town. Hitting that at her current speed would still be a victory of sorts. She had escaped the Tower, but this was no longer what she desired.

Time began to speed up. Still too fast: she had not yet done enough. In one last desperate act of survival, she expelled all her remaining strength into the compressed air beneath her, filling every space with the energy from her core. With nothing left to give she fell, limp and barely conscious. The ground raced toward her, ready to welcome her with its earthy embrace.

As the airy blanket hit the ground it exploded in all directions. Outwards and upwards, the compressed air regained its volume with such power it caused the scrubby vegetation to uproot. Rocks and small boulders were pushed away from the epicentre. It forced her to stop and slightly rise again before falling like a rag doll into the shallow crater it had formed below her. There she lay, flaccid and lifeless on the ground. Out of the Tower and free of its grasp.

***

A great, crashing roar came from outside the town. It caused Angus to stop and stare into the low light off to the north. After a few moments a strong rushing wind, carrying bits of sticks and gravel, hit him in the face. It subsided as quickly as it came but all the crickets and other evening callers were now silent. There was no breeze, no sound, and no explanation.

No-one else was on this path but Angus. The Town's workers followed the sun. When it retreated, so did they. Into their homes, soon off to bed to be ready for another early rise. Thus, it was Angus alone who was witness to this strange event, and his decision alone to shrug it off or explore.

Maima had tried to instil curiosity into her son. Although he had found book learning a trial, he possessed a childlike inquisitiveness, particularly when there may be some adventure. He had found that adventure was not a too-common occurrence, and thus any possibility of it should not be ignored. So, with little thought, and a lot of interest, Angus made his way out of Town and onto the Eastern Slopes as the evening settled.

Carefully making his way over the rough ground, he headed in the direction of the sound and wind. It probably was a boulder that had raced down the side of the slope, crashing into something larger. Still, a sound like that, followed by a disturbance in the air that carried to Town, would mean that it had been one impressive boulder. It must have made a huge dent in whatever it collided with. In Angus' mind this was certainly worth a look. It also was exciting to be the only one who was investigating. It would make a good story for his friends. Some slight embellishments might be required in order to promote the correct response. Even so, he was sure that he could make it into a great story, with danger and a narrow escape that demonstrated his bravery in times of peril.

It was not easy going and the ground would not keep even. He had to make slight detours around great rocks or take extra time to climb over the smaller ones. Still, he had a good sense of direction and was convinced that he was continuing on the right path. Fortunately, the moon rose early that night and provided some much-needed light.

After not too long a time Angus started to notice the presence of freshly uprooted plants scattered around the rocks. Pleased that he had been able to maintain the proper course, he slowed in order to pinpoint the area of impact. He continued, following the increasing concentration of destruction. It was obvious that something had hit with great force. He was excited to see what had happened. Progressing further, he reached a circular area of windswept gravel that was cleared of any vegetation. In the clearing lay a blackened heap.

The light was poor and it was impossible to make out any features. It looked strange. It was a pure, deep black that reflected none of the moonlight and was located right at the centre of the destruction. Approaching carefully, Angus put out his hand and touched it. To his surprise it was smooth, soft and pliable. Not hard and rock-like as he had expected. Leaning down he pulled at the material, revealing the face of a young blonde girl, unconscious and pale. Surprised and unsure what to do, Angus thought of Maima. What would she do in a time of crisis? Remembering that she would always check for injuries, he pulled back the cloak further to look for any blood. Under the robe she was dressed in a similar black tunic. Not seeing any obvious blood, he wondered what else to do.

She hasn't moved. Perhaps she's dead. Maima would always check but, not sure how, Angus just yelled at her. "Hello, hi, are you alright?"

This prompted no answer. A second attempt also failed to provoke a response. Grabbing her shoulder, he gave her a shake. Her head lolled to the side but her eyes did not open. She felt cold to the touch. Colder than anyone should. Still unsure what had happened, and not knowing what he needed to do to help, he decided that the best he could do for her was to get her to Maima as fast as he could. She would know what was needed.

Placing one arm under her back and the other under her legs, he lifted her gently off the ground. Fortunately, he was almost full-grown but, still, there seemed almost nothing to her. She was so light. So frail and light, strange, and yet with a face that he knew he would never be able to forget. Making care to cause as little discomfort as possible he started to make his way back to Town. Surprisingly, this took less time than he expected. All too soon, yet perhaps not soon enough, he was striding down the road into the lower parts of Town. He made his way straight home, hoping that Maima had finished delivering the baby and was already there.

Chapter 2

Angus paced. Maima had not been home when they arrived, so he had placed the girl in his bed and covered her with blankets. Her pale skin was still icy to the touch and she had made no sound throughout the journey home, nor since they had been there. Not knowing what else to do, he boiled water over the fire. This seemed to be something that he remembered was often needed when Maima was working. Still waiting, he continued to pace.

After a time that seemed to last forever, he heard the door of their cottage open. Leaving the small bedroom, he immediately went to find Maima. She looked tired after what must have been a difficult birth. Before she could even sit, Angus pulled her into his room. Looking surprised, she went to the bed and bent over the girl. After carefully examining her, she turned to Angus and with a weak smile nodded and said, "She's alive. Barely breathing, but she is alive. Go and make a hot compress with the water you boiled and leave me to examine her more fully."

Pleased that he had a task to do Angus hurried off, only entering the room again after he was sure that the examination had been completed. Looking expectantly at his mother, he waited.

"She needs rest and warmth. We will just have to wait, but she is young and I could not find any injuries. What happened?" she asked.

Angus related the events of the evening, giving account of all that drew him to finding the girl. Maima listened attentively, pausing him on one occasion to have him more fully describe the sound he heard and the wind that followed.

"Who do you think she is?" he asked. "And how do you think she got there?"

"Who she is, that I don't know. We will have to wait for her to tell us. These robes, however, they tell a very strange story. They are not something we often see. I doubt that there are many here who have ever seen the like or, if they have, would want to talk about it."

"Maima, what do you mean? You're being unclear."

"Did you not look at the robes? Surely you saw them?" she asked.

"Yes, they are black and … soft."

"My dear, have you ever seen such as these before? Did you not notice that they are more than just black? That the light does not reflect off them? They seem to absorb it, releasing nothing."

"I almost didn't see her," he responded.

"Mmm, and what else did you notice?"

"That she was where the sound came from."

"I think that she came from the Tower. I don't ever remember hearing of anyone leaving the Tower unless it was in order to collect another and go back," Maima mused.

"But what does that mean, Maima?"

"I wish I knew. But at the moment she needs our help so we will just have to wait and see."

"I will stay and watch," Angus offered.

Maima nodded. "You will need to keep her warm, so go make some hot packs with the coals from the fire and put them under the blankets. I will stay with her until they're done. After that, watch her, but let me know as soon as she stirs. We don't know who she is or what has happened. There is more to this, I expect, than just a girl who needs our help."

After he returned Maima left to get some supper organised while Angus stood and looked at the girl. Now that he had been assured that she was alive he went over to the bed. Pushing the black hood further away from her face, he brushed the long blonde hair from her cheek. He gazed at the pretty girl who lay unconscious on his bed. Watching carefully, he saw a slight parting of her lips as a gentle breath was drawn in. He sighed, went and got a chair, placed it next to the bed, and sat down. He would be close in case he was needed.

Angus was determined to stay up and watch and so, after supper, Maima brought in a small lamp to give some light to the room before retiring to bed. Sleep, however, often comes far too easily for the young even when they are distressed. So it was with Angus, who awoke halfway through the night, uncomfortable in the chair. In the dim light he saw, but more felt and heard, movement in the bed. The girl was squirming. She looked uncomfortable and distressed but made no other sound. Angus placed his hand gently on her shoulder, making reassuring noises. The movements quietened and her breathing slowed, becoming deeper and more regular. Leaving his hand there, he felt slightly happier that she was starting to show more signs of life.

Morning came as it always does, bringing with it an end to both the restless and the peaceful nights' slumber. As the light crept though the shutters of Angus' room, the girl started to stir once again. The slow, calm movements of someone gradually waking, however, progressively became more fragmented and frantic. Angus again attempted to calm these with a light touch, but this time with no effect. The girl's breathing increased as she flung her head from side to side. Kicking off the blankets she started making a soft, terrified wail.

Trying to hold her down so that she would not hurt herself, Angus called out to Maima to come quickly. Fighting against his restraint the girl kicked harder, flinging her arms about as if trying to ward off something. Hearing movement outside the door, Angus turned his head to see Maima opening the door. Just as he did the girl's eyes clicked fully open. Seeing, but not yet understanding, the girl let out a scream of terror that tore the air. As if hit by a crashing wave, Angus saw a blinding flash of light emanate from the bed, and he was thrown back across the room, hitting the wall with a crunch before sliding to the floor. Maima immediately raced across the room to the bed, placing both hands on the girl's forehead and, with closed eyes, started to chant. In an instant the girl relaxed, ceased her thrashing, and closed her eyes as if asleep. Angus, dazed on the floor, watched with amazement as colours engulfed his mother and disappeared into the girl as she relaxed.

Leaving the girl, Maima reached Angus as he was starting to rise. Reassuring her that he was generally unharmed, he looked intently first at her and then at the girl. Before he could speak, Maima led him out of the bedroom, sat him in the kitchen and said, "She is safe and, for the time being, will sleep."

Preparing them both a cup of tea, Maima sat down on the other side of the table and looked at her son. "The Tower has had more to do with us than you are aware." She spoke softly. "As you know, your father and I were not long together. Circumstances pulled us apart and he was taken from me … from us. What you don't know is how or why."

Pausing, she took a sip of her tea and continued, "I was once one of those from an estate similar to the one you visited last night. I had books and learning and the privilege that came from a powerful father. As a child, my life had everything. All that I could want. As I grew, however, I saw that there was so much more outside the walls that surrounded my world. As a girl I was not allowed to participate in what went on outside the walls. There were so many people with so much less than me. There was so much need, and I could not help. I was not allowed to change things, to make a difference. I was a prisoner in a beautiful cell, nothing more than a bargaining chip, a jewel to be kept in the box of somebody else. This was not what I wanted. It was not who I was, or who I wanted to be."

Angus, forgetting his tea, listened intently to his mother.

"I met your father," she continued, "one day, by chance. He was handsome and charming, clever and kind … and a carpenter. I was forbidden to consider him. I was not to talk to him or see him. Neither of us could bear this. We were made for each other, and I would not listen to my parents or consider life without him. We loved each other and we found ways to be together. But my parents had me watched and knew that we were still seeing each other. One day there was a visitor to our estate. One that came as night was falling. They were like the night, dressed in black and almost invisible in the dimming light. They were dressed like this girl."

Pausing once again she took another sip and recommenced speaking, slowing as she remembered the past. "That visitor stayed only a short time to talk with my parents. What they spoke of, I don't know, but after that I never saw your father again." Her voice cracked with emotion. "I knew that they did something to him, my parents and the visitor from the Tower. No-one would speak to me about it, but it was the Tower that took him from us."

Giving a deep sigh and then a smile, Maima continued, "By that time I was already carrying you, but it was still very early days. I knew that if my parents found out about you then there would be another visit from the Tower, and I could not risk that. I had to get away. So, with just what I could carry and a few things to sell on the way, I fled. We would not be safe so close to my parents so I bought passage as far out of Town as I could. I arrived alone and scared near the Western Slopes.

"I will be forever grateful to a boy I met there in a small hamlet. Seeing my distress and that I was alone, he spoke to me and took me to his mother for help. Without even knowing the truth about me but just that I was in need, they took me in and there I stayed until you were born. It was sometime later, when I felt it was safe, that we returned to Town. You were still very young. I came back to learn of the Tower, to find your father, and to stop this ever happening again."

"I don't remember anything before Town," said Angus, "but is she really of the Tower? She doesn't seem like the one you described."

"She is from the Tower, yes, I have no doubt," Maima concluded. "But, no, she does not feel like one of the Tower, and she left the Tower."

Looking towards his room, Angus asked, "What happened in there? I saw a blast of light as I was hurled across the room. Then I saw you covered in colours that moved from you and into her before she slept."

"Mmm," Maima pondered, "that is a lot to answer. I only know a little. I have tried to find out more, with little success. I do have some experience, but not a lot. There is a thing that they call Influence. It is something of a talent that may show itself in girls of about your age, like this girl. Some families have it more than others, but most families will have had something to do with it. The Tower wants these girls, the girls with Influence. I can only guess that they must give it something it wants. The Dark Ones, those in the black robes, come from the Tower and take the girls. Then, for their families, it is as if their daughters never existed. That they were never born. No-one is allowed to speak of them, although they do, in private and only ever in whispers. The girls are never seen again. Never seen again until this one time … with this child."

"Influence?" Angus asked.

"Yes, it is called that. It is different for each. For this child, I think that she may be able to influence the air. I expect that is what kept her alive when she left the Tower and what threw you to the wall."

"But, the colours …"

"Yes, well … There are other Influences. One may be able to change the way a person feels."

"But, Maima, you …"

"Yes, me. It would appear that there are some girls that the Tower does not take or does not want. I only started to notice that I could help somcone sleep better or feel less pain when I was a bit older than you. By placing my hands on them I try to will the pain away. I have to concentrate and I chant to help me focus. It is hard work and I have to be touching them. I have spent my life learning about herbs and plants that can be used in sickness. I use these skills together with my Influence and I try to help those I can. I suppose that the Tower only wants girls with more Influence than I. But I am careful not to openly display my skill. The colours, that is new. I have never heard anything like that before."

"I saw colours surrounding you and go into the girl," he added.

"I saw no flash of light and have never seen these colours. Perhaps you can see Influence. See it as it is working."

"How? I am not a girl. It's never happened before, and I have been with you many times as you work."

"My dear, there is much I know but about Influence I know very little. I do know that some men may very rarely have some ability. I wish I knew more but my books tell me little about it. Most of what I have learnt has been from others, from memories of lost sisters and daughters." Pausing in thought she added, "I know that you have many questions, many things that you want to know, but now we must be careful. The Tower is able to find the girls who have Influence. They come and collect them without warning, arriving at night, unannounced. Today this child is here, and we do not know who will be looking for her or if they already know she is here. We must decide what we should do."

Angus nodded and asked, "But we are still able to help her?"

"Yes, my dear, we can. How much we can do … we will have to see."

***

Waiting is never easy and waiting without knowing what to expect is even worse. Throughout the morning the girl slept. This time peacefully, uncomplicated by fits of distress and watched over by either Maima or Angus. But, work still needed to be done. By the afternoon Angus had finished the round of deliveries and Maima had set out to visit her patients and check on the mother and baby from the night before. Again sitting next to the bed, Angus waited. Slowly, and this time gently, the girl opened her eyes and looked directly at Angus. Seeing him gazing at her intently she gave a small, embarrassed smile.

"How are you feeling?' he asked softly.

"Sore all over but alive, which I suppose is a lot better than I expected," she said with a wry smile.

"Drink this," he said, lifting her head and putting a cup of tonic to her lips. "Maima prepared this for when you awoke. It will help."

After drinking as she was told, she lay back on the pillow and looked about. "How did I get here?"

"I found you outside the town and brought you here last night. This is our cottage. Maima, my mother's, and mine. You have been resting here since."

"Thank you. You are kind."

"No, you needed help. Who would not help?"

"Many, I expect," she responded sadly. "I am fortunate that it was you who found me."

"Who are you? Where did you come from?"

Looking distressed at the questions, she closed her eyes and swallowed.

"We know that you must have come from the Tower," Angus continued. "Your robes told us that. Do not worry, we will be able to help you," he added quickly in order to reassure her.

"I … I … I did come from the Tower. I cannot go back there. I must keep away from it. Far away. I cannot face it again. Please, don't tell the Tower. I beg you. I can't …"

"No, no, we're not telling the Tower. You don't have to go back. We won't let that happen. You are safe here. I am Angus. What is your name?"

"My name? I … I don't know. I can't remember. I had a name, but that was before, before the Tower. I must have had a family too, but I … I … there is nothing there, nothing left of them, nothing I can remember."

Seeing her getting more and more upset as she tried to remember, but recalled nothing, Angus took her hand and held it. "Do not fret, it will come. It takes time. Maima always says that time is the best cure. You rest here. You are safe. Are you hungry? That can help. Can I get you something?"

"No, thank you. I need to rest. Thank you, you are the first kind face I can ever remember seeing."

With that she closed her eyes and gave a soft, sad sigh as she sank deeper into the bedding.

***

Over the next few days Angus and Maima were particularly vigilant, but neither observed anything unusual about their new charge or in the town about them. Jess, the name agreed to by all, gradually recovered her strength and was able to sit out of bed for longer periods each day. Still weak, she moved slowly around the cottage, often assisted by Angus. Whenever he was at home, he was never far away in case he was needed. Despite their curiosity, Maima had insisted that all questions about what had happened could wait until Jess regained her strength.

On the evening of the third day, Jess was strong enough to sit at the table as Maima prepared the supper while they waited for Angus to return. No longer encased in the black robes of the Tower, she instead wore a pretty, flowing dress that was pulled in at the waist of her slim figure. Her long blonde hair was held back from her face by a ribbon and her sweet and delicate features were relaxed and peaceful.

"I cannot tell you how much you have done for me. I cannot remember ever feeling like this. Thank you," she said.

"My dear, you thank us constantly, every morning and every evening. There is no need. It is our joy to see you getting well," Maima replied.

"You have no idea what it means to me. I'm sorry. I just wish there was something I could do to show how much it means." After a pause Jess continued, "I would like to tell you what happened."

"There is no rush."

"I hope not, but I don't know. There are many things I can't remember but I know that the Tower is vile and takes what it wants, without regard or regret. I don't want you to be pressed by the Tower." Taking in a deep breath, Jess continued, "I will need to go when I am able. I will only be a risk to you if I don't."

As she was speaking the door of the cottage opened and Angus entered, carrying something behind his back. Smiling awkwardly, he walked over to Jess and presented a slightly bedraggled bunch of wildflowers. "I found these just outside Town as I was doing my deliveries," he stumbled.

"Thank you, you're sweet," responded Jess, giving him a peck on the cheek as he bent down. Smiling a bit too broadly he stood up again and spoke in a brash voice, "You do not need to go. Where would you go anyway? You do not know who you were or where you are from." He glanced up at Maima. "You can stay here, with us. Isn't that right, Maima?"

"Indeed, my dear. Of course you can."

Tears in her eyes, Jess nodded and smiled. "I would like to," she said, "but I need to tell you about the Tower. I try to remember what happened, but things are not as clear as they were. I have to tell you now or it might be gone. I might forget and … and the Tower … it might come. If you know, then it might help." As she spoke Maima crossed over to the table and cradled Jess' head to her breast, while Angus stood uneasily to the side.

"Don't worry, my dear. We will work this out. But supper first, and then we talk over a nice cup of dandelion tea."

***

Jess' memory was fragmented. She remembered almost nothing from the time before the Tower. Nothing about her family or where she was from. Her first memory was of the great door of the Tower blocking out the light and leaving her alone with her tormentor in the semi-darkness. Time in the Tower meant little. At times it appeared to crawl at a snail's pace, while at others it seemed to jump forward at a great rate. Much of her time there was jumbled and confused.

Most clearly, she remembered being alone. No sound, no breeze, and no evidence of life. Alone she would wander in the sunless space. Moving through windowless halls and cavernous chambers, finding nothing and no-one. Crying out in these spaces gave no comfort as even the echo of her voice was removed before it could return to her. In the cold, silent darkness she would search for something, anything, that would show her that she was not alone. But she would find nothing except meagre amounts of food and water, left at intervals that were neither regular nor predictable. Eventually, she just sat for prolonged periods in the corner of a room and waited. Waiting and listening for anything. She hoped for something, but feared the nothing she found.

Only once did she remember hearing a voice other than her own. Her tormentor never spoke, and the voice she heard was masculine. This spark of humanity in an otherwise inhuman place emboldened her and she raced toward the sound, feeling the air around her pulsating as if she were in a living thing. But as she ran the voice started to fade. Like smoke it appeared to disperse and lose its substance. Then, turning a corner, her way was blocked by her tormentor.

"They are not to be tolerated," it said, turning as the last of the voice evaporated, leaving only silence. Struck with how fully alone she really was, Jess remembered collapsing in a heap. She stayed there until she woke sometime later, feeling cold and alone.

What she also remembered was that she was there to be tested. How often this occurred she could not say, but the whole point of her being in the Tower was to be tried. Her tormentor would arrive at random times. During periods when the space was filled with a lifeless, silver-grey light or when she had been plunged into the impenetrable blackness of a crypt – it did not matter. Once present, the testing would commence. The mere mention of these trials was enough to cause Jess to go pale and shake uncontrollably. What made up the aspects of the trials she was unable, or unwilling, to recall. She could not, or would not, face the memories of these, and Maima would not press her further about them.

Over time it became clear to Jess that each time she failed to please her tormentor there was a little less of herself present. Bits of who she was became thinner, less distinct. Like her memories, who she was became unclear and harder to remember. Loneliness and despair were her constant companions, feeding her belief of failure and the inevitability that she would be fully absorbed by the Tower, no longer to exist. At her most desperate, she found stairs. Stairs going up. And so, she climbed. Rising higher and higher in the Tower, she eventually reached the only room she had ever found with a window. And, from there, she had jumped.

Chapter 3

Despite the initial concerns about Jess and the Tower, their constant vigilance revealed nothing out of the ordinary. Yet, still being careful, they gradually fell into a new normality. During the day Jess would stay in the cottage and out of sight. She was eager to learn as much as she could about the preparation of tonics and creams that formed the central component of Maima's work. She learnt quickly and was good at what she did. As the months went by her strength gradually returned, but her sleep was still broken by images of the Tower. Most nights she would wake, at times screaming in terror, as images of the Tower would engulf her. She could not tell if these were images from her own imagination or memories of what had happened to others who were taken to the Tower. At times they even felt like a prediction of what would happen to her. With each episode Angus was there, attentive and calming whenever she was in distress. His kind voice and gentle touch brought her back to the new reality about her. It reminded her that she was now part of a family. Either for the very first time, or once again – she could not remember.

When Maima's patients were visiting the cottage, Jess was introduced as her new apprentice, there to learn the skills and be another healer in Town. To further her studies even more Angus started to teach Jess to read. Together, they spent time each evening siting at the kitchen table, heads close together, speaking softly and enjoying the time with one another. Angus also began applying himself to further learning. Emblazed by Jess' desire to learn, he studied all the books Maima had and questioned her mercilessly. He would not stop until he was sure that he understood or, as sometimes was the case, when Maima would have to admit to not completely understanding it herself.

Angus also spent more time being interested in the treatment of the sick. Whether this was a true interest, or so that he could be near Jess, Maima was not sure; but she welcomed the curiosity. One thing that was obvious was that

Angus watched intently every time she would use Influence. He said that the colours were getting clearer. They were more distinct and he could see where these colours dispersed in the body of the sick. It allowed him to see where the problem was that Maima was Influencing. In the more difficult patients this knowledge was invaluable, aiding Maima to be more effective in her treatments. Over time he was even able to detect a slight multi-coloured aura around Maima that diminished when she used her ability. With Jess he started to see that she was surrounded by a pure white light.

Jess was careful never to use Influence. Maima had warned that the Tower had a way of knowing which girls had Influence. It was assumption only, but she speculated that it was the use of Influence that alerted the Tower to their presence. As she herself only had limited Influence she reasoned that it was just not strong enough to be noticed but, as Jess had been collected once before, it would be vital for her not to use her ability in case it was noticed again. It did not take any convincing for Jess to avoid manipulating the air. As far as she could tell, this skill had only brought her misery. And so, for the most part, it was a happy and productive household.

***

The days passed serenely but the nights were still disturbed by Jess' dreams. Excelling at being Maima's apprentice and despite her continuing fears, Jess started taking more and more responsibility for making the basic tonics. This allowed Maima more time to explore her books and experiment with different combinations to improve the medicines. Angus found enjoyment in invention. Applying what he had learnt through study and experimentation, he began creating designs that could help the older townsfolk that suffered from poor mobility. He invented ways for them to get out of chairs, and things to help with washing. He would also make visits to Maima's patients to put these inventions in place. Still only eighteen, he was now receiving almost as much praise as his mother for the improvements he created in the townsfolk's lives.

One evening as he headed home after such a visit, Angus was taken by surprise. Out of the corner of his eye he noted a man quickly disappearing around a corner, coated by a golden light. Startled and intrigued that there was another in Town with Influence, he turned to follow.

The man was moving quickly down the slope into the lower parts of Town, weaving through those still on the streets. It was not someone Angus recognised, and nothing about him would have sparked the interest of a passer-by. He was dressed in the drab clothes of any farmer and carrying a bag over his shoulder. Angus trailed him, unsure what he was doing but wanting to see who this man was and where he was from. The man appeared anxious, continually glancing about him yet, even if he noticed, he paid no attention to Angus following. The sun was almost gone, and the streets empty, by the time they reached lower Town, but the glow surrounding the man made tracking him simple.

In the square in front of the main Town gate the man suddenly stopped. Dropping his bag, he stared straight ahead without moving. Keeping out of sight behind a cart left for the night by the side of the road, Angus watched. Nothing appeared to be happening but the man stayed still, fixed to the spot. Gradually Angus became aware of a field of darkness moving toward the man. It contained a spot of flickering blue light. Others displaying a similar blue light then also advanced on him from either side. Indistinct and undefined, but just visible as voids that were slightly darker than the space around them, they encircled him. Even at this distance they felt cold and dead, as if all the warmth in the air was being drained. He could see and feel the intensity of the golden light begin to build within the man. As the intensity grew, pulses of light shot forth from him toward the voids. The lights exploded, outlining shapes of hooded persons, silhouettes of perfect blackness. The light was then sucked into the blackness and disappeared.

The shadows surrounding the man slowly tightened their net, circling closer and closer. Again and again, bolts of light pulsed into the dark shapes, but faster and faster they were absorbed and gone. With each round Angus saw the man glowing less as the Influence was consumed. Unable to look away, Angus witnessed the voids touch and consume the man as a blue light flared about him. With no sound and no-one else to witness, the golden light was drained from around, and then from the heart of, the man. As if watching the wind erase a child's drawing in the sand, Angus watched the man gradually evaporate, becoming thinner and thinner, less substantial and more transparent until, finally, he was gone. The blackness started to lift from the square. The air regained its warmth.

Angus stayed where he was, too scared to move but afraid to stay. Jess' greatest fear was to be absorbed by the Tower and now, right in front of him, he had witnessed just that. To lose who you were – never to die but never more to think or feel. No longer to exist as you, but to be a part of the Tower, under the full control of another. Now Angus could finally understand what she meant and why it so terrified her.

Staying longer than was necessary in order to be certain that he did not encounter one of the voids, Angus eventually emerged from behind the cart. He walked cautiously into the square to where he had witnessed the man fade. All felt normal and he saw no signs of Influence, but there on the ground was the bag dropped by the man. Picking it up, Angus scanned the square and made quickly for home.

Once safely behind the closed door, bathed in the warm light of the cottage and back in the company of others, Angus finally allowed himself to rest. Never before had he felt so scared. He needed to compose himself before speaking of the encounter. He knew that he must warn the others that the Tower was about, but he did not want to provoke further distress in Jess. He decided that he would speak with Maima first while Jess was practising her reading. So, taking Maima aside after supper, he related the events of the evening.

"And what was in the bag?" inquired Maima.

"I don't know; I simply forgot about it until now," replied Angus. "I left it outside. I didn't want to distress Jess."

"Take it to my room and have a look. It may give us further insight into who he was."

Following Maima's direction, Angus retrieved the bag and emptied it on the bed. A coat and cap, a purse containing a few copper coins, some bread and cheese. But, what was remarkable was a rolled-up piece of parchment, a small bottle of ink, and a quill. Calling Maima to come, Angus showed her the find.

"Someone who can read and write," stated Maima, surprised, as she unrolled the parchment revealing a list of names, all of which were male. Beside each name was written a region of the Bowl and then a number.

"What do you think it means?" asked Angus.

"Can't say. The names are from all over the Bowl and what the numbers mean … there is no pattern."

"This name here, this one is from just outside Town. I should go and see," said Angus, thinking aloud. "He was leaving Town before they … stopped him. These people might know more. They could be in danger from the Tower."

"Or they might be helping the Tower," warned Maima. "We have no idea what this list means. No, you must not go. Promise me."

Giving a non-committal flick of the head, Angus turned to leave the room. "We must not tell Jess about this. She is not ready for it."

***

Angus rose early the next day explaining that he had a number of visits to complete before he could start on the daily deliveries. Waving to Jess as he left, he called back that he should be finished by midday and would return. Turning left he moved in the direction of upper Town but, when out of sight, he made a detour though some alleys in order to head further down through Town and to the main gate. The sun had risen, and Town was alive with the markets opening and tradespeople going about their duties. Passing the site of the previous night's encounter, Angus noted how normal everything seemed. No trace of the deed remained but he paused, just for a moment, to acknowledge the man who once had been. Gaining further determination, he set his face to the west and headed out of Town, making for a small village an hour or so's walk away.

He walked quickly through bountiful fields along a well-maintained road used by the produce carts to deliver their goods to Town. As usual it was a warm, sunny day, perfect to be outside as it was neither too hot nor too cold. On the parchment, he had counted ten names. William Farley was the one he was going to look for. The region written next to his name on the parchment surrounded the small village to which he was headed. Without knowing what William did for a living, or where he lived, Angus thought it best to first visit the general store to inquire where the Farleys lived. He had with him, as a pretence, a small parcel he had wrapped with the name William Farley written on it. He would say that he had the parcel to deliver and had been charged to see that it was delivered to William in person.

Soon enough he arrived at the village, unremarkable in all aspects. By heading down the main street he walked straight to the general store. He opened the door and went in. A few customers were getting orders filled when a girl, slightly younger than he was, returned to her place behind the counter. Standing up straight and putting on his most endearing smile he winked at her. He thought that if he could charm her a little then she might be more forthcoming with the information he required.

"Good morrow, what a charming day, made all the better by a smile from you," he crooned.

The girl giggled and blushed slightly. Angus continued, hoping that he did not sound quite as pretentious to her as he did to himself, "I am new around here and was of the opinion that someone like yourself could aid me. I have an important message for the Farleys that my employer would like me to deliver in person. Can you assist me as to the whereabouts of the Farleys?"

The girl did not answer and looked confused. Feeling a bit deflated, Angus repeated, "Do you know where the Farleys live?"

"Oh," she said, "that's what you mean. Their plot's a ways out on the western track. You'll know it by the sunflowers."

Feeling that he needed to keep up the pretence a bit longer so as not to lose face, Angus responded with the flash of a smile and quipped, "There, I knew that beauty and brains do, in fact, go together," and turned to leave. Once outside again he quickly headed out of the village to the west, feeling a bit silly after the less than authentic way he tried to get the information.

At least it worked. But, perhaps, if there is a next time, I might just be myself.

Time was moving on and he was unsure how much further he had to travel to the Farley plot. Undeterred, he set a rapid pace and scanned the land about him for any glimpse of the tell-tale yellow of sunflowers. Eventually, after walking for over an hour, he caught sight of the tall yellow plants waving in the breeze, off to the left of the road. Finding a rough track that was tending in that direction, he turned and made his way towards the plants. After topping a low rise, he spied a small homestead made up of a cottage, barn and home garden nestled amongst the yellow fields. Heading directly toward these he kept an eye out for anyone who may have been around.

"Hey, hello, is anyone around?" he called as he walked toward the homestead.

An old man emerged from the barn as Angus got closer. Slightly stooped but still retaining the solid build of a man who had worked his whole life on the land, he regarded Angus from under his broad brimmed hat.

"You lost?" he asked in a gruff voice. "There's not much going forward this way. Youse be wanting to head back the way youse came."

"Are you Farmer Farley?"

"And why you be asking?"

"I have come to speak with William Farley," Angus replied.

"None by that name here. You best be going," came the short reply as the old man abruptly turned and made his way back into the shed. After a slight delay Angus followed him into the barn.

"Can you tell me where I can find the Farley plot? I must speak to William Farley."

"There ain't no William Farley, I tell you," the old man responded.

"But if you can tell me where, I will be going."

"Ain't nowhere to go."

"Please, I need to at least speak to Farmer Farley," Angus pressed.

"And so you are," came the terse response.

"You are Farmer Farley? Please ..." Angus started, but as he followed the farmer into the dim light of the barn he noted a pale glow around the old man's hands. Surprised, Angus blurted, "You have Influence!"

The farmer stopped and slowly turned. "Who are you?" he demanded.

"No-one, no-one important," Angus stuttered and then quickly added, "nothing to do with the Tower."

"And why should I believe you?"

"I came because I saw a man, a man ... taken ... taken by things that came from the Tower. He just dissolved ... into nothing. Nothing left. I have to know what happened."

"Why should I know? Never met him and suppose I never will, from what you say," came the reply.

"He had a list, a list of names. William Farley was on it, and he lived near here. I need to speak to him to find out who this man was. He had Influence and the Tower took him."

With the continued mention of William's name, the old man's face lost its sternness and crumbled. His body lost its strength and he sat heavily on a nearby straw bale as he seemed to fold into himself.

"William was my son," he stated simply, his voice cracking with emotion.

Angus made his way to him and laid a gentle hand on the old man's shoulder. "I'm sorry."

"They came, the Dark Ones, the ones from the Tower. We were told ... warned, but they came. It just happened. He didn't do nothing, but they came ... and he was gone. Like you say ... nothing left."

"Why, why did they come?"

"Go, leave me alone. Why do you need to know?" the man spoke irritably.

"Because there are another nine names on that list, and I could easily be added to that list. That's why. I have Influence, like your son," Angus responded angrily.

Looking at him more carefully the old man stood up and started to walk away. As he did, he turned and gestured to Angus. "I s'pose you had best come to the house. At least there's a chair there to make the talking a bit less nasty."

Angus followed Farmer Farley into his house where he was seated in the kitchen at an old wooden table opposite the old man. He sat quietly as the story unfolded.

William Farley was the only son of his father, who had been widowed some years previously. Together, they had run their plot with little interruption from the outside world. William had recently taken over more and more of the responsibility. Farmer Farley had always been good with seeds and growing things. He was able to get things to grow in places where others had failed, a talent that his son had inherited. Angus noted that as he spoke the old man absent-mindedly played with a large bowl of sunflower seeds in the centre of the table. As he did, Angus saw a small burst of green leave his fingers and settle into the seeds.

It was only a few months ago that William had a visit from a man who said that they must be careful. That William had Influence, and it was building in him. They were told that it was too dangerous to let Influence out unchecked. That those in the Tower could tell when more than a little Influence was used at a time. Farmer Farley and his son dismissed this as nonsense as no-one in their family ever had anything to do with Influence. To them Influence was a myth, a story that was told to scare children. The man insisted that it was real. That girls who have Influence would demonstrate it as they grew into women, but for men it could manifest at any time.

"The Tower uses this power, the power of Influence," the man had explained. "It collects girls with great ability, ready to train them … to use them. But the men they destroy. It takes their Influence for itself and the men are discarded."

The farmer and his son scoffed at the man, but he pleaded with them to listen. He said that he would be back soon to help, but that he had others he needed to go to. With that, the man left, and the farmer and his son quickly forgot about the stranger and his visit.

A few weeks later Farmer Farley was milking the cows in the barn. William was repairing the upper part of the barn roof when it gave way and he started to fall. What happened then was extraordinary for, as he was starting to fall, bales of hay stacked themselves on top of each other and formed a platform halfway to the roof on which William landed. Unharmed and bewildered, William climbed down the tower of hay before collapsing in a heap on the barn floor. His father managed to get him into the house where he remained unconscious for a day and a night before waking, groggy, with his whole body aching. He barely remembered the incident but hearing the account from his father evoked in him a feeling of terror, as if his body was turning itself inside out. After a few days he had fully recovered. Through unspoken agreement, the two of them never spoke about it again.

Barely a week after that, as the sun set over the Western Slopes, the Dark Ones came. William was finishing up in the vegetable garden as his father sat on the porch watching the daylight fade. Without any sound, the shapes of darkness appeared and began to coalesce about William. Before either of the men knew what was happening, and while his father watched, the voids reached William. Without a scream or any sound, the father saw his son break up into dust and disappear. By the time the old man had risen and raced to the garden, nothing remained. His son had gone, and the voids had disappeared.

They both sat silent at the wooden kitchen table. The old man, with his head bowed and his body bent, had finished his story and Angus had no words of comfort to give. From what had just been said, and with what he had witnessed himself, there was no doubt that Jess – and possibly even he – was under threat. Looking at the man with pity in his eyes, Angus nodded, sighed and, speaking softly, said, "Thank you. I feel your loss and share your grief. Your words may help others, including myself, so thank you."

Angus stood ready to go. Moving to the door he heard the man say, "The others on the list … tell them. Make them listen."

"I'll try," he responded as he opened the door and left.

Chapter 4

As Angus reached the cottage, he was still unsure what he should say or do. He loved it here and all the people he was helping. Jess felt safe and Maima was irreplaceable to all those she aided. But the Tower was close, and it seemed that men with Influence were in danger. The Tower looked to destroy them and take their Influence for itself. How much Influence could it detect? Was it already aware of him? But then, how could he even think about going, and where would he go? Farmer Farley's son was … gone was the best word he could think of. He had also already seen firsthand what those from the Tower could do. Maima had been here for years and had been using Influence all that time, and they never came for her. Yet, he remembered Jess saying that she'd heard a man's voice in the Tower just before the words, "They are not to be tolerated," were uttered. Perhaps Maima was tolerated but he would not be?

Walking through the door he found Maima at home, working at the kitchen table. That was unusual for her at this time of day.

"Where's Jess?" he asked.

"She's asleep," came the reply.

Angus looked confused. "Why? It's only the middle of the day."

Maima looked up from her work. "I used Influence on her." She continued rapidly, "I had to; she became hysterical. Crying and lashing out. She didn't recognise me. Pleading that I would stop tormenting her. I felt her about to use Influence. I had to do something."

Angus stood there, horrified. "She has never had a fit like that or had one of her terrors during the day. She is so careful never to use Influence. What happened?"

"I was showing her how to prepare a variation of one of the tonics. We were having fun, she was happy, and we were talking of you. Without warning she stopped and turned to look at the door, and her face drained of all colour.

She was so pale. I asked what she heard but she didn't reply. She was just frozen, rigidly staring at the door. She started to wail softly, her face contorted, and she pleaded, 'No, no, no, please no, not again. I can't go back, please!' Before I could get around to her side of the table, she started to draw into herself. I felt the air start to flow toward her. As I got to her, she tried to fight me off and screamed. Before she could release any Influence, I was able to put my hands on her and relax her. She's in bed now."

Angus went to her bedroom door and looked in. There in the bed Jess lay, calm and composed, peacefully asleep as Maima said.

Returning to the kitchen he looked at Maima. "We cannot stay. We have to go." Continuing on, he explained where he had been that morning and what had happened to Farmer Farley's son.

Maima listened intently without interrupting. "We will go to the Western Slopes. We must tell no-one and leave soon. We take only what we can carry," she said.

Relieved that Maima had made the decision, one that Angus felt was far too large for him, he told her about the other names on the list; that he had to try to find and warn them. Furrowing her brows, his mother did not argue but said, "First, you must see where we are going so you can find us again, and then you go."

Angus walked over to his mother and embraced her. Holding him close and stroking his hair she added, "I have done this before, and we can do it again. Together, we are more than enough. Now, I will gather some things. We will leave after dark."

***

The streets were empty with no prying eyes to see them leave. Carrying only a few possessions and staying in the deeper shadows that collected at the sides of the street, they moved cautiously without speaking. Jess had woken, calm and without any memory of what had happened that day. Once she was informed of the potential threat to Angus, she too was insistent that they needed to leave and leave quickly. She helped Maima gather the dried herbs, wrapping them in cloth. These, together with containers of creams and ointments, as well as the mortar and pestle, were placed in a large bag that Angus would carry. Food that would travel well was also packed. That which would not was prepared for supper that evening.

Their last supper in the cottage was quiet and solemn. All were on edge and alert to any unexpected sounds. Keeping the room well-lit lifted their spirits slightly, yet all knew full well that this was, at best, a feeble attempt at providing protection against the voids. They ate not out of hunger but in order to be nourished. There was no knowing when next they may again share a hot meal. In silence they cleaned up the mess from dinner and, leaving the cottage in order, walked out, closing the door silently behind them.

Moving through the Town gate they gave a communal sigh. The first hurdle was over. Without looking back, they continued westward, determined to keep moving throughout the night, putting as much distance between them and the Tower as they could.

As day dawned, with the sun rising behind them, they continued on. Passing through only a few villages and hamlets on their way they had avoided seeing anyone. Now, however, as the workday began, they needed to be more careful to avoid people. Maima knew where they were going. Up ahead was a crossroad where one of the westbound passenger carts would collect and deposit its customers. This was only a short walk further. As the sun reached all areas of the Bowl, they arrived at the crossroad and moved off to the side of the road to rest. They had something to eat and waited for the cart, which arrived as the sun reached its zenith. Paying the small fee, Maima, Angus and Jess climbed aboard.

It was a slow trip, and tiring, but better than having to walk. They arrived at a village as night fell. This was where they would have to stay until the cart left again in the morning. Thinking it unwise to seek shelter in the village in case they were remembered, the three made camp slightly out of town. None of them really slept that night. Each was still far too aware of where they were and what was happening. The shared discomfort, however, was still better than the terror and loneliness that had accompanied Maima's first trip to the west.

Before dawn they returned to the village where the cart was being loaded with items to be delivered to hamlets along the way. As the sun crested the Eastern Slopes they set off once more, hoping to arrive at their destination before it set again.

Each remained locked in their own thoughts as they shared out the remnants of their rations. For Jess and Angus, the further they went from the Tower, and the smaller that it appeared on the horizon, the lighter their fear. For Maima, however, returning to the first place where she had ever remembered feeling freedom brought mixed feelings. She had been happy there. Jim and his mother were so much more of a family to her than her own. It had been such a very difficult decision to return to Town and leave them, yet it was one she felt that she had had to make. She had needed to try and find her love, Angus' father. As she'd told Angus, despite all her efforts over many years she had discovered very little. The Tower kept its deeds shrouded in the same darkness that clothed its inhabitants. She had never attempted to contact her parents. To them, she was merely something to be used to create an alliance through marriage. She was also never able to forgive them for what they had done.

After more time than anyone would like travelling in an open cart, they were eventually deposited in the small, drab square of a hamlet at the end of the line. Maima looked about quickly and started moving off to the west. "It is only a couple of hours' walk and we will be there," she stated matter-of-factly.

"We will be where?" the others inquired.

"Safe, or at least as safe as we ever will be," was the response. "We are going to the plot of James Albee. It was there that Angus was born. He can help us."

Tired and hungry, they made their way along the cart track further west. Despite the sun setting over the Western Slopes, the path was clear and fairly easy going. Finally, after several hours walking, and days of travelling with very little sleep, they saw in the moonlight a neatly arranged plot. Nestled serenely on the plot was a well-kept cottage with light coming from within. Reaching the porch, Maima called out, "Jim, Jim! It's me, Sybil."

The door opened, revealing a young boy who was joined almost immediately by a full-bearded, stocky, middle-aged man. "Sybil, really, it's you?" he cried, surprised. "Alice, Sybil is here. Come in, come in!" Looking at the others, he exclaimed, "Angus, I assume? Come in."

"This is Jess," Angus explained.

"You are welcome, Jess, come in," he added as he ushered them all inside and closed the door.

James Albee regarded them, his eyes bright and his smile broad. "Oh, Sybil, it has been so long. Come, sit, you all must be exhausted. You are all welcome." Looking at Jess, he added, "Sybil has written to me about you and what a wonderful help you have been to her and her work."

A pleasant looking middle-aged woman came towards Maima and embraced her. "It is good to see you, Sybil."

"And you, Alice. I am sorry to arrive like this, but we had nowhere else we could go."

Sitting Maima down in one of the more comfortable chairs, Alice handed her a cup of hot tea. "One thing at a time. You can tell us everything once you have had something to eat. I presume that you are all hungry?" she asked, looking particularly at Angus, who nodded vigorously.

Maima had made it clear to Angus and Jess that here it was safe. That they could be fully open and tell all. So, after what seemed to them to be one of the best meals they had ever tasted, Maima, Angus and Jess took turns to explain the situation. Jim, Alice, and their son, Johnathon, listened carefully without comment until they finished. Thinking carefully, Jim suggested an old, abandoned plot located further toward the Western Slopes. The land around was fertile and there were very few people who came out this way. The only community was the small hamlet that they had passed through earlier that day. There was a cottage already on the plot that was still in reasonable condition, and there was also a small, repairable shed.

Seeing their guests were barely able to keep awake, Alice prepared bedding for them on the floor of a small spare room. Suggesting they retire to sleep, she assured them all that there was a way to help. After a cursory wash of face and hands to get the worst of the grime off, the three lay down. Still in their travelling clothes they were asleep in moments, feeling safe – at least for the moment.

***

The westernmost plot of the Bowl abutted the lower portions of the Western Slopes. Its closest neighbour was the Albee's plot, and could only reached via a rough and very overgrown goat track. They left to make the journey the next day, after collecting some essential items and tools that would be required to make a start on restoring the cottage to liveable status. Taking a small cart that could be pulled by hand, they made slow progress over the rough ground. After several hours they arrived at the abandoned plot. An overgrown home garden was located in front of a small but relatively intact cottage. The roof of the barn was noticeably absent, but the walls seemed sound.

As Jim and Angus inspected the integrity of the cottage from the outside, the women and Johnathon ventured inside. Immediately, they went to work sorting the mess and cleaning.

Over the next week, almost daily trips were made between the two plots. The men would work from morning to dusk repairing the cottage roof, making the floor sound, fixing the shutters, and making sure that the chimney drew sufficiently well to avoid smoking out the kitchen.

The women created liveable spaces. A room in which to sleep. A kitchen in which to cook. They stocked a pantry with supplies obtained from the general store found in the closest hamlet. Johnathon explored the local terrain and located a small flock of goats. Wild goats were not known to be in this area, so these were assumed to be escapees from the plot when it had been abandoned several years before. Together, he and Angus were able to herd the small flock back toward the plot. They secured them in the newly constructed holding pen, near the barn that still needed repair.

The cottage and home garden quickly took shape. By the end of the week, Maima, Jess and Angus had somewhere to sleep, cook and eat. Added to this was the prospect of a milking herd of goats to make cheese and yoghurt. The excess could be sold at market to purchase any other items they would need. With his family now safe and comfortable, Angus restated the need for him to try and locate the other men on the list. Farmer Albee and his wife assured him that they would care for Jess and Maima. Maima and Jess also reinforced that they could cope while he was gone. So, Angus took what little money he had saved and headed back to take the passenger cart towards the east.

Chapter 5

It was several weeks before Angus returned. Having passed by the Albee's plot on the way to his new home, he had been reassured to hear that all had been going well. That there were still frequent trips between the two households. Before continuing on his journey home, he was laden with fresh fruit and vegetables to take back to Jess and Maima.

Striding along the goat track, he was spotted by Jess while he was still some distance away. Waving vigorously in his direction he saw her call out to the house and run towards him. Grinning broadly, he started to trot towards Jess, rapidly closing the gap between them.

Stopping awkwardly a few feet away Angus just gazed at her, taking her all in. Jess looked free and slightly wild, her hair loose around her head and her face flushed. Her natural beauty had been enhanced by the exertion. Feeling all sorts of things, Angus felt his own colour rise. With his heart racing he opened his mouth to speak, but before he uttered a word, Jess launched herself at him. Hugging him tightly around the middle, she kissed him. Immediately she let go, stepped back and stood, a bit uneasily, with her head slightly bowed and her eyes cast downward. Surprised, but emboldened, Angus stepped forward and enfolded the petite girl in his arms, kissing her back. Without speaking they stood there, encased in a moment like neither had experienced before.

For what seemed an age, but passed in an instant, they remained. Without breaking the spell Angus took Jess' hand, clasping it in his own, and they began to make their way back to the cottage. There in front of the cottage was Maima, a witness to all that occurred. Coming towards them both she pulled first Angus to her, and then Jess, her smile and touch saying it all. Acknowledging their feelings, she was bestowing her blessing without words. Then, going inside, she left the two to have more time to be alone together.

***

At supper that evening Angus was able to fill them in on his travels. He had made his way to the various regions to find and warn the men listed on the parchment he had found. Arriving in the various villages and hamlets he would inquire after the family. Often this would yield usable information but at times he would be greeted with suspicion. Anything to do with the Tower was unlikely to be discussed. He had found it necessary to invent numerous stories involving distant relatives. Some of the families were located within the towns and others were farmers. There was no pattern to the names, where they lived or what they did.

On two occasions he had been unable to find any members of a family. One rumour surrounding this suggested that the families may have refused to pay tithe to the Tower and had been punished by the loss of all that they had, cast out to live as homeless vagabonds.

On three occasions the family denied that there ever was a person with the name from the parchment. No amount of questioning or revealing of information by Angus could make them say otherwise.

Only on two occasions was Angus able to find the people belonging to the names in question. He was able to confirm that these were truly ones with Influence as he could see its light within them.

One was only a boy of about seven, living with his family on the outskirts of a town in the north. The parents were tradespeople with little understanding of things outside their own small world. Angus was met with a lack of comprehension and disbelief when he tried to explain about Influence and the danger it entailed. They thought that Angus was some sort of trickster trying to sell them a useless protection talisman for their son. Despite explaining that he had nothing to sell and wanted nothing from them, they politely, but firmly, asked him to leave.

Fearing for the young boy, he had waited in the town until he was able to speak to the child away from his parents. It had not been a long wait as the child was frequently sent on errands for his mother. Taking the opportunity, Angus engaged the child with stories of how Influence had protected Jess in her fall, and how he could see how Influence worked in others. Gaining the boy's trust had been easier than he expected as the child was, in part, already aware of how he could use Influence. The stories of the Tower were equally effective in warning him to be careful, such that Angus left feeling that he had at least given the boy a chance.

The second was a man well on in years. One who had already lost a brother to the Dark Ones. He needed no warning but gave one instead. He told Angus that although being further from the Tower might be safer, all that was within sight of the Tower was still under its watch. For all of them, Influence was a curse. It was something that the Tower wanted and needed, and something that at all costs must be denied to it. Never to use Influence was never, then, to be betrayed by it.

Angus had been unable to speak with the owners of the final two names. One had moved away and was now somewhere in Town. Unsure if he should try to go there or not, Angus reasoned that the man he followed in Town had already visited Town and had, most likely, already found and spoken with this one. Angus also did not want to return to a place where he could be recognised or be forced to explain his family's absence.

The last name on the list he was also unable to locate, although he had found the family. These people at first had been very wary of him. Yet, after mentioning the parchment containing the list of names, they became far more welcoming. They listened intently and finally stated that they already had received a visit by a man wanting to give a warning.

It took some time, but eventually enough trust developed between them that they were more forthcoming. A man had visited them several months ago and spoken with their son. Following his visit, their son told them of some strange events that had been taking place. At random times, he could hear voices in the air. The voices sounded like those of the people he was around. The voices were generally muddled, all jumbled together and incoherent. Occasionally he was able to focus on a single voice and get an understanding, clear and articulate, of what the person was thinking. It happened erratically and even woke him from his sleep. He had felt that he was starting to lose his grip on reality until the visit and an explanation of what Influence was.

Taking the warning seriously, he spent a few days with the visitor trying to learn as much as he could. Eventually he spoke with his parents, saying that he had to go. That there were others like him whom he could help and protect. That the Tower needed to be opposed. That this was something he knew that he had to do.

That had been months ago, and they had only received one message that he was safe since, through the delivery of a single dried, pressed flower. It was his mother's favourite bloom. More than that they were unable to tell Angus. They knew nothing about who or where the others were, or how they could oppose the Tower.

Having finished his tale, Angus looked intently at Maima and looking slightly awkward said, "Maima, I would … I mean, Jess and I would like—"

stopping to look at Jess, he continued, "—we would like to be betrothed. With your blessing, of course."

Maima just looked and smiled. "I have been expecting it, and it is wonderful."

***

Life at the cottage settled easily into a new routine for them all. Jess devoted herself to the household garden, making it highly productive thanks to the many varieties of seedlings given to them by the Albees. Angus cared for the goats and cultivated a small field of grain. He also provided meat for the table through snares laid for rabbits and the occasional butchering of an aged goat. Maima gathered wild herbs and other medicinal plants to prepare ointments and tinctures to sell at the markets. The goats in their turn were generous in their milk, due to the good pasture. The high fat milk allowed for the making of superior grade cheese.

In general things were going well. Angus doted on his wife and his mere presence would animate Jess such that she radiated happiness. Angus and Jess took the bedroom for themselves, with Maima insistent that she would be comfortable in the small second room off the living space for herself.

"You will be needing more room than I will," she said. "Families grow!"

Angus smiled his broad smile. Jess blushed at the thought and looked at her husband with adoration.

Johnathon Albee was also a frequent visitor who loved to go out with Angus and check the snares. Maima took it upon herself to teach him to read, as she had his father. With Jim, Maima worked hard to discover any forgotten or unused books hidden in the region. Over the next year they gradually built a collection of the discarded and forgotten manuscripts. As the collection grew, the small family living at the westernmost plot of the Bowl would each evening read aloud of the many things and peoples and places so different to their life in the Bowl.

Despite this calm and gentle life, not all continued as expected. After an initial lull of many months, Jess started once again to have night terrors. These began slowly and erratically. Over time they were increasingly frequent, with her waking more nights than not after fearful visons of the Tower and what had happened there. Lying quietly next to her, Angus would feel her start to tremble and become restless before she would thrash her arms about as if trying to protect herself. Angus could see Influence moving around her like flames of light and, as with fire, bits of the flame would break off and disappear. At these times he would hold her tight to himself in an attempt to calm and wake her. Eventually, with a gasp, her eyes would open, and he would soothe her with words and caresses before her mindfulness returned and she knew where she was once again.

Jess would not complain but both Angus and his mother saw the continued toll it had on her. Worried, they did not know what to do. Maima was hesitant to use her ability to soothe her as any display of Influence might draw unwanted attention. Yet she was sorely tempted when Jess would not sleep, preferring instead to sit awake though the night rather than endure her dreams.

Even during the day Maima would occasionally see Jess staring out to the east as if expecting something to appear. When questioned, Jess would dismiss the concerns with a laugh saying that she was just thinking about Angus' first return to their homestead. This was not enough to reassure Maima. She observed other things. When making the basic tonics, something Jess had learnt to do so long ago, she would stop and have to ask what it was that she had to do next. Even when they talked of Town, the cottage, and the people they left behind, Jess would at times confuse the markets. She did not always remember their friends. She was not sleeping. She was so tired. The others hoped that all this forgetfulness was due to her lack of sleep. In response, Maima went to the books to look for ways to improve sleep with her herbs.

Angus and Maima were vigilant to any changes but were careful to discuss things privately and not show their concern to Jess. "I'm not sure if it is a good thing or a bad thing," began Angus. "I don't see the light about Jess being as strong as it used to be. When she has her fits, it is brighter, but could being so far from the Tower and not using Influence make it weaker? This may make her of less interest to the Tower."

"We can hope," said Maima. "Do you see the same changes in mine?"

"No, it hasn't really changed. Much as I have always seen it. But then, it has always been less obvious than Jess'."

Maima continued straining the goats' curd from the whey as she thought. "Being further from the Tower could make it weaker. Perhaps you are right. She will be safer if it becomes less strong."

"But the fits come regularly. Your herbs help her to sleep but the terrors still come. It is fortunate that she does not seem to be remembering them as vividly as she once did."

"It is, and for now she does sleep and fears it less. I wonder if this is the herbs at work, or if—"

Maima ceased her thought as Jess entered the room. Looking sheepish but also pleased with herself she went to Angus and kissed him. She wore a gentle, quiet smile that played on the edge of the lips. Her eyes were bright, and she looked peaceful. Angus looked down at her. She hugged him and laid her head on his shoulder. Maima watched this with interest, delighted in the connection the two shared. Taking a backward step away from Angus into the centre of the room, Jess looked at Angus, and then Maima. "I think we're going to have a baby."

The change in the mood of the room was instant. Maima gasped and clapped her hands together, racing over to Jess and embracing her. Angus stood there, open-mouthed and speechless. Releasing herself from the embrace, Jess walked over to Angus and standing in front of him, looked up and said, "You're going to be a father."

Still in disbelief he grabbed Jess in a bearlike hug and then, immediately thinking better of it, released her and held her gently with tears in his eyes as he replied, "We're going to be a family."

***

Time seemed to move at many different speeds. When facing trials and difficulties it crawled yet, in the glow of happiness and expectation, days flew by. Jess was radiant and the night terrors ceased. Angus worked on crafting a cradle and a small bath for future use. Jess and Maima visited the hamlet to buy thread and materials to make clothes and pretty things for the expected arrival.

Angus voiced his concern that he would not know how to be a father. Having never had one, how was he expected to know what he should do? Reassuring him that he would be more than enough when the time came, Maima suggested that he could talk with Farmer Albee if he so desired. Taking the next opportunity, Angus approached the man about the subject and was more than surprised to learn that every potential father feared that he would never be good enough. That this was a feeling that never went away, no matter what their age or how old their children became.

Promising Angus that his door was always open to him, Jim Albee looked at his own son and, smiling, said, "You will know what to do. It may not always be easy and may not always seem best to others but trust yourself. Be the man you are, and you will know what is right."

Taking comfort in the confidence that others had in him, Angus determined to do the best for his family regardless of the cost to himself.

As time went on Jess grew rounder, making stooping over the household garden more of an effort. She persisted but frequently required a nap in the afternoon. Her sore back, slightly waddling gait, and tummy that made a very acceptable shelf on which to place her tea in the evening, were evidence of the size, and imminent arrival, of the baby she carried.

In the afternoon of another sunny day, the butterfly flickerings in her tummy started to grow stronger and more regular. Not yet feeling anything more than discomfort, she sought out Maima who confirmed that the process had begun. Angus was still out with Johnathon checking the snares but would be back before too long.

Inside, Maima set about the preparations required for the delivery while Jess sat and then stood, walked around the cottage, and then sat again, finding it hard to achieve any comfortable position. Before long, the telltale rush of fluid down the legs heralded the true beginning of the birth. As Jess was dealing with one of the strongest contractions so far, Angus, unaware of what was going on, entered the cottage. His first sight was of his wife squatting on the floor, breathing rapidly, and in great pain. Looking worried and confused, he raced to her side and tried to raise her to her feet. He was immediately swatted away as Jess concentrated on breathing through the pain.

Maima took Angus to the side to explain that this was no longer a man's job. He should now trust Jess and Maima to do all that was needed. That it would also be best if he went outside with Johnathon, and that soon there would be a new member of the family.

"Soon" is at term that encompasses many different timeframes – sometimes seconds or minutes, sometimes hours or days. For an expectant father left outside to fend for himself, soon, regardless of its true length of time, feels like an eternity. As the afternoon turned into evening, Johnathon returned home, and Angus entered the cottage. Jess was now in their bed with Maima attending. The lamps had been lit and Maima assured him that all was normal. It was not unusual for the process to take some time with the first child. If he grew hungry, he would have to feed himself. Unable to stomach the thought of food and unable to stay still, Angus paced the common room.

Just before midnight, following a particularly prolonged groan from Jess, a piercing cry cut through the fog of Angus' brain. The door to their room was opened by Maima and he was invited to enter. There upon the bed, her hair plastered to her forehead, Jess cradled a small bundle. Looking tired and drained she looked up at him, smiling the most radiant smile he had ever seen. Walking over to the bed he could see a small, squashed pink face poking out of the clothes, with eyes open and a swathe of black hair. The tiny bundle was offered to him and, for the first time, he looked into the face of his child.

Speechless and with tears glistening in his eyes, Angus knew without a doubt that he could be a father.

Chapter 6

Shan was born healthy and perfect as any newborn should be. With three adults continuously ready to fulfil any whim or desire, the bub grew and thrived. But not all in the cottage did. Following months without night terrors, their sudden return was both unexpected and torrential. It was only a few days after the birth when the first one hit. More real and terrifying than she was used to, Jess woke screaming from her sleep, still able to see the images of the Tower and the Dark Ones with her waking eyes. In blind panic she searched for Shan, believing that they had come to collect another for the Tower. Only after holding her newborn and seeing that Angus was there in front of her could she be consoled.

From then Jess would not let Shan out of her sight. Angus and Maima tried to take some of the burden of the baby's care. Yet, even when with Angus, Jess would watch nervously. Shan was a good and easy child, sleeping well and feeding once, or at most twice, a night. But in addition to this disruption in sleep, for Jess almost every night there would be some additional dark disturbance. Angus tried to calm her but, lacking sleep himself, he found it hard. Jess would refuse Maima's herbs in case they affected her milk.

So, she slept less and worried more. Gradually she lost weight but, despite being constantly on edge, she held onto some normalcy of her life by sheer force of will. Eventually, Maima saw no other option but, on occasion, to surreptitiously use Influence to help Jess get some sleep.

Jess was convinced that the Tower wanted their child. That they were looking for them and getting closer to finding them. Her whole focus was Shan. The household garden was left for Angus to tend. She no longer helped with the tonics and when asked about things she appeared vague and unfocused. For long periods she would just sit, watching Shan sleep. At night she would often leave her bed and sit next to the crib, not moving, and only responding after repeated attempts to communicate with her.

Angus could not understand what was happening. He tried to talk to his wife but would only receive the briefest of responses before she returned to her watching. Maima was equally baffled as to what to do. With Jess eating little, refusing any tonics, and only sleeping when Maima was able to secretly use Influence, her milk supply was dwindling. Shan was no longer gaining weight and would frequently cry with hunger which was not satisfied even after being put to both breasts. It was then that each time Jess slept, Maima and Angus would feed Shan with boiled goat's milk, trying to get more food into the small child.

When Shan was three months old, Jess had her first daytime vison of the Tower. Once again, she was within its walls. The smooth black stone and the silver-grey light. This time, however, she was not alone. About her were ghostly figures, indistinct reflections of young girls. There were many of them and all were unified in one voice, "The Tower, the Tower, we are the Tower."

She looked about herself, terrified. Running down the corridor she passed though many of the apparitions. She felt nothing as she passed through them but an emptiness, a loss, a lack of … of something. They had all lost something. They were no longer complete, no longer individual. Calling to her, they swarmed around her. "You are the Tower; we are the Tower."

She screamed but no sound emerged. She ran but did not move. Falling to the floor she felt something grabbing her arm. She desperately tried to pull away before she realised that it was Angus, helping her to her feet from the cottage floor. Collapsing into his arms she cried; deep, soul-wrenching sobs. Eventually she was able to raise her head and look at him. "It isn't over. I didn't escape the Tower. It will find me."

Angus started to reassure her that the Tower did not know where they were, that they were so, so far away, and it had now been more than two years since they left. Nothing had happened and wouldn't. She had nothing to fear, these were just dreams. Fears coming from all the suffering the Tower had inflicted on her.

Jess looked at him, now calm and with clear eyes. Gently, she took his hand and placed it over her heart. Holding it there she stroked his face, seeing the tears in his eyes at her declaration, "My love. What joy you have given me. When I never thought to know happiness again, you found me. You saved me from a nothingness and gave me love and hope, and a family. What more could I ever want?" Seeing him start to cry she added, "You have Shan, and so I will always be with you."

Pulling her to himself, Angus let his emotions go. He knew that he would not give up. He would find a way.

***

Jess was calmer. She started to sleep better and eat. Although still not her normal self, she made the effort to present an imitation of who she used to be. Her milk supply increased again, and Shan could have a full tummy to sleep. Gradually mushy solids were added to the baby's diet, and an undisturbed night of sleep was even possible. She no longer spoke of the Tower and stopped obsessively watching Shan at all hours of the day and night. Occasionally she would go out for walks, saying that the short break alone did her good.

Angus was cautiously optimistic that the worst was over and that her fear of the Tower was lessening. They would talk of the future, of Shan growing up, of Angus as a father and all the things he would do. Of simple things – the goats and the ripening harvest – but she never would talk about herself. Then one day while Angus was out caring for the goats, Jess said to Maima that she would like to go for a walk. Handing Shan over to her she hugged and kissed them both. Telling Shan to be good she went out of the cottage door without looking back.

The previous day Jess had been weeding in the house garden when a vison came to her. Over the last few months, she had felt Influence being drained from her. In the Tower, each time when she had failed her testing a little bit of her was lost to the Tower. She was now aware that this had continued and was gradually picking up pace. She felt bits of her evaporating. She could no longer remember the cottage in Town or the trip to their new home. That they were real and had happened, she was sure, but there was no longer anything to recall. Meeting Maima was vague, and she no longer had any knowledge of how to make the tonics and ointments. She did, however, still remember seeing Angus for the first time. His kind, handsome face creased with concern as she lay in bed. The way he was always near her to help her as she recovered. These memories were far too precious to lose, and she was determined that she never would lose them. The Tower would not have them. It would not win. She would not let it. She had not let it when she was in the Tower and now, even more so, she would not let it win. She still had one power over the Tower, and the time to use it was now, or never.

Her day had begun normally but, as had become almost routine, a vison of the Tower presented itself to her. Again in the Tower, but no longer afraid, she was once more surrounded by the transparent vestiges of the other girls. As before, they called to her in unison and this time it was clear. She was to be like

43

them. No longer herself, no longer with memories and no longer a mother and wife. She knew that it was close, very close. She did not want to lose a single moment with the ones she loved, yet now there was no other option. Either way, she would be separated from Angus and Shan; but this way she would still be herself. She had decided to do this once before and had found the strength to do it. This time it was harder.

She made her way to the lake. She had been here many times and knew it well, knew where it was deep and where it was easy to access. Gathering rocks from the shore, she placed them in the pockets of her dress and the apron she still wore about her neck. Weighed down, she looked toward the setting sun. Angus was caring for the goats in the pastures of the Western Slopes and would be home soon. Using Influence for the last time, she blew him a kiss with the words "I love you" woven within as she started to walk into the water. Clear minded and calm, happy to take who she was with her, she gazed up at the sky as the water closed about her.

***

Almost back, Angus stopped to take in the view of his home. Things were going well, he thought, and he hoped that they would continue that way. As he stood there, he felt a breeze brush against his cheek, almost like a kiss. It was then that he heard it. Carried on the breeze was Jess' voice, "I love you." Unsure what this meant, he looked and saw a bright light emanating from the small lake that lay beyond the homestead. It rose into the air, broke into segments, and dissipated in all directions. Suddenly gripped by an unnamed horror and covered in a cold sweat, he dropped everything and ran toward the lake. Forcing himself not to think, he ran, heaving in deep breaths, forcing his legs to take him there as fast as possible.

Arriving at the lake breathless and gasping for air, he scanned the shore and then the surface of the water. Nothing seemed out of the ordinary, but then he spied something floating on the water near the shore. One of Jess' hair ribbons. A bit further out he spotted something else. Hurling himself forward, he forced his way through the water until it was too deep. Not knowing how to swim, he thrashed about. Gradually he made his way closer until he could see the long threads of hair resting on the water's surface. Just beneath he could see Jess, still and lifeless. In desperation he tried to pull her to the surface but only managed to drag himself under the water. Too heavy to raise and losing what strength he had left, he let himself fall below the water. In front of him was Jess, eyes closed but looking beautiful and serene, and as cold and pale as when he first found her. How could he have been so wrong? He had promised to protect her. Now all he wanted was to join her. No longer fighting the water he gradually allowed his mind to let go of life and all that it contained. Then he remembered Shan. He was also a father.

With renewed strength, Angus tried to reach the surface, but his water-logged clothes and heavy boots kept dragging him down. Running out of air and only able to look longingly at the sunset playing on the water's surface, Angus was losing hope. Drawing deep into himself and calling on the very last of his strength, he tried one last time. Out of his innermost parts he felt it. A vibration that radiated about him, exiting the water and forming a vortex that reached to the surface, allowing him to gasp a lungful of air. Renewed, he reached for the surface. Sound seemed to radiate from him, causing small waves to form and, without knowing how, he found himself back on the shore.

He was found by Maima who had heard an explosion from the lake. It took little explanation from Angus, as Maima could see what had happened. Revived enough to walk, she took him back to the cottage where she put him to bed and then to sleep.

***

With the help of Farmer Albee, they were able to recover Jess from the lake. They took a little comfort that Jess believed she had avoided the Tower. If this was true or not, however, they did not know. It was a simple burial on the lower slopes. Unmarked except for her favourite flowers, Jess was laid in a place hidden from sight of the Tower. And now, a place that had been their home and full of so many happy memories was haunted by images that could never be forgotten.

Following the burial, Angus sat with Maima looking out across the Bowl. Sitting quietly as Shan rolled about on the grass in front of them, he turned to her. "What else can I do? Tell me. You know that I will do it."

"I don't know, I wish I did, but what you say is true, from what we know."

"How can I? It is not fair on Shan or you."

"There is very little that is fair in this world, my dear. We hope for it, but it rarely comes. No-one can blame you. It happened, and without it we could have been digging two graves. But we know that it is not safe. You said yourself that you saw a red light come from the Tower for several nights in a row after it happened."

"Stretching out to reach each area of the Bowl. Yes, I know."

"Shan and I will be fine, and you will be able to return to us when it is safe."

"But when will that be? If we never use Influence again, they may never find us. It is harder the further one gets away from the Tower."

"We just don't know. I couldn't bear losing you as well. We will be safe here and hopefully you will be as well, in time. Go and find the others. With your talent you will be able to find them and, when it is safe, come back to us."

Returning to the cottage, Angus took his large bag that was already packed. Holding Shan close to him, he breathed in deeply, taking in the scent of his child – his and Jess' child. Looking at his mother he opened his mouth to speak but did not know what to say. She came to him and held him the way she used to do when he was younger. "We will be fine," she said.

Hugging and kissing them both, Angus turned to go. Looking back, he whispered, "I love you, Shan. Remember your mother and father and that we love you."

Chapter 7

There was no doubt that the Tower was impressive. Impressive in a way that invoked wonder, but a wonder that was also tinged by fear. Despite living whole generations under its watchful presence, very few people of the Bowl knew, or understood, what really was going on. For many, its presence did not provoke the slightest spark of curiosity. It had always been there, and it probably always would. Daily life continued, and people lived and thrived. At least, they convinced themselves that they thrived. Things just persisted, mostly in a state of relative calm. The infrequent breaks in this perceived calm were generally greeted, more or less, with acceptance, liberally sprinkled with a touch of denial, allowing the general perception that nothing out of the ordinary ever really happened to continue.

It was only a few, less self-deceptive, inhabitants who were brave enough to admit to themselves that things were not what they should be. That things could, and should, be different. That the separation of families, unexplained disappearances, and enforced rules and regulations were not justified. These unusual few, however, also knew that such thinking was best kept to oneself – or at least contained to the company of other like-minded individuals. Thus, even these relatively unique individuals tended to remain invisible, indistinguishable from the general mass that resided in the Bowl.

***

From the other side of the Bowl, Shan could look down over the cultivated fields, lush pastures, and scattered hamlets all the way east. It was still early and, although the day had commenced and a clear blue sky was seen above, the sun had not yet risen over the towering mountains that made up the boundary of the Bowl.

The goats were both Shan's responsibility and daily companions. Each day they made their way up the lower slopes of the western ranges that were nearest to home. The Bowl was aptly named. A lush, fertile oasis that was fully enclosed by natural walls. These walls rose to dizzying heights and were crowned with permanent caps of glistening white snow. As far as Shan knew, no-one had ever decided to climb these peaks. If they had, then they had never decided to return to talk of the experience.

Gazing toward the Tower, always directly under the path of the rising sun, it was possible to distinguish the first rays of sunshine that crept over the peaks. This was magical. The first rays of sunshine would reach this spot of the Bowl before any other, and that made Shan feel special. Being the first to feel the sun of a new day gave a feeling of renewal and vitality that was never disappointing. It was worth getting up early every morning to herd the goats up the slope just to get this time alone with the sun.

Now that the sun was higher the land looked alive. It was good to have another day to be out and about with the goats who were, apart from Maima, Shan's only companions. They had been playmates from the time of infancy but giving them names like people had seemed a bit silly. They didn't have names for each other so why should names be imposed upon them? They were recognisable by their personalities. This made more sense to Shan.

Simply acknowledging how they perceived each other, and themselves, allowed for commands to be given. As long as these were clear and not too complex, the desired results were usually forthcoming. Goats really were not that clever. They were creatures of habit and base desires. Using this knowledge made life a lot easier, and herding a lot less time consuming. Sheep followed their leader, but goats only wanted to do their own thing. If one, however, was able to link the goats' desire for food, lush grass, and crystal-clear water with climbing up the slope, then this is what they would do without any herding required. Although only thirteen years old, Shan had learnt this very quickly and was able to manipulate the small herd with very little effort.

Spending a great deal of time alone allowed Shan to think and ponder. This was a luxury that many never experienced. It did allow, however, for a lot of unanswerable questions to form and take root. Maima had said that this was a good thing. She encouraged reading once the goats were put to bed. Such a skill was rare, and books were restricted, but somehow Maima provided both. Although, to be fair, reading rarely provided answers to the many questions that circled around in Shan's head. Yet, reading had become as much of a pleasure as bathing in the early morning rays of the sun and, for now, that was enough.

With the risen sun, the task of looking for the herbs and wild foods that Maima would want for their dinner could commence. Dandelion soup was always a favourite, but it often meant a fight with the goats about who could get to the flowers first. Usually, it was just a matter of foraging further afield than the flock. Still, at other times, it required Shan to physically tackle one, or more, of the adventurous goats to the ground in order to prevent the loss of the desirable find. Today, however, they had taken a different path up the lower slopes. This had led them to a meadow sprinkled with yellow flower heads and small, rounded balls of silver tufts that would dissolve into tiny white clouds following any gust of wind that flowed down the mountain side. So, for today, at least, they could all get their fill.

Taking off a canvas satchel, Shan removed a small knife and went to work harvesting the nearest dandelion. Three tiers. First, the flowers. The young flower heads were Shan's favourite. These were sweet and tender, honey-like, and made a wonderful sweet-smelling tea. The more mature flower heads were slightly bitter, but perfect for soup, and were Maima's favourite. The leaves, when tender and young, made salads, while the larger ones helped the soups or were remarkable when steamed. Finally, the roots could be harvested. These would be dried, roasted, and then ground to make a dark, bitter concoction that was added to boiling water for Maima to drink in the evenings after all the work was done. It was enjoyable work, and methodical, which appealed to Shan. Order, predictability, and utility were comforting. Having the knowledge of where you were, what you were doing, and why you were doing it was soothing.

Once enough had been gathered to fill half the satchel and provide provision to create more than a few meals, attention was directed to the search for other ingredients required for that evening's soup. One thing that Shan loved was the inclusion of potatoes, which added thickness to the soup. They created a texture that was smoother, fuller, and more filling. Finding wild potatoes was not usually difficult. They grew in the cooler regions higher up on the foothills. Nothing disturbed them as nothing would eat the toxic flowers or leaves. This, together with their vivid purple bell-like flowers, made them easily seen from a distance against the greys and greens of the rocks and grasses.

Leaving the flock happily gorging themselves in the meadow, Shan started to move further up the slope. It would not take long to get high enough to be in the area where the tubers grew. With the gaining of height, and with the sun higher in the sky and no longer directly behind the Tower, it was easier to see the way it peered over the Bowl. This was particularly true for those living nearer the eastern side of the Bowl, and especially for the inhabitants of Town, located right at the foot of the steep stairs that led to the Tower gates.

Why anyone would put up with being continuously overlooked was beyond Shan's understanding. Having the freedom to be out and about while being unobserved was something that was taken for granted by those distanced from Town. That was the way they liked it. Still, Shan could not help being impressed by the way the Tower appeared to be suspended in front of the mountainous wall that was the boundary to their world. The seemingly-impenetrable inky blackness of the Tower was so black that it appeared to absorb the light itself, never allowing for it to be released again. It was unknown and unknowable. What it was and what it was for, Shan didn't know. It was something that Maima had refused to discuss and always just said, "In time, all in time, my dear. Not before and only when needed." Despite continued efforts and questions, this was the only response that was ever given. With no other option but to wait, no further questions were asked.

Climbing over another rock revealed the distinctive mass of purple that highlighted the goal of the climb. Now the problem was to get down deep enough under the plant to the root system that carried the small round tubers. Once again taking out the little knife, Shan began to loosen the soil around one of the largest stalks. The larger the tuber, the better. This had been one of the first lessons that Maima ever taught; brown good, green bad, and big good, small bad. Fortunately, the soil was still moist with the recent rains and had not been heavily compacted. Still, the work was slow and difficult. Shan hoped that it would be worthwhile. Eventually enough soil was removed to allow for easier access to the root system. Green, definitely not. Potatoes were not without risk.

Shan remembered all too vividly when Maima's teaching had been ignored. Young – yes, Shan had been young – but still that was not an excuse. Potatoes in Maima's soup had always been a favourite and so, logically, if some were good more would be better. Not all of the tubers had been used for the soup. One particularly small and slightly green one had magically disappeared from the kitchen table and ended up in Shan's mouth. It had only been one chew and barely a swallow before Maima had turned Shan upside down, repeatedly whacking the small child's back. This caused a forced expulsion of the remaining tuber from the mouth with such vigour that it hit the opposing wall. That had not been enough. Shan remembered that within an hour, the vomiting, stomach cramps and, being too weak and lethargic to make it to the door and use the outdoor toilet, continual usage of the chamber pot in the corner had begun. It lasted more than a day. The nausea and headaches continued for a full cycle of the moon. So, never again would Shan ignore one of Maima's teachings, especially one that related to tubers.

Digging further led to the discovery of several decent-sized brown tubers almost the size of Shan's palm. These would be perfect, but not too many could be used at once and, as time would turn harvested potatoes green, there was no point in taking more than was needed for today's soup alone.

Putting the precious finds into the satchel and once again storing the knife, Shan looked about. The flock had been left in a perfect place to keep them happy but that did not mean that one, or more, of them had not wandered further off. There were no predators about to cause any concern. These only appeared to exist in the books that Shan read. No-one had ever warned about the need to keep a close watch in order to protect the herd from being eaten. Still, there were streams and slippery banks, caves and nettles that could cause the animals some grief. Hoping that this would not be the case today, Shan started the trek back down.

Back in the meadow all appeared calm. The sun was now well into the western half of the sky. Its rays would leave Shan and the flock earlier than anywhere else in the Bowl. It would soon be time to return home, milk the goats, and put them to bed. Fortunately, by promoting the natural tendencies of the goats, often the desired outcome would ensue. In addition, after much trial and error, Shan had also found that by concentrating hard and then projecting a desire directly into the herd they would frequently follow that desire. Therefore, while giving a loud whistle to alert the flock, Shan also attempted to project into the goats the desire that they wanted to be warm and safe, having a comfortable sleep in the straw at home. It was then a matter of waiting for them to collect nearby so that they could all start down the slope together.

Some goats were just more pliable than others. Shan had yet to work out the reason for the differences but put it down primarily to their personalities. As a matter of necessity, Shan used these differences to identify each individual goat. Calm and Obedient, Homely, Anxious, and Scared were always first to collect. These were then usually followed by Safe and Testy, while Friendly and Excited took a bit longer. In dribs and drabs the others would arrive, but it was always Crazy and Confident that were last to assemble. In all, there were twenty, enough to provide milk and cheese. Occasionally there was also meat, but this was always decided by Maima, and she would undertake the process herself. Shan sent forth another whistle and strengthened the projection of the desire to be safe and warm. Further waiting resulted in Confident slowly joining the others.

Only nineteen. That is annoying. Why is it that Crazy is always the last? If only I knew which desire would most appeal to her most, then perhaps I could control her better?

Looking around the meadow, Shan was unable to see where the obstinate goat could be. Only one thing to do, and that was to leave the others of the flock and go and look. First, however, there was a need to gain any information about where Crazy might be. Obedient didn't like Crazy and always kept an eye on her. Perhaps Obedient could help? Kneeling down in front of the goat, Shan instilled in her a strong desire to headbutt Crazy. Carefully watching Obedient, Shan noticed that she turned her head to the right, looking towards the trees growing up against a rocky outcrop. Shan stood and, before leaving, propelled the feeling of fear of being separated into the flock.

That should at least keep them together. If they do move somewhere else, finding nineteen goats is a lot easier than finding one, mused Shan.

Moving close to the rocky outcrop, Shan noticed a rough track that went through the trees. Following the track led to the opening of a small cave and from within the cave came the soft bleating of a goat – presumably Crazy as there were no wild goats in this part of the Bowl. Crawling into the cave a few feet allowed Shan to hear things better. The bleating was definitely coming from further inside the cave, but it was dark, and Shan was not able to see how far the cave went in or what size it was. It was not possible for Shan to determine if advancing much further was even an option. Without any light Shan would have to feel the way in and, without knowing what was in front, ran the risk of injuries. If the tunnel got narrower it could become impossible to turn around, requiring the unpleasant task of crawling out backwards.

"Crazy, you know that my life would be so much easier if I just left you here or, if I do get you out, I might suggest to Maima that we have not had meat for a while. What do you think? Which is better, that you stay here and die of thirst or I take you home and we eat you?"

No, thought Shan, that is not going to help. I need to get into Crazy's brain. What is it that would make her do this? What is it that she will respond to? What is it that she wants?

Then it occurred to Shan to wonder what was it that seemed to motivate Crazy, what was it that caused her to do such stupid things?

Fundamentally we have only a limited number of desires, thought Shan. We have the desire to stay alive and that requires food, water, and sleep – but these wouldn't make Crazy enter a cave when all this was much better outside. We desire love and friendship but, again, how could this be fulfilled by going in alone, while the desire for safety, avoiding harm and pain are the very opposite of entering a dark, unknown space? So, what about acceptance? This could be possible? Crazy's always doing things that none of the other goats do. Perhaps she is trying to gain respect from the other goats for being fearless. It was worth a go.

Feeling rather foolish for applying human thoughts and feelings to a goat, Shan projected the feeling of happiness at being in the centre of the flock's adoration after surviving a dark cave, at the same time whistling to indicate which way was out. Waiting silently at the cave opening, the bleating ceased, and Shan instead heard some movement. Once again, the desire for acceptance and admiration was projected into the cave. Nothing happened for a while, but after a few minutes Shan heard more movement and the sound of hoof on stone. Further waiting provided the evidence of success as Crazy, covered in grey dust and cobwebs, eventually emerged from the opening.

"Seriously, why, Crazy? You make things so hard!" admonished Shan, both irritated and relieved that Crazy had emerged unscathed. "Back to the herd, you egotistical animal."

They found the herd where it had been left and, just for good measure, Shan projected into it the desire to welcome and celebrate Crazy.

It cannot hurt. If all Crazy really wants is to be accepted, supporting that might make my life that much easier. "Off home now," Shan directed, while trying to project the most intense desire for home and comfort into the herd. Hopefully that might make the trip that much easier. But with this lot, who can tell?

Chapter 8

Inconsequential; what did that mean anyway? Doesn't everyone feel a bit out of place, a bit awkward, a bit different? I might have a little more of that than others, but I am still here, and I still matter. I still have worth.

Molly was getting so used to going through this with herself that it was almost starting to feel like a mantra. It wasn't that people didn't like her or were particularly mean to her, it just was as if they didn't see her. That was all. She just needed to get people to see her, but the more she tried, the more it seemed that they didn't. Being the centre of attention was definitely not something Molly ever desired. But being noticed, considered, being just a bit important, even if only occasionally, would make her life infinitely better.

Once again it had happened. Molly had been sent to the market. It was not a difficult request, just an errand to go and get some fresh vegetables for the family dinner. She didn't understand why, but once out the front door of the house her confidence would fall. The further away from the family, the lower it would get. At home with her sisters, she was bright and happy, fun, and very especially noticed. Once out the door she seemed to fade into herself. She was solid enough, there was no doubt about that. Alright, she was a bit on the rounder side, she had to admit, but then Mama had always said that this was something she should be proud of. She had food and enough of it to be able to be round. She didn't have to hunt and scrounge in order to eat. So, Mama said, "Be proud, walk tall, and be confident." Well, Molly tried. She would walk as tall as she could, but at age thirteen and without particularly tall parents, she was unlikely to be particularly impressive.

This time, however, as she ventured into the Town market things had gone worse than usual. Leaving the front step always took a bit of courage. She felt so loved and accepted at home. She could always be exactly who she was, no hiding, no pretending. Being on the cusp of starting to grow up was not easy and Molly felt it. Mama was always there guiding, supporting, and encouraging. She was no longer a child and had to learn how to care for a house, run a family and look after the household money. Mama was trusting her now to look after her four younger sisters, whom Molly adored. They laughed and played, with Molly creating games that all could play together. Even the youngest, at three years old, could always join in and enjoy.

Molly had a natural gift, intuitive as it was, of knowing how others were feeling. She always tried to consider the way others felt and how things could be difficult or challenging for them. She tried to make them feel free to be themselves and encourage them to take satisfaction in whatever they achieved, even if it was as simple as remembering to go to the toilet before it got a little too late.

Mama needed other help as well, and thus it was that Molly had been sent on her way to the market. Outside the front door she lost the safeness of her home. Feeling self-conscious, she started to imagine how other people would see her. A short, round, nondescript child trying to force herself into being a grown-up because *they* did not seem to worry about what other people thought. Molly knew that she would never be beautiful. Pleasant was the best she hoped for. Mama said that this was exactly the way Molly should be. Beauty may seem like something to crave, but the true light of a loving, caring, and jolly nature shone so much brighter and lasted a great deal longer. Molly appreciated the support, but felt that had she been a bit comelier, less would have been made of her "jolly" personality.

Tuning right and making her way down the street, Molly had decided that today she would try and take a little bit of home with her. In this way she hoped that she would be able to remain more like herself. As she turned into the main street and made her way toward the market square, however, her confidence started to evaporate. As she got closer to the square, more and more people filled the street. People were moving everywhere, in every direction. Carts made their way along the streets. On some, deliveries were on their way to the richer areas of Town. Others were bringing more produce into the market from the farms that made up the majority of the Bowl. Tradespeople moved about from one job to another. Shoppers loaded with purchases returned home from market, intermingled with others on their way there. As the bustle and number of people increased Molly began to feel less significant, less substantial. People started to bump into her as they moved past, seeming neither to notice nor even try to evade her. Molly started dodging from side to side, trying to keep out of the way of people before they would get too close. This, unfortunately, was not unusual for her, but it only made her feel less significant and less substantial.

Finally arriving at the market square, Molly headed towards the stall of a family friend. The vegetables here were always the freshest and Mrs Perkins would often add in something extra, and invariably sweet, to be shared amongst Molly and her sisters. What that was usually depended on what Mrs Perkins had most recently been doing in the kitchen. Sometimes it was jams made from the overripe and unsaleable excess fruit. Less frequently it could be dried fruit strips that stuck to your teeth. However, the undeniable favourite of all the girls were the boiled fruit lollies.

Molly made her way to the stall. There were a few people there before her and so she waited patiently, looking around the stall to see what it was that Mrs Perkins had most recently been doing in the kitchen. Molly enjoyed seeing all the fruit and vegetables stacked neatly into colourful mounds, each appearing to explode with confidence, seeming to shout, "Look at me, I am exactly what I should be." Tomatoes were proud to be tomatoes. Beans were delighted to be just that particular shade of green, while the pumpkins sat dignified and round, exuding self-satisfaction in being orange. Molly wished that she could feel as confident as these vegetables.

As the last customer in front of Molly left, Mrs Perkins turned and stated to busy herself tidying the display. Feeling a bit miffed for being ignored, Molly gave out a small cough. Molly herself could hardly hear this above the market noise and so tried again with barely any greater effect. "Excuse me," she blurted out.

"Oh, hello, Molly," said Mrs Perkins as she turned around. "I didn't see you there. Have you been waiting long?"

Not wanting to appear rude Molly just shrugged and said, "Not really."

"Do you want anything special today? We have just got in the string beans. They are particularly fresh and crunchy as they only got picked this morning. The beetroots are also very good, as are the squash."

"Mama would like some beans, please, also carrots and cabbage, and, if you have any, coriander. She is going to make corn starch soup."

"Right you are," said Mrs Perkins as she deftly collected and placed the items in Molly's basket.

"Thank you, Father will come past on his way home to pay," Molly stated and turned just as another customer walked right up to her, claiming her space at the stall before she had even vacated it. She dodged adeptly out of the way before heading back home.

Molly did not understand how so many people could be in such a rush that they could just walk into her without even noticing. Being careful to avoid a particularly large group that was making its way toward her, Molly moved away from the side of the road. Inadvertently, she stepped into the road itself. Carts were still moving at some speed along the street, but Molly was in full view of the drivers who would be able to slow down. This would allow for her to move past the crowd and back towards the side of the road. The sun was in the west, shining down the road in front of her and lighting it up with a brilliant yellow glow. Molly looked up above the sun to the clear blue sky, enjoying the last of the sun's warmth, totally unaware that the approaching cart was not slowing. Just moments before it reached her, Molly looked back down, threw herself sideways into the crowd with a scream, and scattered her basket with all its contents about her. The sound of the market changed as people about Molly yelled and complained, unaware of what had just happened. The cart came to an abrupt stop as the driver jumped down and raced towards her. "Where the hell did you come from?" he yelled. "You can't jump out in front of moving carts!"

"I didn't!" Molly exclaimed. "I was right in front of you."

"I didn't see you! You couldn't have been. Are you hurt?"

Molly checked herself. No, not hurt; embarrassed, but not hurt. "I'm fine, I'm fine," she mumbled, rising and quickly gathering her things while the crowd milled about and muttered amongst themselves. "I'm fine," Molly insisted, trying to hold back tears. Once she had the basket full again, she lowered her head and made a rapid departure, heading straight home.

"I swear, she wasn't there. I would have seen her."

***

Shan looked down the path toward home. It was not that much really. A simple wooden construction with three rooms, a solid stone chimney, reliable well, and a smallish but generally weatherproof barn for the goats. This was home. Shan cherished it, and Maima. Maima had always been there. The one who took care of everything, taught Shan things and, most especially, gave the gift of reading. Shan didn't remember ever having a mother or a father. It was understandable that there must have been one of each, but for Shan, Maima was both of them combined. She was older now, not as able as she once had been, and so Shan had been doing increasingly more and more of the work that was required to keep the plot going.

Maima never complained but Shan knew that getting around was proving to be painful for her. She often had a list of wild herbs and plants for Shan to collect. From these she would create tinctures and concoctions that she would either place on her aching joints or mix in with her brew of roasted dandelion roots in the evening. Shan was not sure that these mixtures achieved a great deal but was happy if they were able, in any small way, to make things a bit more comfortable for Maima.

Making the final approach home, Shan directed the goats to the small holding pen that was used to separate the unmilked from the milked goats. Not all would produce milk, and even on a good day, only half of them would. The younger ones and, of course, Testy the buck didn't.

Shan would put them in the pen, check which needed milking and get on and do it. Maima would be having a rest at the moment. It wouldn't take that long and then Shan would check on Maima. She would take the milk and start the process of making the cheese, yoghurt and buttermilk that was so important to them. It was these, together with the tonics and ointments Maima created, that Shan would have to take to the small market nearby in order to sell, or barter, for the things that they were not able to get in other ways. And, of course, there was the tithe. One tenth of all their cheese, yoghurt, and buttermilk would make its way east into the town that was at the foot of the Tower.

It was the law and always had been. No-one ever didn't give the tithe. Shan wasn't sure why it was that it was needed, but then there still was a great deal that Shan did not know. Maima had always said not to question and just do it. One day, Shan would work out why. Now, however, the afternoon was drawing on and there was milking to be done. So, Shan set to work, knowing that dandelion soup was to be looked forward to, and then the enjoyment of an evening listening to Maima's lessons or being captivated by a book.

Chapter 9

Some children just seemed to have it all. Well, at least they did to the casual observer. Moira, with her long, sleek, glossy auburn hair, porcelain complexion, gorgeous clothes, and fancy house was a beautiful child of thirteen who would grow into a stunning woman. A girl whose parents could provide luxuries that many would never even consider possible. She certainly had never had to do without, and she knew that her future would be filled with comforts and privilege.

But it is not always the case that outward beauty and advantage will develop the inner person in a way that is desirable. Moira was spoilt. This in itself is not unusual for many children, regardless of their position in life. Most, over time and as they grow, will learn what it is to be spoilt and what it is to be considerate and compassionate and aware of those around them. For Moira, however, this was not the case. Her life was the focus. Her needs were foremost, and her desires were to be fulfilled. This was the way it had always been, and she saw no reason for that to change. Her parents left a great deal of the day-to-day dealings with their daughter to the staff. Whether they thought they were doing the best for their daughter was unknown, but there were strict instructions that their beautiful daughter, who was "such a delight to them", should be kept happy. The staff made sure that she was happy. It was a lot easier if they did. They all hoped, however, that she would eventually grow out of this phase. It was only a phase. They were sure that she would. Well. At least they hoped she would.

Moira, now an only child, had made it her business to run the house the way that she wanted it. It really hadn't been that hard with distant and frequently absent parents. She had originally been the second daughter of the family. Her elder sister had the misfortune to die when Moira was about seven years old, from something or other. Moira didn't know what and really didn't care that much to know. But it had given her the occasion and opportunity to feel that she could cement her position as the most important person in the household. She had been cultivating the talent of producing a convincing cough when convenient to her interests. If denied a wish or desire, she could faint, go pale, and even imitate a slight convulsion. More recently she had developed the ability to create a fever with sweats and the appearance of a rash that, once any objection to her wishes were quelled, would miraculously disappear. This she had found all very useful.

Today Moira had decided to sit, statuesque, on the balcony off her bedroom. It was the bedroom with the best view and had taken her some effort to secure for herself, having been her father's dressing chamber previously. She, however, had been unhappy with the view and wanted a small folly to be created on the grounds of the estate. To this end, a cylindrical tower was to be constructed. A tower with steps winding upwards to a circular room containing four arched windows that faced each point of the compass. The folly was to be hers. Her tower that would allow her to look to all areas of the Bowl, but most particularly allow for a better view of the Tower that had always been there above Town.

She had always been fascinated by the Tower. She did not understand it, but it got a tenth of everything everyone had. She never saw anyone in or about the Tower, but no-one questioned the tithe or failed to give it. *How could this be?* She was forced to give begrudging admiration to the Tower. For whomever was there was able to get the whole Bowl to give something for what appeared to be nothing. She wanted to know why. What was it that made the people of the Bowl do this without question?

Now, if she could get people to willingly do what she wanted, then that would be an achievement. At present it took coercion and persuasion. Yes, she had to admit that she was good at that. Still, she saw, at times, that there was some reluctance, some resentment, to her will. This she expected in the servants and those of lower status than her, but she had also occasionally seen it in her father. That was not good. That could potentially lead to him refusing her and that would not do. For that reason, she planned to study the Tower, to find out as much as she could about it and discover how it got what it wanted without appearing to do anything.

Portraying a picture of perfect serenity, Moira sat on the balcony and contemplated her situation. Young though she was, she knew that beauty was powerful although not lasting. Persuasion and charm worked, but not always. Annoyingly, there were some who appeared persistently resistant to both charm and beauty. Reason was something that she preferred not to address. Most of the time reason would be against her will and desire, and thus needed to be shut down before it had the chance of being considered. But all in all, everything that she really wanted boiled down to the demonstration of power over others. Once one had developed a taste for this it was not easily put aside. Power over others was also not as simple as getting what one wanted. It was, fundamentally, so much more than that. It was being above others and, there-fore, more important. It was control. It was not being questioned – and it was something that she wanted.

***

Mama knocked lightly at the door, gently inquiring if she was alright. Molly really didn't want to answer. She knew that her mother was worried as she had uncharacteristically raced through the kitchen, depositing the shopping on the bench, before exiting rapidly to hide in her room. There really was nothing Mama could do, but her soothing voice and concerned eyes never failed to make her feel more like herself; more solid, substantial, and loved. Opening the door, she allowed her mother to hold her without speaking, soaking in the warmth and care that emanated from her touch.

"What happened?" Mama inquired.

"Nothing important," Molly replied, too embarrassed to admit that she had almost been the cause of an accident.

"No, that's not true, Molly. What happened?" Mama insisted.

In a small voice, Molly started to explain. "I don't understand, Mama. I am me here, but as soon as I leave, I no longer feel like me."

"Darling, you are always you, wherever you are."

"No, you don't understand. I know I am me – but I become less me. Like I'm not really there. People don't see me. It is like I have faded, become thin like air. I don't know why. A cart almost hit me. I had been right in front of it for ages, but it didn't see me, didn't stop."

"Are you hurt? Are you alright? Do we need the physician?" Mama asked, concerned.

"I'm fine, I'm fine," Molly protested. "I fell into a crowd. I'm fine, a sore elbow, that's all."

"Let me see," Mama demanded. Examining the arm revealed a graze and nothing more, but Mama still insisted that it needed to be washed and dressed. Taking Molly by the other arm she led her back downstairs into the kitchen where she gently washed the area, covering the graze in a thick, oily cream before wrapping a bandage lightly around the elbow.

"Molly, how long has this feeling been going on?"

"I don't really know. It has been there for a while, but just seems to be getting worse."

"Molly, think, you used to run around the street and play with no problems. When did you start feeling that you were fading?"

It seemed an odd question. Yes, Molly had used the word fading to describe her feeling, but she did not expect Mama to use the same word. She thought that Mama would scold her for being too sensitive. Give her a talk about holding her head up high or tell her to be proud of who she was. This was one thing that Molly did not expect. "I don't really know. Not that long, I don't think."

Mama closed her eyes. She looked concerned, but when she opened them again, her face was bright. With a smile she sent Molly off to check on her sisters while she prepared supper for the family. As Molly was leaving, she turned and briefly caught a glimpse of her mother, her face tense, holding her hands tightly to her breast before she continued to busy herself with the food.

***

"How are you feeling, Maima? Did you get a good rest?" Shan had finished the milking and had brought the buckets of milk into the workroom that made up the third room of their small wooden cottage. Maima had slowly risen from her chair in the corner and was shuffling slowly around the room, gradually warming up her joints in an attempt to make her movements easier and less restricted by the pains that had been her constant companion over the last few months. Getting rest was never that easy or successful. No matter the position, something always hurt. Cushions and padding had been added and removed, replaced, and altered many times in her chair, with little improvement in comfort. Still, she found it more comfortable sitting. The chair was more comfortable than the horsehair mattress that was the alternative. A rest, no matter the level of success, was needed if she was to continue doing the things that she must. There was still more that Shan needed. There was much more, so much more, to be taught and to be learnt. Time, she knew, was not on her side, but there still was time. She hoped there was still time.

"Enough, sufficiently enough," she lied. She knew that it was not her joints that were the problem. She could see the way her body was no longer filling her clothes. They were beginning to hang on her the way those sacks hung on the scarecrows that dotted the crop fields. Food had lost its taste and appeal; but she still needed time. She had to have more time, for Shan's sake. So, she would force herself to get up, keep some focus of what was normal, and do what she had been doing for thirteen years – protecting Shan.

Disguising the pain on her face, Maima made her way to the rough-hewn table near the chimney. Shan had already emptied the contents of the satchel onto the table. With a smile she looked at her grandchild. "Potatoes, well what else would I expect? Good sized ones, too. It will be a good thick soup to-night."

"I put the milk in the workroom. Two full buckets today," Shan boasted.

"They are good goats. As you will be heading to market tomorrow, we will make sour cream and buttermilk tonight so you can take them with the matured cheese," explained Maima. "The cream will not take long to separate. We will heat it tonight before we settle. That way it will have a strong, sharp flavour by tomorrow. Do you think that you will be able to carry it all?"

"Of course, Maima. I will get Calm and Obedient to pull the cart. It doesn't take long and I will be back before the sun leaves the Bowl."

"I will give you a list of things we need. There is not too much, which is just as well as most of this load will go to the Tower."

"Why, Maima? Why does the Tower get our cheese? They are so far away. They …"

"Shan, we do not talk of the Tower. We do as we must and do not question." Maima's voice was stern. "It is the way it is. It has been that way for a very long time, and it is not always for us to know or understand the way of things."

"But, Maima, you tell me to think and question, not to see just what is there in front, but what is behind. Why is this different? What is it about the Tower? I see it every day, hanging over the Bowl, never doing anything, with nothing ever coming from it. What is there to be scared of? What is it that you don't say? I am almost grown up! I am thirteen … why can't I know?"

"My dear, there is so very much that we don't know. Some things are easy to see and understand, while others are much less so. Not everything is knowable. For some things we just have to wait. Eventually these things may become clearer, but not all will. Remember that although all knowledge can be useful, not all knowledge is good. Be patient and one day you will understand."

Shan, fully knowing that Maima was always wise in her words, reluctantly decided to stop nagging.

"Now, my dear, can you go and start skimming off the cream? We will not want a long night with you heading to market tomorrow."

Obediently Shan went to the workroom, fully determined to revisit this whole question with Maima at another time. One thing about Shan was that once there was something worthwhile to know, there was no stopping in the pursuit of it. But for now, settling into the methodical preparation of the cream for market gave sufficient peace of mind to allow for all sorts of flights of fancy to form and captivate the imagination.

Chapter 10

Days started early when you had demanding and important patrons. Joseph would need to be there and be seen to be working as soon as the sun started to rise. It was only the wealthy who had the luxury of waking to the delicate song of the lark. For the rest, the day began well before the sun rose and it was them who kept things running. And so it was that Joseph was up and dressed, sitting in the kitchen. May, his wife, prepared breakfast, and other food for him to take for nourishment throughout the day. And a long day it inevitably would turn out to be, as always.

Ester sat on his lap, which was one of her favourite places to be. At three she was still delicate but robust enough to put up a good showing with her four sisters when necessary. The others were not yet awake, so this was her time to spend with dear Father. She played with his beard and tugged at his ears with impunity while he tickled her and fed her bits of bread and honey.

May saw to it that a hearty breakfast of fresh bread, sausage and cheese would see her husband well into the day. At times she would send one of the girls to see him. They would arrive sometime in the middle of the day with hot soup, or a pie freshly made. This early morning time together was just as equally special for them. A time to talk and enjoy each other's company, a working man with his beloved wife. Life was good. Joseph had a good and honest job. He worked hard, he could care and support his family, and the worries of having either too little, or too much, of anything did not beset them.

Today, however, was different. May seemed distracted and quiet. Her normal banter and happy smiles were missing, and she looked solemn and worried.

"May, speak it."

"I don't know, Joseph."

"Don't know what?"

"Molly."

"And?"

"It's probably nothing, just a mother's fears."

"May, you are many things, but oversensitive or concerned without cause is not one of them. What is it you fear?"

"You know that Noona had a sister?"

"We must never speak of your grandmother's sister. You know that. It isn't safe. As far as things are, she never existed. She ceased to be, for her family and for everyone, after that day."

"But she did, Joseph."

"It was so long ago and Noona is now so old. What does it matter now?"

"Noona remembers. She has spoken of it, rarely, but she has, and she remembers. She remembers her sister and that day. It happened and nothing, no matter what we are forced to do, can make it unhappen."

"And so, nothing can be undone that is done. How is that causing you worry?"

"Molly."

"What about Molly?"

"They say that it can be passed down through the mother."

"What can be passed down?"

"Influence."

"May, that's silly. Your grandmother, your mother and you do not have Influence, so how can it be handed down?"

"I don't know, but Molly said something very strange yesterday. She said that she felt like she was fading. That is the exact word that Noona said that her sister always used before, before … Oh, Joseph, what if Molly has Influence?" May's face crumpled as a few tears stained her cheek. Ignoring Ester's protests as he placed her on his chair, Joseph stood, crossed over to May, and held her. As she buried her face into his shoulder, he felt her trembling. He wrapped his arms tightly around her and nuzzled her hair.

"There is nothing to worry about, May. All girls feel invisible and misunderstood at this age. It is normal, a stage they all go through. Remember how shy and uncomfortable you were when we first met? You never faded, but at times you wished that you could. Now look at you. The magnificent, strong, confident woman beside me. Molly will be just like you. Give it time."

Yet despite the encouraging words and the confidence with which they were delivered, Joseph felt a chill go up his spine. There never was any knowing about Influence and if Molly was afflicted, then he would need to think. Nothing must destroy his family. Of one thing he was certain: he would not let anyone or anything make Molly, or anyone else he loved, cease to be.

***

Molly woke feeling better. Solid and substantial. Just the way that she liked to be. A good night's sleep really did appear to be the cure for most things. Being the eldest, Molly had the good fortune of having her own room. It was a small, poky little room in the attic but to her it was a magnificent grand boudoir. A sumptuous chamber in a palace, fit for a princess awaiting her prince. Her daydreams saw her splendidly dressed in silver and gold, pearls around her neck and jewels in her hair. Gentry from far and wide would come and gaze upon her beauty, to be charmed by her wit. Gifts of exotic birds, perfumes and spices would be placed at her feet and, if she felt like it, she would flash a dazzling smile at the suitor, who would fall to his knees in gratitude for her attention.

With such stories she would fill her daydreams, for in reality she knew that she was plain and dumpy, and no-one would ever look at her that way; that exotic gifts were fanciful, and even finding a decent tradesman would be a stretch. She looked at her parents and saw the happiness they shared. She hoped that she, in all reality, would be as fortunate as they. To find a man who was good and kind and who loved her. This, she knew, would be a true gift and their home a real palace. Still only thirteen, she hoped against hope that she would grow a bit more. It was unlikely, as she was as tall as her mother already, but a bit taller and she might attain a bit of elegance. Getting a bit less round would help as well. Mama said that it was puppy fat, whatever that meant. But the point was that Mama said that she would lose some of it. Molly hoped she would but wished it would happen a lot sooner rather than later.

The sun was about to rise, and Mama would need help getting breakfast for her sisters. Once Father had left for work, the younger ones constantly demanded attention. Without a bit of help Mama would be forever dealing with little things like, "Can I have a drink?" "I need to use the potty!" "Ester took my doll!" and many, many more variations on the main theme which was, "I want attention, I want my way and I want it now." How Mama managed before Molly was old enough to help Molly didn't know, but Mama never lost her temper, seemed to have time for everyone, solved every argument, found every lost item, and still managed to cook and clean, sew and wash. Molly hoped that all these abilities just magically appeared once you got older or she couldn't imagine how she would cope with a family of her own.

Climbing out of bed, she slowly dressed. The nights were mild and the days were warm, like always, so there was no race to get dressed once she'd left the warmth of her bed. It was something that Molly did not give much thought. She was only vaguely aware that other places had times in the year when it was cold and others when it was hot. In the Bowl, the weather was nearly always perfect. It regularly rained once or twice a week, the sun otherwise shone every day, and crops could grow all year round. There was no need for winter coats. It was just the way things were. Once dressed she left her room, carefully closing the door to prevent prying younger sisters from entry, and went downstairs, ready to lend a hand wherever it would be required.

****

The folly was starting to take shape. Joseph had been charged with its construction and had very strict instructions that the tower must be perfectly round with perfect views across the town and into the Bowl, but most particularly that it must have a perfect view of the Tower through the east window. The things the wealthy desired frequently made no sense to him. Creating a tower that no-one would be able to live in, purely for a girl to sit in and gaze at the world made no sense. Still, it was work and it paid well. It also could mean work for him with others of the elite if things went well. And things *were* going well. He knew his craft and was meticulous in both design and process. So far, the tower was little more than the height of two men, but Joseph was pleased. The addition of the height of another four men should do the trick. This would allow an unobstructed view of the Bowl and the Tower.

About the middle of the day Joseph sat down for a well-deserved rest. The mistress of the house had the servants provide him with water and a place to sit in the shade when he required a rest. That was generous, in a way. That she had stooped to consider him at all was indeed thought to be generous in these circles. So, he was grateful to be condescended to. The daughter, however; now, she was a piece of work.

He had learnt very quickly that to her he was beneath consideration, beneath acknowledgement. He made sure that he avoided her gaze whenever possible. Now he saw the young mistress emerge into the garden. The sun catching her hair made it appear to glow with fire.

Joseph remained in place, tucked off to the side and out of direct sight of the child. This girl's beauty did little to conceal her sharp tongue or the belief in her superiority over all others about her. How one so young had been able to develop such a view of herself was something Joseph did not understand. It made him so much more aware of the grace and splendour of his own wife and daughters.

Moira looked about her as she emerged from the shadows into the sunlight. Why things took so long she couldn't believe. It was just a simple tower, but it had been almost two weeks and it had hardly begun to rise. She would have to talk to Papa if this did not move a bit faster. Still, she had to admit that the wall was beautifully curved with the stone blocks fitting so perfectly that any joint between them was barely visible. She decided that perhaps it was satisfactory for the present, but she would have to keep a close watch.

Gliding along the path, Moira made her way up to a small but charming little terrace. Climbing up the few steps revealed the intricate mosaic patterns that a master craftsman had spent many an hour creating. The muted colours of the tiles enhanced any appreciation of the blue of the sky and pink of the cherry blossom that shaded the area. She sat in a large, cushioned ironwork day bed and waited, listening to the gentle music of cascading water from the fountain nearby. Time means nothing when there is nothing that a person needs to do. But then again, when there is no employment every second can feel drawn-out. Such it was for Moira. She was never expected to do anything except please herself and, therefore, she needed to engage herself in making others around her busy. At present she was waiting, with the greatest patience that she could muster, for her refreshments to arrive.

How can it take so long? It is not hard, and I do not request much, thought Moira. What else is there for them to do apart from what they are told? Is that not why we pay them?

Fortunately, just a moment before her reflections would become less benevolent and slightly more vindictive, a manservant appeared in the garden carrying a tray. As he made his way toward her, Joseph could see the child reposition herself, assuming an even greater air of privilege and haughtiness.

What a child, he thought. My Molly would be about her age and for all this wealth I would never change a bit of her.

"Miss." The manservant bowed as he placed the tray on the small table beside her. The tray contained a crystal glass and a small decanter of sparkling lemon and lime cordial. He deftly raised the decanter and filled the glass without a drop wasted. Next to the decanter was a silver plate containing ripe fruits. Each was glossy and polished, vibrant in colour and mouth-watering in appearance. A small fruit knife lay upon the linen napkin.

"Anything further, Miss?" he inquired before being dismissed with a wave.

Moira looked at the fruit. To her it was merely standard fare, nothing special. As she raised a particularly large and rosy strawberry to her lips, she noted a bruise on the underside. A brown, soft and squishy patch on her strawberry.

Her ire rose quickly. *How dare they? A task so simple and yet they fail.* She glared at the back of the retreating manservant. How dare he bring her this.

Joseph saw her face change as she lifted the strawberry. No beauty was there now. None could call her such at this time. He could feel her rage rise as she glared at the back of the man. The air seemed to be charged with it.

"How, how …" she felt lost for words. "Are you blind?"

Joseph had to blink as something had got into his eyes, making them itch. As he wiped them with the back of his hand, he saw that the manservant was about to turn the corner and enter the house, but instead of turning he walked directly into the tree beside the path. Stopping, shaking his head while rubbing a bruised shoulder, the man corrected his path and continued on.

Moira, also watching the man, let out a laugh of pure delight at his misfortune. *There, perhaps you are,* she thought, feeling justified that the insult to her had been addressed. Recalling her attention to the fare before her, she took a sip of the cordial and chose another, this time perfect, strawberry.

Chapter 11

The market was a few hours' walk away through mainly uncultivated land. Shan had been going there alone for some time now as Maima was no longer able to make the journey.

It was an easy trip along a goat track to reach the closest of their neighbours. Farmer Albee kept livestock for meat and rotated crops, providing a mix of vegetables and fruits that were well known in the area for their quality. Farmer Albee was one of Maima's oldest friends. A widower, his son had more recently taken over the running of their plot allowing the farmer a more restful retirement. Not that Shan ever thought that Farmer Albee would, or could, really retire. The land was who he was and his pride in what he cultivated from the fertile soil of the Bowl was both his life and his joy. And that made perfect sense to Shan, whose whole world had never extended past the hamlet that would be visited that day.

Shan had risen, as usual, before the sun was above the rim of the Bowl and been to check on the goats. Although the plan had been to take the two most docile and compliant animals on the trip, Shan realised that this may not be as wise as first thought. Testy the buck was playing up. One male amongst all the females did put him at a disadvantage at times, particularly when one the younger females was creeping toward maturity.

It was surprising to Shan, who had little experience of the other sex – in fact, had little experience of anyone apart from Maima – at how silly Testy could behave. Bounding around the small herd as if he were an overenthusiastic toddler, Testy was attempting to approach a young doe but was being blocked by several of the older, more matronly nannies. Each attempt to breach the herd was blocked by three steely gazes, heads lowered and ready to rebuff any overly-eager approach.

Shan had no idea how long this had been going on, but leaving Testy in this mood, without supervision and with Maima on her own, may not be the wisest choice. Not that Shan felt that Maima would not be able to control the situation. But with her feeling the way she had for the past few weeks, it just didn't seem fair to make her deal with the potential conflict. And so, fully realising that the trip would be just that much less controlled, Shan decided to harness Testy to the small cart that would be taken to market. Thinking carefully, Shan then collected Calm and harnessed her beside Testy. A sensible, quiet goat might be able to modulate Testy's exuberance. Anyway, it was worth a go, and Shan could rely on Calm to be sure and steady in the face of any of Testy's distractions.

Allowing Maima to rest a bit longer, Shan brought out the sour cream and buttermilk that had matured overnight. Placing then in the copper containers used especially for such a trip, Shan covered the openings with cloth and carefully placed them in the cart, balancing their weight evenly for best stability. The last thing anyone wanted was for the cart to tip, and for the containers to lose their contents. The cheese was collected, already carefully wrapped, and placed in the cart. Yesterday's bread was still fresh enough to take for food and Shan knew that there would be offers of fruit on passing Farmer Albee's plot.

Maima was settled in her chair, still asleep but restless. Shan pulled the coverlet up to her chin and made sure that there was a cup of water beside her. Maima had been everything to Shan. Both the mother and father that had never been there. She was stability, home, love, family, and knowledge – all the things that Shan had learnt were important. Now, sitting there, Maima was frail, small, and vulnerable. It was obvious that things were not right. She never complained, but Shan saw it every day, felt the effort that it took her to put on the front of being herself and knew that, despite everything, Maima was not getting better. Holding back a tear, Shan lightly kissed her on the forehead and quietly closed the door on leaving their humble little home.

Getting into the open air and with a day of being outside ahead, Shan could not help but feel hopeful. Talking with Farmer Albee was always a treat. Learning about the harvests and the best ways to grow the sweetest fruit was as fascinating as reading about the things that were beyond the borders of the Bowl. Maima always said that no knowledge was wasted. No-one could say when a fact from here put with another from there could change the world. She had taught Shan to read, to question, and to always look further than what was just in front. To Shan this had been more a theory than a practice, as the world in which they dwelt was small and comfortable. Yet Maima had insisted that reading was a must. It really had not taken much convincing for it to become central to Shan's every day.

Maima had gone to enormous lengths to procure books. Books from anywhere and everywhere about anything. The arrival of a fresh volume, no matter how old or battered, was greeted with more delight than almost anything else in their lives. Farmer Albee had also been instrumental in this whole process for many years. How and where these books were obtained was never obvious to Shan, for it seemed to be a secret shared only between Farmer Albee and Maima. Still, as long as they continued to appear, Shan felt very little need to venture outside the diminutive real world about them. The whole world was open to them in books.

Setting out along the track to Farmer Albee's plot, Shan led Testy and Calm with a cord. They seemed to be as eager as Shan was to go. As the sun began to crest the rim of the Bowl directly in front of them, they commenced their journey. It was going to be a beautiful day again. This was nothing unusual as most days were sunny and mild. It was not due to rain again for another two days.

Shan had found the weather to be predictable and arranged what would be done, and when, around when the rain would come. It did not require knowledge of the winds and clouds to predict when the rain would fall, although this seemed to be what was required in other places, according to the books. Here it merely required the ability to keep a note of the days and the patterns of when the rain fell. It was not immediately obvious without mapping the falls, but once they had been mapped it showed that the rain days followed a definite, although rather convoluted, pattern. This pattern had been the same since Shan had done the mapping and so it was reasonable to assume that it had always been that way. The rain was just enough to provide for all the harvests to continue, without damaging those that were ripening nor deprive those that were in the peak of growth. And so, at all times, the weather was perfect for planting, growth, and harvest. A situation that Shan had also noted was not normally the case in areas outside the Bowl, where they had things called seasons.

In what seemed almost no time at all, Shan and the goats were looking toward the neat and splendid plot of their nearest neighbour. Just as Shan did, the goats knew that here was the opportunity for some tasty delights. Shan had to hold them back to prevent them racing towards the fields and ignoring the cart to which they were tethered. As they approached the house their excitement grew, with Testy requiring a firmer and closer hold on the lead cord.

What a goat. I knew that Obedient would have been easier, thought Shan, as the desire to rest was projected toward them. If I let them feel tired that should calm them and make them easier to manage.

Shan saw Farmer Albee seated in his favourite chair, enjoying the morning sun with a cup of something steaming hot. Shan was expected. It was market day today but, more particularly, it was tithing day. A day where all must be present to give their tithe. Representatives of Town would be there. As such, it was going to be a big day where the small farming community would be putting on a display.

"Well, young Shan. You have made good time. How is your Maima?"

"She was still resting when I left. She finds it hard these days."

"She is no better? I must go and visit her. Johnathon will be back tomorrow, so tell her I will come the day after."

"It would be best not that day, if you please; it will be raining and she would not want you to be put at risk of a chill," Shan explained.

Surprised, Farmer Albee looked closely at Shan. "You are often right about these things, but how you can tell I never understand."

"I am always right, and she would be upset if I did not warn you," Shan stated matter-of-factly.

"The confidence of the young," smirked the man. "Enjoy such while you can, we cannot all be as blessed!"

"It really is simple," started Shan, "it is nothing more than …"

"I am sure it is, but there is still a way for you to go and I think that you would do better with a pouch full of freshly picked delights."

This was one offer that never needed to be given twice. Shan tethered the goats to the porch railing. About to head to the closest field, Shan was interrupted by Calm bleating loudly. She had just suffered a vicious bite, delivered to her by Testy. Both had started to twist and turn, making the cart unstable and in jeopardy of tipping. Racing to the goats, Shan unhitched Testy from the cart and started to placate Calm by holding her fast and making soothing noises. While Shan was working on Calm, Testy made his break for the closest field, full of strawberry plants and fruit in all stages of development. Shan knew the damage that a single uncontrolled goat could do in a very short space of time in such a place. Yet, leaving a skittish goat with the cart could lead to loss of their tithe to the dirt. Feeling desperate and unsure what to do, Shan held tightly onto Calm and tried to will Testy to stop. Feeling totally ineffective as Testy continue racing towards the strawberries, Shan let out as loud and powerful a scream as possible, "Stop!"

Several things seemed to happen at once. The normal sounds around them went silent and Shan could feel the air become charged and alive. Time itself slowed to almost a standstill and Shan was able to see every detail of what was happening. Still holding Calm tight, Shan could feel the world breathe in. Testy was frozen in mid-bound, all hoofs off the ground, heading straight to the gate of the strawberry patch. The steam off Farmer Albee's cup was suspended inches away from his nose as he was stilled in mid-sip, but Shan could take it all in, observe, and feel a building tension as the world prepared to exhale.

Unsure what to expect, Shan kept watching Testy while wishing him away from the fruit. In one sudden and explosive exhale, the world delivered a direct and decisive response.

Time restarted.

Leaves and dirt rose skywards as a column of air raced forward from Shan towards Testy. As the wind reached him, it lifted the goat's hind quarters several feet into the air. Looking as though he had learnt to walk upside down, he rotated, resulting in the performance of several less than elegant somersaults before crashing to the ground. There he remained in a daze. Shan grabbed the lead cord, raced down the path, and quickly placed it over the goat's horns before checking to make sure there were no serious injuries. Reassured that there were none, Shan pulled the goat to its feet and led the now-docile animal back to the house.

Farmer Albee just looked at Shan, his cup held in mid-air. "Well. That is not something I have seen before."

***

The hamlet really had come alive. Once a quarter the representatives from Town would come for the tithes. As all were required to present and tithe, it was also the perfect opportunity to meet and talk and, potentially, have a flirt or two. Multicoloured bunting festooned the dirt street running though the handful of buildings. The general store always made the most of these days. The more that a festival atmosphere could be created, the longer people would stay and the more they would spend. A series of canvas tents had also been set up, each internally divided into individual sleeping spaces, with wooden cots that could be hired for those who wanted to stay the night.

There were not a lot of opportunities in the area for the young to meet and socialise. On such occasions as this there was always music and dancing in the evening. Once all had returned to their own homes, it was only those who had received some sort of encouragement at such an event who would be willing to continue that acquaintance over the following months. Such it was that the youths and maids would endeavour to present at their best, make the most of their looks, and hide any flaw that they perceived themselves to have.

Yet, the main purpose of the day was to present the tithes. Each family would offer a tenth of their best produce to be taken to Town and presented to the Tower. What each presented was according to their ability. This was duly noted and recorded. How it was the Tower was able to know that a true tithe had been given, Shan did not know, but it did. It did not bode well for those who thought that they could second guess what was known. It was certain, even in this most distant hamlet from the Tower, that many had suffered horribly for undervaluing the tithe. How it was that they had suffered was not clear. That they had suffered was definite. Some said that the eldest child would be ripped from the family to work as a slave in the Tower. Others swore that a whole family had been cursed and suffered painful sores until they all died. The most frequently spouted punishment, however, was the loss of all lands and processions, which was why there was the scattering of empty, decaying hovels dotted throughout the Bowl, marking the remnants of these former lives.

Shan didn't have a lot of experience with people and generally found them strange and unusual. Maima, Farmer Albee, and the goats made up Shan's social group and goats were by far the easiest to understand. There was no lack of confidence in Shan. There was just a lack of tolerance for the stupidity and fakery of people, which, on such occasions as this, was on show in great abundance.

As the sun reached its zenith, Shan arrived with two goats, a small cart, and the tithe still complete. Walking into the hamlet's square, Shan was aware of the change from usual. More colour, more people and, of course, the official Town tent for the collection of tithes. A group of maids, who were well and truly of marrying age, were collected off to one side. They occupied their time by giggling and gawking over an equally awkward group of youths positioned further along on the other side of the square.

They gave Shan a perfunctory look before deciding that further inspection was unnecessary. This did not cause Shan any concern, but highlighted the difference in their appearances. The girls were dressed in bright colours. Their hair was tied back in ribbons and, as far as Shan could discern, they were devoid of any dirt or grime. Shan, by contrast, wore a light beige tunic, pulled in at the waist to allow for comfort and freedom of movement. In addition, there was a fine coating of dirt from head to toe, courtesy of the trip. Dark brown, shoulder length hair hung limply about the face. There was a definite lack of bright colours and, of course, being accompanied by two goats pulling a home-made cart did not scream wealth or privilege.

Making straight for the Town tent, Shan tethered the goats and prepared to present the tithe. Testy had been rather subdued since the event at Farmer Albee's and vastly more compliant than was usual. What had happened there required further thought. Farmer Albee had not seemed particularly surprised and had merely stated that it probably was to be expected. He said that he would come and visit Maima the day after the predicted rain. Then he made sure that Shan had a good selection of some of his tastiest fruits before shooing them onward to market. For Shan, however, the situation was anything but expected and a talk with Maima would be needed.

Taking out the cheese, Shan entered the tent. Two men sat at a portable table on which lay a large ledger. Approaching the table, Shan placed the cheese in front of them.

"Name?"

"Maima and Shan."

"Location?"

"Western Slopes."

"Tithe?"

"Goat's cheese."

"Weight?"

"A tenth of a whey."

The man sitting at the table wrote this in the ledger while the other took the cheese to confirm its weight. After validating that what Shan had said was true, the ledger was turned, and Shan was asked to sign before receiving a stamped receipt of delivery. After only a few minutes Shan's duty was done. The cheese was removed to be placed with the other tithes.

Leaving the tent, Shan made directly for the general store. Maima's buttermilk and sour cream always sold well and so Shan never had to find buyers in the market. It all got sold to the store. The richness of the cream and fullness of flavour Maima had always put down to the abundance of the luxurious pastures of the Western Slopes. But whatever the reason, whether it be the grasses, the goats or Maima's skill, the store would take it all and pay well with items they needed at home.

Entering the store was always a delight. The air was full of fragrances; nutmeg and cinnamon competing with the smell of fresh bread, perfumed soaps and fresh jams, all crying out for attention. For Shan, however, only a few items were required. Flour, particularly, but also spices for some of Maima's special baking. Finally, there were a few more pricy items that it was hoped would ease some of Maima's aches and pains. After emptying the copper containers into ones set aside by the store, Shan collected the required items and placed them into the cart ready for the journey home.

It was still fairly early with the sun just past the centre of the Bowl. Shan unhitched Testy and Calm and placed them in the common area in order to rest and graze before the trip home.

They have done well. Well, mostly, but still, they deserve a bit of a rest, and so do I, Shan mused while taking the bread and fresh fruits from the cart. Heading slightly out of the square in order to avoid the silliness that was beginning to escalate between the maids and youths, Shan sat down in the shade to eat and savour Farmer Albee's fruit, enjoying a break before heading home.

Chapter 12

The sun was already over the western rim of the Bowl when Shan woke up. It had not been a decision to fall sleep but after the trip, and something to eat, sleep just seemed to come naturally. It was now far later than had been planned for the start of the return trip but there really was no another option. None, unless they just stayed and tried to keep out of the way of the revellers who would be awake throughout most of the night. Shan did not like the idea of that, but neither was the thought of traipsing through the dark countryside very palatable. Trying to lead the goats and a cart over some rough ground without causing a wheel to break, or the cart to roll, was not something best done in the dark. In either case, however, Shan needed to check on Testy and Calm. Both goats had now been in the common area for some time. Who could tell what Testy could have got up to in such a length of time without supervision? So, collecting the remaining bread and fruit, Shan made straight for the square and the common area.

It was hard to believe how many people there were. Shan could never remember even having seen so many in a single place before. There must have been over a hundred people in the square where a small band was playing lively dance music. The area was illuminated by numerous torches, revealing over a dozen couples who were dancing energetically, some with a great deal more skill than others. Many others talked in small groups. Youths, most with a tankard in hand procured from the tables of sellers, were positioned around the sides of the square where they intermingled with the girls in their brightly coloured clothes. Flashes of bright, happy smiles and loud, excited voices contrasted with the quite tête-à-têtes that had developed through the evening.

Passing between the groups unnoticed, Shan made for the common area. The goats were not immediately obvious. They were eventually found, without too much effort, standing together in the shadows as far away from the nighttime spectacle as possible. It seemed that it was not only Shan who felt a bit uncomfortable, and out of place, at such an event. Kneeling down, Shan called to the goats while projecting into them a feeling of calm. Scratching them behind the ears and around their necks appeared to reassure Shan just as much as the goats, by providing each a measure of much-needed comfort.

Satisfied that the goats were safe and well, Shan decided to retrieve the cart. It would be best taken out of the square, into a quieter and calmer place, before harnessing the goats to it. By grabbing both handles of the cart, it could be moved without difficulty around a corner into an alley that was a bit further away from the light and noise. Happy that it was now far enough away from the noise to be able to hitch the goats without them being too skittish, Shan turned back. A sound further along the alley caught Shan's attention. Looking through the gloom it was possible to make out the silhouette of two people quietly making their way toward the square. Uninterested, Shan returned to the festival.

***

This was a day that did not come around all that often, so all opportunities had to be considered and made the most of. That was what her mother had told her that morning. There were only the two of them now. It was not that easy tending the plot by themselves, and so, as soon as she was able to get a man, life would be a lot easier for both her and her mother. This her mother had again emphasised before sending her off to the hamlet for the festivities.

"The bloom of youth doesn't last long … and you never had much of a bloom," her mother had reminded her. "You are now over your twentieth year, so you can't be too picky, and you have to put yourself forward."

"Well, what can you expect when I am up at dawn and work outside in the sun every day! Mama, it's not easy and it's not fair that I should have to do this," Agatha complained.

"And so it is, and so it will be, unless you get a man," was the terse reply.

"But what if I don't like any of them?"

"You thought that I liked your father? That's nothing to do with it. If you don't want things as they are, you working like a man, then you need to give out. Choose one that seems quiet and can't look you in the eye. They'll be the easiest to control. You don't want a man who can think for himself. Who could deal with living with one of them? One who wants to do things his way. No, you'll want one who'll do things our way. Surely you can do that. Get a man. They don't breed them smart out here and we all know that there are only two things they want; food and the other."

"But, Mama, I don't know about either."

"You don't have to; it will be too late once you get him for him to find you can't cook. And the other … well, just let him get a sample … but not the whole dish."

"Mama!"

"We need this, so stop complaining."

And with that, Agatha was given a push out the door.

It was true that Agatha did not like working in the fields but, as Mama would not, she had to so that they could eat and pay the tithe. *Oh, how much better it would be to have someone else do this work*, Agatha frequently daydreamed. Without family and not a lot of prospects, it eventually fell to her to get a man so that she and her mother could live more ladylike lives. Lives that they interpreted as doing very little themselves, having most things done for them.

She had done the best that she could with her dress and hair. The dress was not new and was a rather gaudy bright pink that, despite having faded over the years, was still enough to cause people to stare as she went by. Her hair was generally unruly and had to be tied back in order to check some of its enthusiasm. This would work for a while, but only for a short time. Then even these restraints would be overcome. She had a pleasant face, if a bit angular, and a frame that did not tend to the voluptuous. In view of such conditions and in order to allow for a better first impression, Agatha had decided to arrive at the festivities once the alcohol had been flowing and the firelight was less intrusive on one's looks.

She was her mother's daughter but also was not all that her mother was. She did not feel that she could let a man she did not like come near her. And so, as she entered the square that evening, with the music playing and torchlight shadows dancing across her face as energetically as its human counterparts, Agatha decided to look for a man that she could enjoy and not just control. Searching, she eventually spied a few of her similarly-engaged friends. Once detected, Agatha seamlessly joined their group to commence her task for the evening. Her arrival had now evened up the party, with a single maid present for each of the youths.

Conversation was rudimentary. Alcohol had enhanced the confidence and interest, but not the understanding or discernment, of the youths present. The girls excelled in teamwork. Without words, but through gestures and looks, each of them decided on which of the youths was their specific, and unopposed, objective for the night. Once agreement was achieved over this crucial aspect, all flirting and attention toward that single youth was the right and privilege of the agreed spinster. Each female was supported by her colleagues. They would enhance and expand on her qualities and virtues to their respective target. Any interest from a rival's suitor was repulsed and turned instead to its proper recipient.

As such, it was not a surprise that each of the girls was able to fully engage a male's attention. Alcohol still flowed and a female's undivided attention is a powerful aphrodisiac. Gradually the pairs began to split off, moving to other more private, and intimate, areas. Eventually Agatha and her project were the last remaining members of the group in the square. Feeling a bit awkward and uncertain, Agatha suggested a walk. The youth that had been so fortunate as to be aligned with her was a pleasant, slightly bulky-looking man, without the imposition of a great deal of intelligence. He was sufficiently pleasing that Agatha was prepared to be friendly, at least for the moment. Her mother's words continued to echo in her head. She felt, however, that given time she would be able to do better than this and find a man more to her liking. Still, being seen with a man would make her seem more desirable to others. Thus, it was worth spending a bit of time with this one to create the appearance of being in demand.

They left the lights of the square, each with an intended outcome for the excursion. For Agatha it was to waste some time. To create the illusion of being desirable to others with the full intention of finding a more suitable companion a bit later on. Later, when a fair bit more ale had been consumed. By contrast, her escort left with the full intention of getting a bit more than just conversation while he was still sufficiently sober to remember it.

The night was mild and Agatha maintained some distance between them. She made an attempt at small talk. Just enough to make sure that he did not wander off. They strolled outside the square around most of the hamlet, eventually making their way back though one of the darkened side alleys. It was here that Agatha's beau made his move. A last attempt before they would be returning to people and the light of the square.

Grabbing her hand, he pulled her back and up against the side wall of one of the buildings that lined the alley. Adopting a wide stance, he placed his hands on the wall. One on either side of Agatha, whose back was now against the wall, locking her in. A bit flustered and confused, Agatha looked at the moist face of the drunken man a few inches in front of her own. His cheeks were flushed and his mouth was slightly open. As he moved his mouth towards her, she quickly turned her head, resulting in a rather wet sensation in her left ear.

She started to talk softly in an attempt to distract him and give her time to decide how to break free. "Oooooh, it is getting a bit chilly now, isn't it? Might be a good idea to get some warmed ale before the night turns colder," she suggested.

"Ale ain't what you really be wantin'. I knows that," slurred the beau. "You don't takes a man for a stroll, in the dark, without wantin' something more."

Moving a bit quicker this time, he managed to catch the side of her mouth with his lips. Careful not to provoke a man larger and stronger than her, Agatha gave a little smile and said, "You are a charmer; indeed, you are. I picked you out as a man among men as soon as I saw you. But don't you want a drink? I can get you one and sit beside you."

"A woman always knows what a man wants. Now a bit of this … and then a drink."

He grabbed her shoulders and pulled her towards him, planting a huge, soggy kiss directly on her lips. With effort, Agatha was able to pull herself away but found her escape blocked by the wall behind her. Still feigning a bright smile, she looked into her molester's eyes as she felt a hand start making its way under her dress.

***

Shan walked quickly back to the square and gathered the goats to lead them back to the cart. It really was time to go. Testy, and even Calm, was skittish with the lights and noise. So different to anything that they had ever experienced. Moving quickly between the people in the square, Shan re-entered the side alley where the cart had been left. A small commotion could be heard from down the alley. As Shan's eyes adjusted to the gloom it became obvious that two people were up against the alley wall. A largish man appeared to be pinning a girl to the wall while she struggled.

"Get off!" yelled the girl suddenly. The shout was immediately followed by the sound of flesh hitting flesh and a scream. Even to one as unworldly as Shan, it was obvious what was happening. Fear and loathing for such a violation rose instantly within Shan, who felt desperately that something had to be done – anything – and it had to be done now.

Time slowed.

Shan could clearly see a man holding a maid against the wall with one hand. The other was disappearing behind folds of her dress. The girl, fear in her eyes, was holding a hand to her face where blood was dripping from her nose. Not knowing what to do, Shan looked and wished to be able to stop the man. Feeling totally useless and ill equipped, Shan screamed, "Leave her alone!"

As the words broke through the night, the world restarted in a sprint. As the man turned to look, Testy rushed across the space between them at full speed. The girl raised her knee. With skill and accuracy, it forcefully connected with the soft groin area of her attacker. At the same time a column of air exploded forth, racing from Shan down the alley. The impact to the groin caused the man to bend over. He dropped to his knees, allowing Testy to ram him, at speed, in the backside. He sprawled face down in the soft dirt that made up the alley. Moments later, the column of air hit hard, forcing him halfway down the alley and away from his quarry. The girl screamed again. She looked directly at Shan, then ran the other way down the alley and into the gloom. Dazed and disorientated, the man climbed slowly to his feet. He stumbled after the girl without looking back.

Bewildered by what had happened, Shan just stood and looked at Testy without moving. A hand was lightly laid upon Shan's shoulder and a voice said, "Now, that was not a great idea."

Turning, Shan recognised Johnathon, Farmer Albee's son. "Not good, not good at all. We best go … and go quickly," Johnathon said.

"But I have to leave to get home to Maima," Shan objected.

"Not tonight, you don't."

"But I was supposed to be back for supper."

"Well, you weren't, and you can't be." Johnathon took hold of Shan's arm. "There is no need to go tonight. I can take you and the goats in my cart in the morning. I am leaving tomorrow anyway. It will be faster for you than walking. Now, it is best to stay, and better to come with me."

Calling Testy back, Shan hitched the goats to the cart and followed Johnathon as they returned to the square.

***

Johnathon sat opposite Shan in an out-of-the-way corner of the square, voraciously devouring a hearty stew. "I saw you in the square when you came and got the goats. I thought that it was odd that you were still here so late. I followed you to see if things were alright."

"I fell asleep and didn't wake up till after dark," Shan admitted.

"You have all your things?"

"Yes, they're in the cart. Wasn't a lot, just some flour and bits for Maima. She isn't well. I can see it. I don't know what to do." Shan looked hopefully at

Johnathon.

"I will talk with Father; he has a bit of skill."

Shan nodded, thankful that there was someone who might help. "He will be coming so see Maima in a couple of days. The day after it rains."

"I think he will need to talk with your Maima," Johnathon mused. "Things have changed a bit. I saw what happened in the alley."

"I don't understand. It happened twice today."

"What happened twice?"

"The world stopped, or at least it slowed down a lot."

"Well," said Johnathon. "You hit that man and you were nowhere near him. Things like that don't happen. If the Town officials hear of it there will be trouble. We will need to keep you out of sight until we leave tomorrow."

"I didn't hit him, Testy did. I just wanted him to stop," corrected Shan.

"Well, you stopped him, and it was not just me who saw it. Not many will believe what happened to him even if he decides to swallow his shame and tell someone, but *she* will talk about it."

"Why should we worry? We helped her."

"Mmm, well you did, but not in a normal way. The way you did it is not a way that most can do it. She will tell others." Johnathon paused and then asked, "Are you finished?"

"Yes."

"I have a cot in one of the tents. I think that you should use it. I will take you to it and you must stay there until I come and get you in the morning." Johnathon looked and waited for Shan to nod in agreement. "We will leave early, before others rise. We don't want them to see which way we are going. I will house your goats with my horse, and we will load your cart onto mine."

"Why, why is there a problem?" asked Shan.

"I think that it may be time that Maima has a bit of a talk with you," was the only answer Johnathon would give.

Chapter 13

There were few things that surprised Moira. Despite being young she saw the world in a way that was very focused; and that focus was her. She considered it reasonable to put her concerns and desires before all others. She, naturally, considered it normal that others would try to do the same. If one's belief is that everyone is out to get whatever they want for themselves before another can stop them, and that such things as benevolence and selflessness do not exist except in fairy tales, then one would have to expect anything – and not be surprised when such "anythings" occurred.

The challenge was, therefore, to be able to exert your will over others. The best way to achieve this was to make them want to do it. If that failed which, unfortunately, in Moira's experience appeared to be more often the case than not, then the forceful exertion of one's will was required. Lack of success was not a precedent that would be endured. It was *not to be tolerated*. Failure could be interpreted as a weakness. In turn, it could lead to more cases of one's will being circumvented. This was not something to be considered, and even less so should it be suffered.

Fortunately for Moira she was the only daughter of a very well-to-do family. As such, she had control over the servants and the household due to this fact alone. The addition of a father who was generally disengaged from his daughter meant that it was not too arduous a task to get him to agree to almost anything she wanted. He really could not be bothered to argue. Her mother was another situation entirely. Moira avoided contact on that front as often as possible. Thus, getting her will enacted was, in general, not difficult to achieve.

When it came to her tutor, or others not directly linked to the household, however, it was not so easy. She was no longer a child, and tantrums and ill behaviour were not considered seemly. Other means were required. They needed thought and practise. She had mastered the art of pitting one person against another in order to promote her wishes and, while this worked, it was not a method that could be used too often. Playing the poor, sister-less only child also went only so far now that she was older. She had, however, more recently found success with her ability to feign illness or faint. She had also, luckily, developed the ability to create a fever and rash on demand. These symptoms resolved as soon as she felt satisfied that her wishes were being met. After examining various means of coercion, Moira had decided the less taxing on herself, the better. Dreaming up schemes to get her own way filled her thoughts as she floated through, what appeared to others, a charmed existence.

Today, she had felt an exhilaration. It was different to the rush of elation she regularly felt when she had won her way over another. This was new and enjoyable but difficult to pinpoint. Outside on the terrace, frustrating as it was to have decaying fruit presented to her, it had provided her with food for thought. *That simpleton who brought me my victuals: incompetent, really, such ineptitude. I must speak to Father about dismissing him. Yet, he may still be of some use*, she thought.

I felt something as he left. Who wouldn't be angry, but it was something more. Like there was a victory coming to me, a way to be heard without having to try so hard. That he could not see the putrefied fruit he presented before me – only one so blind could have missed it. I felt that and told him, "Are you blind?" And I felt that he was … that he was blind. Only for a moment, as he walked into the tree. But I felt it, I felt that I wanted him blind, and he was. Could this be?

Moira looked about her. She was sitting in the library where she had her lessons. Without the tutor here it was quiet. She wanted somewhere quiet at the moment. Many generations of books had been collected by her family. These were rare. How rare, she didn't really know, but she did know that only a few families were allowed books. Only those families who had proved loyalty to the Tower. What sort of loyalty? Again, she did not know. From what she had gleaned from her tutor and parents it was only those families who were loyal to the Tower that had wealth and power and position and, of course, books.

Learning had been forced upon her. She was quick on the uptake but lacked the desire to exert herself. She rarely made the effort required for full study. Yet here was something that interested her. Moira remembered her tutor describing something that happened generations ago. Families like hers had provided support, backing and assistance, or something like that, to the Tower. The Tower had, in return, given the families their current position.

What was it that they had given the Tower and how was it the Tower had given them their position? she wondered, as she remembered how her grandmother used to always say that their family was special. At the time she had dismissed this as obvious; but what did she really mean?

Turning to the shelves she looked for the family tree. This was an old leather-bound book that recorded the births, deaths, marriages, and children of the family, going back generations with handwritten entries. Finding the book, she took it down from the shelf. She opened it where the bookmark had been left. This contained the entry of her birth, the date, her parents' names, and finally her full name. She was the last entry in the book with many more blank pages remaining for future generations. Turning back a page she saw the entry for her sister. This was written in the same hand and had the same order of information except for a single further line. Date and cause of death.

Turning further back she saw her parents' marriage entered, the birth of her aunt and uncle and then her father, her grandparents' marriage, and so on. Every so often she noted that a page had been cut out, leaving no trace of what was originally there. At first, she thought that these were removed due to errors in putting in the information, but then she realised it seemed to be occurring a bit too regularly.

Surely a date and names are not that hard to get right, she thought. Why had so many pages been removed? Turning to the front of the book she read the first entry:

In gratitude for services given and assurances that these will continue.

It was unsigned and written elaborately in the middle of the page.

One must assume that this refers to the Tower, she thought. That services were given … but what is it that was to continue? What assurances have been given?

Moira needed answers to these questions. They would require more investigation and did nothing to dampen her interest in the Tower.

That is where the power appears to lie, mused Moira, and so, if one knew what that power is and how it is that the Tower has it … Well, that would be of use.

***

Molly felt in her element. At home with her sisters, helping Mama so that things were just a bit easier for everyone. Family was what she wanted, and this is what she had in abundance. At times, she had to admit, the abundance was just slightly too much, but in general Molly would not wish it different. What would happen later, as she got older, however; of that she was fearful.

What if I cannot do what Mama can? What if no-one wants me? What if I do not find a good man and what if I am not a good wife?

Such things haunted her darker moments, but these were few as she still had the hopes and imagination of a child. She filled her days caring for the young ones. Learning how to lead the house, to be a woman in control and make things happen. Also, how to take charge of the money and learn how to use it wisely. Mama took care to teach her all these things. Never too much at a time so that she could take it all in.

Molly tried so hard to remember all that Mama taught her but so much of it seemed so hard. What if she couldn't do it? But Mama said, "It will take time and, in time, it will come."

Molly truly wanted to believe that, but she had her doubts. Father would still come to pay the storekeepers after her shopping as she remained a bit unsure about how to work out the change. "Don't fret, my love, your mother was not good at this either when she was your age," he would say, giving her a hug. "You will get it when you need to." She truly hoped so. At home with her sisters, she was sure. So sure that was something she could do – taking care of little ones.

Today, like so many days, Molly was in charge of her four headstrong younger sisters. Mama was busy in the kitchen preparing for the evening meal. The younger ones would need to eat first as they required supervision, but Mama and Father would eat later when he returned home. As a sign of her age, and the emergence of the beginnings of maturity, Molly was now invited to eat with her parents for the first time that evening. The news had caused great excitement and chatter amongst her sisters. To eat with Mama and Father was an honour that they all wanted. For Molly to get this was momentous. It was something that would now set her apart from her sisters and it had provoked a level of sibling jealousy.

In itself she was excited and proud to be invited, but in truth she felt that it had created a gulf between her and her sisters. Now she was now no longer one of them; but neither was she Mama or Father. It made her again a bit unsure of who she was and who she would need to be.

Ester was having one of *those* days today. Nothing would please her and no matter what anyone did, it was always wrong. On days like this it was best to let her have some space and try and keep the other girls separate from her. This required some skill. The others would, by nature, try and see how far they could go in provoking Ester before she would fall on the floor in a tantrum of screams and kicking feet. To them it was a game. For Molly it was a frustration she could do without.

In an effort to avoid continuous rounds of teasing and screaming, Molly had set up two separate play areas. One solely for Ester, that she had made into a castle by covering two chairs with a sheet. This allowed Ester full isolation from the others.

The other area was for the communal activities of the other three.

"Lucy, where are you going? No, leave Ester alone, you know how she is," Molly rebuked.

"I only want to give her this," protested Lucy.

"I know what you want to give her, and it's not that."

"But, Molly, she took my doll again!"

"Which one?" sighed Molly.

"Hegarty."

"But you never play with Hegarty."

"It's mine and I want it. It's not fair that she can have it, it's mine."

"Alright, I will go and have a look. Stay here, and stay away from Ester."

Molly turned and moved towards Ester's castle, but before she took a single step, a scream echoed about her.

"Owww! That hurt!"

"Well, you shouldn't have done it."

"I didn't!"

"You did!"

"Ava, Elsie, what on earth—" Molly started.

"It wasn't me."

"It was, too."

"Ava, what did you do?" Molly probed.

"Nothing, Elsie pinched me."

"Elsie?"

"She took my crayon."

"I didn't!"

"You did!"

"Girls! The crayons are on the table, which one?"

"My favourite one?"

"I didn't."

"This one?" asked Molly, picking up a brightly coloured red crayon from under the table.

"Yes," said Elsie sheepishly.

"AHHHHHHHHHH!" came a scream from the other side of the room. Turning, Molly saw Lucy emerging from one of the covered chairs.

"Lucy!!!"

"I didn't!"

"I just saw you, what have you got?"

"Nothing."

"Give it to me."

"But it's mine!"

"Lucy!"

Reluctantly, Lucy handed over the old peg doll. Taking it, Molly got onto her hands and knees and started to crawl into the covered space. Behind her, Lucy started crying and Elsie gave out a sharp yelp, indicating a retaliatory pinch had occurred. Ester was bellowing at the top of her lungs as Molly grabbed her. She picked her up and destroyed what was left of the pretend castle. Above Lucy's cries and Ester's bellows could now also be heard the bickering of the older two.

"Girls!" cried Molly. "Girls, listen!" Her cries had no effect, and the noise continued to escalate, each child trying to out volume the next.

"Girls, girls!"

Molly thought, *This is not what Mama is expecting*. She didn't want to disappoint her. She *could* look after the girls, even if they were horrible. She had to be able to do this. This is what she was good at, and Mama needed her help.

"Girls," Molly tried again, attempting to insert what little authority she could into her voice. She would think of Mama and how she could handle anything. Willing herself to be more, more than she was, Molly began to feel bigger, more in control. Better able to manage; stronger, surer, and firmer than she normally did.

All of a sudden, the girls went quiet, each one of them staring, mouths open and wide-eyed, at Molly. Lucy began to whimper, not a cry but a sob. Ava and Elsie just continued to stare silently and then ran for the kitchen as Molly held the now silent Ester.

***

"It is, I know it is, Joseph."

"But, May, it is just their imagination."

"Not both of them. Never both at the same time. They never agree about anything."

"Tell again, what it is they said."

"Molly grew. They were arguing and the little ones were crying. Molly was yelling, and then she got bigger. They say she filled the room."

"How, May? How is that possible? You came straight in from the kitchen. You saw Molly standing there holding Ester. The same Molly as always, the same size and the same person. She was calming Ester, which we know takes effort."

"Lucy wouldn't talk about it. She wouldn't talk at supper at all, but kept looking at Molly."

"But talk about what? They all had a fight, and you know that Lucy is often the one who starts things."

"Joseph, stop. I know. It is. This is it. This is Influence. And they will come. They will come and take our Molly. Who knows what for, but they will. They always find out and they will come."

"We won't let them, May."

"How, Joseph, how? What do we have? What can *we* do?"

"We can hide her. There is no-one who knows about this. If it happened at all it only happened here. No-one else saw. We can keep her at home for a while. Keep her out of sight just in case."

"Joseph, I'm so scared. This is our Molly."

Joseph held his wife as she buried her face in his shoulder. One thing he was sure about was that he was not ever going to let anything happen to his family. Nothing would tear them apart. He would not allow it. He would protect Molly and there was nothing the Tower could do about it.

***

Shan arrived back home well before midday. The trip had been a great deal faster on top of Johnathon's cart than the trip to market. This was despite the goats taking a while to get used to being carried instead of walking. Everything seemed to go smoothly. Johnathon had returned to collect Shan a bit before dawn. As Shan was already awake it did not take long before they had hitched the horse to the cart. They loaded the small cart onto it, together with the two goats, and headed out of the hamlet. They saw no-one awake and only a few rough sleepers, sleeping where they lay after a heavy night on the ale. Once at Farmer Albee's, Shan hitched up the goats again and made rapid progress home.

Finally home, Shan's first instinct was to check on Maima, but the goats needed to be made safe and secured. So, the cart was quickly unloaded, and the goats returned to their kind, left to graze in the small paddock off to the side of the shed. Making haste to the cottage door, Shan called out as it was opened, "Maima, I'm back. Sorry, I fell asleep and had to wait till this morning …"

But Maima was not there, nor was she sitting in her chair. Looking about the room, everything appeared just as it had been the day before. In fact, exactly as it had been. Even the cup of water was there beside Maima's chair, untouched.

"Maima, where are you, Maima?" Shan called, but there was no answering call. After checking the workroom, which was empty, Shan made directly for the other room that Maima infrequently used as a bedroom. There was Maima, lying limply on the horsehair mattress. Her hair was covering her face and her shoes were still on. Racing towards her, Shan brushed back the hair from her face and felt her cold and clammy skin.

Chapter 14

The rain started on schedule as Shan continued to sit by Maima's bed. Since finding her the previous day, only the slightest signs of life had been observed. Her breathing was shallow, but regular; however, she had yet to show any awareness of what was going on around her. This had been a blessing in some small way. For as Shan tried to make her comfortable by removing her shoes and her outer garb, it became clear that her underclothes were soiled. These had to be cut off and the mess cleaned. While tending to Maima, Shan tried to remember the love and care that she had so often shown to others. Now, with her face wiped and dressed once again in clean undergarments, she lay unmoving on the horsehair mattress she so detested.

Shan also sat, unmoving, staring at the same spot on the wall that had been watched since the afternoon before. Having not eaten, and only racing away when it was absolutely required, Shan had been there beside her since arriving home. No tears had fallen. It was still too raw and any sense of what had happened was yet to be digested. At present just being there, no matter what, seemed to be the most important thing to do. Barely having slept in case Maima was in need, Shan existed in a daze. Unable to feel and hardly thinking, time just passed with waiting and watching for any sign.

If only was a frequent thought, but Shan could not face taking it any further. It was just too painful. And so, as the rain fell on the roof above them and with no-one else there, the best thing to do was to remember anything that could be done that might help. Wetting the clean cloths that had been brought in, Shan moistened Maima's lips, then tried to dribble a little into her mouth. Water was essential, that was something Shan always remembered. Without water things could get even worse than they already were.

Around noon Shan noticed the first signs of movement. Small and fleeting, but a definite flickering of the eyelids. Something, not a lot, but enough.

Enough to give a feeling of hope to a child left alone with the imminent loss of the only family they'd ever known. The slight twitching in the right little finger may have been imagined, but there it was again. Like a breeze shaking the twigs of a tree, subtle and wavering but definitely there.

Feeling totally parched, Shan had to leave the room to replenish the jug with water. Scared to leave in case … but knowing that it had to be done. They both needed water, or neither would do well. All the stored water in the cottage had been used. Mostly in cleaning and making Maima comfortable, but, fortunately, fresh rainwater had been collecting in buckets placed outside. This could now be used instead of drawing water from the well. Thankful that the buckets had been put out, Shan brought them into the bedroom. Placing them on the floor and turning to sit back in the chair beside the bed, Shan saw that Maima's eyes were open.

"Maima, I'm here, it's Shan, I'm home. Maima?"

Her head rocked slightly toward the right and her eyes looked directly at Shan. There was thought in the gaze. Maima was in there.

"Maima, are you alright? What happened? I'm sorry I wasn't here, it all happened at the market, I fell asleep, I'm sorry …" Shan started blurting out all in a rush with tears already running down both cheeks. But Maima said nothing. Shan stopped short and watched as she tried to open her mouth. She attempted to speak but only the side closest to Shan moved. Making no more than a slight gurgling noise, Maima closed her eyes again. Her head lolled back to the left, allowing saliva to dribble out of that side of her mouth. Shocked, Shan just stared and, not knowing what had happened, checked again to make sure that Maima was still breathing. She was, but this time the breaths were quicker and shallower. Taking a clean compress, Shan gently wiped away the saliva and waited.

Eventually Maima opened her eyes again. This time Shan was more composed. Looking at Maima and speaking softly Shan said, "You will need some water. Do you think you are able to drink a bit?" Then, taking a fresh compress soaked with water, Shan gently opened Maima's lips and squeezed water into her mouth. This was followed almost immediately by Maima coughing and choking. It took a minute or more to resolve. Shan tried again but squeezed in only a few drops. This resulted in no distress and so, every minute for the next hour, the process was repeated. Finally, Maima again closed her eyes and drifted off to sleep.

Somehow, she looked more comfortable. Now, as she had at least had some water, Shan allowed sleep to overtake emotion and, with head supported by the back of the chair, fell into a deep slumber. Only once in the night did they both awake. Shan repeated the process of squeezing water for Maima to drink. Again they rested, and Shan slept until the morning sun filtered through the bedroom window.

The rain had stopped sometime in the night and the new morning dawned with the promise of a warm, sun-filled day. Waking, Shan looked towards Maima. She seemed uncomfortable and worried. Not sure what had gone wrong, Shan got up to examine Maima and noticed a wet patch on the sheets covering her legs. Immediately looking up and thinking that the roof had leaked during the night, Shan could not see any water damage on the ceiling. Getting a new sheet to replace the damp one, Shan noted that the wetness centred around Maima. Taking in a deep breath and holding back tears, Shan turned to look at Maima, whose eyes were open.

"I'm sorry, Maima. I should have thought. It's my fault. I will have to change the sheets and also the undergarments. I'm so sorry."

Taking time and covering her modesty with the clean sheet, Shan removed the sullied undergarments. As Maima was still unable to move herself, Shan rolled her onto her side in order to remove the wet lower sheet, and noticed red welts on her skin from lying on the hard mattress. Thinking about what to do Shan folded several of the soft goats' hair blankets under her before rolling her back. At least things would be a bit more comfortable.

Once clean and covered, Shan gave Maima more water. She appeared to be coping with the water better now. She was able to accept more at any one time. She even made some coherent sounds, although their meaning was unclear. When she was once again sleeping, Shan felt confident enough to go and clean up.

It had been over three days since Shan had left the westernmost plot for the market. With all the travelling and not washing over that time, things were beginning to get rather pungent. There were also the fruits and vegetables that had been given by Farmer Albee. So, after a wash and a change of tunic, Shan returned to sit by Maima, eating some of the bounty from the Albee's plot.

***

"It was then that I saw Shan in the alley. It was Agatha Figgit. It wasn't hard to find out who. She never would keep quiet about something like that. By later that evening it was being talked of all about the square. It was fortunate that neither of them could see who it was who screamed out to them. By that time, Shan was already in my cot and out of sight. No-one saw us leave, but the

Town guards were still there. They heard all of this and they *will* report it to the Tower, even if the Tower doesn't know already." Johnathon paused and looked at his father. "What should we do? The Tower will know that there is a strong Influencer here and will come. After all the protections that Maima put in place. It won't be enough. Shan isn't safe."

"No, you're right. Shan isn't safe. But if they come it won't only be Shan who's in danger. Maima's not as strong as she was. The toll of her gift. Also, don't forget what else is here. I was going to see her. After the rain falls, I will make the trip. Not as young as I used to be. We must talk and decide what needs be done."

***

"Goats, there were goats, and they obeyed his every command. Large, hairy, vicious things," sobbed Agatha while surrounded by a multitude of people. She was sitting in the square the morning after "the incident", making the most of her newly found popularity. Stories of supernatural forces and demons sparked the interest of all the rural folk. Agatha was not going to waste this opportunity with merely stating the facts. Being the centre of attention, regardless of the reason, was new for her, and she was enjoying it.

"He was standing in the shadows, huge he was. He saw us in the alley and bellowed at us. I think he was trying to curse us," she uttered, before breaking down into tears again. A mug of ale was handed to her. Taking it, she clasped both hands about it and drained it. She was not used to getting drinks given to her. No male companion had ever seen the need.

"And then the huge animal with him battered my intended as he was on his knees in front of me. I am sure he was about to propose." Wiping her eyes theatrically, Agatha observed her listeners. "It was followed by a rushing gale of a wind that threw us both down the alley with its force. We barely managed to escape. And now my love is too afraid to reinstate his intentions to me. He immediately left to travel back to his home."

This last statement was accompanied by a general state of bewilderment as the women came and tried to console the distraught thespian. The men just stood about looking concerned. As they continued to murmur together one of the Town guard forced his way through the circle of people around Agatha.

"And, Miss, can you describe this man you speak of … this huge, bellowing man?" he asked, looking at her with disdain. Aware that she was not fully convincing Agatha stuttered, "He was huge and … and a man."

"Not much of a description to go on, Miss."

"It was dark, and I could only see a shadow."

"Then how do you know he was huge?"

Not sure how to be believable in her answer, Agatha took the safer route and burst into tears. The women about her turned to the guard. They berated him for his insensitivity to a girl who had just lost her betrothed. Looking at her again with poorly concealed disbelief, the guard left, allowing the tale to be told and retold until it was embellished to a level that barely had anything to do with the facts.

***

Jim Albee arrived at the westernmost plot of the Bowl at about midday to find the goats unmilked and still in their holding pen. It all looked quiet, with an air of uncertainty resting uneasily on the place. Walking cautiously up to the cottage door, fearful of what might have already happened, he called out, "Shan, Sybil, are you there?" There was a prolonged silence before he heard Shan's voice from inside call back.

The door opened and there in front of him was the dishevelled Shan, blinking at the sunshine that was now reaching onto the balcony.

"Oh, I'm so glad you're here. I hoped that you would come when you said you would."

"Why, what's happened?"

Shan led Jim through the cottage to Maima's room where she was now propped slightly up on the bed. Awake and aware of them both, she uttered some incomprehensible words while saliva dribbled out the side of her mouth. Looking at her, Jim noted that the lower left side of her face drooped as if it was made of wax that had started to melt in the midday sun.

"Sybil, I'm here. We will sort this out." Turning to Shan he asked for the full account. Following that, he turned back to his friend. "My dear, Shan has done well and so you are still with us." Then directing his attention back to Shan, he started to give instructions. There were things that would be needed to make Maima more comfortable. They would also need more help. Shan must go to Johnathon to get the items and Johnathon would be able to give the help required. With a list of things to remember, he sent Shan off, promising not to leave Maima alone. First, however, he directed Shan to the handcart out the front to appease any lingering hunger before heading off to find Johnathon. Once Shan had left, Jim sat down facing Maima and held her hand.

"My dear friend, it is time I am afraid. I know that all these years you have been here to protect Shan. But now, it is time." Jim told her of the incident at his plot and then the one that also occurred at the market. How Shan had harnessed the air. Just as Jess had been able to do and, like Jess, the Tower would see the use of a major Influence and would eventually come. In this Agatha Figgit may have been a hidden blessing, being of more use than harm. Her exaggerated story telling could lead them down a few dead ends, providing a bit more time before they came. Yet they both knew that the Dark Ones would eventually come.

What would happen when they came, now that was less certain. Males were absorbed and girls were gathered to the Tower. For Shan it was unclear. Only women were known to be able to influence the elements. Some could also control people – their perceptions or even their bodies. Men had other talents. But Shan was different. The son of Jess and Angus could harness the air and influence animals. There may even be more Influences than these. It was time that he was made aware. Alerted to the Tower and what they knew. Maima watched him as he spoke. Tears in her eyes told him that she understood. Giving a small but definite nod she gave her approval to his words. She then closed her eyes and sank further back into the bed.

It was dusk by the time Shan and Johnathon arrived back at the cottage, bringing a larger cart that could transfer Maima to the Albee's cottage. There the three of them would be able to provide her with better care, and more easily get anything that might be required. Maima was once again awake. This time she was able, with some difficulty, to swallow some porridge. Shan was even able to understand some of what she was trying to say. These improvements in her gave some hope, limited though it was.

The next day, having collected all Shan and Maima's necessary items, the men placed Maima on a mattress contained within the larger cart. Covering Maima with a blanket to keep her warm and protected, they slowly left the westernmost plot. Before they did, Johnathon spoke to Shan about the goats. They could not be brought with them at present. They must be let out. They would be safe on the slopes and well fed. It would not be too hard to find them again as they would stay as a flock. Shan, distressed at having to say goodbye to his daily companions, knew that it was necessary, hard though it was. Giving each a gentle touch allowed for the projection of a feeling of love into the flock. They were encouraged to stay together and to remember them, Maima and Shan, for they all were family.

The trip was slow and difficult as the trail was narrow, but through determination and brute force, the cart traversed the distance without incident.

Eventually they were once again looking at the Albee's well cared for plot. Carrying Maima inside, they placed her on Jim's own bed and made her comfortable as she fell asleep. Johnathon went to prepare something for them all to eat while Jim and Shan went to sit on the porch in order to talk.

Chapter 15

Molly was confused. Many things confused Molly, particularly numbers, but normally her family did not confuse her. The girls had been acting strangely for a few days now. She could not work out why. Lucy would barely look at her while Ava and Elsie were overly considerate and obedient. If she asked either of them to do anything, instead of the usual, "Why me?" off they would go without complaint. It seemed like they were looking for any excuse not to be in her presence. Only little Ester was unchanged, still wanting tickles and cuddles, demanding this and that just as she always had. She thought about speaking to Mama about it, but she felt that it might just all be in her imagination. The girls were all well, just acting a bit strangely. Mama had also seemed a bit out of sorts lately. Jumping at small sounds and wanting to know where Molly was at all times. Not wanting to add any more worry to her mother's day, she decided to say nothing.

Molly had not been outside for the last few days. She had been sent on no errands to the market. Mama just said that she needed Molly's help with the girls and that Father would be able pass by the market to get things on the way home. Molly didn't really care about that as she felt safer at home, but a break from the girls would be nice, just in order to go for a walk. Once they were having supper she might go outside for a bit.

"Molly, where are you?" echoed through the house. Molly gave an exasperated sigh.

"Just in here, Mama. I had to take Ester to the potty," she said as she washed her hands after wiping the small child's bottom. It felt like Mama was not trusting her the way she used to. That hurt a bit.

"When you are done, come to the kitchen, please."

"Yes, Mama," yelled back Molly.

Returning Ester to the central room and the care of her other sisters, Molly entered the kitchen. There was Mama, hard at work preparing dinner for the girls.

"Molly, could you peel the potatoes, please. Enough for a cottage pie. We will have that with your father after the girls have finished their dinner."

Having dinner with her parents was still a treat. She loved listening to them discuss the day and what had happened. Molly was particularly engaged in the tower Father was building. More particularly she was interested in the girl who it was for, beautiful but terrifying. Father said that she was something else, although what that something else was he did not say. Imagine having a tower built just for you and for your amusement. A damsel in a tower, a dragon holding her captive as she waited for her prince to arrive and rescue her. A fantasy in real life. She hoped that she may be able to take Father his lunch one day and see the tower for herself.

"Molly, are you alright?" asked Mama, bringing Molly's thoughts back to the here and now.

"Yes, Mama, just a bit cooped up. I think I need to go for a walk."

"I think that I will need you here to help with the girls."

"Just a short one, while they are eating. You don't need me then and I will be back to bathe them after supper." Reluctantly, Mama acquiesced as she was unable to find a suitable excuse to keep Molly at home without relating her fears.

"Alright, but keep close to home just in case."

Molly rolled her eyes but was careful to have turned away from Mama before she did. *Really, I am not a child anymore. It is not like Ester is going outside for a walk*, she thought, although said nothing and continued peeling the potatoes.

Once the girls were all seated with their supper placed in front of them, Molly gave Mama a kiss on the cheek saying that she would not be long. She then put on her bonnet and walked out the door. It felt like a little piece of freedom. The last few days Mama had been keeping her busy with all manner of things. Now she just wanted a bit of quiet and a nice walk by herself. This time she turned right to go away from the market and all its hustle and bustle and started a slow wander. The sun had reached the Western Slopes and the shadows were long. Soon it would be dusk and time to be back home, but until then she would enjoy a bit of solitude.

Engrossed in her own thoughts of a tower and a prince, Molly wandered aimlessly through some of the narrow streets. Eventually she arrived at the edge of Town. She looked over the rugged, rocky eastern slopes that abutted the houses. The now crimson sun to her left created patches of light and dark across the barren land that gradually led her gaze to the Tower. She had never liked the Tower. She didn't know anyone who did. It was so different to the way a tower should be. Nothing like the ones in her daydreams. These were encased in vines and flowers and surrounded by trees with a spring of water at the door, illuminated with the colours of the setting sun. The one before her was black and impenetrable, giving forth nothing. It seemed to take and take until there was nothing left for it to take. She shuddered. It was time to turn back before it got dark.

Slightly unsure of exactly where she was, Molly started to retrace her steps. The narrow streets were starting to get darker as she hurried on her way. Making a few wrong turns she had to backtrack to find an alternate route. All this was taking more time than she had hoped. Gradually, the light began to fade as the sun dopped below the Western Slopes.

Fairly sure now that she knew where she was going and that it would not be too much longer before she saw the light of her cottage welcoming her home, Molly decided to take a few shortcuts through some of the narrower alleyways. Keeping alert to anything about her, she turned into a dim and dirty lane. This one should take her more directly to her home.

Halfway along the lane a figure emerged from the shadows to block her path. Stopping short some distance away, she looked at the bedraggled figure. An unshaven, dirty, and ill-kempt man looked back. For a moment neither moved. Unexpectedly, the man started walking towards her. Shaking, she started to speak but no sound emerged. Nauseous and rooted to the spot she stood, unable to move. No thoughts came to her except a vision of her mother, strong and in control, commanding the household. Channelling her mother, Molly rose to her full height and, in a voice that she placed all the authority that she knew she could use on the girls, she commanded, "Stop that!"

But instead of a forceful command that required all who heard it to obey, there emerged only a timid squeak. The man slowed slightly and chuckled under his breath. Desperate and not knowing what to do, Molly continued to stand rooted to the spot, her mind blank. As the man approached closer, Molly felt her fear turn into anger. *What right does he have to do this to me?* As her anger flared inside her she felt stronger and more in control. More solid, more real, making her unyielding, with weight and substance.

The man stopped and looked surprised, his mouth agape and his eyes wide open. Then without a word he turned and shuffled quickly away from her and out of the lane. Molly stared straight ahead, unsure what had just happened. Gradually she began to feel more like her normal self. Not as solid, but a great deal calmer. Carefully she picked her way along the lane until she came to its end. She recognised the street in front of her and now knew exactly where she was. Soon she would be home, but she would make extra sure that she did not pass through any of the smaller paths to get there.

Turning left she followed the now empty road down the slope to her home. Coming to a bend she saw the man standing alone in the middle of the street. Moving quickly to the shadows of the buildings on the side, she waited and watched. He was just standing there looking quickly about him. There was nothing else there that she could see. The air was cool. There was no breeze, but she heard a soft sound like wind in the branches of a tree. In the fading light the street seemed to get suddenly darker with shadows moving, swirling about the figure. The darkness collected about the man, and she heard him scream, a sound that was quickly muffled as if he had been suddenly immersed in water. The man looked as though he was struggling, trying to break free from the air about him. Gradually he became less distinct. That which separated him from his surroundings became blurred. What was him and what was not him started to meld together until he was just no longer there. Gone. From her hiding place Molly saw, but also felt, the darkness lift from the street. What light was left of the day now returned, and the air was that little bit warmer.

Remaining in place a bit longer, wanting to be sure that there was nothing still there in front of her, Molly slowed her breathing and waited. Nothing further happened. Feeling that it was now safe to emerge, she quietly and quickly recommenced her way home. Constantly looking about her as she walked, she kept control of her fear. Eventually she saw her house in the distance. The door was open and light was flooding the street in front. Racing toward home, Molly felt a chill on the back of her neck. Turning, she imagined that she saw the shape of a person in the shadows behind her. On a closer look, however, there was nothing to see. Dismissing the thought as just her overly active imagination, Molly sped to the door and pulled it shut behind her.

***

The routine tasks of bathing the girls and putting them to bed grounded Molly after everything that had happened. She felt safe and secure in her own home with her family. Later she would be able to take time to think about what had just occurred. But for now, doing was better than thinking, and that is what she did. Dinner with Mama and Father would be soon, and she would feel a lot better after eating. She could also talk to her parents about what she saw. She thought it best, however, that she did not tell them everything or she may not be allowed to go out again by herself. She had learnt her lesson. She would not be allowing that to happen again, so it didn't really seem too important to fill them in on that aspect.

Father had arrived home while she was bathing Ester. He had stopped by the market and had brought something special for them to have after their supper. It certainly was an advantage to eat with her parents. She was also very careful not to tell the girls about the treats that they missed out on. That would just make things even more difficult between them. So, once the girls were in bed and quiet, the two adults and the one not-quite-yet adult sat down to their supper.

Father spoke further of the tower he was creating. He took great pride in his work. He spoke at length about how he was ensuring the walls were smooth and circular. Within the tower the spiral stairs were put in place as the walls rose. It was now possible to climb to the unfinished top that rose to the height of three men. From the top a view of Town and the Bowl, as well as an even more direct view of the Tower, could be taken in. Molly listened with interest to the description of the tower. She was even more interested in asking about the mistress who would own the tower.

"The lady who wants this tower, what of her? Did you see her again?" Her father looked stern as he recalled seeing Moira that day.

"She is not one who is easily pleased." He continued by relating what he saw as he worked. He had seen Moira enter the tower garden in the late morning. She strolled about the garden with a servant holding a large parasol above her head. The garden was already quite shaded. The item thus seemed rather unnecessary. Still, the young lady appeared to take joy in making things difficult for the servant. Joseph observed that the poor man walked into the raised garden walls, grazing his legs. He would frequently stumble over the cobblestone path. At each misfortune, the young lady would just smile or turn her head and giggle. Joseph was quite convinced that she was one of the most entitled and unpleasant girls he had ever encountered. Turning to Molly he patted her arm and smiled. "You, dear Molly, are worth a hundred of her. Do not change. Always remain the sweet, kind girl you are. You are perfect the way you are." Molly blushed. Her father's praise was like a tonic to her. She took particular note of the tone of his voice so that she could dwell on his words later.

Once dinner was done and they each sat with a cup of fresh brewed tea and a small sweet currant bun, Molly spoke of what she had seen that evening. As she spoke, she could feel her emotions rise again as she relived the shock and fear of seeing a person just disappear. Her mother mirrored her fear while her father looked very grim.

"Where did this happen?" he asked.

"Just a few streets up Town, toward the Tower."

"Did anyone see you?"

"No, no-one was around. The streets were empty apart from him." She remembered turning as she reached the front door of their cottage. She hesitated – she had looked more closely but there was no-one there. "No, nobody saw me," she repeated. Joseph looked at his wife and said nothing.

May turned to her daughter and explained. "Molly, listen carefully. What you saw were the Dark Ones from the Tower. They come at night. The Tower has overseen the Bowl for a very long time. They care for the people here. They do what they do without us knowing why. But I think that it is best that you do not go out in the evening again. We stay at home then and go out, if we need to, during the day."

Molly could see that her mother was not saying all that was on her mind, but she nodded and felt better that she had not told her parents everything. As an act of generosity for all the effort Molly had given to the girls that day her mother relieved her of the task of cleaning up the supper things. She sent her up to bed, wishing her a peaceful sleep. As Molly left May looked silently at her husband who stared back, deep in thought.

***

Moira had had a wonderful day. It had been extremely entertaining and enlightening. After an extensive search of the library, she had been able to discover a leather-clad volume describing some of the obligations agreed to by her forefathers. These were in return for what appeared to be status and protection from the Tower.

Pouring over the tome for several hours the previous day, she had been able to discern several hitherto unknown facts about her life. Firstly, and unsurprisingly, that the Tower was in control but deemed it more effective to decentralise the power of governing the Bowl to the great families. These families maintained order within the Bowl. They collected the tithes and saw to it that any specific wishes of the Tower were seen to.

Secondly, the great families had been chosen by the Tower to be the great families due to specific qualities found within their blood lines. Originally it was from the great families that the Tower was able to draw its inhabitants, choosing them carefully when they displayed specific abilities. Moira, however, had not been able to find any further details of these qualities in the text despite reading and rereading it. What was clear was that only females were to be selected. If selected, they had no choice but to attend the Tower. In return for their allegiance to the Tower, the great families maintained their wealth and status. In addition, the Tower would sustain the commercial system, the agriculture and its produce that kept the people of the Bowl well fed and productive. How this was to happen? On that the text was extremely vague. Moira was fascinated that the Tower still was able to maintain its grip on the great families, and therefore the Bowl, with a mere promise. She wanted to know more.

Searching well into the evening, she eventually stumbled upon a small book, well-worn and blemished, containing handwritten entries. Each entry consisted of a name followed by two dates and then only one or two more words. These were names she had never seen before, but they appeared to be family members, and all were female. Once again pulling down the family tree, she searched for the names by using the first date of the entry. To her delight she found that the dates coincided with the missing pages within the book. It was not much of a leap for her to determine that each of these names corresponded with one of her ancestors. That it was these women who must have been selected by the Tower.

The second date varied slightly. It was a date somewhere between twelve and fifteen years after the first one. Moira thought that, as the most momentous date in anyone's life must be their selection, this date must be the date they entered the Tower, there to become one of its inhabitants and a ruler of the Bowl.

The words she saw after the names were often repeated. Fire, Fire, Fire, Physical governance, Fire, Earth, Fire and so on. Each name had only one of these. There was no pattern to the words and the word fire outnumbered all the rest put together by a ratio of two to one. This puzzled her, provoking further rummaging through the old manuscripts of the library. Eventually too tired to look further she retired to bed, determined to continue the search the next day.

Rising early and directing her breakfast to be brought to the library, Moira continued her search. In the appendix of a volume on ancient lore she found reference to the Influences. It stated that each of the great families were selected due to an inherent ability of some of their women to demonstrate control over one of the major elements: air, water, earth, and fire. When used together, these Influences could control all aspects of the Bowl, its weather, and the land. More rarely there were women who displayed other Influences. These could more directly impact the others about them and were highly sought after by the Tower. These women appeared to be desired by the Tower as a means of maintaining its control over the people of the Bowl. Further reference to these other Influences, however, was lacking.

Still fascinated, Moira pondered what these other Influences might be and how they would be able to be used in order to maintain control over others. She thought about her heritage and of the number of powerful women in her family who had left to join the Tower. She became more certain that she, too, was predestined, and that one day she would be selected for the Tower. Now she just had to make sure the Tower knew that as well.

Leaving the library, she returned to her room to dress for the day. Choosing something particularly fetching, she put on an emerald-green gown that, through contrast, enhanced her alabaster skin and fiery red hair. As she was dressing, she practised her trick of creating a rash on her skin and then making it disappear again. Remembering the episode with the strawberry, she mentally prepared herself to try again, to see if she really was able to project her wishes on another.

In the late morning she emerged from the house and into the garden, with a servant attending her. She did not need the parasol, but she did need a test subject who was near and whom she could observe closely. Strolling slowly about the garden where her tower was progressing, she concentrated on making the servant fall. She was not exactly sure how she should do this, but she knew that she really, really wanted him to fall. It was her deepest wish that she could wield power like the Tower; but she would have to prove that she could. She had to be able to do this. She knew that she could. Now, she must do it. It was a fundamental aspect of her, a need that was hardwired into her.

The servant stumbled and hit his legs hard against the garden wall. She yielded back, surprised, and unsure if this was a result of her power, or merely carelessness from the servant. She tried again. This time he tripped slightly on the uneven cobbled path. Pure delight flooded her. She could not hold back a laugh of triumph. Several more times she tried. For the most part, the outcome was sufficient enough to indicate that she was, indeed, affecting the man. That she was controlling him and his movements in some small way.

Such a rush of joy. She did it and she knew that she could. Practise – she would need practise, and then the Tower would notice her. If it did not, she would just have to go to the Tower and show it. Exhausted after the walk she retired to her room. It took effort, but what a discovery. One that would change her life forever.

Chapter 16

Shan sat on the porch with Jim Albee, exhausted but finally feeling safe now there were others about to help. Not everything was to be placed on his shoulders alone. Before now he had not had time to allow himself to stop and think. With Maima so sick he had to be there in case he was needed for anything. Alone and staring in the dark, he had sat and watched. He'd waited through two nights hoping for any sign that Maima would come back to him. He had not allowed himself to feel. If he allowed tears then he might miss something, not be ready if she required anything. It was safer to lock these feelings away. They would only get in the way, and he didn't want to feel them, anyway. But now Maima was resting and had shown some improvement. This in itself was enough to give a bit of comfort and some hope for the future, so he could allow himself to stop, just for a moment.

Shan sat in his chair. Never had he ever felt so tired. After the last couple of days, everything else in his life looked like one long holiday. Going out onto the slopes, into the open and isolated lands that rose up from the westernmost plot to care for the goats, his friends, who returned the care by providing food and fleece. He had exulted in the rising of the sun, feeling the gentle warmth of the first rays of a new day as he looked east over the fertile fields of the Bowl. Then coming home to Maima to speak of the day and share in the exploration of anything and everything through her books. These had been joys in his life.

But now, it was different, things had changed. He was not so young that he did not know that things would never be the same. How could he care for Maima and the goats? He could not leave her to soil herself again. He would have to be there with her, but then how would they survive? They needed the goats for their milk, to make the cheese, to take to the market in order to get what they needed to live. He could no longer go to market. Even if he could,

Maima could not make the cheese for him to take. He could gather plants. Perhaps he could plant the ones they needed near the cottages so he would not have to go and look for them. There was pasture near the cottage, too. The goats would have to stay near the house. Perhaps he could milk them one by one near the door of the cottage so that he could hear if Maima needed him. He would just have to make it work.

These thoughts swirled around in his mind. Gradually the pain that he'd tried so hard to lock away behind a barrier of pure will began to leak through. There was an unmistakable aching of loss; loss of what had been and what would never be. Without Maima, what was there? What would he do? Despair started to coalesce around him, gaining weight as it lay on his chest like a crushing force. He was only a boy. What could he do? His breathing became difficult and he gasped for breath. Why was it so hard to breathe? As he placed his hands over his mouth, he felt that his cheeks were wet. Why? Where did the water come from? Unable to sit upright any further, Shan bent forward and, to his own surprise, let out a long and guttural sob. He couldn't stop. It just kept coming between the laboured breaths.

He felt arms around him. Solid, tangible, secure arms, holding him as he slumped forward. It was as if his whole body was turning itself inside out. There was nothing he could do. He clung to the security of those arms. Not seeing anything, only feeling them. They were an anchor, a sure foundation. The only thing about him to hold on to. How long this continued Shan did not know, but eventually his sobs started to ease. Little by little he became aware of Jim kneeling in front of him. He was holding him, sure and firm. Solid, when he needed something sturdy to ground him.

Jim said nothing but his face showed that he understood. That he understood the pain and the loss. This was a man who had known loss and what it felt like, and that no words would make it better. Shan held tighter to the older man. So thankful for him. Knowing that he shared the pain. Finally, he was able to let go and sit upright again. Drained and empty but better, so much better, than he had been before.

Looking at the boy, Jim noted how small he still was, not yet coming to any form of physical maturity. It was not fair. Jim knew this. Anybody would know this. But the Tower – the Tower would come. It did not care if it was a child and if the child needed help. It would come. He felt there was a little more time yet, but it would not be long. It coveted these things, the Influences, for its own purposes. It let nothing get in its way.

Sybil had been careful. She had placed protections about Shan, but no-one knew if they would work. Living in the westernmost plot meant that there were never any unexpected visitors. No passers-by and no intruders who would know them. She had made sure that any who had contact with them thought that it was only Maima and her granddaughter who lived there. Up until now, only girls had ever had the major Influences. The Tower absorbed any man who demonstrated any significant ability. If Shan did demonstrate an ability, possibly the Tower would just assume that he was a girl and not destroy him. At least it might give him a chance. To this end, she had allowed Shan's hair to grow and had dressed him in ways to obscure his sex. *At least Shan still can pass for a girl as he has yet to reach the change*, Jim thought.

But time was short, and Shan needed to know all that had been part of him from before his birth. Why things would change. About the Tower and what it wants. So much was still unknown, but through their searching Jim and Maima had discovered some things that could help. Not least of which was a list of those who had challenged the Tower.

When Angus, Shan's father, had to leave, he went looking for them. Looking for the others who could help and protect him. Like the others, he would oppose the Tower. Yet, right now, Jim did not have the heart to place more onto the shoulders of a boy still struggling to deal with what had just happened. *There is time, I am sure that we have a little more time. I can let Shan rest for a bit before he has to know more. He needs a bit of time.* Jim just hoped that he would not regret the delay.

As he was thinking, Johnathon emerged onto the porch, declaring that supper was ready and that Maima was awake. She had asked to see Shan. Shan jumped to his feet and raced inside. Arriving at Maima's bedside, he could see that she looked more like herself. She was still frail, with one half of her body not moving, but her eyes were bright. She gave him an odd half smile as his bent over to kiss her on the cheek.

"My dear, are you alright?" Her speech was slurred but understandable. "I'm sorry you had to go through that. I don't remember a lot. Johnathon told me that you were there alone. For two days! I am only here because of you. Thank you."

Shan felt relief that she did not remember the sheets and the underclothes. "Oh, Maima," he half laughed and half cried as he hugged her and she stroked his hair with her good hand, staying there until Jim came up behind him with a bowl of thickened soup.

"You need some food, young one," he said, "and so does Maima. So, you go off and eat while I make sure she gets to eat as well."

Shan got up, kissed Maima again and, looking back several times, left to get the food that Johnathon had prepared.

"Sybil, he is a good boy and resilient, but don't worry, he will not be alone. Johnathon will be going with him. We spoke about this. He wants to go. We know that Angus will care for him once he knows."

Maima looked at him, tears in her eyes.

"You will stay here. We can get help. There is many a young girl who is looking for employment. There is still much for us to try and discover. We can help those who challenge the Tower's control. It will be fine."

He started to carefully feed his friend. Slowly, giving one small but nutritious spoonful after another, allowing time for her to swallow each tiny bit before attempting the next. He had had some practise with this; but that was a time he preferred not to remember.

In the kitchen Shan sat across the table from Johnathon, a full and hearty stew in front of him. Beef – now that was rare for him to have. It gave as much delight as seeing Maima be more herself. Shan felt lighter than he had a mere hour ago. A weight was no longer there, despite the future, and how he could care for Maima, remaining uncertain. Somehow it would work, he was sure of it. She would get better. He could take care of her. Things might not get back to the way they were before, but they would still be together. He ate the stew with gusto. Johnathon was a good cook.

Johnathon watched as Shan ploughed his way through the bowl in front of him, taking some comfort from providing joy to a boy who had been through so much. Johnathon also observed that Shan was remarkably controlled, particularly considering the talk just had with his father on the porch. It was hard, but they had to leave the Western Slopes and Maima in the morning. This might also be their last chance for a decent hot meal for a while, so they needed to eat well tonight. As soon as Shan finished, Johnathon filled up his bowl again. They would both need their strength for what was ahead, and Shan was rather skinny.

"We can only take what we absolutely need. Travel light so we can disappear quickly and easily if needed," Johnathon said.

Shan looked confused. "Are we going back to get the goats?" he asked.

Now Johnathon looked confused. "No, when we leave in the morning. The goats will have to stay on the slopes. They can look after themselves."

"Then why are we going to the slopes in the morning?"

"We're not going to the slopes. That is the very place that we must leave."

"You're not making sense. Why would we leave the slopes?"

Johnathon stopped. "Did my father talk to you about any of this?"

"Any of what?"

Jim entered the room with an empty bowl. Johnathon looked at him and Jim looked at Shan. Shan looked at one and then the other before asking, "Why am I leaving? Maima needs my help, and I must be here."

Jim walked over to Shan and placed a hand on his shoulder. "There are a few things that you need to know. Your Maima needs to tell you something. I think that she should do it now."

Shan looked towards the bedroom door as Jim nodded to him. "Johnathon and I will come to help fill in the details so that she doesn't get too tired." And so, the three of them carried a couple of the kitchen chairs into the bedroom and sat down next to the bed, with Maima the centre of attention.

***

It was a joint effort. Maima was there to nod and confirm what was said while Jim gave the details. He and Maima had spoken of this moment many times in the past. About how the story needed to unfold. Jim spoke of the Tower. Of what it meant and what it wanted. Of the Influences that gave the Tower its control over the land and its people. From the murder of Shan's grandfather to the escape of his mother and of his father, Angus. How he was a builder, an inventor who cared for people. But most especially, his family and his baby son. How Jess, his mother, had been tortured and tormented until her only escape was the lake. Of her Influence on air, her ability to fold and bend it to her will, and what this meant. Of Angus and the reason that he left – that the Tower would absorb him, destroy him, if he stayed, and the risk that would put Shan in.

He explained why Maima had come to the Western Slopes and why they had lived so far from Town. Of the difference to the Tower between girls and boys with Influence, and how they were treated. To this, Maima tried to add more, but the effort was too much for her, so Jim continued. "Your Maima has tried to protect you from the Tower. Keeping to the slopes has meant only a few people know you. Apart from us they all think of you as Maima's grand-daughter." Shan looked surprised. "It is strange, we know, but we did it in case you ever displayed Influence. If you did, the Tower might leave you alone, or at least not be so eager to erase you, if you were thought to be a girl. You are different. The only male ever known to have a major Influence. And because of this Influence, the Tower will come."

113

Shan looked at Maima, who gave a slight nod of agreement with Jim's telling. In the silence that followed, Maima rested her head against the pillow with her eyes closed. After a while she opened them again. With great effort, she spoke gently, "And now, my dear," she paused and then slowly continued, "you have shown your mother's ability. The Tower feels this. It will come for the one with Influence. It will think you are a girl. It will come quickly. You must go. It must not find you."

Jim continued "There are those who oppose the Tower. Johnathon will help you find them. We know only a little, but we know that your father is with them. You need to head to the northern reaches of the Bowl. There are some there who will know how to direct you further. They keep themselves secret from almost all and move about frequently."

Shan's mouth opened and then closed without saying anything. Silently, he looked from one adult to the next, finally resting his gaze on his grandmother.

"I'll be fine, dear. It doesn't want me. It has had many a chance to come for me. It never has. But you, you are special. It will want you."

"But I don't want to go."

"No, you don't. I don't want you to have to go … but go you must," Maima responded. Shan went over to the bed and rested his head on her chest. She continued to speak as she stroked his hair with her good hand. "It will be just for a while. Jim will take care of me. I want you to take care of Johnathon."

Having completed the telling, Jim nodded at Johnathon and they both rose, silently leaving the room to allow Maima and Shan time to be. Time to accept the way things were, so that they would be able to say goodbye the next morning.

***

Dawn came with its usual regularity but was not accompanied by the feeling of restful refreshment that was normally the case for Shan. Sleep had been difficult to come by despite the physical exhaustion that had weighed on him from the previous few days' responsibilities. Leaving the westernmost plot had not been a stretch. He had seen it only as a temporary measure to allow Maima to recover. In his thinking, they would have returned and been able to continue life as normal with only some minor changes. Now, however, it was nothing like that. This was a full break from the only life he knew.

Having never travelled further than the market in the local hamlet, the rest of the Bowl, and what happened there, had always been more theoretical than anything, having no practical impact on his life. He didn't distrust what Maima had said, but how could it be that the Tower knew it was him who used Influence? Surely if it came and he was not found, he could just come back? He'd just not use Influence again. Live as he always had.

He decided that he would go, but not for long. They all thought that this was important, so he would do what they said, in a measure at least. He was also interested in learning more about his father. He had never felt fatherless. Maima had been both mother and father to him. He did feel a bit odd when he thought about meeting his father for the first time. It was a mix of excitement and nausea. This was also the feeling he got when he thought about leaving the Western Slopes. These thoughts swirled around in his head, allowing him only to sleep in patches as he lay next to Maima's bed.

As the sun rose above the Tower and the Eastern Slopes, Shan was awake. He was mentally prepared to go on a trip. One that he considered should not last more than a week. A trip that would see him reunited with his Maima before too long. Johnathon and his father had prepared two sacks the previous night, one to be carried by each on their journey. Only the essentials could be taken, and thought had been put into each carefully selected item.

Breakfast was an extensive fair with great effort put into making copious amount of food of different varieties. Fried sausages and eggs with toasted bread, fluffy pancakes covered in honey, and fresh berries in cream were all on offer. All were gratefully consumed. Maima was even able to have a soft-boiled egg and a cup of dandelion tea. With very full bellies, Johnathon and Shan prepared to leave.

Standing next to Maima's bed, Shan felt a burning in his eyes that made them water. An affliction that also seemed to be affecting Maima. She hugged him to her and kissed him repeatedly before letting him go. "I will be here when you return. Remember all that you have read. All that you know. All knowledge can be useful, even if not all knowledge is good."

Kissing her one last time Shan turned and left the room, determined that he would be back again, a lot sooner than Maima thought. Together with Johnathon, he picked up his sack and, saying final farewells to Jim, headed east. They left the Albee's plot and headed toward the eastbound passenger cart that they would take from the hamlet.

Chapter 17

May and Joseph spoke well into the night. It was no longer a matter of conjec-
ture but an accepted fact between them. Molly was inflicted by the Influence
and the Tower may have noticed. Their hope was that the Tower did not know
who Molly was or where she was to be found. From her family history, May
knew that if the Dark Ones came, they would come in the evening. Speaking
to her grandmother Noona, May had tried over the last few days to piece together the series of events that preceded the loss of Noona's sister. The
memories were now fairly vague. Although tinged with melancholy, one thing
remained clear – that once the Dark Ones came, there was nothing that the
family had been able to do to stop the collection of the child.

Noona remembered her sister as a kind and caring girl, three years older
than her. Prone to shyness, she was uncomfortable in the presence of strangers.
She avoided large gatherings of people she did not know. How she was selected
by the Tower, Noona did not know. She remembered that her sister was often
scolded by their parents for removing herself from situations where she felt
uncomfortable, but her sister would swear that she never did. She said that she
just faded into a corner while continuing to observe the proceedings. Staying
there and being ignored by the other participants.

The collection happened without warning. One evening after supper a darkness fell about the family as they were tidying up and getting ready for the next
day. The younger children were already in bed. Noona was teasing her older
sister about the colour of her hair, which was a nondescript brown. Without
any sound, the door of the cottage opened. Several figures entered the lamplit
room. The figures cast no shadow and all light appeared to be cancelled as it
hit them. They appeared as voids that glided through the air. Terrified, Noona
hid behind a chair and closed her eyes. What happened next, she was unclear
about. When she opened her eyes again her sister was surrounded by the voids.

They formed a barrier between her and all else.

They started to move toward the door, forcing her sister to move with them. Her terrified sister tried to call out to her mother, but no sound could be heard. Her mother knelt, weeping, on the floor over the unconscious form of her husband. She could only watch as her eldest daughter disappeared out the cottage door which shut once again. From that time onward no-one ever mentioned her sister. They never spoke her name again. No-one, except Noona who would try to remind others that her sister had indeed existed.

So, what to do? There would be no warning if the Dark Ones were going to come. There was no knowing if the Tower already knew that Molly had Influence. If it did, then where she was had to be kept secret. How, how was this to be kept secret? No place within the Bowl was out of reach of the Tower. Would remaining in Town be as safe as being further from the Tower? If they did take Molly away from Town, where would they go? How would they manage? There were also the four other children to consider.

May and Joseph spoke around and around in circles about it. Unsure what they should do, there was only one thing that they did agree upon. Molly needed to be told. In the morning, May would have to try and explain it to her. Joseph would leave earlier than usual to start work so that he could be back home before dusk fell. Finally feeling slightly calmer now that evening was over, and the Dark Ones were less likely to come, Joseph led his wife upstairs to bed, willing them both to get some sleep but not convinced that either would.

Morning found them both up and in the kitchen earlier than usual after a less than acceptable amount of sleep. None of the girls were yet awake. It was even too early for Ester to assume her regular spot on her father's lap while he ate breakfast. This would provoke a howl or two when she discovered her loss once she did awake. But Joseph was determined to get to his tower before the sun rose so that he could return home before the sun set that evening.

They looked at each other across the kitchen. It was an unusual silence that lay between them. What words were left to be spoken were few. Those that lay unspoken were more than either could face. May was packing her husband a substantial midday meal. She did not want to send any of the girls out to deliver anything today. She wanted to keep them close by. She wanted to be able to see and hear them. It was, at least, an attempt to try and mitigate her anxiety.

Joseph understood his wife's moods. He could read her fear on her face as she worked. He, too, was anxious. Anxious that he would not be able to protect those he loved and was bound to care for. There had to be a way for him to shelter them. Yet, despite hours and hours of worried thinking, very little had revealed itself in the way of actions that could combat the Tower if it came to his door.

Finishing his morning meal, he rose and held his wife as she trembled slightly in his arms. He released her and left to make his way uptown to his tower. He hoped that the day would pass quickly, without incident. He hoped to do without seeing the young mistress of the estate. He did not feel that he had the stamina to deal with a girl so wholly unworthy of the fortune that surrounded her, particularly when his own Molly was under threat. Things were unfair. This he knew well; but to see that spoilt, vindictive little creature get all she wanted and still not be happy could potentially drive him to say or do something that he would later regret.

May stood at the sink after her husband left. It was a blankness that filled her mind. Like a daydream without colour or thought. How long she stood there she was unsure. Eventually she was roused by the sound of the kitchen door opening and the patter of little feet on the flagstone floor. Ester had arrived and would need consoling after she realised that her father had already gone. Pricked back into motion and her motherly role, May picked up her youngest daughter and started her day anew.

***

Moira woke rested and in a very good mood. Life was getting more and more delightful. She was certain that she would be ready for the Tower when it called. In her mind it was a matter of "when" and not "if". She would make sure that the Influence she wielded was noted, and then how could it not want to select her? She looked forward to that day with anticipation, as a fitting recognition of her importance to the Bowl and its people.

What this would mean for her parents interested her little. She always knew that she was just a bargaining chip. Something to be used to shore up the family's political strength and social standing. For her to be seen as anything more than that seemed unlikely. But, if she was of the Tower, she would no longer be the chip but the player at the gambling table. It would be her family and all others being used by her as she willed.

As her parents' only remaining child, she knew that joining the Tower would be the completion of this family line. No further children would be forthcoming – a fact that pleased her for some inexplicable reason. What would become of the family estate and who would eventually call this their home barely raised a thought in her head. It would be as it would. She did not have to see, or be part of, any of it. But up until the time that her presence would be requested by the Tower, she would continue to run things the way she wanted, and practise on her own.

Still in bed, she concentrated on slowing her own heart. She was getting better at controlling things. Feeling the pulse in her neck, she was able to count the beats as she watched the ornate shelf clock on the mantlepiece. Sixty, and then down to fifty, a minute. In stages she slowed and slowed her pulse, eventually dropping it to a mere twenty beats a minute. This made her feel lightheaded and slightly nauseous, which was why she practised when lying in bed. Today she would take things a bit further. She would have to wait just a little longer to satisfy her curiosity.

Finally, as her patience was starting to fade, her maidservant entered the chamber to draw the curtains and start the day's preparations. She was there to get Moira dressed and ready.

Staying in bed, Moira watched and concentrated. Projecting her thoughts, she started to feel the maid's breathing and the blood as it was pumped around her body. Gently probing about, she was able to focus on the heart. She started to use Influence to slow its rate.

Moira could feel it slowing. She did not have the patience to take things gradually this time, so she pushed the Influence hard to rapidly reduce the heartbeat. Moira now had two visions of the maid. Physically, with her eyes; and feeling, almost seeing with her mind, the heartbeat. Watching it slow, causing the blood to linger for longer within the organs, even as the breathing rapidly increased. She saw the maid's face go pale as she gasped for breath and fell to the floor in a faint.

Satisfied, Moira withdrew the Influence. She felt the maid's heart rate rise again. Moira continued to watch as the maid regained consciousness, gradually stumbling to her feet before giving an apology and rapidly retreating from the chamber. *Yes, it was going to be a good day*, she thought to herself.

Wearied with the effort required to exert Influence, Moira remained in bed a while longer before rising. A toll was exacted when Influence was used, but it was transient. It may lessen with practise, she reasoned. Still, it was worth it, and would not curtail Moira's efforts. So, rising from bed, she made short work of the morning tray prepared by Cook before looking to dress and prepare herself for the day. She could complain about the lack of a maid to aid her. However, she was feeling generous after the delightful start to the day. So much so that she brushed her own hair after dressing, and sat down to a second cup of tea.

***

Molly entered the kitchen while her sisters were already eating. She went to help herself to the porridge from the pot on the stove and sat down next to the youngest sister, Ester. Ester loved all attention. She was happiest if she was the centre of it. Very different to Molly, who preferred to remain on the edges, observing how others behaved so that she would know what was expected and not stand out. When together, however, they were able to modify each other for the better. The exuberant nature of Ester emboldened Molly while the quiet nature of the elder calmed the toddler. They took comfort in being together. It made for a good start to the morning.

Once the girls finished their morning meal, Molly would normally take them outside to get some air. This allowed Mama a bit of quiet so, as the dishes were placed by the sink and the table was being cleared, Molly started to get things organised. It was then that Mama informed her that the four younger girls would be having a morning at their aunt's place, so that Molly and she could have a bit of "grown-up" time.

Aunt Joy lived slightly further down toward the Town gate and had two daughters of her own still living with her. It was always a treat to see them. All the girls got on famously. Despite the delight in the unplanned excursion, however, the two next oldest sisters looked at Molly with envy. Once again, she was being given a privilege not yet on offer to them. Molly looked back at them sheepishly but still felt very special, even in the face of their poorly disguised jealousy. Time alone with Mama was almost as coveted as having supper with Mama and Father.

With faces washed, and clothes inspected for any traces of their morning meal, Molly led the other girls out of the house and down toward their aunt's cottage. She held tightly onto Ester's hand. It was the only reasonable way to control the wanderings of the child. Ester tried to drag her this way and that. She wanted to look at everything along the street and talked constantly. Everything was exciting to her. The more people that filled the street as they moved closer to the market square, the more animated and enthusiastic she became.

Why can't I be like that? thought Molly. Four times older than Ester and it still scares me. I just need to take a little of that excitement she sees in everything about her. Make it my own, she thought. If she is not scared, then what do I need to be fearful of? With that thought, Molly started to try and see things from Ester's point of view. She found that she could enjoy a bit of the colour and odours that encompassed them. That, as she embraced them, perhaps they were not really so alarming.

After a short time they arrived at their aunt's door, who welcomed them in with a smile. She had planned to do some baking with the girls helping. This was greeted with universal delight as not only would it be fun but there would also be something delicious to eat afterwards. Giving her farewells to all, Molly left, returning home for her own special morning with Mama. The trip back was uneventful as Molly continued to try and enjoy the sounds and bustle about her. She achieved a modicum of success and did not once feel like she faded.

Once home again, Molly saw that her mother had made tea. She had also brought out a pair of the good teacups to use. These, with slices of the raisin cake made the previous day, were placed by the two best chairs in the sitting room. Molly saw that these were ready for mother and daughter to sit and talk about whatever it was that grown-ups talked about in this sort of situation. Mama pointed to one of the chairs and suggested that Molly should sit. Nervous and excited, Molly went to the chair that was only rarely used and sat down. Mama brought out the teapot from the kitchen and placed it on a mat on the table between them. Molly just watched, unsure what she was supposed to do.

"Molly, love, how are you feeling?"

"Well, I think."

"No more fading?"

There it was again. Mama used the same word that she had used to describe what had happened to her. Why did she do that? It sounded odd when she did. There was silence as Mama waited for Molly to answer.

"No, not really." She thought of explaining that she now had times when she felt more solid, more real, and didn't fade. Also, that after seeing Ester this morning she thought that she would have less of a problem with the market. But she just left all of this unsaid and ended her answer with a slight shrug. May observed her closely but appeared satisfied. She looked more relaxed than she had when she sat down.

"Molly, love, there are things that, as we grow up, we need to know. These things are for adults to know. Not for children. As you are now almost an adult it is time for you to hear these things." Molly just looked at her, waiting for her to continue. Mama poured them each a cup of tea. She offered Molly a piece of cake. *So, this is how adults talk*, Molly thought, as her mother continued.

May started with the Tower. She stressed that it was the Tower that governed the Bowl. It kept the law, but that it also needed people to help to run the land. She spoke of their own family history. Of Noona's sister, and how she was selected to be one of the ones to help the Tower. May did not elaborate on the way in which Noona's sister was selected. The Influences were mentioned as abilities that could help the Tower in its work. That only special girls had these gifts. If these girls did not want to leave their families and help the Tower, then they would have to not use the gifts. Then the Tower would not select them to help.

Carefully, May spoke of the Influence that Molly's great aunt had possessed. How it revealed itself. Gently, she drew comparisons between Noona's sister, and Molly. She tried to delicately lead Molly to discover that she had the same Influence as her great aunt. Molly listened with interest. Yet, she was totally unaware that her mother was making a direct link between her and selection by the Tower.

Finally, May commented that as Molly was now almost a woman, it was not wise for her to be out on the streets by herself. Particularly in the evening, as there were men who might try and take advantage of her. To this Molly definitely saw a link. She was ready to agree that this was indeed not a good idea.

As Mama concluded, she asked if Molly understood what had been said. Did she have anything to say or anything to ask? Molly looked thoughtful before replying that it would have been dreadful for her aunt to have to leave the family to help the Tower, and that she hoped that none of them would ever have to do that.

Her mother looked satisfied with the answer and poured them both anther cup of tea. She then suggested that later she should teach Molly how to make her father's favourite supper. Once the morning tea was packed away, May left Molly at home while she went to the market to get the items needed.

Now left alone, Molly considered her mother's words. How dreadful to be asked to leave your family. Surely they would ask you first if it wanted you to go help the Tower. She knew that she wouldn't. But she, fortunately, would never be asked. There was nothing special about her. She had no special abilities, so there was nothing in that story to alarm her. Yet, with the incident the other night, she was more than aware that there were others in Town whom she would not like to meet on her own. She wholeheartedly agreed that solitary evening walks were best to be avoided.

Chapter 18

The morning was bright and pleasant as they walked towards the hamlet. They said little, both immersed in their own thoughts. Shan was observing and trying to remember everything around him. He was attempting to create a store of images that he could pull to mind whenever he wanted to feel like he was back home. He was convinced that it wouldn't be long before he would be walking back along this path but, until then, he wanted to keep himself firmly grounded in this land where he had spent his whole life. Maima needed him. He was confident that Farmer Albee would care for her well enough; but he knew that he would be able to do it so much better. Well, at least with a greater level of determination. So, leaving was not saying goodbye to Maima and the Western Slopes but merely a "be back soon".

It did not seem long before they were entering the market square. This had reverted to its usual drab appearance following the conclusion of the festive atmosphere of the previous market day. The eastbound passenger cart would be leaving in about an hour. Having arrived the previous evening, it had exchanged its cargo for other items destined for inhabitants further to the east. Johnathon indicated that there were a few other things that would be useful to get from the general store before they boarded. Therefore, after paying the cartman the fare for two, they made their way toward the store in search of the desired objects.

The general store always smelled so good. It was a treasure-trove of delights for the senses. Every time Shan entered its doors, he had to stop for a moment to adjust to the onslaught of all the sights and smells. It was no different today. While Johnathon looked for the needed items, Shan was free to explore and investigate what was new or exciting. He ran his hands through the various grains, held in large sacks, and indulged in a bit of fantasy about exotic and strange lands. The irony of this did not escape his notice. Here he was, dreaming of far and distant places, while he was in the process of being forced into a journey against his will. All he really wanted was to stay at home. While he was contemplating the absurdity of dreaming about one thing while wishing for another, Johnathon gave him some bundles to hold while he went looking for a few more things.

Shan heard the shop door open, announced by the telltale tinkling of bells.

"Morning, Madam Toolly," came a thin, strained voice.

"Morning, Mrs Figgit. I hope you are well and have come to settle part of the account," was the less than welcoming reply.

"My daughter will be here shortly. I'm sure she can address you."

"And what is it that you are requiring today?" was the barely polite response.

Johnathon arrived at Shan's side, making signs to be quiet and remain concealed from sight behind the high storage cabinets. "We will need to make a quick and quiet exit before Agatha arrives and sees us or, more particularly, you," he warned. "Stay here while I go and pay. Watch for my signal and then we will leave." Leaving Shan where he was, Johnathon made his way to the counter, forgetting about the things Shan still carried. Unable to avoid a meeting with Agatha's mother, Johnathon placed the items he had on the counter. He nodded towards the small woman.

"Ahh, Master Albee," she cawed.

"Mrs Figgit, I hope you are well."

"My daughter, Agatha, will be here soon. She would enjoy seeing you again."

"And what a pleasure it would be to see her as well. I am afraid, though, that I have a pressing matter to attend to."

Having paid for the items, Johnathon put them under his arm and made for the door. As he did so he looked back and nodded to Shan. Seeing the gesture, Shan left the cover of the shelves. He made his way to the entrance just as the door opened. There was Agatha Figgit, in all her glory, blocking the only exit. Coming face to face with Johnathon, she put on her most endearing smile, reserved for only the most eligible unmarried men of her acquaintance.

"Master Albee, oh what a delight in seeing you here. It was such a dreadful fright I had the other night. I do not know how I could bare it. And I hardly saw you that evening."

"Well, I am sure that your attention was directed more on your beau than me," he replied.

"Oh, that was heartbreaking. I am sure he was about to propose. But for that horrible incident. And now, now, oh now I fear that he will not be able to follow his desires to …" As she spoke, she looked past Johnathon and directly at Shan. Stopping mid-thought, her face changed from the coy and coquettish smile to sudden horror. "There, there!" she screamed. "That's the one, the one with the goats!"

Madam Toolly followed her gaze and looked directly at Shan. "What? Sybil's granddaughter! What on earth are you going on about, Agatha?" But this did not distract Agatha, who continued to stare at Shan with terror before collapsing against the wall by the counter.

"Shan." Johnathon indicated the entrance with his head. With a rush, Shan raced for the closing shop door. Agatha's mother and Madam Toolly looked on in astonishment.

"He was huge, and a man, you said. Shan is anything but that. You have terrified her!" admonished the shopkeeper. Agatha continued pointing and staring. Shan exited the store, still carrying the bundles Johnathon had given him.

"Agatha, control yourself. There is no-one here like you described," her mother demanded.

"But it was, it was!" Agatha insisted.

"Thank you, Madam Toolly," inserted Johnathon, stepping over the girl still cowering in the doorway. "I hope you feel better soon, Agatha." She just looked at him as he passed by, her mouth pressed tightly shut and her eyes wide with fear.

Johnathon caught up with Shan as they rounded a corner into one of the alleys off the square. "Well, we can be thankful that Agatha's tendency to exaggerate seemed to work in our favour," he said. "Still, we best move away from the square. We can wait for the cart a bit further out."

So, making their way down the alley, they circumvented the hamlet and eventually made their way onto the eastbound road to wait for the passenger cart. It was only then that Shan realised that he was still carrying Johnathon's things. Horrified, he swore to himself that he would definitely make sure that he would pay for them as soon as he was able to return.

They did not have to wait long before they saw the eastbound passenger cart making its way toward them. Flagging it down, they boarded, feeling that at least the first part of their journey was over.

***

Moira had climbed to the top of her unfinished tower and gazed at the ominous black one on the slopes above her. She wondered for the umpteenth time what it was like to be in the Tower. How could she make sure that she was noticed? Her home, so full of light and colour, with broad balconies and large windows that allowed the fragrance of flowers to unite the indoors with the out, sat in direct contrast to the object of her desires.

Pure black, an outline with almost no details. That was how the Tower appeared. Even in the colour of the setting sun it had no depth. It reflected no light. Mysterious, enigmatic, and powerful, it held its place as it had for generations. To only a few were its secrets revealed. Moira wanted to be one of the chosen.

What this would mean for her parents gave her little concern. She had learnt that it was easier not to feel dependent on any other person – doing so only led to disappointment. She had idolised her sister. Had looked up to her. Had depended on her. Then one day she was gone, leaving the young Moira alone. Moira hated her for that, leaving her alone with a cold and fashionable mother. A woman so beautiful, but as unsuited to motherhood as one could be. So jealous that, if the spotlight was not on her, she would devour her rival – no matter who it was. Moira had seen her pet wolf spider do the very same to its offspring.

Moira was purely entertained by her mother as a necessary evil. Her presence was required to cement the family's position. Her attention was not something that needed to be encouraged or fostered. As for her father, Moira didn't even really know that much about him. Her limited contact primarily occurred when she would be presented to him before bedtime, when she endured being patted on the head and told to be a good girl. Despite this, she had learnt enough to be able to manipulate her father. It was not hard. He just didn't seem to care, as long as he wasn't bothered. She had learnt to avoid her mother.

What she desired most, however, was not something that she could order the servants to arrange, or coerce her father into providing. There was no-one she could ask, so her only source of information was the family library. The Tower made its own choices. It selected its own candidates. She would just have to keep on practising and demonstrating what she could do so the Tower would notice her.

***

To journey by cart may appear at first to be a pleasant experience, moving at the pace of the walking horse in the open air surrounded by nature and its beauty. Reality, however, is frequently less picturesque. There never were a lot of passengers who travelled from as far as the Western Slopes. For these travellers it was a choice of the cart, finding their own form of transport or walking. The rarity of passengers and lack of choice provided little incentive to supply any semblance of comfort or hospitality on the cart. The traveller could simply take it or leave it.

Boarding the cart just outside the hamlet, Shan and Johnathon took their places on the hard wooden plank that was the designated passenger seat. This was supported on either side by the walls of the cart, with various bits of cargo placed around it. As the trip progressed more cargo would find its way into the cart, gradually diminishing the space available to passengers. The road was not that frequently used. It was generally overgrown and peppered with potholes that made it fairly rough going. This, for half an hour, might be enjoyable. But after an hour or two of the constant bumping and jolting on a hard, backless plank of wood, attempting to avoid being hit by tree branches hanging low over the roadway, any gloss was well faded.

Finally, after six hours, they arrived at the first stop of the trip. Carefully and delicately they both climbed off the cart and stretched. They were bruised in places that they thought would never have to suffer from such abuse. Gradually they loosened their joints by slowly walking around the cart. Only after they had stretched did they stop to look at the place in which they had arrived.

This village, in comparison to their own hamlet, was quite grand. Instead of the hardened dirt that formed their square, this opulent village had cobblestones to allow for a mud-free market even during times of rain. Erected in the centre of the square was an obelisk. Inscribed on it were the names of previously important inhabitants. Around the square were several shops. These were substantially more elaborate and welcoming than the solitary general store from their home. Milling around the shopfronts were people dressed in clothes that, in Shan's experience, would only have been seen on the most special of occasions. It all seemed very different, and a world away from where they had been.

They decided that they would leave the cart and start their journey north. It had been a choice between enduring another day travelling east before intersecting with one of the northern routes – while having their rear ends battered and bruised from the hard wooden plank – or making their own way northeast before once again connecting with a main roadway. There they could purchase passage on one of the more substantial, and user friendly, passenger coaches that travelled to the northern regions of the Bowl. The option had been considered as plausible after two hours of travel on the cart. It had become definite once the four-hour mark had been passed.

Walking as if they were wearing britches two sizes too small, they wandered around the square. In one corner was a public house that advertised room and board. More importantly, it announced counter service for food. It was mid-afternoon and although it was too early to get food, the allure of a hot meal after such an ordeal was irresistible. They decided that they could wait and take a meal before starting their journey north.

Meandering around the square, they were aware of people looking at them. After travelling since early morning, including walking for several hours before undertaking the six-hour open-cart ride, they were covered with a layer of grime. It had worked its way into every fold of clothing and clogged the pores of their skin. It was also probably fortunate that there was a slight breeze blowing though the square. The sweat mingling with the dirt from the road generally did not make for a pleasant odour. This was particularly noticeable when experienced within a confined space. Feeling embarrassed by the impression they were giving, they headed away from the store fronts to the furthest point of the square. There they found a pump and horse trough intended to provide water to the animals. Filling the trough with fresh water, they started to scrub their faces and arms free from the worst of the grime.

Shan was about to remove his tunic in order to make an even better attempt on the grime when Johnathon suddenly stopped him. "No, don't take it off. It is best they don't suspect."

"What?"

"Listen, Shan. I know you are a boy, and you know you are a boy, but the rest of the people here … Well, your Maima did this to protect you. It is probably best to keep up the ploy. Just for a bit. At least until we get to your father."

Shan stopped what he was doing and looked at Johnathon.

"Do you really think that the Tower would come all the way out here for me?"

Annoyed, Johnathon replied, "Did you not listen to my father? Think of what happened to your mother and your father. Don't ever ignore the Tower. It will always come for what it wants."

Still not convinced that the Tower would come, let alone know who and where he was, Shan put his head directly into the trough. He scrubbed his hair while underwater. Squeezing and then shaking the water out of his long hair after emerging, he just shrugged and let the water drip onto his shoulders.

"I will make a pretty dreadful girl if anyone speaks to me."

"Then don't speak. Let me handle things. You are my younger sister. We are going north to family after our mother's death. Okay?"

Shan reluctantly agreed.

Now that they were slightly cleaner, if still rather damp, they decided to gently stretch their legs again. They would walk about the village while they both dried, and pass the time until that could get their supper. Leaving the square, they followed the eastern road that would head directly toward Town and the Tower. With the sun at their backs, they wandered this way and that as they watched their shadows lengthen. Finally, it was time to return to the square.

Now dry, and somewhat aired, they made directly for the public house. There were a few tables set outside for patrons to enjoy the last rays of the sun. The space within was already fairly full of men who had finished their day's work and stopped for a quick one on the way home. Going up to the counter they waited until the matron of the inn approached them.

She looked at them closely, taking particular note of Shan, whose hair hung limp about his face. "You'd be best to sit outside. A young miss like this would be better there," she directed, after Johnathon had ordered and paid for their meals. "'Tis not often we get those that are from further west than us. It must have been a slow trip," she added politely, while gently probing for more information.

"We had a death in the family. We go north to other relatives. My sister still needs a woman in her life. That is not something I can provide," Johnathon responded as Shan glared at him. The matron looked again at Shan and nodded.

"Shan't be long," she said as she waved them outside.

Once outside, Johnathon smiled at Shan and his discomfort. "You certainly would be a dreadful girl. Let's hope no one looks too closely at you!" As he was speaking the matron appeared at the entrance with a pint in each hand.

"Beer has never done me no harm. I'm sure you and your sister could do with one. On the house." Putting down the mugs, she placed her hand into her apron and removed a long pink ribbon. "One can hardly see you with all that hair about your pretty face. Men don't seem to know the first thing, do they?" She looked at Johnathon as she started to brush back Shan's hair with her fingers and tie it with the ribbon. "There now, that's better. No hair in the stew and you look more like the girl you are." Smiling, she left them with Shan looking straight ahead, hands clenched beneath the table.

Johnathon unsuccessfully stifled a smirk. "You look very pretty," he said, totally unable to resist the comment. Raising one finger toward Johnathon, Shan just glowered and said nothing.

The stew was excellent and the bread fresh and light. Even with a ribbon in his hair, Shan's enjoyment of the food could not be dampened. The beer was also something of a delight. Having never tasted it before, he had been a bit wary. But, after the long day and with good hot food, the beer just made everything seem even better. He finished the pint to the praise of the matron, who checked on them at regular intervals. "There, my girl, a pint is as good as a poke in my books."

Thanking her for her kindness and generosity Johnathon helped Shan to his feet. He was feeling just a little lightheaded.

"A beer can do that," Johnathon said, "but it's unlikely that you will be any the worse for it by the morning." They left the square and started their way north through the village. The sun was now just a glow in the west. They made their way onto the northeast track that would connect them with one of the major northern routes. They had decided that they would walk for a while, before resting by the side of the track until morning came and they continued on their way.

***

Molly felt proud and very nervous. This would be the first time that she had ever made supper for Father. It was his favourite. Mama had spent the afternoon showing her how to prepare it, but she had done all of the actual preparation and the cooking herself. All the ingredients were fresh from the market that day.

Now, with everything done, Molly waited expectantly for her father to arrive home. Mama had said that he was going to be home early this evening as he had started the day a bit earlier than usual. The girls had already been washed and were just finishing their own supper when Molly heard the cottage door open and saw her father enter the kitchen. Before approaching his wife, he nodded to the girls. He embraced their mother before turning to acknowledge each of them in turn. His gaze lingered for a moment longer on Molly, who blushed slightly. As the girls tidied their things, Molly wiped and reset the table so that she and her parents would be able to eat.

While Mama went to settle the girls in their rooms and Father went to clean off the fine white dust from his clothes and hair that was the trademark of the stonemason, Molly undertook the final preparations of their meal. Hoping against hope that she had remembered to do everything correctly, she carefully filled the bowls with the rich, hot rabbit stew and dumplings. Placing the full bowls on the table she waited for her parents to return. Before too long they were seated. Molly watched anxiously as he tried his first mouthful.

"May, you have certainly outdone yourself tonight," he said as he wiped his mouth.

"No, I don't think so," she replied. Joseph looked confused as she added, "It was Molly who outdid me tonight." Surprised and delighted at her parents' praise Molly just beamed at them and thought, *You know, I think I really might be able to do this.*

***

The moon had yet to rise and the way was dark and difficult. Shan felt light. The bow was still in his hair but that didn't really bother him anymore. In fact, not a lot was bothering him. The world in general seemed to be a much better place since their visit to the inn. With a full stomach, and an overarching agreeable disposition to everything about him, he meandered along behind Johnathon. Gradually the distance between them increased until he was only just able to make out Johnathon's silhouette against the darkness.

Without warning a hand covered his mouth. Several others grabbed him about the waist. They lifted him off the ground. Unable to yell or scream he tried to kick at his attackers. They forcefully held him on the ground as they bound his feet and arms with straps. Before they removed the hand from his mouth a knife point was place against his neck with a warning not to make a sound while they gagged him. A bag was placed over his head. Left helpless, and with difficulty focusing, Shan could only imagine where he was being taken.

Chapter 19

The guests were arriving for yet another glamorous and politically useful affair. Moira would be required to make a brief appearance. Then she would be quickly ushered out of the away to allow her mother to retain the central positions of both hostess and most beautiful woman in the room. Reluctantly Moira descended the tower's stairs. She needed to be ready for her entrance at the moment when her father deemed it most efficacious.

Tonight, she needed to look her most stunning. Her hair was twisted into an elaborate style that framed and accentuated her heart-shaped face. The green of her dress enhanced the fiery red of her hair. It contrasted with her porcelain skin, lending her an otherworldly beauty that was almost ethereal. Nearly of an age to be used as one of the most valuable bargaining chips to enhance and secure the family's fortune and status, Moira was tonight to be exhibited to the parents of all her potential suitors for their consideration. Moira felt as if she were a prized heifer, there to be offered for sale to the highest bidder after having her teeth and udder closely examined. She could hardly wait for the Tower to come for her.

Waiting outside the family's private entrance to the ballroom, Moira stood patiently. She could not sit, as this would crease her dress and flatten the small train that trailed behind her. The maids had begun preparing her several hours previously. She had not been able to sit for some time. With hands folded demurely in front of her, she stood and waited. Posture was important. Grace was a necessity. She could hear music coming from beyond the door and the general hum of conversation was felt as vibrations through the floor.

Finally, the door began slowly opening. Already in place and perfectly framed in the doorway, Moira waited as the music ceased. A hush fell across the room. With all eyes upon her she glided across the marble floor. She floated into and through the mix of people, who parted before her. As she reached her father, he took each of her hands in his. She kissed him lightly on the cheek. Beside him she could see her mother, a smile painted on her face but eyes hard with jealousy because Moira had assumed the spotlight. The coldness that emanated from her was palpable to Moira. It was a kind of hatred that only the most self-absorbed people could justify.

Continuing to hold her by a single hand, Moira's father gracefully turned her to face the crowd.

"My friends, tonight I have the great pleasure to present my daughter, Moira," her father announced. To this Moira gracefully bowed her head in acknowledgement. "The pride and joy of our house and the heir to the great name of Keep." The assemblage applauded gently in welcome. Moira's father passed her to her mother, who took her hand and led her away. Away from the centre of attention and back to the side of the room.

In a perfectly gentle and melodic voice, that still could not hide the iciness behind it, Moira's mother said to her, "You will remain here until my maid comes to collect you. You will not move. You will not talk. It is fortunate that you managed to look acceptable tonight. At least you did not embarrass us."

Saying nothing further, her mother turned and flowed back to the party, prepared to endure all the ill-conceived congratulations from incompetent, but well-meaning, women about the grace and beauty of her daughter. All Moira could do was look on. She concealed her feelings behind a mask of serenity.

Moira watched her mother working the room, actively ignoring the daughter whom she had left standing on her own – out of the way and, hopefully, out of sight and mind. All Moira could think about was what a wasteful and useless life this would be. One that she was determined to avoid. The Tower would want her. It must want her. She would make it want her.

Projecting her thoughts into the room, Moira could feel each person. There was a myriad of heart beats. The air was moving as the guests breathed in and out. Gradually she focused and was able to feel her mother. A cold chill ran through her as she probed a bit deeper. A light, quick pulse with short and shallow breaths, probably due to some tight corsetry that allowed her mother to maintain the figure she so desired.

Perhaps a little tweak. Maybe a faint. Why not? She would be the centre of attention and that is what she wants, Moira thought. Focusing hard, she started to slow her mother's heart rate. Just a little. Make her a little dizzy. She will have to sit and crease that dress of hers, she laughed to herself.

The heart slowed a touch but then rebounded. Moira tried again and the heart rate slowed in response. Once more, it got away from her control and returned to normal. Frustrated that it was not working the way it was supposed to, Moira tried harder. This time she slowed the rate much more, which reduced her mother's blood pressure and provoked a rapid rise in her rate of breathing.

Her mother revealed little of what was occurring internally. Her smile stayed rigidly in place. Her pale skin only exhibited a slight glow from the film of sweat that had formed on its surface. Moira felt resistance to the Influence. She could not let herself fail. The Tower would know, and would not want her. Despite all her efforts, the heart rate would not stay low. It doggedly returned to normal. Feeling panicked, Moira put all that she had left into it. Her very self she poured into reducing her mother's heart rate. All she wanted was for her to faint.

It was a battle for control. Moira was winning. The rate was falling. Her mother was losing. It took energy, all that she had, but Moira would do it. She had to. Without warning, her mother's eyes locked with hers and Moira felt her mother once again break free from her control. The heart rate rose dramatically and the blood pressure exploded upward, no longer dampened by Moira's control. Having exhausted all that she had left, Moira fell to the ground in a faint. The last thing she remembered seeing was her mother's face, flushed with blood as her eyes rolled back in her head and she, too, collapsed to the ground.

***

When Moira awoke, she was lying on a daybed in one of the ancillary rooms off the ballroom. A maid was seated beside her. As her eyes flickered open, the maid rose, offering her a glass of water. Still dressed in her finery, Moira awkwardly raised herself on one elbow and accepted the glass with a nod. The lamps were still lit but it was quiet. No music nor conversations were to be heard.

"You alright, Miss? Is there anything I can get you?"

"No, thank you," Moira responded, still feeling a bit vague and disorientated. "What happened?"

"You fainted, Miss. When your mother …" She stopped midsentence, unsure of how to continue.

"When my mother what?" Moira demanded.

"When you mother fainted, if you please, Miss."

"My mother fainted?" she responded with surprise.

"I best get the housekeeper. I must inform her you are awake," said the maid. She got up quickly and left the room in a hurry, leaving Moira alone.

Gradually remembering what happened just before she fainted, Moira looked about her. The party should still have been underway. A fainting fit was not unusual at such events. This was primarily due to the vanity of women who bound their bodies, ever so tightly, to achieve the prized hourglass figure. No, something more must have happened. She remembered that it had been a battle. This had never happened before when she practised on others. Never had anyone resisted her use of Influence. The whole thing had drained her strength completely. She still felt the effects of her efforts. The maid said that her mother had fainted, but it seemed likely to be a bit more than that. She pondered this as she waited for the housekeeper to arrive.

Within a few minutes Moira was being examined by the housekeeper who, when convinced that it had been nothing more than a fainting fit, looked directly at her. "Your mother had a turn at the party. Your father is with her."

Curious if her mother would have said anything about the battle that occurred between them, Moira asked, "Did my mother say what happened?"

"You mother is not yet awake. The physician has been with her for some time."

"And what does he say?"

"I think it best that your father tells you more, when he is ready. I will get the maid to take you to bed."

"I would like to know what is happening," insisted Moira.

"When your father is ready," was the terse reply as the housekeeper rose and left the room, ignoring Moira's demanding looks.

The maid returned immediately and helped Moira to her feet. Slowly they made their way to Moira's chambers, where the maid helped her out of her gown and into her bedclothes before taking down her hair.

Looking at the maid, Moira asked, "What happened? And do not think that you have any other choice but to answer me."

Looking timid and unsure, the maid searched about her for a means of escape.

"It will not go well for you if you do not answer me truthfully," threatened Moira. Seeing no other alternative, the maid crumbled and related the events of the evening.

Both Moira and her mother fell to the ground at the same time. Moira had been largely unobserved, except by the servants. They had gathered her up and placed her on the daybed where she had rested for several hours before awakening. Her mother, however, appeared to have had some sort of a fit as she collapsed. In the middle of conversing with several ladies, her eyes rolled back in her head and, with neck arched, she went rigid before crumbling to the floor. Since then, there had been no response from her. No movement and only occasional gurgling sounds. On occasion her breathing would cease, causing much alarm before it would start again. Gradually it would become deeper and deeper, before steadily reducing and getting shallower once more.

The physician had been called but, despite being there for hours, had said that there was little that could be done. In short, Moira would more than likely be motherless by morning.

***

Shan, bound and unable to see where he was, stayed still. He tried to think. Who these people were and what they wanted evaded him. They were not from the Tower, that was obvious, but could they be working for the Tower? Had he been identified? Was he on the way there already? What about Johnathon? Was he also here, bound and blindfolded? If it was the Tower, he needed to continue the pretence of being a girl. Maima seemed to think that was important. So important that all but a few who knew of him already thought of him as a girl. So, as much as it wounded his pride, he would continue the deception.

He was lying on a cold, hard floor. Apart from the sound of movement on what would be the floor above him, all was quiet. How long he had been here he was uncertain. An hour, perhaps, or more. The trip here had been uncomfortable as he had been slung, he thought, over someone's shoulder. Every so often he was passed to another. Any movement on his part resulted in a quick smack to the head or face. He had soon learnt that it was best just to go limp and avoid any further abuse. Now he appeared to be alone, but his arms and legs were tightly bound. His movement was severely restricted and he could not see his surroundings. He waited and thought about how he could defend himself if required. No-one was going to absorb him, no matter where they were from.

Eventually he heard the sound of a door being unlocked. Footsteps came towards him. He stayed very still, waiting, unsure what was going to happen. Several hands grabbed him at once and pulled him into a sitting position. They held him firmly from either side. All of a sudden, the bag was pulled off his head. He saw that he was in the basement of some building, sitting on a hard stone floor. The only light was coming from a window high on the wall behind him, that would have been just above ground height from the outside. Three people were in front of him – two men and a woman. The men he did not recognise, but the woman; she was the matron from the inn.

"Hello, deary. We must get you a bit more comfortable, mustn't we? You're here with us now." Bending over and looking Shan directly in the face she added, "Your brother won't find you and he will stay safe and well as long as you behave." Shocked and unable to speak due to the gag that was still in place, Shan just looked at her in horror.

"We will look after you, don't you worry. You are very special, and we mustn't damage the merchandise. Undamaged and cared for is what we all want. Now I am just going to have to check. Going to see if the flower has yet bloomed." As she spoke, she gradually undid the bindings around Shan's legs and tried to pull his legs apart. Shan kicked at her wildly but the men on either side each quickly grabbed a leg, holding them apart while the matron started to lift Shan's tunic. Writhing futilely against those restraining him, Shan tried to call out. Only a muffled cry emerged from the behind the gag. Frantic, he could no longer think. He could only fruitlessly try to free himself from his captors.

The room went silent. Everything stopped. There was no sound and no movement as those around him remained motionless, frozen in time. Shan could feel the air about him, like a blanket covering him or as water engulfing him. Regaining some composure, he pushed at the air with his mind. It flowed away from him. Willing it to come back, he gathered it about him. It could expand and be compressed.

Remembering what had happened in the alley, he concentrated on pulling the air towards himself. If he compressed it far enough, could it expand when needed? Enough to push these people away from him? He tried, pulling air to himself, holding it tightly compacted. A buffer between him and those next to him. He drew more and more to himself, holding it, crushing it against his body. Building layer upon layer as protection.

Time started again.

Slowly at first, but quickly gaining speed. The matron's hands were raising the tunic with his legs held apart. Desperate for this to work, Shan concentrated. He willed the air to come to him. Holding it there, he tried to add more and more until it was too much. He was no longer able to hold it in place. He lost control. Just before the tunic exposed his true identity, the air exploded outward in all directions. With Shan at its centre, it expanded. Both men lost their grip and flew away from him. The matron was tossed backward like a leaf in the wind. She landed heavily on her back. Bound and gagged apart from his legs, Shan, however, remained still.

Now what? he thought. I pushed them away from me, but they are still here and I'm still tied up. They will just continue. How stupid. This achieved nothing. Gradually all three captors rose to their feet and stood, looking at him.

"I think that we will want something better for you than I first thought, deary. There are those who pay a very good price for someone like you. They are very particular about who they select," the matron said in a syrupy voice. "Best make sure that she does not hurt herself, boys," she then directed as the men grabbed Shan and rebound his legs. "Boys, we need to send a message to the Tower."

Alone, bound, gagged, and locked in the basement of some unknown building, Shan had revealed himself to the Tower. Now all he could do was wait for the Dark Ones to arrive.

Chapter 20

Molly lay on her bed. She had been relieved from any of the cleaning up from supper, since she had cooked. It had been a good day. Tea with Mama and success with Father's supper. *I outdid Mama's rabbit stew.* For the first time, Molly actually started to believe that she could do this; be an adult, a mother, and wife like Mama. It felt good knowing that she was starting to get the hang of it. Mama had always said that she would. But then, Mama always said things to make you feel better if something went wrong. Molly had never been quite sure that Mama really thought that she could do it, despite her words. Mama had always been there to help. She was there to make things right if they started to go awry. But Molly knew that Mama would not always be there. She could not constantly make things better. Molly herself would eventually have to rely on her own abilities. *Now, perhaps,* Molly thought, *Mama doesn't always need to be there to make things better. I might be able to do it myself.*

Full of excitement at all the possibilities, Molly was not feeling tired and was still in her clothes. She wanted to do something. Something she would remember. Something that would mark this day as the day when she started to get it right. When she knew that she would be a good woman, wife, and mother. Not being one for taking risks if she could avoid them, Molly considered the possibility of doing something to challenge herself. She looked out the window. She had always wondered what it would be like but had never dared. Her friends had done it, but she had never felt brave enough. She decided. Tonight was the night. She would do it. This would mark the first day of the new, more confident Molly. A woman in the making.

Dimming the lamp, Molly walked over to the window. She opened it. Pushing the shutters aside, she looked at the roof just outside and at the lights of the town beyond. Hers being an attic room, she was already in the roof, so it was not far to go before she would be on the roof itself. There she could sit, looking at Town from a new and exciting vantage point.

Holding her breath, she pulled up her skirt to her knees and climbed onto the windowsill. Feeling a breeze on her face, she carefully put one leg and then the other outside the window frame. Carefully she put part of her weight on feet that were finding their grip on the roof's shingles. Still holding onto the window frame, she gradually lowered herself onto the sloping roof. Now fully outside the house, she felt a rush of exhilaration.

Not yet finished, she looked up. Steadily, she started making her way to the roof's peak. She planned to sit at the very apex of the house. Right at the top, straddling both sides of the house, where she could see the eastern, southern, and western parts of Town by merely turning her head. It turned out to be easier than she expected. The slope of the roof was not great and the shingles were not slippery. Before she knew it, she was sitting where she had always been too scared to go. The air was warm and the breeze light as Molly embraced the experience. The scattered lights about her were like fireflies in the night, and she could hear crickets call to each other. She let the noises of evening waft over her. Her sense of delight in the experience was only heighted by the tinge of danger.

Sitting on top of the world, Molly revelled in her newfound confidence when, without warning, the world suddenly went silent. The breeze stopped. Everything went still. The lights of Town and the stars above became dim. The air got just a little bit colder. Having been so aware of her surroundings at that moment, Molly felt the change as strongly as if she had been drenched with iced water. A chill raced up her spine. Her breathing quickened. The night was now darker and less welcoming than it had been. Molly sat, now too terrified to move.

***

May and Joseph worked as one. Washing and drying, replacing and resetting the kitchen as they had done most evenings since their marriage. It did not take them long before the kitchen was back to its normal orderly appearance. Then they sat down at the kitchen table to a cup of tea. Joseph looked at his wife. "So, did you get to talk with Molly?"

"We did. I said that the Tower needed girls with special gifts to help with its work, and if the girls did not want to go, they should not use their gifts. She said that she never would want to go. I think she understood. She won't use Influence."

Looking worried and unconvinced, Joseph asked, "You are sure that it was clear?"

"As clear as it could be without terrifying her. You know how Molly is. She's not like Ester. Molly takes things to heart too much. She's at such a difficult age. So much is changing for her." May shook her head as she spoke. They both knew that it was out of their control. All they had was a wish and a belief that their family would survive.

"We have to hope that the Tower has seen nothing of us. We will have to keep Molly out of harm's way. Keep her at home until she is older. Hope that the Tower loses interest. We are lucky she won't find it difficult to keep close to home."

Silence rested heavily between them. May looked at her husband with eyes glistening as she clasped his hand and asked, "Joseph, what do we do if they do come?"

"Whatever we can, May. There must be some way to stop the Dark Ones. They, too, were once someone's child. They must remember what it was like. Molly wouldn't survive them coming," he responded solemnly. Remaining in silent thought, they held hands as if this physical link between them was there to protect their children. Rising, Joseph went over to the door leading out onto the street and uncharacteristically bolted it. "Whatever we can," he said again as he tidied the cups and placed them on the sink.

Dimming the lamp, they rose to go upstairs to bed. Leaving the light on was not something they normally did. At times like this, any light might be a better protection than none in the presence of the Dark Ones. Together they started for the stairs when May noticed the light behind them flicker and dim. Turning, she watched in disbelief as the bolted door silently swung open. There, in the doorway, was a shadow darker than the night outside. Muffling a scream, May clasped her husband's arm to warn him. This was unnecessary as Joseph had seen. He was already armed, having grabbed his brick hammer, the one he used to split stone with the long, chisel-shaped blade. Standing his ground, having pushed his wife behind him, he faced the threat as it entered their kitchen followed by two others.

The world become thin about them. There was no sound. The air was still. May could see Joseph yelling at the intruders but heard nothing. Joseph, too, must have been aware of the lack of sound as he ceased his attempts. He stood there between them and his family. The shadows took on the form of hooded figures once in the light of the kitchen. They were all covered, head to toe, in garments so black that it was like looking into eternity; an infinite emptiness, a chasm that never ended and could never be filled.

Three had entered the cottage. Two stood behind the first. All just waited. They stood there, appearing to do nothing. Without a word the Dark Ones moved forward. Joseph raised his hammer ready to strike the first that made for the stairs. As one, the intruders raised their arms in front of them. Joseph felt the air leave his lungs and refuse to fill them again. Defiantly he maintained his stance. Not for long though, as the lack of vital oxygen caused him to drop to the floor. No longer able to retain his hold on the hammer, it fell. He opened and closed his mouth in a futile attempt to breathe. May saw but did not understand what was happening. She could only see that her husband was choking before he hit the floor and lost consciousness. She raced towards him, unhindered by the visitors. He was still alive, attempting to take short, rapid, shallow breaths.

The figures glided passed them. They began their ascent up the stairs. On the first floor the doors to the two bedrooms opened by themselves. Ester, in her parents' room, stirred slightly but did not wake. The three older sisters, strewn across the large single bed that dominated the second room, also remained unaware of the forms outside the door. Wasting no time, the Tower's representatives moved around the landing and started up the narrow stairs to the attic.

***

Molly looked about her. She couldn't stay up here, no matter how she felt. She had to make her way back to the window and into her room. With great caution and purpose of movement she shifted both legs to the same side of the roof. Now, looking down, the roof suddenly seemed a great deal higher than it had a few moments ago. Sliding down the roof's slope on her backside she made slow but steady progress to the attic window. When almost there, she found that she was unable to advance further. Looking behind and up she saw that her dress had caught the rough edge of one of the shingles. Giving it a tentative tug, she tried to release the trapped material. Nothing happened. She gave a slightly firmer pull. Frustrated, and not wanting to climb back up the roof to fix the problem, Molly was about to give a final jerk in an attempt to tear the material away from the snag when, out of the corner of her eye, she saw a hooded apparition appear though her window. Startled, she lost her footing. The dress tore from its tether. She started to slide down the shingles.

No longer concerned with the shadow, Molly wildly scraped her feet against the tiles, attempting to find any foothold to slow her descent. Instead of regaining control she picked up speed. She passed the attic window, making for the edge of the roof. Beyond was the drop to the street below. Without warning her progress ceased and she sank into a pillowy softness that encompassed and held her. Although her feet were over the edge of the roof, they appeared to be pushing against marshmallow. Pressing them against the unseen force that protected her from falling to the ground, Molly scrambled back up the shingles and to her attic window. She grasped the sill tightly as she felt herself start to tremble.

Gradually regaining some composure, Molly climbed in through the darkened window of her room. Making it inside without further incident, she sat on the edge of her bed to slow her beathing and calm herself. Only then did she become aware the room seemed darker than it had. Much darker than it should be, even with the dimmed lamp. Looking up, she came face to face with an apparition. A dark outline against the poorly lit room, only feet away from her, standing silently but with a presence she could feel.

Seeing a nightmare with her waking eyes, Molly felt coldness immerse her. She tried to scream. No sound emerged. Engulfed by fear and unable to move, Molly could only stare uncomprehendingly at the shadow, waiting for it to strike. It remained still. Two others approached the bed. Then from the void in front of her Molly heard a voice; deep, melodic, calm, and unmistakeably female. "Tonight, your life will begin. You are privileged to be selected by the Code. Only those who succeed will rise. Those who fail will still be able to serve. You will come now, neophyte. The Tower awaits."

The figure turned and moved toward the door. Molly remained on the bed, unmoving. Without slowing or turning, the figure said, "The rest in this house are of little consequence to the Tower. Remain here and observe the Tower's discipline on those you call family."

Fearful of what might occur, Molly rose and followed the figure. The two others let her pass and fell in behind. Going down the stairs Molly saw her sisters asleep in their rooms. There at the base of the stairs was Mama, cradling Father's head in her lap as he lay unconscious on the floor. With tears running down her face, Mama appeared to speak. Molly heard nothing. Seeing her father and the distress in her mother's face, Molly held back her fear. "Mama, it's alright. It'll be fine." Turning to the figures Molly asked, "Will they be left alone if I go?"

"They are of little consequence to the Tower. They will remain as they are," was the reply.

Trailing the dark outline as it headed for the open door to the street, Molly looked directly into her mother's eyes. "I love you," she mouthed, exaggerating her words so that Mama might understand even if she could not hear her. Lingering a moment longer their eyes said all that could not be voiced. Molly turned. She followed the apparition and entered the street, silent tears flowing down her cheeks. She looked back and saw the door silently close behind her.

***

The walk through Town to the Tower was a blur. Flanked by escorts and hardly able to see through the tears that coated her face, Molly neither saw nor heard anyone on the way. Without fanfare or welcome they arrived at the steps of the Tower and started to climb. It was a long way from the street to the great door above. Molly was breathless by the time they stopped before it. Silently it opened, revealing nothing but an inky blackness beyond. Hesitant, she was moved forward by the Dark Ones behind her.

It was cold and silent in the huge antechamber. Molly turned to catch one last glimpse of the outside world before the great door glided closed. What light had crept its way through the entrance was now gone. Molly was left in a cool greyness that hardly illuminated the walls about her and did not reveal the ceiling above. She found that her escorts had gone, leaving her standing alone, not knowing what she was supposed to do or where she should go.

Trembling, both with the cold that emanated from the black stone about her and from the dread of this place that had only ever been spoken of as a nightmare, Molly warily made her way across the floor. It was smooth and hard beneath her feet. Placing her left hand on the wall and keeping it there she carefully started to walk away from the great door. She thought that if she kept her left hand on the wall at all times, she would always be able to find her way back to the entrance by simply placing her right hand on the same wall and walking back the way she came.

Off the antechamber there appeared to be three passages. She took the first and continued. The light in the passage did not alter. She heard no sound apart from her tentative steps. "Hello, is anyone here?" she called out. The sound of her voice was muffled. She heard no echo off the walls. "Can anyone hear me?" No-one answered. Continuing on, Molly made her way through circular chambers, more passages, and small alcoves, but nothing seemed to change. The air was still. No sounds were heard. There were not even any cobwebs in the corners or dust on the floor.

Deciding that there was no point continuing her exploration, Molly elected to return to the great door. *Perhaps I was supposed to wait there for them to return and tell me what to do,* she thought. So, turning around and placing her right hand on the wall, she started to make her way back again. This time she walked faster, always being careful never to take her hand away from the wall beside her. *They might get angry with me if they find I am not there.*

Every room looked the same. No corridor differed from the one before, but Molly knew that she had to find her way back to the door. Father had taught her this trick in one of his stories. It had stopped the hero getting lost. On she went, unable to tell if this room was one she had been in before or not. *I should have been there by now.* But there were only more corridors. More chambers like the last. Molly continued on but was starting to get more and more anxious. *Where is the door? I kept my hand on the wall at all times.*

Eventually, after having walked for far longer than she should have needed to, Molly stopped. Exhausted, she rested her back against the wall. She slid down it until she was sitting on the floor. Desperate, tired, alone, and scared, Molly could not understand why she had not found the entrance. She knew she was lost. Curling up into a ball with her arms hugging her knees to her chest, she sat. Feeling the cold of the stone penetrate her clothes chilled her even further. With no Mama or Father there to help and not knowing what else to do, Molly lowered her head onto her arms and silently sobbed.

Chapter 21

The bedchamber was quiet when Moira awoke. She had slept late. The sun had risen but the curtains were still closed with the daylight creeping in around the edges. This was odd. Normally the maid would have attended to the chamber while she was still asleep, preparing for the day ahead, drawing the curtains and bringing her morning fare. Raising herself out of bed Moira looked about the room. No breakfast and no refreshments of any sort on the small table. Annoyed, as she was feeling hungry after the exertions of the evening before, she climbed out of bed. She rang for the maid as she saw to her personal toilet. After completing her ablutions and waiting for what seemed an extraordinary amount of time, Moira became frustrated. Her maid was not overly efficient, but she was normally prompt and punctual. Good maids were hard to find. Moira had been through a number of those who had been less than acceptable. She was not keen on trying to find another, even if this one was not ideal.

Resigned to getting herself ready for the day without the aid of her maid, Moira made her way to the robe. She chose a simple pale-green garment that reached almost to the floor. Elegant but fitted. Easy enough to don by herself without a maid to button up the back. Once dressed, she approached her dressing table to organise her hair. Today she would let her locks flow around her face and allow the sun to enhance their natural brilliance. It was only then that she noted the black veil covering the mirror.

Memories from the night before returned to her. The presentation ball "in her honour". Her honour indeed. It really was an auctioning house, designed for others to place their bids in an attempt to purchase some of the family's power and status through acquiring an asset – namely, her. She remembered the cold and disdainful looks from her mother. The woman who despised her as a rival for attention in this wasteful, self-flattering world of indifference. Then there was the use of Influence on her mother. The ensuing battle for control, that ultimately led to them both collapsing. And now her maid was absent. The mirror was covered and the curtains undrawn.

Her mother was dead.

Moira sat there in front of the shrouded mirror. She wondered how people were supposed to feel when their mother died. She assumed that many would be in great distress. Crying or wailing, beating their chests, and falling to the ground in demonstrations of grief. It all seemed a bit pointless, really. Much of this, she assumed, was an act for others to see. A way to show that they had really loved their mother despite the arguments, lack of communication, and thoughtless absences that put distance between them. Once certified by the physician they were definitely dead. Nothing would change that, so why put on the pretence?

In silence, Moira examined her feelings. Looking deep inside herself, she found nothing. She did not feel much, even knowing that her mother had died. The woman who had given birth to her had done very little over the years apart from shun and ignore her. Moira may have inherited her mother's looks, but they had been strangers. They had never shared a conversation, let alone demonstrated any form of affection toward each other. *Was she a hardened, soulless, and emotionless creature?*

In her life feelings had always been considered a weakness, but she was not emotionless. She remembered how upset she was seeing the small, injured bird she had rescued die in her hands. She did have feelings. To date, however, she just had not had much of a need for them. Her mother and her death did not provoke any feelings. The loss of her mother would also mean very little practically as well. Soon the Tower would come to collect her.

Well, I am not going to look like I just got out of bed for the rest of the day, she thought. So, removing the veil from the mirror, Moira picked up the silver-handled hairbrush. She started smoothing her hair. It was soothing brushing her hair. Even in the dim light it appeared to burn with an internal fire. Hardly concentrating, Moira relaxed into the repetitive movements.

Out of the corner of her eye she saw reflected in the mirror a dark figure standing on the other side of the room. Turning to look, she saw nothing there. But again, in the mirror, she saw it. It moved a bit closer towards her. As it neared her, Moira could see in the shadowy figure some subtle features. Tall and slender, it was made of a mist that eddied and swirled within the confines of its outline. It was wearing a long, flowing elegant dress.

Moira felt a chill run down her back. The figure moved even closer. Mesmerised by the spectacle, she sat still, fixated on the image. Where the face should have been was just a churning mist without features. The room became colder. Moira could see her breath condense in front of her. The figure reached her.

Turning again, she couldn't make out anything behind her, but she could feel the cold and still see it in the mirror. It bent over her, bringing the churning void of a face close to her right ear. In an instant the mist coalesced into the features of her mother. The apparition whispered into her ear, "Your end is preordained." The mist immediately faded and dispersed about the room until no trace of it remained.

Trembling, Moira stood up and turned to view the empty room. Racing to the curtains she pulled them open, letting in the midmorning sun, flooding the chamber with light. The warmth of the sun lifted the icy coldness that lingered about her. Carefully examining the space, Moira confirmed that she was alone. Bracing herself, she returned to the mirror to complete her task. To her horror she saw that the mirror had turned an inky black. In its reflection she appeared like the shadow of her mother in the lightened room. Throwing the veil once again over the mirror, Moira lifted her dress and ran from her room. For once in her life, she needed company. The company of people, anyone, no matter their station.

***

The early morning sun was working its way into the basement through the small window set high on the wall behind him. Shan sat on the ground. His arms and legs were still bound but, following a warning from the matron, they had removed the gag from his mouth. If he made any noise in an attempt to attract the attention of those outside, the act would be followed by the swift removal of his tongue. She said that, from her experience with the Tower, it did not appear to mind if those it collected were able to speak or not. This threat was accompanied by a mock demonstration as to how the aforesaid tongue would be removed. Then the presentation of the instrument that would undertake the task. For Shan, further persuasion was unnecessary. The means, and the will, required to perform the task had been displayed in abundance. Silence, in many instances, may be golden; but in this case it would also be a lot less painful.

He had not slept much. Lying on the cold, hard floor without any coverings, unable to move his arms and legs, was uncomfortable. It had been a long night. He felt dazed by the lack of sleep and was also nursing a slight headache, most likely from the ale he had drunk the previous evening. This was combined with aches in both arms and legs, he expected from the restriction of their movement. The whole process was particularly intolerable. The discomfort even overshadowed the concern he had about the impending arrival of the Dark Ones.

After his demonstration of Influence, and removal of the gag, Shan had been left fairly much alone. The door had been locked and, from what he could hear, a guard was stationed outside. One further concession was that his hands had been bound in front of him instead of behind his back. This meant that at least the meagre provisions they provided were able to be consumed. Also, that he could lift his tunic to relieve himself in the bucket in the corner when required. He had tried to work at the bindings on his wrists to loosen them but without success. His captors certainly knew how to tie a knot. They also checked on him regularly enough to identify if there had been any progress in freeing himself.

What a fool he felt. He had not thought it through. He had failed, once again, to control the effect of the Influence. Surely there must have been a better way than using Influence? *So what if they found out I was a boy?* he thought. *They would just have had to let me go. I wouldn't be worth anything to them if I wasn't a girl. Now I have to make sure they, and the Tower, think I'm a girl.*

This, of course, came with its own dilemma. What did he need to do to keep them convinced that he was a girl? Not having any experience with real girls apart from Maima, he was at a bit of a loss as to how to play the part. One thing he did consider important was squatting instead of standing at the bucket when relieving himself. Apart from that, he was not really sure of the differences between boys and girls. This was something he was able to consider during the long hours he remained in captivity. He also wondered what had happened to Johnathon. They had said that he was safe. He hoped that they had left him alone. He was reluctant to ask any more in case it resulted in harm coming to Johnathon as well.

So, all he could do was await his fate. He had to keep up the pretence that he was without family here in the western part of the Bowl. Fortunately, as a thirteen-year-old girl with Influence, he was valuable to the Tower. This meant that he was not destined to warm the bed of a single purchaser, if he had been lucky, or the beds of many on an hourly basis if he was not. There was enough to worry about here in the present moment without adding to it the anxiety of the Dark Ones and the Tower. In his thinking they would just have to be dealt with, each in their turn. At the time they had to be, and not before.

While pondering the predicament in which he found himself, Shan heard the lock of the door click open. Light flooded the basement. A shadow emerged against the light, its features obscured. As it made its way towards him, Shan recognised the shape of the matron.

"Now, deary, I sees that you've been a good girl. Nice and quiet. We are expecting a few visitors later today. They tend to like the evening best and we like here to do our best for our guests. We have standards. You do have a spicy aroma about you. Not sure that our guests would be too pleased with that. So, a bit of a clean-up might be in order."

Shan tensed. The matron noticed and, looking slightly troubled, added quickly, "No-one is checking the honey pot, deary, but you need a bit of a tidy. We will let you do your own cleaning. But if you don't, we will do it for you. We pride ourselves that we only provide top-notch products. We ain't gonna offer anything less."

Behind her, two men brought in a small wooden tub and filled it with water. A large bar of laundry soap was placed next to the tub.

"In you get. And take the soap with you."

Confused, Shan just looked at the tub and then the soap. *How am I going to do this?* he thought. Slowly crawling towards the tub, he grabbed the soap and tossed it in. Pulling himself upright by grabbing the side of the tub, he sat on the rim. Flicking his legs over the side, he fell into the cold water inside. Satisfied, the matron turned to leave. "We will be back in a bit when you're done."

Shan searched for the soap under the water. Once retrieved he was able soap himself up under the tunic that was floating about him. Despite the bound arms and legs, he succeeded in cleaning most of his front surface. He then made a reasonable attempt to wash his hair. Once rinsed, he pulled himself out of the tub and sat shivering on the hard floor, dripping wet with a soaked tunic, but more or less clean. Eventually the door opened. One of the men threw a couple of old towels at him. Grateful that they were at least dry, he attempted to squeeze out the water from the tunic to dry it, and himself, as far as possible.

Shortly after, a tray of bread and water with a bit of cheese was delivered to the room. Hungry, Shan made quick work of this. He was then left alone by his captors to await the evening, and to gradually dry.

***

Moira wandered through the corridors of the place she called home. All was quiet. She encountered none of the servants. For a place that was noted for its bright and airy feel, an estate that allowed natural light into almost every corner of every room, and where mirrors reflected the light onwards, the whole place felt dull and morose. Every mirror had been covered. This hindered the progression of the sun into the apartments. Moira also noted that all the clocks had stopped at one minute to four. Unsure if that was the doing of her mother, as her spirit roamed the estate, or a tradition to mark the time of death, Moira left them well alone, not willing to provoke another encounter with the entity that had once been the lady of the house.

She was hungry. She was yet to break her fast from the previous day. She headed towards the breakfast room to see if any food had been provided. Once there, she was disappointed when she encountered merely a polished table with neither napery nor china service, let alone the food she desired.

Against her better judgement, she headed for the servants' area below stairs. She should find someone who would be able to receive her request for sustenance. This was a place she had never been. It was unseemly for one of the family to be seen below stairs. It was fortunate that she had a vague impression as to where to find the kitchen. Climbing carefully down the uneven stone stairs, she entered the realm of those who were habitually present, but were often unseen and frequently disregarded.

At the end of the long corridor she heard voices. Feeling uncharacteristically timid and disorientated by the way the day had been unfolding, Moira quietly crept down the corridor. She listened intently for any approach so that she could reinstate her dignity before her weakness was observed. As she got closer the voices became more distinct. She was able to make out the conversation. It was clear that all the servants were collected in the kitchen. They had been charged to remain there until further notice by order of her father. Making it to the door she stopped and, remaining hidden, listened to what was being said. She wanted to find out what was going on. She obviously was not important enough for her father to inform her himself.

"… here we stay. Least we get food."

"Really, John, is that all you can think about?"

"Better than starvin', Polly. I expect the young miss might be feelin' it by now."

"Quiet, you two. We have our orders, and we stay out of harm's way. Be grateful we have no mirrors here and *they* won't come downstairs."

"But why, Mr Colin, why do we?"

"Madam was not without her 'interests', Polly. Over the years we have received many a strange visitor late in the evenings."

"Polly … the Tower," whispered John.

"And the mirrors? What's that about? Mrs Poole was very strict not to look into them."

"Yes, Polly, never look into the mirror when someone dies," came a voice that Moira assumed was that of Mrs Poole. "Particularly when the person who has gone had delved into the things that Madam did."

"But why? When my grandpa died, we never did such a thing."

"Madam was different. She was never one to give up easily. When she decided to do something, she would do it. She always said that she would never leave this place while her daughter was here. And I expect that she won't," was Mrs Poole's reply.

"They're taking her body out to be burnt today. They say the Tower will see to it," added Mr Colin. "But that is just her body."

"They say, Polly," came the voice of John, "that the first person in the house who looks at themselves in a mirror after someone dies will then be the next to die. You wouldn't want that, I expect."

"As unlikely as that may be under normal circumstances, John, when it comes to Madam, I would not pretend to assume that she would not see to it," was the cold addition by Mrs Poole.

Moira wanted to hear nothing more and crept back along the corridor. She found that she was trembling. Her hunger had now gone. It had been replaced by a churning nausea that was located low down in the pit of her stomach. Afraid to return to her chambers, and no longer desiring food, Moira made directly for the garden. At least there the sun was shining. The world would appear to be continuing in a normality that she could understand. Glad to feel the warmth on her face, she emerged from the house. She climbed onto the small mosaiced terrace where the cherry blossom was falling, but the soothing sound of cascading water from the fountain was no longer evident. The water was still and undisturbed in the shallow pool at the base of the structure. It was here that she decided to stay. To be in the sunlight and away from the shadow of the house. Away from the presence of her mother.

Chapter 22

Black and cold. That pretty much described everything. The walls were black and cold. The floor was black and cold. The air was dark and cold. There was no sound, no breeze and no-one else. Molly had hardly slept. She had been unaware of all the sounds that normally surrounded her through the day and even throughout the night. The creaking of the house, the wind as it blew through the trees, the insects that called at night, the birds that awakened the dawn. All these she had never appreciated, until they were no longer there. Their silence was as threatening as the Tower itself.

She had no idea if it was morning or not. There had been no change in the light. There was nothing that she could use to identify if the sun had risen or not. She felt that it must be a new day outside of these walls, but she could not be sure. The only change she did note was the appearance of a small sack against the wall next to her. How it had got there and who put it there she had no idea. Yet it was there. Unsure if she should open it or not, Molly considered the possibilities. They had brought her here. They could do anything to her they wanted. There was no-one here to help her. So, what did she have to lose?

Preparing herself for the unexpected, but resigned to whatever the outcome would be, Molly undid the pull cord. She opened the sack and turned it over to expel its contents. No slimy beetles and no slithering snakes emerged. Just a small loaf of bread and a corked stone bottle fell to the floor. Uncorking the bottle, she gave the contents a sniff. Nothing. She poured a little onto her hand. It looked like water. She tasted the liquid that was still on her hand. It had no taste. Water? Well, that was what she would have to assume.

Unsure if she was hungry or not, Molly looked at the rations before her. How long had she been here? Would this be all she would get? Hardly knowing what would be ahead of her she decided that she should eat and drink. If things could suddenly appear then they could, presumably, suddenly disappear and leave her with nothing. *Best take the opportunities as they arise and make the best of what is on offer,* she thought. Taking a small bite out of the centre of the loaf, she chewed. Not bad. Not as soft and fine as Mama's bread but not the worst she had had. That would still have to be Aunt Joy's daughter's first attempt at making bread, when she had forgotten the yeast and put in far too much salt. Molly's first attempt had been better than that, despite it having been a bit undercooked.

Molly surprised herself at this train of thought. How could she be thinking of normal things that at a time like this? She would no longer be seeing the girls. Not eating with Mama and Father. Never would she to be going back to the market or working out the change that would be required. Everything she had ever known was now gone. She knew of no way that she could get them back. She was here now, locked in a dark Tower with no-one around. In a place of semi-darkness that excluded the rest of the world, she had no way of knowing what was going to happen to her. She felt like crying again but she could not let herself wallow in the situation. She would think of Father. What would he do?

Having finished most of the loaf, Molly decided to keep the last bit for later, just in case. *In case of what?* she thought. *In case I do actually get through the day and need something else to eat, I suppose.* She hoped that nothing bad would happen. But now there was another more urgent problem. One that she would have to face. Just because she was no longer at home did not mean that some of the normal daily routines were no longer routine. There was only so long that a person could hold on. She only had the clothes she was wearing. There were no others with the food sack, and there was nothing worse than soaking your clothes just because you did not make it to the facilities in time. So where were the facilities? She had wandered through these dark chambers and corridors for many hours the night before and had not seen anything that would remotely suggest the whereabouts of a privy.

Getting up, Molly put the bottle and remaining bread back in the sack to bring with her. She started heading in the first direction that took her fancy. She had no idea of where she was and, despite using the trick of her father's the previous night, had never made it back to the entrance hall. So, not caring which direction she was taking, she moved at speed down the corridor. Nothing had changed. The walls were still dark and cold, reflecting no light and appearing to absorb what little light was present. Passing through further chambers, past small alcoves and along passages, Molly found nothing new. Things were getting a bit more uncomfortable now. She would have to do something, and soon, before the decision was taken away from her.

Eventually she stopped by one of the small alcoves. She looked about carefully, embarrassed despite never having seen a single soul. Mortified at the indignity of having to relieve herself in such a way, Molly crouched and did what she had to but even so felt the heat rise in her face at the ignominy of the situation. Now in much less physical distress, she returned to the corridor.

In spite of her best intentions, she glanced back towards the alcove. Nothing. To her surprise, there was nothing there. No evidence. Although she did not want to, she could not help looking closer. Nothing was wet. No sign that anything had happened there. Relieved as well as horrified, Molly considered her options. She would need a privy in the future and this, although lacking in many things, was at least 'tidy' she thought. She decided to try and mark it in some way so she would be able to recognise it again. Taking the stone bottle from the sack, she tried scratching the surface of the wall, with little effect. Taking aim at the corner of the alcove, she swung the stone bottle as hard as she could. A loud, sharp crunch ensued but neither reverberated nor echoed about her. A small chip was flung away from the wall. It was not much but there was now a distinct flaw against smooth finished walls. Looking once again at the alcove before moving quickly away, she thought, *This is a very strange place.*

***

Moira made her way to the small orchard off to the side of the estate. No-one had been near her all day. She had remained outside the house and was feeling very unlike her usual self. A tornado of words circulated within her head. Around and around they went, but no matter how many times she heard them, they were no clearer in their meaning than the first time. Moira was not one for silly superstitions. No-one really believed that the first person to look in a mirror after a death would be the next to die. That would mean that once there was a death in a house no-one would ever look at themselves again for fear of being the first. That was obviously something that just did not happen.

But her mother; there was more to her than Moira had ever expected. What were the things that she had delved into? The Tower appeared to have taken an interest into what had just happened. Although Moira didn't really know, she suspected that the Tower didn't normally get involved with funeral arrangements. Not even if it was for a powerful family. Did they know of the battle between mother and daughter? Was that a good or a bad thing? She didn't know but felt uneasy about it.

Moira reached up and grabbed a ripe apple. The lack of any food since the night before was making her feel sick in the stomach. Eating something, anything, should help. There had been no-one to offer her food, so she had decided to get it herself. She was not ready to re-enter the house after what she had seen and heard earlier that day, so she did not know if any other foods had been laid out. She decided that she would make do with the orchard. Taking a bite, she let the sweet juice trickle down her throat.

As well as her looks, Moira had inherited her mother's determination. Having once decided to do something, or get someone else to do it, it would be done. Her mother was still here; or, at least, some variation of her mother from what she had experienced that morning. *What does "end is predetermined" mean?* thought Moira. *My death. Unlikely, but if so, it was hardly specific. And why would Mother never leave while I am still here? It makes no sense. They said the Tower was coming to get her today. She will have to leave then. Feet first, I expect. The staff will see to that. They won't want my mother looking back at them and delivering a final curse. They really believe the silliest things.*

Despite her belittling of the staff's superstitions, Moira still felt a bit unsure about it all. She had not yet decided what she would do when the sun started to get lower in the west. It did not appear that anyone would be looking for her. Her father had confined the household staff to the servants' quarters, and she knew that he would never go looking for her himself. That was if he even remembered her. Returning to her chambers would need to happen sometime, but perhaps not quite yet. Avoiding mirrors seemed wise. Also, she would try to stay where the rooms were well lit. Company would not be forthcoming so a solitary endurance would need to be undertaken.

Picking another couple of apples, Moira returned to the garden terrace. Silence was still evident from within the house. Even the wind and the birds were quiet. Nothing stirred about her, making her feel even more isolated than she had before. Instead of sitting, she made her way to her tower and gradually climbed the stairs.

Reaching the top of the unfinished structure she came face to face with the Tower. Her mother must have had some Influence. How else could she have put up the fight she did? And now the Tower was coming to claim her. What did this mean? Would she now no longer have any chance to go to the Tower? Would her mother hinder her in this as she had in so many other things? How would she bear a life here as a pawn for someone else's power?

Standing and staring longingly towards the Tower while the sun gradually dimmed as it fell below the mountains, Moira sensed a change. Something was happening. There was still no noise. No-one was there to be seen. Yet, important things were transpiring. Not understanding how she knew, Moira raced down the stairs and directly into the house. There was something she needed to see and, hopefully, be a part of.

***

How long? How could she know? The water was gone, and she had finished the last of the bread. Nothing else had changed. She sat against the wall just waiting for something, anything, to happen. *Surely something must happen. There must be a reason they brought me here.* Yet, as hard as she listened and often as she looked, there was nothing to hear. Nothing new to see.

Time goes slowly when nothing happens and nothing varies. After what felt an age, Molly was starting to get hungry again and her back was sore from sitting against the hard wall. She climbed to her feet and stretched. *If I weren't so bored, I probably would still be scared.* She pondered her dilemma. There really was no benefit that she could see to just sitting still. Perhaps the corridors were a maze that needed to be figured out, and then …

Well, "and then" was where she preferred to leave it. If the Tower had come to get her, specifically her, it would want her for something. That probably was not for sitting against a wall. Mama had spoken about gifts. How Noona's sister had been asked to come to the Tower to help because of her gift. *But I don't have any special gifts and they certainly didn't ask if I wanted to come,* Molly thought testily, crossing her arms. *So what do they want?* She tried to think of anything that might make her special, different, and of interest to the Tower. Mama said that her great aunt was able to disappear. She could also do some other sort of things that Molly couldn't remember.

Thinking back on it, Molly had the impression that Mama was trying to imply more than she was saying. *But me? Really, why would Mama think of me in the same way as Noona's sister?* Yet she had to agree that, apart from being dragged from her home in the middle of the night, there had to be something similar between them – or why was she here? Then she remembered the cart. *I was right in front of it for ages and still he said he didn't see me. Said that I jumped right out in front of him. I never did. And Mrs Perkins said that she didn't see me … and, and people would walk right into me. But that's silly, everyone else can see me.* But Molly was now not quite so sure. Perhaps she had been using Influence without knowing it. The Tower had seen this and now wanted her to help it.

Out of the corner of her eye Molly saw a movement. It gave her a shock, causing her to reel back against the wall. Looking again, she saw a figure, just

157

like the shadows that came to get her from the cottage. It stood there alone, a darker black than the wall behind it.

"Hello," squeaked Molly, "I'm Molly." She waited vainly for a reply. The figure just turned and moved away from her. Not knowing what else to do, Molly followed. They moved down one of the long, dark corridors. They finally entered a square room that contained a single closed door that faced them from the opposing wall. The figure stopped. It turned toward Molly and gestured, with what Molly assumed was an arm in the cloak's sleeve, to approach the door. Tentatively, Molly moved forward. As she neared the door, it opened to a lamplit kitchen and the sounds of laughter. Thrilled to be seeing and hearing anything that was normal, Molly crept closer. As she did, she recognised Mama's voice. She saw Ester run across the room into Father's arms. Overjoyed, Molly raced to the door, crying out, "Mama, Ester, I'm back!"

***

Moira reached the house and heard her father's voice greeting visitors. She knew that he would not want her anywhere near visitors. Not unless she was specifically summoned to be present should she be there. Carefully she hid behind the curtains of the drawing room. This was where visitors were normally received and waited upon. She hoped that she would be able to find out what was really going on and not just have to make do with the servants' gossip. Her patience was rewarded. After waiting only a few minutes, she heard people enter the room.

"We will not stay long. We will claim what is ours and go."

"There was nothing that we could do. The physician tried throughout the night." Her father was nervous. Moira had never heard him like this. No, never before. Everyone in Town always bowed to him. He never bowed to anyone. *Who could these visitors be to make him act so?*

"It was ordained. Your physician was pointless. Mortella knew this. She came back for nothing less. We will take our own and leave."

"She's downstairs. All has been done as you instructed."

"No, she is here. What is downstairs is merely a shell, ready to be disposed of."

Moira listened intently, piecing together what she heard. They must be of the Tower. None other than they would speak to her father so. And they knew of her mother. *She came back to die, and she is here? Now?* Moira felt a chill run down her spine. She didn't want to have to face her mother again. Not like the last time.

There was silence in the room and Moira stayed hidden behind the curtain.

Scarcely breathing for fear that she might be heard, she gradually and gently drew air though her open mouth. Without sound or force, the curtain behind which she was hidden lifted high towards the ceiling, bringing her into the lightened room. Revealed to all, and in front of her father and the visitors. Moira lifted her chin and faced them. Cowering was beneath her. She would stand tall and face the consequences.

She saw a figure clothed in a black robe. The hood had been lowered, revealing her face. She was a woman of maturity but what was most notable was the air of authority and confidence that emanated from her. This was not a woman who bowed to anyone. She would not be in the habit of having her orders questioned. Behind the woman stood Moira's father, who appeared diminished in stature when in the woman's presence. Further behind him were two other black-hooded figures who stood unmoving just inside the door of the room.

"As I said, she is here," the woman continued.

"But that is my only daughter. What …"

"You will remarry and produce another heir," was the dismissive reply.

"And you," said the woman, raising her hood again to hide her face, "will come with us to the Tower."

Shocked and delighted in equal measure, Moira raised her head higher and straightened her back just a little more. Walking past the figures, she looked directly at her father before turning at the door and saying as she left the room, "I will never again be your prized cow to be offered at auction to the highest bidder."

Not pausing to consider the servants in the hall, Moira walked serenely to the front door. It opened, unaided, allowing her to leave her home, once and for all.

Chapter 23

The kitchen felt light and airy after the bleakness and closeness of the Tower. Molly looked in wonderment at the place she thought she would never see again. Father had just returned from work and had been greeted by Ester running enthusiastically to welcome him. *He was alright. They had not hurt him.* Molly felt light at the thought. *They have not destroyed our family.*

Mama was peeling vegetables at the sink, obviously busy preparing their supper. Lucy, Ava, and Elsie were still at the kitchen table finishing off their supper. They looked longingly at their father as he went up to greet Mama before coming to kiss each of them in turn. Molly could only watch the familiar scene in silence, taking in every little movement, every nuance of what occurred between the people she loved. She was going home. Everything over the last two days would never have happened. She didn't have Influence. There was no need for the Tower to want her. They were sending her home. Spellbound, she remained at the door drinking in the love that connected her family.

Molly looked over her shoulder. The figure was still there, black and unmoving in the dark and foreboding chamber. What if this was not what it seemed? What if they were only showing her this so they could take it away again? Molly felt her heart start to race as she realised that she was not yet there. She was not yet home. Terrified that the door would close on her, keeping her apart from her family, Molly turned. She made a dash through the opening into the well-known room she saw before her.

The light was real. She could smell the onions simmering on the stove. She could hear the chatter of her sisters as she stopped and looked behind her. Now, instead of an entry into the cold and breathless Tower, behind her was the door into the sitting room. She had entered the kitchen through that door a million times. She was home. She really was. Trembling all over, her heart racing, Molly called out, "I'm here, Mama, Father, I'm home!" as she raced forward to hug Mama. All her focus was on her mother. The one who was always there. Mama, whom she had last seen on the floor cradling Father's head in her lap. Mama, who was weeping as she watched her daughter being taken from the house. Mama, who always cared and was always ready to help.

Moments before reaching her, her mother turned to face her with that gentle, knowing smile that continually reassured them that everything would be alright. Molly let out a slight squeal of excitement at seeing her mother look at her. She raced to embrace her, and then stopped short, unsure of what she saw in front of her. In less than a moment, the look on her mother's face had changed from a lively kindness and love to one of disappointment and disdain. Her mouth closed tightly. There was thinning of her lips. Her brows were furrowed, and her eyes narrowed as she looked down her nose at Molly.

"Mama ..." Molly started.

"You, you're back," came the response, delivered in a flat, emotionless voice. One devoid of any warmth or welcome. Shocked, Molly was sure that she had heard wrong.

"Mama, the Tower let me go."

"S'pose I cannot blame them for not wanting you either." Unbelieving, Molly turned to her father who barely looked at her.

"Father, you're well, they ..." Molly stumbled.

"What are you doing here?" It was a frozen, lifeless voice that drilled into Molly's heart, making her shiver at its coldness.

"The Tower let me come home," she started amid a sudden flow of tears that went all but unnoticed. "I came home," she cried to all in the room. Looking about her, she pleaded for any form of acknowledgement that she was home. Turning to Ester, Molly held out her arms for her to fly into them and be twirled off the ground as she had done so many times before. But Ester just looked at her in horror. She began to cry and raced to the side of Ava who comforted her, while glaring at Molly.

Uncomprehending, Molly just stood in the centre of the kitchen, not knowing what she should say or what she could do. This was the one place that she had always felt sure of herself, solid and loved. Now she was faced with something she could not believe. No longer wanted, no longer loved, she felt so much less than she had moments before; diminished, small and insignificant.

"There she goes and does it again," Lucy chimed in. "Every time she doesn't get what she wants. She just fades. Can't face what's real. She's such a baby."

Molly looked at her sister, who met her gaze with a steely look and a curled-up lip.

"Such a baby," all the others repeated, again and again.

Molly felt less and less substantial. Less of who she was, she turned to run from the kitchen. She made for the sitting room door, ready to push it open and race through it. She had to leave the voices behind her. But, try as she might, the door would not budge. It was not one that could be locked. It normally would fling open with such ease that even Ester had no problems coming through it. This time, there was nothing. It would not move. Looking down at her hands, Molly was shocked. She was able to see through them to the door beyond. Trying again and again in desperation, Molly could achieve nothing. She was as insubstantial as a ghost.

The mocking voices continued around her. Unable to leave the room, Molly turned to face them. All she could do was cover her ears and close her eyes as she sank to the floor and curled herself up in a tight ball. Bringing her knees to her chest, she lowered her head and rested her back against the door. To block out the sound, she started to repeat to herself over and over again, "It'll be right in the end, right in the end, right in the end."

How long this continued Molly didn't know, but no-one came to comfort her. She was left alone with the jeering voices only partly obscured by her efforts. Silently crying and shivering with a cold that appeared to come from within her, Molly stayed as she was.

Unsure when the voices had ceased, Molly stopped her chanting. All was quiet. Cautiously, she opened her eyes. She was no longer surrounded by a friendly glow. Now she was once again coated in the silver darkness of the Tower. She was curled up on the stone floor of the Tower. Her back was against the wall, and she was alone. Slowly climbing to her feet, Molly was aware that she was no longer dressed in her own clothes. Instead, she was shrouded in a robe as black as the Tower. Light and warm, it flowed easily about her. Not knowing how this had happened, Molly just resigned herself to the fact that it had and chose to ignore it

Hardly bearing to think of the door and what had happened, Molly forced herself to focus. How could Mama say that? She had never been so hard before, or Father so cold. Ester has forgotten me so easily, she thought. Did I imagine it? It was so real, but how could it have been?

Molly knew that she had been a failure at many things. She couldn't do the math needed to get change for the shopping. She had no longer been sent to market after almost being hit by the cart. How disappointed her parents must have been in her. Perhaps they were better off without her. They had more suitable and intelligent daughters than her still remaining. Those much more worthy of their efforts. *They probably only realised what a burden I was when I left. That was why they were so disappointed to see me.*

Molly also recalled that there were others in the room. Others that also rebuked and belittled her. *Comments supported by Mama, so they must have been true,* Molly thought. Who these others were, Molly was unable to remember. That was of little consequence as, whoever they were, her parents had agreed with them. Feeling deflated, she was weighed down by a grief she had no words to describe. Once again, she curled up on the floor, pulling her robes around her. She lay on her side, all alone and miserable in the dark and breathless corridor.

***

The light had faded before Shan again heard the lock of the door unbolt. He was glad that the wait was over. Whatever would happen would happen. Now he could face it square on and not just wonder about what would occur. Would they straight away see that he was a boy and not a girl? That could determine whether he was taken to the Tower or if they tried to absorb him. He knew they destroyed any male with a strong Influence.

Well, he would soon find out. Either way, he did not intend to make it easy for them. Surprisingly, he was not nervous. *Several days of boredom will do that,* he thought. *It's just not possible to keep being anxious all the time.* It was while he was sitting on the cold flagstones, waiting to dry after his bath, that he realised he was no longer fearful but just fed up and bored.

He pulled himself to his feet and waited expectantly. He was not going to cower under this threat. As he had just recently learnt, that was not his family's way of dealing with the Tower. They fought back. That was what he intended to do as well. As the door opened, light flowed through, but no-one entered. He saw no shadow in the entrance. Unsure what was going on, Shan waited expectantly, facing the opening. After a few minutes with nothing eventuating, he half shuffled, half jumped towards the door as best he could with his feet and hands still bound. Looking into the lighted corridor just outside his door he saw and heard no-one. There was a chair. It was next to the door and leaning against the wall. Empty. On the small table beside it was a half-eaten plate of food and, much more importantly, also a knife that had been used to cut the meat and cheese.

Totally baffled as to what was going on and feeling slightly paranoid that this was just a little too strange, Shan sat on the chair. He grabbed the knife and started to cut away at the bindings securing his feet, slowly and methodically. Constantly looking about him for any evidence of someone watching, he continued. Eventually he succeeded in cutting though a single length of the bands that were hobbling him. Removing them, he rubbed his ankles where the straps had caused more than a little irritation. Now able to stretch his legs and walk normally, he took the knife and made an attempt on the straps securing his hands. However, not being a contortionist or having the luck of finding a knife-handle-shaped hole in the wall in which to secure the instrument, there was no way that he could free himself.

It must have taken him at least ten minutes to free his legs from the restraints. Yet still there was no-one and nothing apart from himself in the corridor. He became aware of the lack of any sound coming from above. If the previous evening was any indication, normally the inn would be doing a busy trade at about this time. He should be hearing the thump of feet and scrape of the stools on the floor above. There was only silence.

Now even more wary that things were not as they seemed, he took the knife and held it out in front of him as he silently crept along the corridor. He stayed in the centre. If someone was watching, they would have seen him already. If not, he would prefer to have some space about him if he were surprised.

At the end of the corridor were some stone stairs leading up out of the basement. These he assumed led into the inn above. Where in the inn they would deposit him, he had no idea, but they were the only way forward. That was the way he would continue, if he continued at all. Halfway up the stairs he stopped and listened. Silence. No voices, no sound of any kind. Only his breathing, which he tried to keep steady and quiet. After a few minutes he recommenced the climb. He arrived at a closed but unlatched door. *Really*, Shan exclaimed to himself, *they must think I am a total idiot to think that this is not some sort of trap. Anyone who has read anything would know that. As Maima always says, if it doesn't make sense, then you're looking at it the wrong way. So, what way should I look at it?*

He considered what he knew.

The matron was selling him to the Tower, so he was considered valuable.

They still thought he was a girl.

The Dark Ones should arrive that night.

Someone let him out of the basement.

No-one was around.

The first was definite. The second and third were most likely. The fourth was accurate but the intention behind it was unknown. The fifth, however, was pure assumption. *To assume something without further evidence often leads to error*, Shan pondered. *So what if I remove point five and assume that people are around? Why are they* quiet? If three is true, then that would explain the lack of activity in the inn and why there is quiet. The "who" behind four could also be the Tower. That leaves the reason. Maima said that their reasons are their own. If it were me, why would I do it this way?

Shan was mesmerised by his own thinking. He stood, unmoving, on the second top step before the door to the inn. If I were stupid, I could have thought I would have some chance of escape. That I could get away. That is very unlikely from what I know both of the matron and the Tower. I can assume that I am still their prisoner and will not escape. The only reason I can see for doing this is to test me. See how I react to having my hopes of escape dashed. I would bet that just beyond that door are the Dark Ones, there waiting for me. I think it is time that we meet. And we will. Meet on my terms and not theirs.

Shan placed the small knife gently on the step. It would be useless against anyone unencumbered. He still had his arms secured in front of him. Standing tall with shoulders back and head up, he reached for the door. He pushed it open and stepped out of the stairwell onto the wooden floor of the inn. All was in semi-darkness. Light from the moon was coming in through the windows, giving slight illumination to the space, but it was of little help. Shan's eyes were yet to adjust to the darkness after the light of the basement below. There was no sound. He scanned the space about him and caught the glimmer of blue light at three different points off to the right. They were not close. Most likely near the windows on that side.

Turning to face the lights, he took two steps in their direction. Planting his feet, he looked directly at them. Then in his most polished and polite tone he said, "Good evening. I apologise for the delay. The knife provided was a little dull. I hope that you have not been waiting long." As he spoke the light came up, revealing the room and three dark, hooded figures located exactly where he had seen the lights. They glided towards him and Shan had to muster all of his determination and strength not to run away. He held his ground before them.

As they approached, the figure in the middle spoke in a smooth and melodic voice, "The Tower has need of you. You will be taken from here to commence as a neophyte of the Tower." The tone of the voice was gentle. Shan could almost detect a hint of a compliment there.

"We trust your treatment here has been satisfactory?" As this was spoken, the hooded figure turned and looked in the direction of the matron who had just appeared in the room. "If not, we are sure that amends can be provided by your host." Shan looked at the matron who, without meeting his eye turned and quickly left.

The figure continued, "We doubt that such things will be required," as the bindings around his arms fell to the floor. This took Shan by surprise, but he tried not to show it.

If they can do that there's not much I can do against them, he thought.

"It is time. We go to the Tower." The figures turned and left the room through the front entrance. Shan hesitated only for a moment, thinking, *What if I go the other way? I might get out.* But then he considered it a bit further. *If they are so confident as to just turn and leave, expecting me to follow … then they know I have no choice. If there is no choice but to go with them, it is better to go unbound.* With that he started walking towards the entrance of the inn. He emerged into the square and joined his captors for the journey to the Tower.

Chapter 24

Moira could hardly contain her excitement. The day had finally come. She was free of her father. Free of a meaningless existence as a political pawn of someone else's power. She was now on her way to be part of the very centre of authority. She waited outside the entrance foyer of her father's house for her escorts to the Tower to attend her. *Not one, but three Dark Ones have come to escort me. They must consider me to be of some importance,* she modestly thought as she contemplated her future.

As the Dark Ones exited, Moira turned and started to descend the stairs ahead of them. The stairs led down to the sculptured garden entrance of the estate. Barely halfway down the flight, her feet became fixed to the marble steps. She almost fell forward as the unchecked momentum of her upper body fought against the resistance to any movement from her feet. Barely maintaining her balance, she watched as the three figures regally glided past her. Once again, she was able to move her feet and recommenced the descent. The Dark Ones said nothing. They gave no indication that anything had happened but merely continued their path to the elaborate gates. Once in the street they turned right to make for the Tower itself.

Moira followed in their wake. No-one was about in the streets surrounding the estate. There was no-one to witness her ascent to the Tower. Of her inclusion in the centre of power and authority of the Bowl. *It is unfortunate,* mused Moira. *I would have preferred for all of them to have seen this.* To have seen her rise above them all. *But it is of little consequence. They will know soon enough.*

They moved quickly. The figures in front moved with speed and ease. Moira found herself having to lift her dress. She had to trot along behind them to keep up. This was not elegant. Not the way she thought it should be. Her arrival at the Tower should be graceful and momentous. As they neared the Tower and the stairs that led to the great door, Moira was out of breath. Her hair was dishevelled. She was sweating profusely, and she had almost called out more than once for them to wait a moment to let her catch up. It was only her pride and self-will that had stopped her from doing such a demeaning thing.

On arriving at the lowest step, she stopped. Bending over with her hands on her hips, she attempted to regain her breath. Looking up at the climb before her, she had to mentally prepare herself for the final ascent.

The Dark Ones were already at the great door before Moira had taken her first step on the flight before her. She climbed, slowing as she attempted to hold herself erect. She wanted to exude power and authority as she ascended. But the casual observer, had there been any, would have just seen a small, tousled figure laboriously climbing the stairs. One that was struggling upward in an attempt to join three ominous voids waiting at the summit. Certainly, there was nothing in the figure that would have evoked a sense of wonder. There would be no admiration in the seer, only a mild feeling of concern that this individual may not, in fact, make it to the top before collapsing in a heap on the stairs.

Eventually gaining the summit, Moira now stood before the great door. She suddenly felt small and insignificant, feelings not normally in her repertoire of emotions. It was even more unsettling to her than it had been for the many others who had stood in a very similar position before her. Without a sound the door opened, revealing behind it the huge antechamber. The Dark Ones entered the space. Moira stopped and gazed ahead, feeling, for the first time, slightly unsure of her choices. Almost reluctantly she followed then into the cavernous space. The great door closed behind them.

Looking around her, she saw nothing in the space and turning to the figures asked, "Who will show me to my chambers? I would like to refresh myself before presenting myself to the others." Silence followed her question. The three figures stood unmoving and unresponsive. In the cold, grey light of the chamber, the figures were only visible as voids that were of a deeper darkness than the black walls about them. It seemed impossible that indignation could be seen in their stance, yet the clarity of their disdain for Moira's request was palpable. Without a word the figures turned and faded into the darkness. Moira was left alone, with her question answered in a very definite way.

Confused and annoyed by her treatment, Moira examined the antechamber. It was vast, with several corridors leading off it. It contained no furniture of any kind. The ceiling was not visible. The steely light that illuminated the space appeared to emanate from the air itself. It was cool, which she found somewhat refreshing after the climb, but there was no refreshment. Nothing to appease her thirst nor any sustenance to ease her hunger after a long day where she had only consumed a few apples. Realising that there was no point remaining where she was, Moira headed off down the central corridor in front of her.

Walking confidently down the centre of the hallway, Moira continued for quite some way. She encountered no turns or rooms. She heard nothing. She saw no-one. She felt not a single bit of movement in the air. Feeling less sure than she had when she started down the hall, she stopped. She decided to return to the antechamber and choose a different entrance to explore. Turning to retrace her steps she was shaken to find that where the corridor should have extended behind her there now was a wall. It contained a door that was partially open.

Cautiously, she approached the door. Opening it, she revealed a luxurious chamber with a central table laid out for supper. Famished, she entered the chamber. The door closed behind her as she made straight for the table. She poured herself a goblet of water, quickly draining it before pouring herself another to quench her thirst. She drained this one, too, and put down the goblet. Now, as she turned to investigate the food on offer, she felt a cold chill, like icy water running down her spine. Stiffening, Moira held her stance as she slowly turned to look behind. She came to face the swirling vortex that she recognised as her mother. Suppressing a squeal, Moira glared at the wraith. Her mother's features gradually formed within the churning mist.

"Your end is preordained," emerged from the ever-changing contours of her mother's mouth, and the dark sockets where eyes used to be drilled into Moira.

"You've said that already, Mother," Moira retorted contemptuously. "Do you have anything else to add? Something that might be a little more informative?"

The wraith moved past Moira towards the table. "You were never wanted," it sneered. "It should have been you and not your sister who died. I knew I should have taken the herbs to expunge you from my body when I had the chance."

"Oh, Mother, do you really think I ever thought you loved me? That you wanted me? I am no longer a child. I know what you are. I have despised you for as long as I can remember," Moira spat. "What you think of me has as much effect on me as a drop of rain in the desert."

"And a desert you will be," answered the wraith as it glided through the table, causing all the food upon it to darken and decay before Moira's eyes.

"But no more of a desert than you, dear Mother. A heart barren of anything but greed and avarice. At least now you look more like you than you ever have before." Moira felt the hatred for her mother boil through her, burning off any fear and leaving only contempt for the woman who used to control her existence. "No longer, Mother. You have nothing to do with me. I am no longer your daughter. I am a Dark One." And, speaking in slow, determined and venomous words, "I am no longer beholden to you. Go back to your own special hell. Leave me alone. I will never regard you again." With that, Moira turned and walked away from the table. The room dissolved about her and, once again, she was in the long corridor.

Exhausted, Moira slumped to the ground. She realised that she was no longer in the long pale-green gown. Instead, she was clothed in a black, hooded robe that enveloped her body. Beside her was a small sack. Opening it she found a stone bottle filled with ice cold water, together with cold meat, bread, and cheese. Feasting on the fare before her, Moira felt more whole than she ever had before. She was further enlivened as she remembered the hatred and vitriol that had flowed through her. Now refreshed and satisfied she lay down where she was and fell asleep.

***

It took a day for them to arrive at the gates of Town in the enclosed carriage. Shan was surprised. He was sure it should have taken a great deal longer to get there. They had started the journey almost at the Western Slopes. Town was situated in the most easterly part of the Bowl, abutting the Eastern Slopes. Yet there they were at the gates. There was the Tower itself, rising above the highest reaches of the town.

The sun had almost set as they entered the gates. They passed through the lower market square. Making its way to the Tower, the carriage moved smoothly with none of the clattering that was normally associated with traversing the cobbled streets. As the last of the sun's rays left the town, they arrived at the steps that led to the great door. The carriage door opened and his captors appeared to flow out of the carriage. Shan climbed down after them. He looked at the stairs before him and started to climb, following the lead of his jailers. It felt good to be able do something physical. Climbing these was hardly an exertion after years of hiking through the lower slopes of the western mountains.

There was a breeze as he ascended. He looked behind him as he climbed and was able to take in the vastness of Town below, with all its buildings. Then he looked longingly at the silhouette of the Western Slopes against the darkening sky. There was home, and where he hoped that both Maima and Johnathon were safe. Arriving at the landing before the great door he found the three figures awaiting him. The great door opened, and they turned and entered. Shan followed after stealing one last look at home.

When the door closed, Shan became aware of a multitude of lights of various shades that hung in the air and wove complex designs. They moved as if performing an intricate dance to unheard music. The blue lights were now once again easily visible about the hooded figures. It lent them an eerie glow in the semi-darkness of the antechamber. Standing silently before him, the central figure raised its arms and offered him a bundle. Stepping forward, Shan put out his hands. As he touched the item, he saw sparks of light erupt from it and then engulf him in a shower of flashing embers. Looking down he was surprised to see that now he was cloaked in a black, hooded robe. At his feet was a small sack. Looking up again he saw that the chamber was now empty. He was alone, surrounded by an ever-changing pattern of coloured lights.

Shan opened the sack and looked inside. It held a corked stone bottle, a small loaf of bread, some cheese, and dried meats. Not feeling hungry he closed the bag and continued to contemplate his surroundings. The lights incessantly cascaded about him like colourful fireflies. Putting out his arms with palms held upward he waited as some flew almost close enough for him to touch. He felt no heat. They were just pinpoints of colour that were forever moving. They were both beautiful and disturbing. Obviously, they were there for some reason, although what was not yet clear. Illumination was certainly not their purpose. The walls were still cloaked in darkness and he could not see the antechamber in its entirety. Its roof was hidden in gloom.

Seeing nothing else of interest in the chamber Shan grabbed the sack. Taking it with him, he moved off to explore the passage that led off to the right. The coloured lights continued down all three corridors, so it was a random choice between the three. There was little to distinguish between them. He might as well start with one and explore the rest in turn.

Leaving the chamber, he walked down the smooth black flagstones. What had started as an entrance large enough to drive a horse and cart through began to narrow. Shan felt the walls begin to close in on him. The corridor narrowed to such an extent that he could simultaneously run a hand along each of the walls. The ceiling, however, was still shrouded in darkness. The air was still without any sound. Shan attempted to call out, but his voice sounded small and distant, muffled. It was as if it had been dampened by layers of velvet, leaving it without any depth or echo. The effect was unnerving. It made him feel small and insignificant and provoked a desire to proceed in quiet submission.

Silently he made his way deeper into the Tower. He knew that it was evening when he entered but there was no sense of time passing here. How long he had walked, he couldn't say. That he had walked a long way, he was sure. He was now tired and hungry. Stopping, he sat down on the cold stone with his back against the wall and opened the sack. The water was cold and refreshing. The dried meats, cheese and bread were almost as good as he had ever had. All except for Maima's goat's cheese, naturally.

Looking about he watched the dancing lights, pondering their purpose. Off to the left he saw a larger amber glow. It was not moving in the haphazard manner of the other points of colour. It was coming down the corridor directly towards him. Unsure what to expect, Shan drew his knees up to his chest while he watched and waited in silence.

The glow became a light, suspended in mid-air at about chest height. It moved slowly towards him. It neither slowed nor veered off track as it passed him and continued on its way further down the hall. He watched it as it gradually disappeared into the darkness. There had been no change in the stillness of the air. There was no sound to accompany it. But it was different. Different to all the other lights. It was larger and it had purpose. Had he just thought a bit faster he would have followed it. In fact, he decided he would. So, quickly, he packed the remaining things in the sack and raced down the hall in pursuit of the light.

Chapter 25

What, what did I do wrong? Molly cried over and over to herself as she settled into a troubled and restless sleep. Not knowing how long she skirted between wakefulness and oblivion she was finally woken by a cold and disturbing presence. Opening her eyes, she was confronted by a dark silhouette. It stood silently in front of her, stationary, against the opposite wall of the chamber. Confused for a moment she forgot where she was. She wondered why she was not in her attic room bed. Assuming that she was still dreaming she rubbed her eyes, willing herself to wake up. All too quickly, however, any illusion of a dream was shattered. The Tower had reasserted itself on her consciousness.

Feeling the figure observing her, Molly clambered uncomfortably to her feet. She was slightly lightheaded as she rose. The water bottle had been drained some time past. She had had nothing further to eat than the bread a day ago — or was it longer than that? She no longer remembered. Once upright she stood, supporting herself with the help of the wall behind her, and waited.

The figure said nothing. Molly was no longer surprised by this. Since she had been in the Tower, not a single word had been spoken to her. There had been no noise to hear. No light to see and no breeze to feel. Nothing but an empty, lifeless space shrouded in a semi-darkness that enveloped everything. It was the lack of noise she had found particularly difficult to bear. The incessant chatter of her younger sisters was something she thought she would never miss. Now, what would she not endure just to be able to hear their babble? Molly continued to wait. She expected something to happen, but the figure just stood there observing her. She felt she had no option but to remain as she was.

Feeling more and more uncomfortable under the gaze of the Watcher, Molly started to fidget and play with the cuffs of her sleeves. She was getting tired and restless. There was also something on the wall that was pushing into her lower back. Turning, she was startled by the presence of another door whose handle was poking into her and causing discomfort. She moved away from the wall and the door began to open by itself, allowing her to see through it to the realm beyond. Cautiously Molly approached and looked through. Through the doorway she could see the sitting room of her house. Beside the two best chairs was the small table, set with two teacups and Mama's best cake.

She watched as Mama entered the room. She sat in one of the chairs without pouring the tea. It looked as if she was waiting for someone. On an impulse, Molly walked through the door. To her delight she was greeted by the loving smile of her mother who indicated for her to sit in the other chair. Overjoyed at being acknowledged, Molly sat and smiled as Mama poured the tea.

"Molly, love, we need to talk," started Mama as she added a teaspoon of sugar to Molly's tea. Waiting expectantly, Molly accepted the cup as it was passed to her and took a sip. It was cold and bitter. It must have been salt that Mama had added. Her face screwed up at the taste; however, she quickly re-composed herself and said nothing.

"Have you been having a nice time with your new friends?" Mama continued, not noticing Molly's reaction to the tea.

"Oh, Mama …" Molly almost wailed.

"I'm so glad that you are," her mother continued, cutting her off. "Your father and I both thought that it was time you went."

Molly held back a gasp. Her mother continued in her sweet, gentle voice. "There really was only so much we could do for you, my love. Not the sharpest knife in the drawer, are you? Then again, you're also not the prettiest of pictures." She took a sip of her tea without flinching at the taste and with only the smallest of pauses continued. "Now Ava," she gushed, "now she should be able to marry well. Already been calculating the change from market. Oh, this saves Father so much time now that he doesn't need to go down there each day after work. Growing so tall and slender, as pretty as … And what a change she has made to the attic room. You wouldn't recognise it, so pretty and sooo clean."

Molly was dumbfounded. Ava had always been a bit shorter than her at the same age. But now she was becoming what Molly always hoped that she would be. She didn't know what to say. She knew that she had had difficulty with the shopping money. She had always tried so hard. Yes, she was short and a bit plump, but she used to think there was at least something a bit pretty about her. At least she thought Mama did.

"The rest of the girls are coming along beautifully. So much better behaved than before … well, before, when you were supposed to look after them. It really has been such a blessing." Mama took the plate laden with her best cake and offered it to Molly who barely registered its presence. Giving a slight shrug, her mother took a piece for herself. Taking another sip of tea, she said, "It really has all worked out for the best. We have so much more room now. We are happier. It is so good to know that you are as well, love. I don't expect we will see you too much more. Don't worry, the girls won't be distressed. They hardly remember you. In fact, Ester not at all."

Putting down her teacup, Mama continued, "Lovely to see you. You best be going. Not much point being here now, is there?" And with that, Mama rose from her chair and waited for Molly to do the same. In a daze, Molly stood up. She followed her mother as she led her to the cottage door and ushered her out. "Don't be a stranger. Well, probably best send a note before you come. Just to let us know. Oh dear, I forgot, you don't know how to write. Well, I'm sure it will all work out."

Molly faced the closing cottage door, still in a state of disbelief. She remained there staring at the closed door for a few minutes longer. Eventually, unprepared and not knowing where to go or what to do, she turned towards the street, only to be confronted by the cold, dark chamber once more.

***

Shan raced down the hall anxiously seeking the light that had passed him. Through one chamber after another he sped. He was surrounded by the small pinpoints of coloured light but was unable to see the purposeful movement of the amber glow. Randomly choosing one direction over the next when there were multiple corridors to choose from, he continued.

Feeling a sort of desperation, he almost stopped in defeat. There was something about that light. He did not know why, but it was important. Different to the others spiralling overhead. This one was important. He had to find it. Forcing himself to keep going he entered a massive cavern. Larger, even, than the antechamber. So large that he was unable to see the wall opposite him, if there was one, let alone the roof above.

There in front he saw the amber light. Assuming it was the same one, he approached it slowly. It was no longer moving but hovering, stationary, an arm's breadth from the stone floor. Its light oscillated, gradually dimming, and then flaring slightly. The other pinpoints of light circled it as if it was the centre of a vortex. A sun with its many planets orbiting. The walls nearest him appeared wet and slimy, as if covered with oil. In the silver-grey light that permeated the space they cast a sickly red hue. They seemed to pulsate in time with the light. He could feel the beat penetrating to his very bones.

As he came closer to the light Shan felt a sense of loss and hopelessness coming from it. This was not something good. He stopped. He was unsure if it was a threat to him or not. As he watched, the points of colour above swirled faster and faster about the amber light, leaving a trail of colour behind them. The amber light pulsated faster and faster, and the thumping quickened, both now in unison with the points as they churned. There was no sound. There was no wind as they moved but Shan could feel a building crescendo.

Oily liquid began to flow onto the floor, spreading the redness. Not knowing what was to happen next, he stepped away from the light as it suddenly expanded. Getting larger and larger, the spherical ball of amber light rose high into the air. As it expanded it became less intense. Then it rapidly contracted and exploded into thousands of yellow pinpoints of colour. The air gave a shudder, as if quivering with delight. The yellow pinpoints fragmented, only to meld with the coloured points of light and become indistinguishable from them. Then, in an instant, the dots of colour resumed their normal erratic movements. The walls returned to their black state. The beating ceased.

Warily Shan made his way to the place the light had been hovering. There was no sign that it had ever been there. There was nothing to explain what had occurred. All he knew was that after seeing the amber spots disperse, he had a feeling of inexplicable loss.

***

Molly was dazed and confused. The sudden changes in location were unsettling. It took a little time for her to adjust to being back in the Tower. Her heart was racing as she looked about for the Watcher, but it was no longer there. Finding it hard to catch her breath, and with legs shaking, she sank down against the wall. Trembling, her mind could only focus on a couple of things. Mama wanted her gone and her attic had been handed over to someone else. No longer wanted, no longer needed, no longer loved. Molly knew now that she was an outcast from her own home, not wanted back.

Feeling a chill that pierced her heart, Molly pulled the black robe about her. She lay down on the hard stone floor. Holding herself close, she curled into a tight ball and remained still. Nursing the grief inside her, she stayed unmoving. Unthinking, she was buried under a mountain of pain that she felt would never be lifted. Being set adrift from those she loved and needed more than anything else had removed any purpose or motivation. No longer feeling any hunger she remained where she was. She had no food anyway, but what would be the point if she did? It would be of no use. It could do nothing to lessen what she felt. So much better not to feel this than to endure a pain that had no remedy. Molly remained on the floor, unmoving. She hoped for oblivion. It could only be better than this.

***

Shan moved away from the cavern. He felt the loss of something. He did not know what it was he mourned for. Something bad had happened here. Of that he was sure, but he could not explain what it was that had occurred. Whatever had happened, he wanted to get as far away from it as possible.

Without looking back, he started to run. Unconcerned about which direction he took, he would keep running until he could run no more. The Tower must have an end. There must be a window somewhere. He would keep going until he found something.

He ran. In the cold, silver light, he ran. Surrounded by swirling points of colour, he ran. Uninterested and no longer wanting to have them anywhere near him, he ran. Passing through chamber after chamber, racing along corridor after corridor, nothing seemed to change. The light was the same. He saw and heard no-one and there was nothing apart from the cold, black walls beside him and the hard stone floor beneath him.

Eventually he could run no longer. Gasping for breath, he would not stop. He had to keep going. Now walking with head down and panting for air, his determination was all that he had. He would not give up. He would not stop. Barely able to put one foot before the next, he continued. There had to be more. There had to be something. His mother had survived this, and he must as well.

Nothing, nothing seemed to change. The walls were the same. The floor was the same. No steps, no slopes, no windows, no doors, just the continuing hard stone floor and the impenetrably high black walls. Entering yet another chamber indistinguishable from the multitude that had come before, Shan had to rest. Just for a moment to catch his breath. Bent over, breathing deeply, he felt an emptiness that was growing inside of him. One that was mirroring the space about him. What was the point? What did they want of him? They brought him here. Why? He could understand why his mother had jumped. Jumped — she had jumped! That meant that there was a window, a way out. He could, he would, make it out. Feeling another spark of determination, he stood up, ready to move on again.

But there by the wall, on the other side of the chamber, he saw another hovering, glowing light. Not one of those pinpoints of colour. This was a substantial turquoise glow that remained stationary in mid-air. This time there was no swirling of the points of light about it. No pulsation. Still there was a feeling of desperation and hopelessness that emanated from it. Shan moved forward with anticipation, approaching it gently. He held his hands out in front of him as if he were trying to calm a small, timid, and scared animal.

As he drew near the glow remained unchanged, but he felt that there was more to it than he saw. Eventually, he was standing directly in front of it. He moved his hands closer. There was no heat to it, but he felt a prickling sensation that caused the hairs on his arms to rise. Passing his hand though the light he was shocked to get the impression of a girl. A tired, lonely, and lost girl. He felt her, but there was no-one there.

***

Molly rested her head on the flagstones, looking into the chamber despite having nothing to see. She didn't mind the cold that much now. It seemed fitting that she should be uncomfortably cold while lying on a hard, unforgiving floor. That was all she deserved and all she could expect, so why put up a fight? This was it. She just lay there. There was no point getting up. There was nothing to do. Nothing to see. So why not just remain here? She was not sure how long she would be able to stay like this but, eventually, she was sure that it wouldn't matter anymore. She wouldn't have to think about things. Wouldn't be a disappointment. It would be best just to stay and do nothing.

And so, she remained long after the hardness of the floor was hurting her hips. Not wanting to rise, she wished the pain she felt would purge her of her failures. Through her pain, she felt a warmth touch her. It was the tenderness of compassion. It had found its way to her. It was soon followed by the impression of a boy. One who knew loss but wanted to help. This roused her. Where was he? It was the first time she had had any contact with anyone in the Tower, apart from those Watchers.

Desperate, she quickly rose and looked about. She saw nothing, only the empty space with the cold, silver light. She could feel him. She knew that he must be somewhere nearby. Where was he? Emboldened with purpose, and a desperate need, she used all that remained within her, forging a steely determination to find him.

***

Things were changing. The turquoise light began to flare. Terrified that it was going to happen once more, Shan stepped away. He could not bear to watch this again, but something held him there. Someone needed to be there. To be a witness for the end of something, so that it did not happen in isolation, without someone there for the passing. So, he watched and waited to acknowledge an end.

But instead of the light beginning to pulsate and points of colour to churn and swirl, a shadow began to form before him. Transparent at first, it gained in substance and form. Before he was aware of what was happening a black-hooded figure appeared and suddenly raced towards him. Startled, he only had time to put his hands up to protect himself from the onslaught before two arms were firmly about his chest, hugging him tightly. He heard a girl's voice crying into his ear, "We're not alone!"

Chapter 26

Not that she had ever really specifically thought about the internal workings of the Tower, but this was definitely not the way she would have envisioned it. With power came privilege, and privilege brought with it certain luxuries; and luxury was definitely not epitomised by the presence of stark black walls and cold stone floors without any form of comfort whatsoever. It would have been an understatement to say that she was disappointed by her treatment, but she was yet to find anyone to put her concerns to.

Moira sat, leaning against the wall. Having slept little, she was feeling tired and irritable. She had finished the food provided her and was wondering what other indignities would be in store. Peasant rations were one thing and sleeping on the floor was cold and uncomfortable, but they were not the worst of the ignominies she had had to face since arriving in this place. No mirrors to allow her to fix her hair could be forgiven. But to force her to relieve herself like an animal ... now, that was not something easily forgotten.

It was a thing that would be impossible to forgive. It was of no comfort that the evidence did not remain. The mere necessity of performing such a humiliating act provoked the need for retribution, of a type that would take a special sort of planning. The level of pain inflicted would be in proportion to the offence received. Visualising such punishments was how she had been passing the time while she waited for the next thing to happen.

It had felt good to have been finally able to say what she really thought of her mother. To be able to say that directly to her face. If it really was her face. But even if the thing in the chamber was not really her mother, it allowed her to have the final word. She was still here, alive, whilst her mother was decaying somewhere in a shallow pit. This thought, however, unexpectedly made her remember her sister. The only one who had looked after her and truly cared. The one and only friend in her life. A sister who had been taken from her when she had no defence against the malicious and spiteful woman who was their mother, or protection from the absent, detached man whose only desire was for domination over others, that called himself her father.

The remembered tenderness of her sister's embrace caused Moira to brush back a tear. She despised herself even as she did so. Such weakness was of no use. Who needed a softness like that in their lives? She was much stronger now. She knew the working of the world in ways that would have surprised the most cynical of observers. There was no-one who was on your side. You could only depend on what you could achieve. Never trust anyone. Never allow them to know your weaknesses. They would only exploit them, either in an attempt to destroy you or to gain an advantage over you. Dependence on others was failure. That was why she would succeed here, in the Tower. Let it humiliate her, force her to sleep like a beggar, and starve her. She would never let it defeat her. She would do this on her own. In her own way. Of this she was certain.

Now feeling angry but revitalised, Moira was impatient for something to happen. *Let me show you who I am and what I can do*, she silently pleaded. As if in answer to this plea, a figure emerged from the darkness. It waited across the chamber from her. In no mood for civility and impatient for answers, Moira made directly for the figure while deriding it, saying, "So, now what? Are you going to talk to me this time?" The figure was unmoved and simply directed Moira's attention down the nearby corridor.

Looking down the corridor Moira saw a light. Intrigued, she made her way down the hall towards it. As she did, she found herself once again in the servants' passage outside the kitchen of what had once been her home.

"Where is that girl? I tell you, she will be trouble. She is never around when you need her."

At least this was something that Moira understood. She knew that finding a good servant was almost impossible. As she stood there listening, Mrs Poole came into the hallway. Glaring at Moira, Mrs Poole bellowed, "Where have you been, you horrid girl? Leaving all the work for others while you laze on your backside. You worthless little beast!"

Grabbing Moira by her ear, Mrs Poole dragged her into the kitchen. This hurt and Moira glared at the cook. "How dare you—" she started. Without warning, she received a hard slap across the mouth that was delivered with such force her head snapped backward. She felt her lip swell. On bringing her hand to her mouth she found that it was bleeding.

"Never talk back to me, you loathsome creature. Those fireplaces need cleaning. Finish them before I return."

"I will never—" Moira began, before once again receiving a stinging blow to the cheek.

"No-one cares what you think. Mr Colin will not be as generous as I, so I suggest you begin. Polly, come, we are needed upstairs." And with that, Polly left the kitchen without looking at Moira, followed by Mrs Poole who carefully locked the door behind her.

She was left alone. Her face was flushed as much from anger as from the blows she had received. She looked around. She had never been in the kitchen before. It was mostly below ground level, with windows located high on the walls above. There were two enormous fire pits at the end of the room, each full of ash and the remains of the fires required to cook the food that fed the estate. Starting to feel hungry, she looked about but there was no food to be seen. A strange situation for a kitchen this size, but so it was. Trying the door, she found that it had been secured and would not open.

She knew that this could not be real. The servants would never have dared to treat her this way. It must be a trick of the Tower. What was it doing? Unsure what point was being made, Moira sat at the table and waited for what would happen next. She was ready to avoid being struck again and planned to deliver a stinging blow of her own.

Her waiting was eventually rewarded and she heard the door unlock and open. She sat and watched. In the doorway stood the tall figure of her mother, sneering at her through parched and cracked lips with bloated cheeks and black, mottled skin. Despite her resolve Moira was only partially successful in hiding her surprise.

"Welcome to your own special hell, my darling," the apparition contemptuously scoffed, spittle leaking from the side of her decaying mouth. "You thought that I was so easily dealt with? Oh, that is sooo delightfully naive of you. What fun it will be to … *educate* you into some of the more charming aspects of the Code."

Her mother entered the kitchen and ran her cadaveric fingers along the wall opposite Moira. She continued in a tone of derision and contempt, "You think that this is a trick, do you? Just a diversion made for your entertainment. Let me assure you, just as a little bit of advice, that this is as real as anything you have known before. Anything that happens here will have its consequences." The apparition stopped. Then it moved with such speed that before she could react, it was face to face with her, one clawed hand held tightly against her neck, speaking sweetly, "One misstep here and you may wish you had never found Influence."

Before Moira found her voice the apparition was gone. She was alone once more, but this time with the door open. Moira jumped off the table and made quickly for the door. As she reached the opening it was suddenly blocked by a large form that pushed her to the ground. Looking up she saw Mr Colin scowling at her.

"Mrs Poole told me about you," he said, making to strike her with the back of his hand. Shuffling out of the way, Moira narrowly missed being hit. She continued crawling way from him as he roared at her, "One word out of you and you will not be able speak again for many a day, you maggot! I'll give you one chance to do it right and no more."

Terrified, Moira clambered to her feet. She ran away from the man to the fire pits at the other end of the kitchen. There she fell to her knees and started to pull out the unburnt logs from the deep ash. Unsure how the work was supposed to be carried out, she tried to look as if she was attending to the job. She hoped that it would be enough to avoid further strikes.

***

Eventually Molly let go and took a step back. Tears running down her cheeks, she smiled and said, "I'm Molly." Shan looked carefully at her, assessing her and the potential risk. She was slightly shorter than he was with a round, pretty face and wearing the same black robe he was. Her voice was light and timid. She looked real and certainly was able to give a pretty decent hug. She did not look like the Dark Ones and definitely did not talk like them – if they said anything at all. Also, the Dark Ones all had a blue glow that surrounded them. Molly's was different. Hers was a bluey-green and seemed more vital and alive.

"I'm Shan," he replied. "How long have you been here?"

Slowly and tentatively, she replied, "I don't know. I can't remember. I don't think that it could be that long, but I'm not sure."

"I got here yesterday ... I think," Shan responded. "It gets very confusing without being able to see the sun."

"Yes," Molly responded sadly. "I miss that ... and the birds ... and ... and ..." she stopped, her voice cracking with emotion. "But, they don't miss me," she stated matter-of-factly.

"Who?" asked Shan.

"Mama and Father ... my sisters. I thought that they would ... but its best that I'm gone now."

"Why do you say that?" Shan was surprised.

"I'm no good. They don't want me. Ester doesn't even remember me and

183

the others, ahhh … the others …"

"Your other sisters?"

"Ummm yes, ahhhh, I think so. I can't remember. But they didn't want me either."

"How do you know that? We're in here and they're out there. Families don't forget each other."

"But they do. I know. They told me so," Molly insisted.

"How?"

And with that, Molly told Shan of her visits home. Of how Ester had been scared of her. How everyone had made fun of her and called her a baby. She spoke of Mama and the disappointment her family had in her. Of the dreadful tea, and how something important of hers had been given away. Shan listened closely, letting Molly ramble and repeat again what had happened. How she had been able to go home and how she had returned. Finishing, Molly said, "It just doesn't make sense. I thought that Mama would always be there."

Under his breath Shan repeated to himself, "If it doesn't make sense, then you're looking at it the wrong way."

"Sorry, what was that?" Molly asked.

"Oh sorry, just something my Maima always says. If it doesn't make sense, then you're looking at it the wrong way. Are there other things that don't make sense?"

"Well, the tea was strange." Molly pulled a face. "Mama has always been very particular about the tea. It was dreadful, but she drank it anyway." Stopping to think, she continued, "Ester always loved getting picked up and swung around but she was so scared of me. Father's voice was different. I remember that my sister was getting taller than me, but she's always been shorter." Thinking further, she slowly said, "I also can't remember who else was there, but there were others."

"Were your other sisters there too?"

"Ummm, I think so. Ester was and … ahhh, another one …" Molly started getting upset again. "I can't remember their names. I've got other sisters. I can't remember what they look like. There's Mama and Father and Ester and …. What's going on?" Molly sagged to the ground. "If I can't remember them, of course they won't remember me," she whimpered.

Unsure of what to do, Shan sat down next to Molly. "Are you hungry?" he asked, opening up his sack and inspecting the remnants of the food he had been provided.

"A little," Molly responded.

"Here," he said as he took out the bread, cheese, and dried meats. "I'm sorry, there's not a lot." He handed them over to Molly who took them and started to nibble.

"Better than what I got," she said. "That cheese is not bad."

"Well, you should try my Maima's cheese. She makes the best goat's cheese in the whole Bowl."

"Really, I've never had goat's cheese."

"You've missed out. You'll have to try it once we're out of here."

"Out of here?" Molly pondered "I've never even thought about getting out. Do you think we could?"

"Why not? We came in. There has to be a way out."

After sitting in silence for a while as Molly ate and Shan thought, Molly suddenly asked, "How did you find me?"

"By your light."

"My what?"

"The blue-green light that is with you. I saw it. It's very different to all the other points of colour around us."

"I don't have a light and I've never seen a light that is blue-green before." Puzzled and looking around her, Molly continued, "What points of colour? There's no colour here, only darkness."

"But it's right there now, surrounding you. When I first saw it, it was a flame that was just sitting in mid air. When I touched it, I saw you."

"And I saw you, or at least felt like I saw you. A boy who was looking at me."

"After that, your light got brighter, and then there you were, right in front of me," continued Shan.

"I knew that I had to find you. I wanted to, so badly."

"And you did."

They both fell into another silence thinking about what had been said. Shan pondered how he had been able to find Molly and all the lights that he could see but she couldn't. Molly turned to Shan, "Do you have any water? My bottle's empty."

As Shan passed over what was left in his bottle he looked back at Molly and asked, "What Influence do you have?"

"I don't have one."

"We all have one or we wouldn't be here."

"Well, I don't know."

"There's only six. Can you make water or fire do things they wouldn't normally do?"

"No."

"How about air or earth?"

"Not that I know of."

"The only other two are being able to change the way a person acts or how they see things. You must have one of those."

Molly stopped chewing and looked directly at Shan. "Mama said that my Noona's sister had Influence, so the Tower wanted her to help. She could make it seem like she was not there when she was."

"And you?" Shan prodded.

Things suddenly started to get a lot clearer for Molly. "Mama wanted to talk to me about Influences just before those Watchers came and got me. She used the word faded, which was odd, because I used to say that when I felt people would ignore me. A cart almost ran over me. He said that he didn't see me, but I was right there in front of him."

"Okay," said Shan, "that must be it. You can influence how people see things. I can do things with air. Not very well, and things keep happening without me really wanting them to. I got that from my mother, but my father also had Influence."

"No-one in my family ever had any. Well, no-one apart from Noona's sister," Molly added. "I don't see why I had to get it."

"They say it runs in families. I think I also got my dad's one as well. Maima said he could see other people's Influences as a colour. I think that's why I can see the coloured lights but you can't. I found you by your colour. I was able to find the Dark Ones when they came to get me at the inn. Have you finished?" he asked. Molly nodded. Pausing to look around, he started to gather up the things and put them back in his sack.

In a quiet voice, Shan whispered, "I don't think that they want us to know that there is anyone else here in the Tower but us. They want us to think that we are alone."

"Why?"

"I don't know. Why are we here to start with? It just is, otherwise why couldn't we see each other before? Nothing seems to happen here without someone in control." Thinking further, Shan continued, "It also means the Dark Ones think that we can't see each other. They make us think that we are the only ones in the Tower when we're not. They won't know that we know we aren't … Who knows how many others are in here with us?"

Getting up, Shan gave Molly an awkward pat on the shoulder, took his sack and walked over to the other side of the chamber.

He waved at her as she started to look worried. "Don't worry, I'm not going anywhere. We just have to make it seem like we can't see each other in case they return. I will wave at you or something if I see someone's colour coming."

Seated against the wall on the other side of the chamber, Shan continued to think. If he could see Influences as colours, then it made sense that the points of colour all around were something to do with the Influences. He remembered the amber light. So like Molly's; but it had exploded. Eventually fragmenting and dispersing throughout the chamber until it was intertwined with all the other colours. Maima said that his mother had thought that the Tower was alive. That it took what it wanted without regard or regret. It was this that she had feared more than anything. To lose herself to the Tower and to become one with it. To lose everything that made her, her. Was that what he saw? The amber light becoming one with the Tower. Correction – a person with an amber light being absorbed by the Tower. So now it just remained as a countless multitude of yellow pinpoints of colour. If this was true then all the coloured points had once been a person, living, breathing, hoping, and then … There would be countless numbers of people who had been taken by the Tower. People like Molly, like him. People who were now no longer themselves, being part of a composite whole. Never again to be themselves. Never to think and never to feel again. The thought made him sick. An eternity of subservience to the Tower. This was a fate much worse than the death his mother chose. He understood now why his parents and Maima had wanted to fight against this.

Chapter 27

Covered in ash, Moira had cleaned and swept the firepits. Once she had started to clean, she had been left alone with the door again locked. She had no idea if this was how it was supposed to look, but it was done. "One chance to get it right" was definitely a threat. She had to hope that it was. Now finished, she waited. It gave her time to think. She was here because she had Influence, major Influence, so why didn't she use it?

She berated herself for failing to do so. Previously she had had to plan to use it. She would gradually and subtly introduce changes, keeping the subject unaware of her efforts. That would not work here. Here she needed to be fast and direct, not gentle. A sudden and catastrophic blow should do it. How would this work? She had not practised this method and if she got it wrong then another beating would most likely ensue. She would have to choose her time. Assess the situation and then attack.

She knew that her mother was dead, but here in the Tower she was unsure if the apparition was a trick or really her mother. She would have to be careful. Alive, her mother had been more than Moira had been aware of. She knew about Influences. She had been able to counteract Moira's probing of her at the ball. The Tower had come to collect her and now she seemed to be around to make things difficult for her. This just made Moira more determined.

And what of this place? First there had been a banqueting table and now it was a kitchen. What was the Tower doing? It couldn't be real; well, not all of it. Her mother might be. She had been warned that the things that happened here had consequences.

Moira sat on the kitchen floor and continued to wait. She had considered it prudent to complete the task set. It gave her time to think and reassess. What was the purpose of all this? When she got a new servant, and she had been through a fair number, she would set chores for them. Test them. Give them difficult, or even impossible, tasks to do. Although she enjoyed wielding the power she had over them, it was not her fundamental reason for doing it. She wanted to see what they were made of. How they would cope with both the mundane and the impossible. Then she would know if they were suitable. Could all this be a test? A way that the Tower assessed those with Influence. A way to work out who was worthy and who was not? If so, what were they testing?

Moira remained still, deep in thought. She had always had a particular intertest in the way power could be exerted. One's position in society could often provide a level of authority that may, or may not, be deserved. Here, however, it had been made clear that she had no position. Cajoling and coercing also would not work. None of the Dark Ones would speak to her. Manipulation and playing one person against another would not work. So here it must be the person's inner strength. A resistance to being belittled, degraded, and debased. To be able to exert control with just what you fundamentally had at your disposal, including Influence, Moira reasoned.

If this was so, she needed to stand up to Mrs Poole and Mr Colin. Show no fear. Use what she had. Using Influence took its toll though. There was only so much she could do before it exhausted her. She had gotten better and developed more stamina, but it still was a limited resource. Best to use it only when it would have the greatest effect.

As she sat contemplating, the kitchen door once again opened and in came Polly, one of those servants that Moira had only been peripherally aware even existed. "Mrs Poole asked me to check on you," she announced. Walking down to the firepits she gave them an appraising look. "Not too bad for a first timer," she said, giving Moira a slight smile, "but if we just give this a bit more of a sweep and then lay the beds for the next fire, you'll be set." Without waiting, Polly took up the broom and gave the pits one last clean before walking over to the wood stacks. "If you see these, these little bits go in first. Easier to take the fire. Then when they're lit, bigger ones go on." She took several handfuls back to the pits and lay them in the centre of each before returning to the stacks.

She repeated several trips to lay slightly larger twigs and sticks around them. "All set," she said as she gave her hands a wipe on her apron. "Up you get. It's time we be out of here."

Moira looked at Polly, unsure and slightly confused. "Why did you do that?" she asked.

"Do what?" Polly replied.

"Finish the pits."

"Well, Mrs Poole won't be happy unless it's done right. One can't expect a newbie to know. Next time you will." Unsure of how this could be used against her, Moira stood and followed Polly out of the kitchen and into the hall.

"We best get you cleaned up. Can't have you traipsing about like that. You'd be a dead sitter for one of Mr Colin's sessions." Moira just looked questioningly at Polly. "It's not something you'd want," Polly responded. "You'd not be able to walk too well after the beating," she added, gently touching Moira's arm. "Just round the corner and in you go. Throw out your clothes before you get in the tub." Moira looked into the small room. In the centre was a roughly hewn wooden tub. "We don't have much time, so in you go," Polly added.

In the room Moira saw that there was only a sheet that could be dropped to close off the entrance. She looked in the tub. It was half filled with greyish water. Bits of oil and dirt were already floating on the surface. "Chop, chop," Polly directed, "we can't waste time. Get out of those things and I'll get you some fresh ones."

Reluctantly, Moira removed the black robe, which she handed to Polly, but left on her underclothes.

"Oft best to leave those on when the tub's already had a few uses," Polly suggested. Moira held her breath as she put one foot into the cold, murky water. "All the way in, now. There's soap on the floor beside it."

Moira looked. She saw a large chunk of laundry soap that had obviously seen many previous users. Tentatively picking it up, she put her second foot into the tub. Polly pulled down the sheet to cover the door and went off to get fresh garments.

Against everything that she had ever felt was her due, Moira sat down in the tub. She shivered as the water enclosed her. Making sure to keep her head well above the water, she attempted to wash off the soot. She knew that her hair was filthy, but it took all her resolve to put it into the oily water to wash it.

Rinsing her hair, she squeezed out the excess water before twisting it onto the top of her head. Satisfied that the worst of the ash had been removed, and certain that any further effort would not add to her cleanliness due to the state of the water, Moira stood up and climbed out of the tub. She saw a couple of old towels hanging on the wall. Taking the one less soiled, she started to dry herself. She was well aware that the odour of the harsh soap now clung to her. Before she finished, Polly returned. Placing dry undergarments and a plain rough-woven dress on the floor where it was still dry, she looked at Moira.

"Hurry up. You'd think that youse been one of the upstairs lot."

Removing her sodden undergarments, Moira quickly dressed herself in the coarse, prickly fabric and, after finding her slippers, entered the hall.

"We're late but there should be some left," Polly said. "Come on." Setting off down the hall, she moved with a speed the caused Moira to half walk and half jog beside her in order to keep up.

"Where are we going?" Moira asked.

"You'll see. There's been a party 'n we get to have what's left. Quick."

At the end of the hall, they started to climb the stone steps that would take them into the *real* part of the house. Polly looked giddy with anticipation. "I've never had what the upstairs lot get to eat. I see it, I prepare it, but Mrs Poole won't let me try it."

Moira looked at Polly. "Why don't you just try it anyway? I'm sure that no-one would ever know?"

Polly looked shocked. "Because that's wrong, that is."

Moira mentally took a step back. She knew that she would have tried it. Now she felt as if she had been reprimanded by that one simple phrase. Looking at Polly, as if for the first time, she saw a girl who was perhaps one or two years older than she was. Pretty, but not beautiful, with a kind, soft face and a mouth that tended to rise at the corners. Her hair was covered by a simple bonnet revealing no hint of its colour. Moira now felt exposed. Her hair was tied in a simple wet bun on top of her head, threatening to come loose at any moment.

Reaching the landing, Polly moved off to the left. They finally arrived at a door familiar to Moira, one that led into the dining room. Knocking gently, Polly waited. Receiving no answer, she opened the door slightly and peered in. Seeing no-one in the room, Polly opened the door fully and stepped inside. Her face was aglow with wonder and delight as she gazed upon the near-empty dishes that remained on the table. Going to the sideboard she opened one of the drawers and took out two tin plates and forks. Handing one to Moira she gleefully said, "Here we are. I don't know where to begin!"

Moira looked at the foods on the table. It was fairly standard fare with nothing particularly exotic. But noting one of her favourite dishes she stopped and, pointing to it, said to Polly, "Try that one, it's particularly good." Eagerly, Polly went to the dish and spooned a small portion onto her plate while Moira pulled out one of the chairs and started to sit.

"No!" Polly squealed, causing Moira to start. "Never, never sit. It they ever found out ..." Moira looked at the girl, seeing fear and desperation etched in every part of her face. Quickly she stood up and pushed the chair back into the table. Polly looked quickly around the room and only started to calm when she could see no-one else there with them.

"Sorry," Moira said, truly feeling sorry for the fear she had caused. "I wasn't thinking." Polly returned a nervous smile.

"I'm sure it'll be fine, but we best be quick in case an upstairser comes." Finishing off the small portion she had served herself, Polly looked longingly at the other dishes about her. "We need to go."

"But you only had the one," Moira objected.

"And youse were right to point that one out!" Polly gushed.

"So wouldn't you like to try others?" Moira pressed.

"It isn't for the likes of us. One's enough to fill m' dreams," answered Polly as she turned and left the room.

As Moira began to follow, the door closed. A voice behind her sneered, "I've never seen you look better."

Turning, Moira was confronted by the liquifying countenance of her mother, barely a palm's breadth away from her own face. The putrefying smell of decay and death surrounded her. She took a step backward. "Mother dear, how good to see you. And in such a *well-preserved* state."

Mortella grinned at her, showing yellowing teeth against blackened gums. "Much more so than you could ever believe."

The apparition made its way to the head of the table and sat, directing its gaze straight at Moira. "Are you enjoying your little vacation? Do not presume to think that you are anything special. We of the Code have never considered you. It was Clara we desired. You, you are nothing but the curse that has hung about my neck from the first day that you were unwantedly conceived."

Moira felt a searing pain at the mention of her sister, lost to her when only seven years old.

"My darling, you look pained," mocked the apparition. "Perhaps you are in need of some refreshment." Rising, she held a crystal goblet containing a ruby-coloured liquid. "It was your father's favourite," she said as Moira reluctantly took the glass. Despite her better judgement, she took a small sip and immediately spat it out. She glared at the form before her.

"He had some rather unique and perverse tastes in the marital chamber," scoffed the apparition.

"A pity that he did not take things a touch further, my darling mother," Moira shot back.

"We tried to, my dear, but as much as we tried … you just refused to die."

"Well, my dearest mother, you didn't refuse, so why don't you just stay buried."

Moira made for the door, but it wouldn't open for her.

"Oh, my sweet child, death is never quite what one would expect."

Turning back to face the spectre on the other side of the room Moira said, "No, I expect not," and then added sweetly, "but I am sure it suits you well."

She spun to the door and pulled hard. It opened as her mother retorted, "I shall give your best to your sister, shall I?"

Ignoring the final taunt and without hesitation, Moira passed into the hall, closing the door behind her. Seeing Polly anxiously waiting by the stairs to the servants' area, she ran quickly towards her. Together, they started the descent.

***

Shan waved in Molly's direction, only to see her wave back at him. Heaving a deep sigh, he waved more vigorously and pointed down one of the corridors. Molly finally got the message and stopped waving. She looked down at the floor, surreptitiously making sure that she was still able to see Shan. He had seen a blue light making its way up the corridor. Only one. From what Molly said this would most likely be one of the Watchers. As the light got nearer a shape formed out of the darkness. It stopped in front of him.

Risking a glance at Molly, it was obvious to Shan that she saw nothing of the figure. Standing, he faced the figure and pointed at it with both hands hoping that Molly would get the message. Out of the corner of his eye he saw that Molly was now also standing but being careful not to look in his direction.

The figure turned and began retracing its steps down the corridor. Shan, now looking directly at Molly, indicated that he was going to follow. He gestured for her to come after him. Molly nodded but indicated that she still saw nothing.

He began down the corridor, abruptly coming to a dead end. In the wall was an open door that led into his cottage on the westernmost plot. Intrigued, Shan approached. Looking closely, he saw Maima sitting in her favourite chair. The Watcher indicated for Shan to enter. Not inclined to do so, Shan remained where he was. The Watcher remained still, unmoving. Further up the corridor he saw Molly also stop and wait.

So, what now? he thought. *It's a stand-off. What if I just walk away?* Trying to take a step back up the hall, however, was almost impossible. It was like trying to walk though treacle. Every movement away from the door was met with resistance. *So you are going to give me no choice. I just hope that I don't lose Molly.* Finally, he turned to face the opening but not before attempting to indicate to Molly

193

that he was going to enter.

He stepped through the door and into their cottage. The familiar smell of freshly brewed dandelion tea wafted around him. As he arrived, Maima rose from her chair. She turned to face him, but before she said a word, Shan let out a dry, humourless laugh. Ignoring the Maima in front of him, he spoke aloud. "It is very well done. Very accurate, right down to the stain on the rug. But you have missed something. We moved everything out of the cottage before I left. And yes, one other thing, Maima could hardly talk, let alone walk."

Turning to the Maima before him he smiled as tears gathered in his eyes and gently said, "I hope that you look as well as you do here, right now." As he spoke the room dissolved and he was again in the corridor, but this time there was no dead end. The Watcher had gone. To his great relief there was Molly, still standing, surrounded by her turquoise glow right where he had last seen her. Quickly checking that he saw no blue lights, he raced to Molly. "Did you see that?"

"No, I only saw you."

"They took me to our cottage at the Western Slopes."

"Umm, you never moved. You flapped your arms down the corridor and then the next thing, you were running up to me."

"I didn't go? You could see me the whole time?"

"Yes. You didn't go anywhere."

"Did you see the dead end … the door?" Shan sounded confused.

"There wasn't any door. You were standing in the middle of the corridor."

"Mmmm." Shan paused and slowly said, "Molly, I don't think we can believe anything we see here. It isn't real."

Chapter 28

Polly had taken Moira directly to her bed chamber. It was a small, cramped room at the furthest reaches of the passageway with only a narrow slit of a window high on the wall opposite the door. There was barely enough room to stand beside the single wooden bed that was pushed up hard against the left-hand wall. The bed's slats were covered by a thin horsehair mattress without any linen. At the head of the bed was a tiny stand holding a flint, the butt of a candle, and a small, framed picture.

On their journey from upstairs to downstairs Moira noted that everything became dimmer. The natural light was certainly less as they were below ground level with only tiny windows to let in the sun's glow. Yet, the whole feel of the place was dimmer with less colour, fewer things, and a starkness that felt sad. The saddest bit of downstairs was now before her. This tiny room was damp, with some sort of mould growing on its unfinished walls. It was without personality, giving nothing away about the person who lived there.

Polly turned to Moira, "Here we are then. You'll be bunkin' with me."

Moira looked confused. "There's only one bed and the sun has yet to set."

"Never you mind. There's more than enough room if you just make it. We're up early as we've to light the pits to get them burning for Mrs Poole," replied Polly, removing her apron and folding it neatly before placing it under the bed. "Do you want top or tail?" she asked.

"Sorry?" responded Moira.

"Top or tail?" Polly repeated.

"Top or tail of what?"

"Of the bed, silly. Do you want your head up here or down there?"

Moira looked at her in disbelief. "Umm, what do you suggest?"

"Nothin' really in it. But I do like to have my family near me."

"Family?" Moira asked, confused.

"This," said Polly, picking up the small, framed picture and showing it to Moira. Looking at the picture, she saw a poorly executed miniature portrait of four figures. A man and a woman seated with two small girls standing beside them. It was almost impossible to make out the details of their faces, primarily due to the lack of technical skill by the artist.

"That's my Ma an' that's my Pa," said Polly, pointing to each figure, "an' these are my sisters."

"Oh, it's lovely," lied Moira.

"It's the one thing I still have of 'em. I look at it every night as I go to sleep."

"Then you should take the top," said Moira.

Polly smiled and gave her a quick kiss on the cheek. "Thank you." Polly took off her slippers and proceeded to remove her outer garment, again folding it neatly and placing it under the bed. "Do you need some help?" she inquired sweetly.

"No, no I'm fine," replied Moira as she followed Polly's example and folded her dress, also placing it under the bed. Still in her undergarments, Polly climbed onto the bed, facing the portrait. She indicated to Moira to do the same at the other end of the bed.

"Best to face the wall and keep m' feet at your back. It's not been my day to bathe," Polly added apologetically. Moira followed the instructions and found herself only inches away from the unfinished wall, trying not to breathe in the mould that she could now so clearly see.

"Good night, sweet dreams. I certainly shall, I can still taste that food," said Polly as her breathing gradually became softer and deeper, leaving Moira awake and alone.

***

Shan looked back down the corridor and spotted another sack similar to the one he already had. He picked it up and opened it. Taking out each item in turn he found another stone bottle of chilled water, a slightly larger loaf of bread than previously, cheese, some dried meat, and an apple. There also was a second smaller bottle which, when he opened it, reminded him of the ale at the inn. Looking at Molly, he grinned. "We're in for a feast."

Sitting on the floor with the hoard spread between them, they shared the food out evenly.

"So, what did you see?" Molly asked as she took some cheese and bread.

"It was as if I was in our cottage again. And there was Maima," said Shan with his mouth full. "But it wasn't real. It looked real, but it didn't feel it. And

196

though Maima was there, it wasn't Maima."

"Why wasn't it?" asked Molly after taking a drink of water.

"Because when I left, Maima was sick and couldn't talk and definitely couldn't walk. And we had to move everything out of our cottage to go to Farmer Albee's so we could look after her. Could you pass the water? Thanks." Continuing after a drink, Shan said, "It was like what it used to be. Like a memory. But not a real one. Something close to, but not really."

Molly reached for the other bottle.

"I wouldn't drink that," warned Shan. "That got me into trouble when I tried it."

Molly opened the bottle and had a sniff. "That's ale," she said, "not something my father says a good girl should have." She replaced the stopper and put the bottle aside. "And all that happened when I could see you the whole time?" Molly asked.

"It seems so," replied Shan.

"So, it's not really real?"

"How could it be? You saw me but never saw the dead end or the door. And they were gone when I came back to the same place I was to begin with."

"But you never moved."

"Exactly. So, it can't be real."

"Like a memory but not really," Molly repeated. "That's like Mama and me. Because I'm almost a woman I got to have tea with my Mama in the special chairs. That's when she talked about my Noona's sister and the Influences. When the Watcher came, I saw Mama with the tea. But the tea was wrong. Mama didn't seem like Mama. So you think that that wasn't real?"

"Very likely. You said it was like a memory, but not really, and things felt wrong."

"Yes." Molly paused and then, sighing deeply, asked, "Then what they said wasn't real?"

"How could it be?" answered Shan.

Molly was quiet as some of the tension left her body. She suddenly leant over and hugged Shan before saying, "We have to get out of here."

***

Moira was awoken by having her shoulder shaken. Rolling over, she saw Polly standing over her.

"Time to be up."

There was no light coming through the window. The only source of illumination was the small candle on the stand. Polly was already unfolding the clothes she had stored under the bed. Moira retrieved hers and did the same. In almost no time they were ready, and Polly blew out the candle. Taking Moira by the hand, she led her along the passageway in near total darkness.

"Don't fret, I've done it many a time," Polly said encouragingly. "We'll be able to get some light in the kitchen." As they made their way along the corridor Moira could hear the snores and heavy breathing of various sleepers in the rooms off the hall.

"It's oft the best time of the day as it's only me. But now it'll be even better. Now you're here," Polly stated plainly. "It'll be good to have a friend here."

Moira remained silent, unsure how she should respond. Previously even the notion of conversing with one such as Polly would have raised her ire. Now it almost seemed a reasonable suggestion. She settled with, "I'm not sure how long I will be here."

"Never you mind. We'll make the most of it anyway," Polly happily responded. Still holding Moira's hand, Polly turned several corners, eventually arriving at the kitchen door. It was still dark. Dawn was yet to break and cast some light through the windows.

Feeling her way along the counter on the right Polly found the flint and candle that was left there specifically for this purpose. Expertly wielding the flint, she had a flame sitting on the candle in next to no time. Waving Moira on, they found their way to the firepits.

"Now we just light what we set yesterday. We need to get a good blaze going. Mrs Poole needs the fire to settle and then the coals will do the cooking," Polly explained. "Watch me." Using the candle, she brought the flame close to the bits of chaff which caught it quickly. Gradually she placed twigs and small sticks on the flame. She waited until they, too, were ablaze before placing larger sticks, and then logs, onto the growing fire.

"We want just enough to make the coals but not too much that the fire won't settle," Polly said. "Now, your turn." She handed Moira the candle.

Moira followed Polly's method and soon she also had a roaring blaze. The fires were pumping out such heat they both had to move away from the pits.

"It takes a bit of time. We just need to wait and feed the fires," Polly said. Then, putting her hand in her apron, she pulled out some items. "How about a game of snobs?"

"Snobs? I don't know how to play."

"Not know how to play snobs?" exclaimed Polly, showing Moira five small bones.

"Oh, you mean knucklebones."

"If you say so. Will we play?"

Polly handed Moira the bones and watched. She made a fairly poor attempt, only getting to threes before missing a bone.

"What poor luck," Polly said as she took back the bones and proceeded, with expert coordination, to get well into the fourth or fifth variation before making a mistake. Laughing, she handed them back to Moira, gently giving her a few suggestions to help.

Back and forth they went, giggling and laughing at both the successes and failures of each, as they fed the fires and watched them gradually settle to form the coals required for Mrs Poole's cooking. Without Moira even being aware, the sun had risen. The household was stirring as she, and a friend, shared some fun.

***

Having packed what little remained of the food and leaving the original sack behind, Shan and Molly chose a direction at random and started walking. As they went, Shan explained what he saw. "They aren't really lights. They're more like points of colour. Lots of different types of colours. They're everywhere."

"And me?" asked Molly.

"You have a bit of a glow about you. The colour is something between a green and blue. It sort of outlines you," replied Shan.

"What about you? What colour do you have?"

"I don't know," answered Shan. "I never thought about that." He looked at his arms and then down at his feet. "Mmm, I don't seem to have any. Perhaps my Influence doesn't have a colour."

"Or perhaps you just can't use Influence on yourself," suggested Molly.

"Oh, you might be right. When you used to fade, could you still see yourself?"

"Of course. I never really faded. I was always there."

"But not there to other people," Shan observed. "So the Influence didn't work on you."

"No, I suppose not," admitted Molly. "Have you seen other lights like mine?"

"Not like yours, no," answered Shan. "But I did see a yellow light that was floating down the middle of the corridor."

"What happened?"

"I don't think that it was good, whatever it was that happened," he said softly. He retold the last moments of the amber light before it melded with the points of colour.

"It sounds horrible," said Molly. "What do you think really happened?"

Shan paused. He turned to Molly and, taking one of her hands, said, "I think that there is a lot more to the Tower and it isn't good."

"And?" she waited. "Go on. If we are going to get out of here …" Molly tightened her grasp on Shan's hand and continued, "We *are* going to get out of here and if it's important, I need to know, too."

Sitting down and pulling Molly's hand to make her sit as well, Shan began his explanation. "My mother was chosen, just like us, but she was able to escape the Tower. She jumped out a window."

Molly looked excited. "So there is a way?"

"Yes, but it was a long way down. She had to use Influence on air to break her fall, which only barely worked." Molly looked less enthusiastic.

"She always feared the Tower," he continued. "She thought that the Tower was alive. That it would take whatever it wanted. She was terrified that she would be absorbed by the Tower. To completely lose herself, no longer be her, but just be a part of the Tower. Just after I was born, she felt that she was losing the fight to remain free from the Tower," Shan paused. "She took her own life to stop it winning."

"Oh, I am so sorry!" Molly cried. "That's dreadful." She squeezed his hand.

"I never knew her," replied Shan coolly. "I only found this out a few days ago. Maima was all I ever needed. She was my mother and father."

"What happened to your father?" inquired Molly.

"After my mother died, he had to leave us to protect me," Shan sighed. "He had several Influences, and the Tower doesn't like men with Influence. They would have come to absorb him."

"Ohh," was all Molly could say. And then, "So what about you?"

"Well, supposedly only girls can Influence air, but I got that one from my mother."

"But you're a boy," pressed Molly.

"Yes; but everyone but you thinks I'm a girl. Maima said that was the best way to protect me. Pretend to be a girl."

"I won't tell,' promised Molly.

"Just as well," laughed Shan, "or I might just have to push you over with a gust of wind."

Molly challenged, "It would have to be a pretty big one. I know how to stand my ground." After a slight break she asked, "What do you think happened to the amber light?"

"Well, I think that that could have been the very last moment of someone like us."

Molly held her breath. "How do we know if that is going to happen to us?"

Shan waited. He was not going to scare Molly more than she already was, but he thought it was already happening to Molly. He remembered the feeling of desperation and hopelessness that came from her light when he first found her, so like the sense from the amber light. And she was forgetting things like his mother did. It seemed that each time the Watcher came, she lost a little bit more. But instead of saying these things, he just said, "We won't let that happen."

***

Mrs Poole had arrived in the kitchen and given the firepits a thorough inspection. Satisfied with them, she just nodded and sent them to the other end of the kitchen to start peeling the potatoes that would be needed later in the day. Polly smiled at Moira and gave her a quick pinch on the arm.

"Oww. Why did you do that?" demanded Moira.

"For balance, of course," answered Polly.

"You really don't make much sense at times, Polly," was the exasperated reply from Moira.

"You don't know much, do you?" laughed Polly. "One must balance things," she said simply. "When something good app'ns then best balance it … to stop something bad coming."

Moira sighed. She was aware of the many superstitions that were held by the masses. Up until now she had largely ignored such things. Still, she was in a good mood. "Well, thank you, Polly. I will then expect the rest of the day to go very well."

Polly giggled. "I should have pinched you harder. Then we might have got the day off." Moira supressed a giggle.

Once they were well into the second bucket of potatoes the room suddenly seemed cooler and darker. Looking around, Moira saw that in the doorway was the bulky form of Mr Colin. Walking up to Mrs Poole, followed by John the under footman, he stopped in front of her and demanded, "Who was last to indulge in the residuals last night?"

Mrs Poole looked over to where Moira and Polly were busy at work and pointed. "They were late," was her reply.

201

Nodding at John who immediately left the kitchen, Mr Colin stormed over. The two continued to work, both keeping their heads down. Polly's hands were visibly shaking as she attempted to continue peeling the potato she held. Moira, who had already narrowly missed a beating from Mr Colin, kept quiet.

"You," he bellowed, pointing at Polly. "Stand up when I talk to you."

Timidly Polly rose, followed by Moira who was already planning what she would do if he threatened her. Hard and fast. Like a punch to the face but worse. No gentle slowing of the heart rate now. More like completely stopping the heart. Just let him try. She was ready.

Gabbing Polly roughly by the arm he half dragged her into the centre of the kitchen. "This abomination, this piece of filth that we brought in, out of the kindness of our hearts, when she had nowhere else to go. This trash went and sat – yes, sat – in one of the master's dining-room chairs. And this filthy bit of refuse left a stain on that chair."

Throwing Polly to the ground he kicked her in the stomach with his massive shoe. Painfully winded, Polly could only squirm on the ground, unable to make a noise. Moira stood shocked at the treatment before her. Her mind blanked as she tried to comprehend what had just occurred.

Moira watched as the man dragged Polly towards the firepits. When he was almost there, John arrived back in the kitchen. He carried in one hand a long, supple leather cord, and something small in the other. Provoked to motion Moira raced down to the other end of the kitchen, unsure of what she would now do.

Taking the small object from John's hand, Mr Colin pushed it towards Polly's face. "Do you see this? This is what happens when you get above your station."

Moira could see that he held the small frame that had been by Polly's bed. The only item in that room that meant anything.

"You see it?" the man repeated, as Polly looked up, sobbing.

With a heartbreaking voice she pleaded, "Please, please sir …"

"You'll know now what respect means," he continued as he raised his arm, ready to slam the object into the centre of the fire.

"No, it wasn't her. Leave her!" screamed Moira.

She was smacked hard across the face by a raging Mrs Poole, felling her to the ground. "Silence," she hissed.

From the ground Moira saw the frame leave Mr Colin's hand. It flew into the firepit making a smashing sound. Polly was made to watch her family burn in front of her. She let forth a harrowing scream of hurt and loss. A sound so tormented that Moira could never have imagined that it could come from a person. Now Polly was just a crumpled heap on the floor. Mr Colin, still enraged, dragged her back down the kitchen and out the door with the strap ready in his hand.

Chapter 29

The two of them walked on. The corridors continued just as dark and just as empty as before but now, for Molly, they were nothing like they were before. She knew that she was not alone. That there was hope. The Tower lied. That had not been her Mama. She wanted to kick herself for allowing the Tower to do that to her. *Mama would never say those things. How could I be so stupid to believe she would?* Now warned and prepared with this knowledge, she almost looked forward to another dance with the Tower. *Let it try again and let's see what will happen*, she thought.

Shan, meanwhile, kept a close watch on everything. He watched to see if the colours changed. To see if they started moving differently or if there was a different sort of light that moved with purpose. *If Molly's here, there may be others*, he thought. *Others that are also trapped here and want to get out. Perhaps if there were more of us ... it might be easier.*

Locked in their own thoughts they kept going, hoping, but not expecting, for anything to change. Eventually stopping for a rest in one of the larger chambers, Shan opened the sack and removed its contents. Together they emptied the remaining water from the bottle and finished off the last bits of food. They both left the ale well enough alone.

"The food doesn't go as far with two," said Molly. "I'm sorry."

"Sorry for what?" asked Shan.

"For taking your food. They don't seem to give me any," she sighed.

"Don't worry, we'll find more," he replied, once again looking around them and down the corridor. "Nothing seems to change. Do you see anything different?"

"No, it's just the same," shrugged Molly. "Do you still see the colours?"

"Yes, they're always there ... but nothing new." Shan hesitated. Down in the dark depths of the corridor across from them he thought he saw some movement in the colours. "Molly, I think there's something down there," he whispered as he pointed down the passageway. "We best move apart." Gathering the sack and bottle he stood up and moved to the left where he could still see the colours. Molly moved a way off to the right.

Looking intently, he watched as numerous colours coalesced and gradually grew in brightness as if making their way up the hall. As the lights got closer he was able to see that they outlined a figure. Carefully he looked over to Molly so as not to make it apparent that he could see her. It was evident that she, too, was able to see something.

Giving his attention back the approaching figure, he waited. He was unsure if this was wise but was aware that he really had no other choice. The figure eventually emerged into the chamber. It was a tall, elegantly clothed woman. Who, looking directly at him, gave an acknowledging nod before turning slightly to face Molly and presenting a similar greeting. Around her was a halo of coloured lights. They were turquoise like Molly's, and amber, as well as violet and red, with a touch of green and pure white. They surrounded her, encasing her. "How unusual," she cooed. "You two are here together." Pausing, she lifted both arms and made a welcoming gesture. "My darlings, please come closer. Your secret is safe with me."

With really no other viable option in front of him, Shan walked slowly towards the woman. Molly, seeing him do so, did the same. As she got closer, she saw that the woman was very beautiful. Tall, slender and with long, fiery red hair that twisted elegantly onto her shoulders and down her back. Her gown was of a flowing, sparkling silver-grey material, the like of which Molly had never seen before. A figure of pure beauty and grace.

"The Tower has never played host to such as you two before," the woman said sweetly. "You must be very special to be able to break Influence."

Looking from one to the other she gave a slight laugh. "I should know, my dears, for it was once I that wove that Influence." She paused. "But then, no-one ever broke through that." Still looking between them she enquired, "Which of you has the Influence of perception?"

Molly looked at Shan who gave a slight shake of his head.

"We don't know what that is," he answered.

"Mmm … yes, it can be one of those that does creep up on one … but, my dears, you can trust me. You are already here. The Tower selected you. It will not be difficult to discover which of the Influences you have." She waited.

Molly took a step forward. "I think I might have that one, the one that changes how people see me."

"Oh, my sweet child, how quaint," scoffed the woman. "It is so much more than that."

Molly just looked at her not really knowing what to say. The figure observed her closely. "And you broke the illusion of solitude?" she asked with a tone of disbelief.

"Yes," answered Molly defiantly, "I did."

"Mmm …" she replied.

"So what if you don't believe us. It's broken now," said Shan. Turning to him, the woman gave him a closer examination.

"And you, what Influence do you have?"

"Air," he replied.

"Mmm …" was the response. "I suppose that you are hungry? The Tower does tend to ration the portions." She waited but neither responded. "Well, are you?" she demanded.

"A little," Molly acknowledged.

"Then follow me," she said as she turned and seemed to float down the corridor from which she came.

Molly looked at Shan who shrugged as both of them followed along behind the woman. Down the corridor they moved until she stopped in the middle of the hall and turned to face the wall. As Molly watched, the wall melted away revealing stairs going up. Without explanation the woman started to climb. Looking at each other, they followed. After a single flight they entered a chamber with a chandelier and a long table set for supper. By the wall was a second table containing plates of meats, cheeses, fruits, and bread. With a single gesture the woman offered to them all that was before them.

Shan nodded, took a plate from the table, and started to fill it from the sideboard. Molly held back, unsure.

"Nothing to lose," Shan said as he gave her a wry smile. "If they want to, they could starve us or poison us. The end would be the same, but I would prefer to have a full tummy."

"I suppose," she murmured, "but I would prefer neither."

With plates full they sat at the table. The woman indicated the decanters. Pouring a small amount of liquid into the goblet before him, Shan shook his head. "Just water, please," he asked as the woman indicated the other jugs on the table.

The food was excellent. Better than the provisions supplied to them earlier. Both of them ate their fill while the woman stood by the stairs and watched.

Finishing the last strawberry, Molly turned to her. "Thank you," she said simply. "It is very kind of you." After pausing she continued, "Are you a Watcher?"

"A Watcher?"

"She means one of the Dark Ones," helped Shan.

"Oh, darlings, I am not one of the help," she answered smoothly.

"I'm sorry," Molly added quickly.

"They are merely the lowly servants of the Tower. They go and fetch like the obedient animals they are. No longer really human anymore. More of a mobile form of the Tower, if you will."

Shan looked at Molly. "Where did they come from?" he asked.

"Oh," she said, sounding surprised. "Where you all come from, dear." She took his face in her hands and, looking directly into his eyes, said dryly, "They didn't do well here. Well, they did better than some …" then added quickly, "but only have limited uses." Examining him closely, she continued, "Talent is one thing, how to use it is another. Now, my darlings, we must go," she said, leading them down the stairs and back into the dark corridor. Behind them the wall reformed, hiding the stairs once more. "We shall meet again, my dears. At a more convenient time." Turning to leave she added, "We may be able to help each other," before fading into the darkness without even moving.

***

Lying on the ground nursing the side of her face, Moira stayed still. She heard the characteristic slapping sound of leather hitting skin followed by Polly's cries. She was too terrified to move and too ashamed to think clearly. All she could do was replay over and over again the sound of Polly's inhuman wail as her family burned before her. Finally, the disciplining ceased, and all was quiet. Mrs Poole also seemed to have left the kitchen, leaving Moira forgotten and alone.

To have cared so deeply about something that it could bring such pain showed Moira how empty her life had been. As a child she had adored her older sister. But had she really cared that much for her? She had blamed her for her own death. She then hated her sister for having left her with a hateful mother and dismissive father. *Did I ever really mourn her?* Moira thought. *In truth, I just thought about myself. Of what I had lost and how my life was harder*, she finally admitted. *There has been no-one I have ever truly cared for*, and then, pausing, she continued the thought, *and there has been no-one who has ever truly cared for me.* Polly was the only friend Moira had ever had. Then, at the first opportunity, she had let her take the blame for something that she had done.

Despite all the fine words she had said to herself, she had failed. She had been going to stand up to Mrs Poole and Mr Colin. Show no fear and use what she had. It was going to be a sudden and catastrophic blow. And what did she do? She froze. She did nothing as her friend was abused and beaten. A friend who had shown her only kindness, without motive or desire to use her. Her friend who had nothing … but shared it anyway. Moira curled tighter into a ball on the ground. She felt the weight of her betrayal pressing down on her making it hard to breathe.

There she stayed, unthinking and unmoving. Finally, she was able to rouse herself out of the mire of self-pity by realising that, once again, she was only thinking about herself. More of the same. No better than her mother. Polly needed her. She was failing her again. Now she was more than ever aware of the need to be the Moira who depended on no-one and did things her own way.

With determination Moira picked herself up from the ground and hastily made for the kitchen door. Looking though it into the hallway, she saw no-one. Listening carefully, she was unable to hear any sounds or get clues as to where Polly would be. Entering the corridor, she took the opposite direction to the time before and carefully made her way along the wall.

Glancing in each doorway she saw no-one. Eventually she arrived at the laundry where she thought that she could hear a quiet sobbing coming from within. Entering the room, she saw what looked like a figure huddled in the furthest corner. Fearful that Polly would not want her there she hesitated.

"Polly," she whispered. "Polly, is that you?"

The figure did not respond. It remained as a crumpled heap in the corner.

Tentatively Moira took a few steps towards the figure. "Polly, I'm sorry." She spoke softly. "I didn't know what to do. I didn't mean for this to happen." Without any response, Moira stopped again but then slowly took more steps. "Can I help? I know you must hate me but tell me what you need, and I will do it."

While she was waiting for a reply, Moira heard someone else enter the room behind her. She turned quickly. This time she was ready to release all the anger she felt. One massive blast of hate. She turned hoping that it would be Mr Colin. Instead, a familiar voice derided her. "I didn't know what to do," it mocked.

There in front of her once again was the putrefying form of her mother. "Oh, sweetie, how low you have fallen," she scoffed. "I thought that I taught you better than that. Consorting with the help!"

"Mother, I have no time for your contempt. Go back to your crypt. There none of us need hear nor see you."

"What a pity, is that all you have. That's no fun," replied the form in mocking sadness. "Where's that little bitch that reminds me so much of myself?"

"I'm nothing like you."

"Oh, darling," she laughed, "you are everything like me. Don't think that this fling with emotion will last. You're far too shallow for that."

Moira just glared at her mother before turning her back on her. She made towards the form in the corner.

"No-one ever likes you, dear. It never lasts. Remember that little puppy you got for your tenth birthday? Even that silly creature couldn't last. Running away as far as possible from you within the first week. At least it had the sense to keep running," she sneered.

Moira continued to ignore her mother. Gradually, she approached the figure. Gently putting a hand on the form, she found that it had no substance. It was just a pile of dirty linen that had been left in the corner for the next day's laundry. Shaken far more than she realised, Moira silently slid to the ground by the pile. Her mother was gone. Now, so had Polly. Once again alone and friendless, Moira just sat with eyes burning. Her mouth was dry and she was unable to think, finding herself in a haze of pain and emptiness.

***

"Who was she?" Molly asked as soon as they were alone.

"I don't know, but she's different," Shan responded.

"How?"

"She's not a Dark One. They and the Watchers all seem to have a blue light. Hers was many colours. She had yours."

"My what?"

"The same coloured light as you," he said, "and yellow and red … and green and purple. The lights were all around her, like some sort of protection."

"Well, she seemed nice," Molly added.

"Seemed nice but there was something not quite right about it." Shan paused. "She wants our help. To do what, I wonder?"

"She's better than anything else we've found, or not found, in here," Molly said. "As you said, they already have us here so they can do what they want with us."

"Yes, but there's something I don't like about her."

"We'll just have to be careful then," Molly stated very matter-of-factly.

"You're right, Molly. So where should we go now?"

"Let's go the way she was going."

And so they walked down the dark and nondescript corridor in front of them. Despite their concerns they were both feeling in quite a good mood. The food had been good. Having a full stomach did wonders for confidence and motivation. It had also shown them that there was much, much more to the Tower than these corridors. If only they were able to work out how to see these differences, then …

As they were pondering these things, they entered yet another large and dark circular chamber. Like so many others before, except for one small detail. Near the corridor opposite Shan saw a red light. It hovered a few feet off the ground. He stopped and stared. Quickly he pulled on Molly's arm to get her attention.

"There's a light here," he whispered.

Molly immediately moved away from Shan while looking at the floor.

"No, not a blue one. This one's red," he explained.

"Where?" Molly asked.

"By the corridor over there," said Shan, pointing.

"Is it moving?"

"No, just sitting in mid-air. Like when I saw your one."

"What should we do?"

"It might be someone like us. We can't just leave them."

Shan walked slowly over to the light with Molly following a step behind. "Last time I just touched it."

Stopping next to the light Shan moved his hand slowly toward it. Again, there was no heat. Unsure, yet determined, Shan put his hand into the light. Once again there was a prickling sensation up his arm. For a moment, just for a moment, he felt that there was a girl there. This one was sad and felt hollow. He could sense her emptiness. Turning to Molly he said, "It's a girl. She needs help." Then, grabbing Molly's hand, he started pulling it towards the light.

"What are you doing?" complained Molly.

"Oh, sorry. I wasn't really thinking," answered Shan, letting go of Molly's hand. "Umm … I thought that if I put your hand in the light then you might be able to see her too and break the illusion."

"Oh, alright," answered Molly. "Let's give it a go," she said, giving her hand to Shan.

Gently, he moved her hand closer to the light. "Do you feel anything?" he asked.

"No, nothing different," Molly responded.

"I feel tingling in my arm and the hairs stand on end," Shan explained.

"No, nothing like that," said Molly.

Moving it even closer and still seeing no response from Molly, he put her hand directly in the light.

"Nothing?" he asked, disappointed.

"Sorry, I don't see or feel anything."

"But you were the one who broke the illusion. It is your Influence that can do that. I can only find them," he complained. "Do you remember what you did?"

"Well, when I saw you, I knew I just had to find you. I just concentrated really, really hard and then, there you were."

"That's not very specific," noted Shan.

"It worked, didn't it?" shot back Molly.

"Yes, I'm sorry. It did, you're right. Can you do it again?"

"I can try. What does she look like?"

"I don't know, I only got an impression," Shan paused. "She was sad and alone. She's right there in front of us, she—" He stopped and said quickly, "There's someone coming."

Molly immediately walked away from Shan who ducked into the corridor in front of him. He watched a disembodied blue light come and stop in front of Molly.

Chapter 30

The marketplace looked exactly like it always did with people moving here and there, carts delivering produce to the stalls, and others making deliveries to the more important residents of Town. There was Mrs Perkins, busy tending the customers and providing them with the best and freshest items available. At least, according to the sign that was always placed before the booth. The sun was shining. A slight wind blew through the square, keeping the whole place pleasant and free of the stifling odours of ripening fruit and body sweat that could so easily prevail without the breeze.

Into this familiar scene Molly suddenly found herself. The transition had been instant. There had been no door through which she could choose to walk, or not. Slightly blinded by the light she stood where she was, trying to orientate herself before further assessing what was happening. Yet, just by standing still she seemed to act as a magnet for people. They continually brushed against her or bumped into her without notice and without apology.

It isn't real, she told herself. None of this is real. It's just some sort of memory. She moved to a more open area in order to avoid being hit so frequently. Mama would never have said those things. Ester would not forget me.

Looking about her, Molly wondered what was the point of this, this thing of the Watcher? As she searched the marketplace, her eyes were drawn to a tall figure making its way effortlessly through the chaos that epitomised the square. Even from a distance the figure's hair burnt a brazen orange in the sunlight. As it got closer, Molly recognised the woman from the Tower. Making her way directly towards Molly, the woman glided forward as a path opened in front of her before falling, once again, into its normal bedlam as she passed.

"My darling, wonderful to see you out and about," she crooned.

"It's only a trick," Molly responded.

"Indeed, my dear, but the sun still feels warm, and the breeze is refreshing.

Is it not, after the dark, cold and still corridors?" she asked sweetly.

"I guess so," Molly paused, "but what is the point, what is it for?"

"Oh, my dear, is that not obvious?" came the reply. "The Tower only wants ones who are worthy to rise." After a pause she added smoothly, "Not that those unable to rise are not of use. The Tower will still keep them … and their Influences … for use." The woman looked carefully at Molly. She appraised her before asking, "I assume that you would prefer to remain … unabsorbed?"

Molly looked shocked. "So it is true. The lights?"

"Oh, my darling, do not fret, those lesser ones are happier now. And they have purpose. They are much better able to assist their superiors as they are than as they were." Looking closely at Molly's face she pointedly asked, "Are you one of their superiors?"

Fumbling for an answer Molly dropped her head. She looked anywhere but at the woman in front of her. In a small voice, she responded, "I don't know."

"Mmm, we shall have to see what you can do."

"I don't know how to do anything. I didn't really know I had Influence," Molly confessed.

Responding quickly and sharply in a tone less gentle than before the woman snapped, "If you do nothing you will join those melded with the Tower. So, I suggest you try."

"But how?" cried Molly.

"How did you break the illusion of solitude on the other one?" was the taut reply.

"I just really wanted to … and … and it happened. I don't know how."

"Exactly, my dear. You *wanted* it, more than anything," answered the woman with a gleam in her eye as she watched Molly work it though.

"If I want it bad enough then … it happens?"

"Oh, my dear, why such contemplation? Just do it and find out."

"On what?"

"On anything."

Molly looked around her. While they had been talking the crowd had provided a space about them or, more likely, around the figure with her. It created for them a small oasis from the constant movement in the square. Molly moved out of this eye of the storm and into the melee that surrounded it. Immediately people started to bump into her. They pushed their way past her and through her as if she didn't exist. This time, Molly did not jump out of their way or avoid those coming towards her. She instead willed herself to be more solid, more substantial. To be a person that others would notice and not run into.

Remembering what if felt like to desperately want to find Shan, she reached into herself. She looked to find the desire to be more than an insignificant, plump girl on the cusp of adulthood. She wanted to be noticed. To be acknowledged.

"It is a start, my dear," was the retort from the oasis as Molly started to feel bigger and more substantial. People began to go around her instead of trying to push through her. "It lacks finesse, yet it is effective."

"What happened?" asked Molly. "I can't see any difference."

"Yes, it is unfortunate that one's Influence does not work on oneself. Suffice to say, you did appear bigger. More as one of those troll-like creatures one hears about in the stories. Not a good look, dear." But for Molly, this was praise. She had managed to use Influence when she wanted to.

"When we use Influence, we need to weave it and construct what we want. Craft it, develop it, and then spin it. You can be whoever you want my dear. Tall and beautiful or short and fat. Whatever it is that you need for the occasion. With work, you can be invisible."

"I think that I already have that one worked out," giggled Molly.

"Mmm, have you? That normally takes quite some training or a fair bit of natural ability," mused the woman.

"Well, no effort for me," stated Molly. "I always seemed to be making myself invisible."

"Really? Mmm. That would seem to be adequate." Then after a pause the woman continued, "Let us see what else you can do." With that, she moved away from the centre of the square to the busy roads that led towards it. "Come, my dear."

Molly watched the crowd close in on her without the presence of her companion. Moving forward, she had to dodge her way through the masses. She trailed the eye of the storm as it made its way to the edge of the square. Finally catching up, she entered the calm space once again.

"Weave and construct. You *need* to plan. To create the detail. It must be realistic in order to trick the senses. The texture, the size, the colour, and the feel of it must be determined. Without these anyone can see through the illusion. Then, the most important thing. You must want it, desire it, yearn for it. It comes from you. The more you need it, the stronger it becomes. The finer the detail the harder it will be to break." The woman looked at Molly, drilling into her with those green eyes. "Do you understand?"

Molly nodded despite not really knowing what she was supposed to do.

"Very well, then. I want you to stop all movement into the market from this road."

Molly just looked at the woman, stunned. "Stop all movement along the road?" she repeated.

"Did I not speak clearly enough for you?" was the curt reply.

"Umm. Yes … but how?"

"However you want. But be quick. I cannot stand indecision."

Molly looked down the road. There were carts laden with produce coming up it for delivery to the stalls. Shoppers were making their way both to and from the market. The tradespeople were crisscrossing in front of her. The whole thing was awash with people. Molly looked in wonder at the task set. To stop all movement along the road to the square. *Weave and construct, desire and build. Make it happen*, she thought. She couldn't let down this woman who was helping her. She didn't want to be made part of the Tower. She had to think of something. *Think and build. What should she build?* Her mind was blank. She had never even dreamed about blocking off a street before. What sort of thing would do that? Then she had an idea. Something that she had dreamt about in her little attic bedroom. From that thought she created an image in her mind. She gave it details, trying to make it look real, taking time to think of how it would feel.

She wanted to make this happen. She needed to succeed. She was not a failure. She was not destined to be absorbed. She had to want this so that she would be her and remain her. She so wanted just to be Molly. All these feelings Molly put into the image that she had formed in her mind. *What now?* she thought. *How do I make it happen?* But then she just let go. Let her feelings flow into the image and let the image take on a life of its own.

As she allowed the two parts to meld, she watched people down the street start to look up. Startled and giving forth small cries of terror, they started jostling with one another as they began running back down the road. Baskets, both full and empty, were flung away in haste, their contents strewn across the ground. The nearest horse reared onto its hind legs, tipping over the cart it was pulling before breaking free to follow the exodus down the street. The driver was thrown to the side as the cart tipped. Picking himself from the ground, he looked up. Without a second thought he followed his horse as fast as he could. Further down the road other drivers were able to control their skittish mares. They rapidly turned their carts about before retracing their steps, only narrowly missing the fleeing shoppers.

Beside her the woman was laughing. "Oh, my darling, crude but effective, I'll give you that." Turning to Molly, she smiled a dazzling smile at her and said,

"You will do, my dear. I really think that you will do. I'm so pleased." With that she turned and disappeared into the crowd that was blissfully unaware of what had just occurred. Now alone, Molly pulled back the image. She let the feelings that she had fed it evaporate. Exhausted, she sat on the ground where she was, too tired to even think about doing anything more than just sleep.

***

When she awoke, she was back in the dark chamber with Shan sitting beside her. There was an open sack beside him, and items of food laid out, ready to be eaten.

"I was hoping you would wake up soon. I was getting hungry. How are you feeling?" he asked

"Like I haven't slept for a week," Molly replied.

"Well, things must have gone well," he said as he pointed to the sack and food spread out over the floor. "There is even a slice of cake!" Molly gave a weak smile. "Here, have a drink. It will make you feel better," suggested Shan as he passed the bottle of water to her. "What happened? I watched as you just stood where the Watcher came to you. Then after a while you collapsed on the ground, and you have been sleeping for some time."

"So much happened," Molly began as she took some bread and cheese. "Remember the lady who fed us? Well, she was there. She wanted me to use Influence and showed me how." Molly continued to explain how both the thought and the desire for something to happen must join together. "The stronger the wish is for it to happen, the better the result," she concluded.

"What was it that you made to block the street?" Shan asked, also taking some more bread and cheese.

Molly blushed a little. "Well, I used to imagine that my little attic room was a palace. I was a princess waiting for a prince to come. And what is a prince without a dragon?"

"You made a dragon?" Shan sounded impressed.

"I think so. My Influence doesn't work on me, so I didn't see anything. But it seemed to work, and the lady was pleased. She said that I would do. I won't be absorbed by the Tower."

The last statement was uttered with such an air of relief that Shan was able to see how much this had scared Molly. He also felt relief. He had truly felt that Molly had been in danger of exactly that.

"Do you think that it is the same for all Influences?" asked Shan between mouthfuls.

"What is the same?" asked Molly.

"That first you create a picture in your mind, then let everything that you wish and want make it happen?"

"I don't see why not. They are all Influences. You can always try it out," suggested Molly.

Without another word, Shan stood up and closed his eyes. Concentrating hard, he pictured an eddy of wind swirling above them where the lights were dancing erratically. Wishing and willing it to be true he allowed the image to gain power from his desire. He tried melding them together. Letting go, he watched as the lights above them started to spin for a short time in roughly a circle before they slowed and regained their haphazard movements. Shan sat down again, smiling to himself.

"What did you do?" asked Molly.

"Oh yes, sorry, I forgot you can't see the lights. I made them spin around above our heads. It worked just as you said. It will take practise but now at least I have some idea of how to control it. Better than letting it loose when I don't want to," he said, thinking back to the incident in the basement.

"Oh, what about the other girl?" interjected Molly. "I forgot about her. Is she still here?"

"Yes, I think so," said Shan. "Her light has not moved from before the Watcher came. Do you think you could do something?"

"I can try. I know how dreadful it is to be all alone in here. We have to help her."

Getting up from the floor Shan made directly for the light, followed by Molly. It was still hovering, unmoving, above the floor. Just where it had been previously. Placing his hand into the flame he once again felt the presence of a sad and lonely girl. Taking Molly's hand, he placed it together with his into the flame.

Molly closed her eyes and tried to feel the illusion. She thought of what it had meant to her being found by Shan. The feeling of loss and despair that had enveloped her had been transformed in an instant to hope. She wanted to help. She so desperately wanted to give support to this unknown girl who was like she had been.

Feeling a flood of emotions fill her, Molly remembered the love and care of Mama. All the trust and affection of Ester and the joy of pleasing Father. This is what she wanted to share with this girl. Pouring these feelings into the image of a sad and solitary figure, Molly began to see the barriers that had been set up between them. Slowly peeling back layer upon layer of darkness and despair, she was gradually able to discern the outline of a figure lying on the floor. It was surrounded by what looked like piles of clothes.

Shan watched as Molly concentrated. He watched as her breathing quickened and she became pale. Her face glistened with sweat in the poor light. Gradually he was able to see a figure lying on the floor in front of him. A ghostly shape without colour or substance. He also watched Molly as she started to waver and stumble. He was there to catch her before she fell to the floor, unconscious.

***

Moira had fallen asleep amidst the dirty laundry. Sad, alone and lost, she had not the will to get up and move on. She had simply stayed where she was until sleep softened her misery. Her mother was right. No-one had ever liked her. No-one except Polly, who would now also hate her for what she had done. But what could she do, left alone and unloved in the estate? Avoided by her father. Actively hated by her mother. She had no-one who had ever taken an interest in her. She had never had the chance to let someone like her. No-one until Polly. And now she had proven that she was her mother. Selfish and thoughtless of anyone but herself. Much better not to think about this and know that she was alone and unloved. Better to let the Tower take her and be done with it.

Stirring in a restless and broken sleep, Moira felt the presence of others. Fearful that she had been found by John, or worse, Mr Colin, she forced herself wake. Quickly scanning the room, she failed to see that anyone had entered. She was still alone, scrunched up in the dirty laundry in the corner of the room. Half hidden from sight. Trying to will herself back to sleep, she was continually nagged by the lingering notion that she was being watched.

Raising her head, she looked more carefully. She saw the outline of two figures. One lying on the ground, with the second bent over it. They appeared to be located somewhere in the wall to her left. It was as if she was able to see through the wall while it still remained solid and unyielding. She tested it. Yes, it was there. A rough, unfinished stone wall, as solid as the floor on which she lay. Yet there they were. Seemingly only a few feet from her, but unattainable.

As she watched, the one that was standing turned towards her and took a step forward. It was looking directly at her. The features were indistinct, but it appeared to be speaking. She heard nothing. When she did not respond, the figure raised an arm and with an open hand waved at her. Not sure why, Moira responded in kind. The figure, appearing to be satisfied, went back to tending the one on the ground. Moira watched, spellbound. Unsure what it meant but

218

hoping that it would be something positive. The figure did, at least, look friendly.

***

Molly gradually regained consciousness. Shan had placed the rolled-up sack under her head and was there offering her water as she opened her eyes.

"Rest," he commanded. "It takes a lot out of you."

"Was it working?" were Molly's first words.

"See for yourself," replied Shan, directing her attention to the ghostly figure that was facing them. It appeared to be watching them intently.

"Oh!" cried Molly. "Really? I did it?"

"Well, almost," answered Shan, "but you will need rest before you do anymore."

Molly raised herself on an elbow and waved at the figure. "Can she hear us?" she asked.

"I don't think so. I tried to talk with her. She responded but I couldn't hear her."

"Poor thing. It must be terrifying not knowing what is going on. More so if we look the same to her as she looks to us."

"Drink some water. You should eat something as well. Using Influence drains a lot out of you. This can only help."

"Just a little. We have to keep going. We don't know if one of the Watchers will come back."

Shan just nodded. It was true. They could arrive at any moment. Then their chance to help would be gone. After some water Molly got up and, with help from Shan, moved closer to the figure.

"I'm going to undo some more of the layers," she said to the figure as she closed her eyes and opened her mind to the illusion before her. She could feel the barriers, layer on layer, that separated the girl from them. Gently she felt where the edges were and, with a limitless desire to help, lightly peeled the top off the one beneath, freeing it from the others just for it to fade away by itself. Shan noticed that the figure was getting clearer. He could hear a small, muffled voice.

"We're here to help," he said. "We're not of the Tower," as he raised his arms in a gesture of welcome.

The figure seemed to recognise something that he said and nodded, although her words were indistinct.

Molly continued. She rested at intervals with Shan supporting her and providing her with water and food as she required. The toll on her was obvious but she would not stop. Weary beyond anything she had ever felt before, Molly persisted. Nothing was going to get in the way of helping this girl. Not the Tower, and certainly not any weakness of hers. With such determination, she knew that she would succeed. Finally, with the last layer stripped away, there was Moira, seated on the ground before them. She was clothed once again in black and looking in wonder at the two of them. Molly, giving her a broad, happy smile, once again collapsed into Shan's arms.

Chapter 31

"Is she alright?" asked Moira, looking about and feeling a bit wary of how things had suddenly changed.

"Yes, I think so," replied Shan. "It just took a great deal out of her to break down the illusion between us."

Molly was once again sleeping soundly after the effort exerted.

"Why did she do that?"

"Well, wouldn't you if you found someone who needed help?"

Moira looked down and remained silent. She was not sure that she would, or even could, after what had just happened with Polly. "Did you find anyone else?" she asked.

"No, there was only you. Why, was there someone with you?"

Not wanting to disclose more about what had happened, Moira simply shook her head and demanded, "But how did you find me? How do you know there was no-one else?" She waited and then added in a far gentler tone, "I haven't seen anyone in the Tower since I got here. Well, no-one normal."

Shan ignored the outburst and replied, "Neither had we until we found each other. Molly was able to break the illusion of solitude." Shan paused and looked closely at the girl in front of him. "Sorry, I'm Shan, and this is Molly." He added slowly, "Well … it's one of the things I can do. I can see peoples' Influences. I see them as coloured lights or flames. Yours is red and Molly's is a bluey-green colour. If anyone were near, I would see their light."

"I've never heard of that being one of the major Influences before," declared Moira, "so which one do you have?"

"I can influence air. Molly, well she has perception."

"Oh yes, I'm Moira. Mine can influence the physical body," she volunteered, "but it doesn't seem to be as good as it first sounds. So how did she do that?"

"You will probably have to ask her, but we did meet one person here, a woman who has been helping us. She said that first we have to imagine what we want and picture it clearly in our minds. Then make it real with our wishes and wants. The more we want it, the stronger it will be. But, it does take its toll," he added as he looked over at Molly.

"Yes, it's exhausting," Moira admitted. "Even with practise I found myself only able to use it on occasions and then needed to rest after." She looked at Molly. "It must have been very hard for her."

"Yes, but there was no stopping her. She was going to get you out."

"But you don't even know me."

"Why does that matter?" asked Shan. "You wouldn't ask for an introduction before saving a drowning man, now, would you?"

"No, I suppose not," Moira replied, knowing it was the right thing to say. But even as she did, she was aware that it had not been part of her previous practice. Normally, she would want to know what motives were behind the person. If they were wanting more from her than she would be prepared to give. Here and now, however, this thinking just showed her up to be the selfish image of the mother she hated. This she was determined to change. She was not going to be her mother.

"How long have you been here?" asked Shan.

"It is hard to be sure. At least a few days, but time seems to run a bit differently inside the Tower. I expect it is the lack of sunlight that does that."

"Yes, I think so too. Probably only a few days for each of us as well. That is, if we go by the food they have provided." He paused again before saying, "You know, you look very familiar. But I can't have seen you before."

"Well. I was rather well known outside the Tower," Moira responded with some pride.

"That couldn't be it," Shan mused, totally missing his cue. "I would know if I had seen you before." Looking beyond Molly to the food that still remained he asked, "Are you hungry? We still have some food left. Molly seemed to do quite well in the last encounter with the Watchers."

"The Watchers?"

"Oh, sorry, that's what Molly calls the Dark Ones in here."

"Yes, them," Moira waited.

"Well, the Watchers always come before a challenge. I expect you have been having them as well."

"Yes," was all that Moira said.

Molly began to stir and gradually opened her eyes. After a few moments they focused on Moira, and she gave her a smile. "Oh, it worked. It really did. I can't believe it. Hello, I'm Molly."

"And I'm Moira."

Molly pulled herself into a sitting position as Shan passed her the bottle of water from which she took a drink.

"You're very beautiful," Molly stated, without any note of jealously or derision.

Moira nodded in agreement but added, "I must look an absolute mess. I have yet to find either a brush or a mirror in this place."

"No, neither have I. Not that it would make much of a difference even if I had."

"Oh, I'm sure that you never need one," Moira stated, "and you have such a sweet smile," giving Molly a genuinely stunning one as she made her way over to her. Sitting beside her, she looked into her eyes and gently said, "Thank you. I can only think of one other person who has ever been as kind to me as you have."

Molly reached out and hugged Moira tightly. "I am so glad that you're here."

Awkwardly returning the hug for a moment, Moira rose and looked at the food. "I am a bit hungry. I always just seem to miss the opportunity to eat when it arises."

"Well, help yourself," Shan said. "We're happy to share whatever we have." He began to help Molly up from the floor and back towards their makeshift picnic.

"You are sure?" inquired Moira.

"Of course," added Molly, "better that we all get something to eat instead of two of us being full and one going hungry."

Moira was not sure whether to believe that things were really going this well. She expected that there was some twist coming to catch her out. Still, she sat by the provisions as Molly and Shan joined her. The food was meagre, but the mood was bright. Moira even tried the second bottle that had come with Molly's sack, declaring it a very passable red, but still had no success in getting the others to try it. The conversation was light and easy. They ignored the space about them as they spoke of the Western Slopes, or of the games played with one's sisters, and even of a tile terrace shaded by cherry blossom and surrounded by the music of running water. Eventually the food was gone. They all felt that it was probably time to try and get some sleep. Whether it was nighttime or daytime didn't matter anymore. What mattered was getting food when they could and sleep when they were able. Shan explained to Moira that they would also need to pretend not to be able to see each other if one of the Watchers came. He would make a cooing noise to warn the girls if he saw one coming. With that, they dispersed to separate parts of the chamber to try and rest and prepare for whatever was to come.

***

Shan woke with a start. He hadn't been sleeping that well anyway but now he was wide awake and felt worried. He looked about. Molly was asleep, lying on her side against the wall to his right, but Moira was sitting up and looking around like he was. He caught her eye and shook his head. "No, no Watcher," he mouthed without making a sound.

The lights had not changed. Yet something felt wrong or, at least, different to usual for, as he looked around, what could be called right about this place? Climbing to his feet he went to look down the first corridor to the left. The colours meandered erratically down the hall as normal. There was nothing else discernible. Moving to the corridor nearest Molly he saw the familiar blue light of a Watcher some distance down the hall.

Turning to Moira he cooed softly. Quickly he made his way back to his place in the chamber and waited. Before much time had passed, he saw a black-robed figure emerge from the corridor. He took a moment to prepare himself for his next trial. To his surprise, however, the Watcher did not approach him but stopped in front of the sleeping form of Molly. It just stayed there, poised above her, unmoving.

Confused, Shan looked at Moira. She made it obvious that she could see the Watcher as well, as it stood over the recumbent Molly. Then he heard a familiar voice coming from behind him.

"Oh, what fun, my darling, they found you as well." Quickly Shan turned and saw the woman of the Tower. She glided into the chamber from the other passageway, still shrouded in a multitude of the many coloured tiny lights.

"Mother, won't you ever leave?" Moira fired back. Shan hastily looked at Moira and then back at the woman. Yes, the similarity between them was obvious.

"There is no need to, my dear. I have everything I need right here," came the smug reply.

"And what would that be?" Moira asked sweetly. "Darkness to hide your rotting flesh? No-one to smell the decay you wear as a perfume?"

"Oh, darling, I won't be staying in here much longer." Her mother paused. She looked over at Shan and then at Molly. "As I said, I have everything I need,

224

right here."

Suddenly suspicious, Moira approached her mother. "Say what you mean, you putrefying corpse."

"Mmm. Is that all you have, dear? Try to keep up. Innovation, darling. We must always try to use our intellect."

"Mother. I stopped you once—" started Moira before she was interrupted.

"Yes, you did make this rather inconvenient," was the curt reply. But then, gesturing to Molly, she said, "Darling, I see that you have met my protégé. She does have ability. It is a pity about the packaging but fortunately that is all just perception … and so … easily altered." Shan looked from Moira to her mother, trying to follow the conversation between them with little success.

"Mother!" Moira demanded.

"You deprived me of my body," her mother spat back before in a calmer tone adding, "It has been an inconvenience, to be sure." Looking over at Molly she added, "The Tower can sustain me in here, but it is not possible for it to give me the freedom to leave. For that, I need a living body.' She stopped and looked back at Moira. "One with Influence in the blood. One preferably with *my* Influence." Gesturing with one hand in the direction of Molly, she added, "One must settle with what one can get … but she will do."

"Mother, I won't let you," threatened Moira as she took a step towards the woman.

Laughing, the woman turned her back on Moira. Slowly, she moved towards Molly, scoffing at her daughter. "I'm already dead, my dear. What do you think you can do? Make my cold … dead … heart be still?"

Moira engaged the Influence, pushing forth her senses. She could easily detect Shan's pulse, beating firmly but quickly. Molly's was slow and restful. But for her mother, there was nothing. No pulse, no beat, no breath. There was nothing that she could feel. There was just a cold void where her mother was standing.

Reaching Molly, Mortella turned back to face her daughter. "You should stay and witness this. You are privileged. It is not often that the Tower allows one to take another's body. You might learn something."

Turing to face the Watcher, Mortella gave a simple command, "Let me enter."

The Watcher gave no indication that it had heard but, as Shan watched, the beautiful red-haired woman before him began to change. She no longer wore the figure-hugging emerald gown. Instead, she wore a loose white tunic that hung from wasted, angular shoulders. No longer standing straight and tall, the body started to droop. It leant to the left, allowing one lifeless and withered arm to drag against the thigh. Her stunning, heart-shaped face with the flawless alabaster complexion was slowly replaced by a hollowed-eyed, sunken-cheeked horror. The skin was a decaying dusky green-black that had started to peel away from the bloodless tissue beneath.

Within moments the transformation was complete. The thing that was Moira's mother then remained as still as the Watcher beside her. With the transformation came the overpoweringly sweet smell of decay. It clogged the sinuses and could be tasted on the tongue.

"What was that?" Shan demanded as he turned to Moira.

"That ..." she responded with vitriol, "thing looks exactly as she has always been. It is a vile, selfish and venal creature that I have had the immense pleasure of calling my mother."

"What is she doing? What is happening with Molly?" Shan asked.

Moira glanced at him. The she looked straight into his eyes, as if she were allowing herself to be seen for the first time. "She's dead," she said simply, "and she wants to take Molly's life as her own." Dropping her eyes she continued, "I'm sorry. I didn't know, didn't know until just then."

"And?" demanded Shan.

"And what?" said Moira.

"And what can we do to stop her?"

"I killed her once," Moira explained but then added quickly, "I didn't mean to, but I did. Now I can't stop her," imploring Shan with her eyes. "I would if I could, but my Influence only works on people who are alive."

"So, what is she doing now?" asked Shan.

"I don't know, but I can feel Molly. Her heartbeat is steady and strong. I think she would try and resist if she could?"

Shan turned and ran headlong at Moira's mother. Head down, he rammed his shoulder directly into her back. He ricocheted off the figure and onto the floor without causing her even to totter slightly at the impact. Rapidly climbing to his feet, he stepped back. He recalled Molly's first heart-wrenching embrace. The delight he felt at having a friend in a place like this. He focused on his desire to rescue Molly from the Tower and from the thing before him. Concentrating on his need for Molly and all the things they shared, Shan felt the air become physically tangible in his mind. He was able to compress it and concentrate it. He could bind it together. Pull it from all around him to create a ball of energy. Hold it together with his being and ready it before releasing it to follow his need.

He held it all together as he added more and more until he had no strength to hold more. Directing it at the Watcher and the figure beside it, he let go, allowing the full force of his efforts to explode towards them. Immediately, a torrent of compressed air hit the figures. It rebounded off them, hitting Shan and throwing him back across the chamber. He hit the floor hard. The figures, however, remained exactly where they were. The explosion had merely blown back the hood of the Watcher and torn, and almost removed, the tunic of the creature next to it, revealing a decaying form beneath.

Shan rose slowly from the floor, exhausted with the effort but determined to keep trying. He saw Moira also rising from the floor where she been thrown, on the other side of the chamber. He limped towards the figure, finding the effort required to do so almost beyond his powers. He saw that all was almost exactly as it had been. Yet, for the first time, he saw the face of a Watcher. It appeared to be made of dried and flaking parchment, masquerading as skin. This, together with sullen cheeks and sparse, dry whisps of hair that emerged from an almost bald scalp gave it the look of a dried and dehydrated creature that had perished in a desert. Such an image was created when all that had once made it alive had been sucked out. Only a dry, lifeless shell remained. The eyes, however, where different. They glowed with the same blue light that he saw about the Watchers. As he looked, Moira came up behind him. She caught him just in time, and he collapsed to the floor.

***

Molly had been sleeping soundly. It had probably been her best sleep since arriving at the Tower. Yet, it was all too short as she awoke, groggy and disorientated. It took her a moment to arrange her thoughts but then, even from her position on the floor, she could see that things were different. The same cold, silver-grey light immersed her, but the air felt cooler. It was even more silent then normal. As she slightly raised her head, she could see that she was no longer in the same chamber as before. This one was small. It was only a few strides across in both directions and there were no openings. She sat up and saw the woman standing at the end of the chamber, at her feet.

"Where am I? Where are the others?" she cried out, distressed.

"Oh, darling, you're awake," came the cool reply, totally ignoring Molly's questions. "I have been waiting for some time. Keeping someone waiting is impolite," she admonished.

"But, Shan and ..." Thinking better of it, she refrained from adding more.

"Shan, as you call her, is where she should be and," she continued, giving

227

Molly a conspiratorial little smile, "Moira, my dear, is also where she is and should be."

"You know?" Molly was surprised.

"Of course, my dear, why should I not know?"

"I, well, I just …" Molly stuttered.

"It is of no consequence. That is for the Tower. I am here for other things." The woman walked around Molly and stopped. "Get up, dear," she commanded.

Molly climbed to her feet as instructed. She stood facing the woman in front of her.

The woman looked at her. Her face was gentle and sad as she spoke. "Now, my dear, there is such an important task that I need to ask you to do for me. Do you think that you could? Do you think that you could help me?"

Molly looked back at the most beautiful face that she thought she had ever seen. The eyes were indeed sad. There were tears in the corners. "Of course, if I can," Molly responded. "You have been so good to us. I must at least try."

"Oh, my dear, you are sweet."

The woman raised both her hands towards Molly, indicating for her to take one hand in each of her own.

"My dear, I need you to relax and let your mind go blank. Do you think that you can do that?" Molly noticed that the woman looked concerned.

"It doesn't sound too hard," she said with a smile.

"Good, then shall we begin? Just hold my hands, relax, and think of nothing."

***

Exhausted as he was, Shan was not going to let something happen to Molly. He was thankful that Moira had caught him before he hit the floor for the third time. He allowed her to help him back up to his feet as he supported himself against the wall. He looked carefully at the figures before him.

The Watcher was immobile and mummy-like, with a blue aura. The same blue light was in the eyes. The Watcher seemed less of a threat than the other one. The other was a moist, rotting cadaver with fluid still oozing from the tissue that was falling off in places all over the body. It was still surrounded by a concentration of many different colours. He now knew that these were most likely pieces of other peoples' Influences. They were being used to allow this thing to exist. This one wanted Molly. It wanted to take her and make her its own.

As he watched, the colours started to swirl. They moved in a complex pattern about the form they enveloped. A white vapour gradually started to leak out of the creature within. Before he could decide what was happening Moira was speaking. "I think it's starting," she whispered. "Molly … her breathing is getting faster. Her heart beats are quicker but heavier."

"What's happening?" Shan demanded, furious with himself for not knowing what to do as he turned on Moira. "What have you let happen to Molly?"

"Nothing," she shot back. "This is not me. This is her," she said, pointing at the figure in front.

"But we have to do something," Shan cried, now grabbing the shoulders of the bodily remains before him. He only succeeding in removing several layers of decomposing flesh without moving it at all.

"But what? It's already dead and I cannot affect it. Your wind did nothing," Moira stated, looking horrified as the milky white mist snaked its way toward Molly.

Shan quickly made his way around the figures. He knelt down over Molly. "Molly … Molly!" Shan yelled as he shook her. "Molly, wake up!" but with no effect. Molly remained as she was, as if asleep. Looking back at Moira, Shan commanded, "Help me move her away from it," as he grabbed one of Molly's arms, bringing it above her head. Moira grabbed the other one and they pulled as hard as they could. Molly remained determinedly fixed to the spot.

"The lights are keeping your mother alive. If we can get rid of them …" Shan thought out loud.

"I can't see them," Moira responded. "You will have to do that." The mist reached Molly and slowly started to enter through the nostrils. "I might have an idea," Moira hesitated, "but, it could be dreadful."

"What? More dreadful than Molly being taken?" Shan shot back. "Anything would be better than that." He watched the lights and tried to work out what he could do. As he continued to watch, they gradually started to spin off the remains of the woman and re-joined those randomly moving about the chamber. As more of the mist left the body, more of the lights left as well.

"The lights are leaving your mother!" Shan cried. "As the mist leaves, so do the lights."

"It might be the only option." Moira winced as she turned to face Molly.

***

Molly took the hands as offered and tried to relax. Trying to think of nothing was a lot harder than she thought it would be. Random thoughts would just pop up into her mind without her thinking of them first. Playing with Ester. Making Father's favourite meal. Shan finding her here in the Tower and really being a boy, not a girl.

Then she felt her. A distant twinge on the periphery of her mind. A dark and soulless thing that was hungry, very hungry, for something that Molly could not place. Then within her mind she heard her voice.

"Oh, sweetie, how fascinating … a boy. Not been one of those in the Tower for a very long time. Never had one as a neophyte before. This will require a closer look."

In her mind, Molly now was able to see the woman that had been before her. "What's happening, what are you doing here?" she cried.

"Oh, didn't I explain? My error … merely an oversight. You kindly offered me your body. I unfortunately … lost mine, and needed another."

"No, I didn't!" Molly exclaimed

"Mmm, really, well, my mistake again then. But it's a little too late now, my dear." The woman seemed to move closer to her. "Don't worry, you will still be here," the woman added sweetly. Then with a laugh she added, "Just a little bit of you," and Molly felt a wall start to form about her. A wall similar, yet a little different, to the ones that had most recently surrounded her in the box-like chamber.

"I won't let you!" Molly screamed at her.

"But you already are, dear." Molly felt another two walls surround her. Almost fully enclosing her, yet still allowing her sight of the woman as she gradually became more distinct. "You will be safely tucked in here," the woman appeared to smile, "well out of my way. And there, my dear, you will remain for the rest of our life." The woman was now fully visible to Molly. She was still beautiful, but with eyes that looked at her with condescension and contempt. As if she were insignificant, worthy only of spite.

Frantic, Molly looked about her. She was starting to feel faint. Finding it difficult to breathe. Things were starting to get blurry as she tried to think. The woman now appeared less defined. Molly could no longer hear her talking. Her final thought as she lost consciousness was, *Why?*

***

While Shan knelt by Molly, he saw the lights leave the remains of the woman, who began to slump forward. Any semblance of life became less and less. The mist was continuing to slowly enter Molly. He had no idea what to do. Floundering, he could only wait and watch his friend being violated by the thing before him. Turning to Moira who was kneeling beside him, he saw that she was still and concentrating.

He could see that Molly was getting paler and colder to his touch. He brushed back the hair from her face. Her lips were blue. Thinking that she was cold he began to vigorously rub her shoulders and arms, hoping against hope that she would be able to face and defeat the woman's invasion. He knew it was unlikely. As the last of the lights left the figure, it sank to the ground with a wet, sodden sound. The Watcher turned and silently left the chamber. Moira gave a deep, guttural groan as she too fell forward, panting deeply. It was then that he noted Molly was no longer breathing. Her mouth was slightly open. Her face was drained of all colour.

Desperate, he turned to Moira, tears running down his face. "What's happening?" he sobbed "What's going on?"

"I tried," Moira wailed. "I really did. I really tried," she wept. "I didn't know what else to do. It was all I could think of." She looked at Shan, tears in her eyes. "I couldn't let my mother take her. I had to do something … You said anything would be better."

"What? What did you do?" Shan cried.

"I'm sorry, I thought that it might work," Moira sobbed as she wiped her nose on her sleeve.

"What might?" Shan demanded desperately.

"Mother needed—" Moira abruptly stopped, her attention drawn to Molly. The milky mist was no longer entering their friend, but was starting to return to the inanimate corpse that lay beside them. As it tried to re-enter the corpse it would instead dissipate and dissolve into the air. No longer attempting to reclaim the corpse, it made for Moira and Shan who brushed it away with their hands. Some remained by Molly but it, too, gradually evaporated.

Shan looked at Moira. "It's gone, but Molly is cold and isn't breathing."

Shocked at what she saw before her, Moira was silent until Shan's words sparked her back to life. "Get her onto her back," she commanded. Without questions, Shan helped Moira roll Molly onto her back.

Pushing Shan out of the way, Moira put both her hands onto Molly's chest. Pressing them hard against the cloak, Moira bent her head and let out a scream. A scream of loss and heartbreak. A scream that made Shan look at her and wonder at the amount of hurt that could produce such a sound. As he waited, red light flowed from Moira to Molly, encasing them both in a reddish hue. Removing her hands Moira looked at the cold, unbreathing form of Molly before her. Shan also watched as the red receded. Nothing had changed.

Again, Moira placed her hands on Molly's chest and let forth a scream full of hatred and disgust. "YOU BITCH!" she bellowed. A torrent of vivid crimson rushed from Moira. As the yell subsided, Molly convulsed on the ground before taking a deep, rasping breath. Moira collapsed on top of her.

Shan quickly pulled Moira off Molly. He checked both of them. Moira was breathing quickly, if shallowly, as he rolled her onto her side. When he looked at Molly, he could see a difference. She was no longer blue and pale. Her lips had colour. She was breathing slowly but deeply. He also rolled her onto her side. Once again, he could do no more than wait. He sat alone, wishing and hoping for someone he cared for to wake up. But before too long, he was overcome by exhaustion and fell asleep.

Chapter 32

Moira woke first. It had been a deep, dreamless sleep and she felt rested. Beside her Shan and Molly were still sleeping. Nothing seemed different in the Tower, but she knew that it was. Everything had changed, and how could she ever be the same again? She did not want to dwell on what she had done, or the inevitability that made her do it, but it had worked. In some small way, it allowed her to offer herself a measure of forgiveness for what she had failed to do for Polly.

Climbing to her feet, she stretched. She was amazed how quickly she had gotten used to sleeping on a hard stone floor. It was so different to the down-feathered bed to which she had been accustomed. That life seemed an age ago, although she knew that it had only been a few days. How much more would yet change for her, she had no idea.

All things considered, the happenings in the Tower had moved in a way that made her feel better. She was now more of the someone that she had always wanted to be. She never would have had the chance if the Tower did not come for her. She was always alone in the estate. Abandoned by her sister, ignored by her father, tolerated by the servants, and actively despised by her mother. In here, however, she had been seen as someone to value. By Polly, for simply being a friend.

As for the two who still slept beside her, they had tried to find her without hesitation. Once they had, they welcomed her openly, without asking for anything in return. They had willingly shared what little they had so none of them would be any worse off than the other. She was yet to fully understand what motives could be behind these actions. There must be something more that she was missing. She was unable to work out what it could be. But, for the present, she was genuinely content not to understand. To just accept it for what it was.

She was also getting used to the silver-grey light, the still air, and the lack of any sound. Over time this had dulled her to any sense of danger. What was there to fear anyway? The Tower would do what it would, regardless. So what was the point of being scared? From what Shan had said, she was surrounded by a multitude of absorbed souls. Her mother had implied these were those who had failed in the Tower. They remained trapped in a void somewhere between life and death. No longer individuals, they were here only to serve the Tower. Kept in a limbo of life that allowed their Influences to persist, solely for use by others.

Intermingled with these failed souls were the Watchers. The mummified remains of what she assumed had been slightly more successful neophytes. They wore the black robe but also no longer appeared to have the capacity for independent action. They existed exclusively to carry out the wishes of the Tower, or those in charge of the Tower. She knew also that there were other Dark Ones. Ones who were not like the Watchers. Ones such as those that came to the estate to collect her. All this suggested to her an order in the Code. That there was a hierarchy of power and authority that existed within the Tower, similar to her experience outside the Tower. Those with the power directed the rest. She decided that would be her goal here. As for her mother, she had certainly been from a very different mould to the others. Yet she had still been subject to the Tower. This would require further thought, but for the present she was tired and satisfied with her deductions.

Now fully awake she was aware of a gnawing feeling in the pit of her stomach and a dryness of her throat. She noticed a shadowy pile located on the other side of the chamber. Curious, she wandered over to have a look. On top of the pile were black robes. They were of a lighter material than the one she currently wore. Altogether, there were three.

Looking back at the others and seeing them still asleep, she stripped off her robe and put on a new one. It was soft and silky to the touch, almost sensuous. Although still black and matte, without shine or glimmer, it hung gently about her body. It felt warm, with a breathability that she had only previously experienced with some of her best silk gowns.

Under the robes were three sacks. They were larger than the ones she had seen before. Now really starting to feel the hunger, she opened one of them expectantly. She was not disappointed, for inside she discovered a still-warm loaf of bread and several thick slices of juicy roast beef, with cheese and fruit and two corked bottles. Placing these carefully on the floor, she opened the second sack. Here she found half a roast chicken with all the other additions.

The third was similar but with a number of slices of ham. Once all these were laid out on the floor Moira looked longingly at them. She wondered how hard it would be to wake the others. Fortunately, as she was debating with herself how she could do this without seeming to be the cause, Shan yawned and opened his eyes. "Something smells good," he said.

"Food," was Moira's only reply.

Slowly pushing himself to his feet, he made his way over to Molly and placed a tender hand on her shoulder. As he did, Molly opened her eyes.

"How are you feeling?" he asked gently. Looking directly at him, she gave a small smile.

"As if the cart *did* hit me," she replied.

"Are you hungry?" he asked, looking over to the bounty Moira had set out before them.

"We ate all the food we had," Molly responded.

"All the food we had, but not all the food we have," Moira corrected, and then added, "A whole lot more came while we slept."

Crossing to the others, she helped Shan get Molly onto her feet and they made their way over to the food.

"Do you remember what happened?" Shan asked Molly, helping her to sit beside the feast.

"Mostly, I think," was the response as she took a drink.

"Well?" prompted Shan.

"I'm not sure what to say," Molly began.

"Well, let me then," interrupted Moira. "That woman, the one you met in here … who was helping you … she was planning to destroy you," she said plainly, before continuing with unconcealed loathing. "That was one of the vilest of creatures, one driven entirely by her own desires and incapable of considering or feeling anything more than her own needs." She paused. "That thing … that vile creature … was my caring, loving … mother." Molly looked at her with shock. "Mother dearest needed you …"

"But Moira stopped her," interjected Shan. "If she hadn't done what she did …" Shan looked at Moira. "I'm sorry, I should never have blamed you for what was happening. I was wrong."

Moira returned the look. "Yes, you were. But you know that now, and it is over." Turning her attention to Molly, she asked, "What happened with my mother?"

Molly lowered her head and closed her eyes. She explained what followed once she awoke in the small room, finding herself alone apart from Moira's mother. "I don't remember anything more until waking up here with you," Molly concluded. "Moira, what did you have to do?"

Shan looked at Moira who raised her chin and casually said, "Mother was already dead and needed a living body to be able to continue her loathsome existence." She gave a nonchalant wave of the hand as she added, "I just made sure that that was not possible." After a further pause she continued, "I don't expect that we shall ever need to endure her presence again." Looking defiantly at her companions, and then at the food, she added, "It certainly has given me an appetite."

They started devouring the food that had been provided. It was Shan who stated what was on all their minds. "Three robes and three sacks." The other two looked at him. "Well, then, they know we are together, whoever *they* may be." After taking another bite he said, "And they seem to be okay with it. At least for the present."

"And the food," said Molly. "It's better than we had before."

"Yes, and food normally only comes after a trial with a Watcher," added Shan.

"There was a Watcher," stated Moira.

"Yes, and a trial," said Shan.

"So, you think that the Tower had Mother here solely to be a trial?" asked Moira.

"I don't know. How can we know? But all of us were here and there are three sacks and ..."

"So the Tower made all this happen to test us?" Molly exclaimed, outraged.

"Or used what was already here," suggested Shan.

"But then it must know everything, and see what happens in here." Molly sounded concerned.

"Well, yes, that would seem to be the case," Shan nodded.

"Then it would know," she whispered.

"Know what?" asked Shan.

Molly looked at him apologetically. "The woman found out when she started to ... started to ..."

"Started to take you?" suggested Moira.

"Yes," answered Molly.

"Know what?" pressed Shan.

"That you're a boy," Molly blurted.

Moira looked stunned. "But no male has ever had a major Influence!" she exclaimed, and then added triumphantly, "I knew that seeing Influences as colours was not part of a major Influence."

"So?" asked Shan.

"Well," started Moira coolly, "if it knows that, then it might be best if you were not here in the Tower."

"I saw it happen once outside the Tower," said Molly in a small voice, "and we were planning to get out anyway," she added.

"If it knows and doesn't like it, then why am I still here?" asked Shan.

"Why was my mother here?" asked Moira.

"Good point," Shan conceded. He looked about the chamber but did not see any new lights approaching.

"So, what should we do?" asked Molly. "Remember how your mother got out?"

"Your mother?" Moira looked surprised.

"Another time," Shan said before turning to Molly. "But how do we find the stairs?"

"She said that everything about us is part of an illusion. A part of perception. Perhaps if I can break some of it down …"

"I do remember that when that wall dissolved in front us, the colours about the wall were a bit different than elsewhere," Shan thought aloud.

"Do you think that you would be able to recognise it again?" asked Molly.

"I can only try," Shan shrugged as Moira looked at both of them.

"Well, I think that we still have some time before anything is going to happen … if it is going to happen," she said.

"Why?" asked Shan.

"Why would they still feed you if you were no longer needed? What would be the point of providing a new robe?" she explained, indicating the other two robes still by the chamber wall.

Shan nodded.

"It would be a total waste. They should just have got on with it … if they were going to … as soon as your use was gone," Moira added. "I would have if I were going to get rid of you."

Molly looked warily at Shan as Moira spoke, her eyebrows furrowed, and lips pressed together. "Well, be that as it may," she began, pointing a finger at Shan, "you are going to have to stay close to us at all times from now on. If you ever see another Watcher come, you let us know."

"Oh no," interjected Moira, "no, no, not a Watcher." The others stared at her. "There are always three. I doubt that a Watcher would be able to absorb anyone," she continued matter-of-factly. "No, there would have to be three. There would have to be a proper Dark One to do that."

After looking at Moira in silence for a moment Molly continued, "Well, you will let us know if you see any of them coming, and especially if there are three."

***

Having all eaten their fill, packed away the remaining food and changed into the new robes, they decided to head out of the chamber and along the central corridor. Shan was not yet convinced that the Tower knew that he was a boy. Even if it did, it didn't seem to bother it. Even so, as he had already said to Molly, they were going to get out of the Tower. There was now no reason to delay the search for a way out.

His plan, as he explained to the others, was to make their way to the outer-most wall of the Tower. This seemed to him the best place to find stairs that might lead to a window or a way out of the darkness.

"So that we don't just keep wandering in circles, we need to follow a plan whenever we come to more than one passage," he said.

"Like when I kept my left hand on the wall as I wandered here on the first night," suggested Molly.

"Yes, something like that, but if we do what you did, we could just walk in circles," Shan explained.

"We need to keep taking a path that will move us away from the centre of the Tower," said Moira.

"Yes," replied Shan, nodding at Moira, "at the first choice we will take the one that goes left."

"And then the one after that we will take the one that goes to the right," said Moira.

"Absolutely," said Shan, looking at Moira with a new level of respect. "That way we will not walk in circles and the corridors will keep pushing us outward from the place we started."

"How does it do that?" asked Molly.

"By simple geometry," said Moira.

"Geomtree? What's that?"

"Just a form of torture invented to make the day go slowly," responded Moira.

"I quite liked it," objected Shan.

"Anyway, that would work in a normal tower," said Moira, ignoring Shan's comment, "but may do nothing here if what we see about us is only perception and not real."

"Well, we have Molly who can help with that, and I am able to see any changes in the movement of the colours."

"I'm not totally useless either," Moira added irritably.

"Of course not," soothed Molly, putting a hand on Moira's arm and giving her a smile. "Without you I wouldn't be here." And then, looking about the darkness she added slowly, "If you can do what you did then, if more than Watchers come, we're going to look to you."

Shan nodded at Moira. "That's true," he said.

Moira looked from one to the other. It was true that she was their best defence. She felt content that others knew that as well. The Dark Ones were not at all like the Watchers and, as long as they were alive, then she knew what she could do. It also felt good to be part of a team that was working together, even if the goal was basically impossible. She was not at all convinced that she would want to leave the Tower even if given the opportunity. What was waiting outside for her? A life controlled by others. A poor option compared to what the Tower might provide. Still, she gave them a smile and nodded her approval.

They arrived at the first choice and took the passage on the left. Shan noted the lights continued to move in random patterns with no order or obvious purpose. Thinking back on the time the wall dissolved before them, he remembered there had been an abundance of the bluey-green colour. He was unsure, however, if this was just him being aware of Molly and her aura or if it was the woman surrounded by her lights. Still, as Molly's Influence was perception, it would make sense that a concentration of this colour could indicate where the perception was being used to greater effect. It at least gave him something to look for.

They continued on. They took the next right and then, after that, the left-most passage. They were also being careful to try and maintain some sense of their original direction. Although it was hard, they were doing their best not to be fully turned around by the maze of corridors and heading back in the direction that they had come. Through chambers and past alcoves they went. Nothing and everything seemed familiar. Without any real distinguishing features anywhere, they could not be sure that they had not already passed through any particular place earlier. Of one thing only were they absolutely sure; none of them had ever found their way back to the antechamber with the great door.

After what must have been several hours of walking, they finally sat down in the centre of a larger chamber with six corridors leading off it.

"How big is this place?" complained Molly. "From the bottom of Town, it looked big," she continued, "but it takes me less time to walk from the market gates to the north side. And that has to be further."

"We must have got turned around," said Shan.

"Not necessarily," challenged Moira. Shan looked at her expectantly. Happy that she had their attention, she continued, "I have studied this Tower my whole life, so I think I know a few things."

"And?" Shan prompted. "We're listening."

"Town rises up to the Tower and the Tower then rises high above Town, but backs onto the Eastern Slopes."

"Yes. I see it from my attic room," said Molly.

"Well, it backs onto the Eastern Slopes," repeated Moira. She waited without either of them responding. "So, who said that we're still in the Tower?" she added, in an exasperated voice.

"So, you think that we are in tunnels … under the mountains?" asked Shan.

"It would explain why we can keep on going and going without ever getting to the Tower wall," Moira surmised.

"But then there could be hundreds of layers of rock above us right at this moment," Shan said.

"It could also explain why there has never been a breeze, and why everything is always so quiet," Moira added.

"But then, what do we do?" asked Molly, looking at each of them in turn.

Shan remained silent, unsure of what to say. If they were truly in passages within the mountains, they could be a very long way from the Tower itself. They had already walked for days. That could put them leagues away from the great door. "So, what do you suggest?" he asked, looking at Moira.

She looked directly back at him. "That we have a drink and see what the Tower has for us next," she said, taking out one of the water bottles, unstoppering it and taking a drink. Once finished, she passed it to Molly who had not quite been paying attention. She fumbled the bottle, allowing it to fall to the floor with a loud crack. The stone bottle met the stone floor, spilling some of its contents. Against all laws of nature, the sound did not reverberate around them. There was no echo. The sound stopped as sharply as it began, as if it had hit the walls and been engulfed by them.

"Sorry," said Molly, "I was just trying to remember what sunshine felt like."

"Don't worry, Molly, we have the other two bottles with water, and those other three if we really are desperate," soothed Shan before returning to his own thoughts.

Moira got up and began to look down each of the corridors. "Not much of a choice," she commented.

"No," said Molly as she played with the small puddle of water that was starting to trickle towards her. "They all look the same and all lead to more of the same."

"Yes," said Shan hopelessly. "Just more and more of the same."

"Well, we can't just stay here. Which one do you want to take?" asked Moira.

Looking up, Shan shrugged. "Does it matter?" Then, looking over at Molly, he cocked his head on the side and watched. "Molly, did you make that trail of water?" he asked.

"No, the puddle did that. It looks a bit like a one-legged chicken now."

Shan looked behind him where a corridor led off from the chamber, indistinguishable from any of the others. He took one of the bottles of wine from the sack and uncorked it.

"It is good wine," said Moira.

"I'm not drinking it," said Shan irritably as he got up and entered the corridor. He poured a puddle of wine onto the floor and waited. Gradually it began to move slightly toward the chamber. "We go this way," he said, pointing up the corridor.

"Why?" asked Molly.

"Because this one leads uphill, and uphill must get us closer to the surface."

Going back into the chamber he packed the sacks. "Come on," he said, "we just have to keep going uphill. We have enough wine to see which corridors do that."

As the girls rose Shan took another look around the chamber. Something was a bit different. He was not sure what, but the coloured dots seemed a bit less erratic in their movements. They were moving in a more regular, circular orbit about the room. Unsure, but unconcerned, he turned and led the way into the passage that took the three of them away from the chamber and uphill.

Chapter 33

Molly was watching carefully as they walked. She knew that Shan would look out for her, but she was not so sure that he would do the same for himself. He certainly did not seem to feel a matching level of urgency as hers to get out of the Tower. She had determined to just keep checking on him for any sign that something had changed. She would not just let him shrug it off and ignore it if there was.

Moira and Shan were talking as they walked. It was something about heights and depths, but she was not able to follow half of what they said. She was not sure about Moira. Shan said that she had saved her from the woman. She believed that, even if she was unsure of what had been done. Neither of them would give her much more detail, apart from that Moira had stopped her mother. That meant that the Tower's power to keep her alive had ended. Again, this was not something that she fully understood. How could someone who was dead still be alive? Dead was dead, but then, this was the Tower.

Moira was beautiful. She knew many more things than Molly did, but also seemed a little bit too comfortable with the Tower. Molly found that odd. She also had been less than excited about the idea of getting out of the Tower. Then there was her mother. Her mood could change in an instant from being friendly and open to cold and distant. Shan was a bit awkward at times, but he was always consistently himself. Molly was not sure how to deal with someone like Moira. Someone who could change so rapidly. She might even be hiding things. Shan wasn't, but Moira … Molly felt there was a lot more behind that perfect face than she was saying. She was also determined to keep a watch on Moira. If the woman was a test, then perhaps Moira was as well.

They had been walking for some time, stopping at each passage junction to pour some wine on the floor and see which way it ran. At times it was not very clear which corridor was best to take, so a joint decision was made, and they continued on. Every so often Molly would ask Shan if he saw anything that was different. To this he would reply, "No different to anything I have seen before," but Molly was sure that he was not telling her the whole truth. She would not say that aloud but would just look at him until he looked away in confusion, thus confirming her impression.

Shan was continually scanning the air about him as he walked. He was enjoying talking with Moira. The topics were many and varied. Apart from Maima, he had never had a chance to talk to anyone like this in his whole life. Maima. He had not thought about Maima in days. That made him feel very guilty. How was she? Was she getting better? Was Farmer Albee able to get the girl from the hamlet to help? Did Johnathon get back home? What did Johnathon think when he went missing? What did Maima think? She would naturally think that the Tower had him. Would that make her get sick again? So many questions with no answers, and no way of letting them know that he was alright. Well, they would get out. Then he could send them a message. It probably would not be safe to go back there, but they would know that he was okay.

He was still not sure how they would get out. But he was determined that they would. He had promised Molly that they would. Moira, on the other hand. She might not want to go. Her whole life she had been looking at the Tower and wanting to be part of it. Was it what she expected? He thought not, but then, what had she expected? Her mother had obviously been linked to the Tower. Moira did not seem like her mother. Talking with her made him feel that she could not be like her mother. She wanted to be different. She wanted to do something with her life. How could that be bad? Like him, she had studied. She knew things. That meant that she must know that their Influences and knowledge should be used to help those who could not help themselves. Like Maima did with her herbs and healing skills.

They stopped for a rest and something to eat. There was not much left, but it was enough to relieve hunger pains. They were all tired and conversation was sparse. Molly made sure that they did not rest for long. She was determined to keep them going until they had at least arrived somewhere that showed they had achieved something. Chiding them until they rose to their feet, Molly took the lead into the passage, calling on the others to follow. Reluctantly they did. Both were unconvinced they would ever get anywhere that would satisfy Molly.

Moira started off and immediately began to lag a few paces behind the other two. She was tired. She would never admit that to anyone. She would not be the one to succumb to fatigue first. Exercise was not something she was used to. She never had to go and fetch as everything had always been brought to her. Thinking about it, most of her day had been sitting in one place or another. The occasional stroll when she was bored. Bored, yes; she had been bored all too often. She had not been a good student, trying her best to avoid the tasks set for her by her tutor. Speaking with Shan, however, she realised that she really had learnt quite a lot. She had never had a chance until now to use such knowledge, but with Shan it was fun. His excitement about learning and books startled her. How could anyone feel that way? But the more they spoke, the more she started to feel a twinge of regret that she had not put more effort into her studies.

Moira's experience with boys was limited, to say the least. It had solely consisted of seeing the stable hands muck out the stalls. Her experience with men was equally limited. They had viewed her as merely a means to an end, paying her attention only to win favour with her father. To get a step closer to the power they would derive from a connection to her family – a connection that would be gained through an association with her. None of them had ever been interested in her, in what she said or what she thought. Shan, however, listened to every word she uttered and weighed it thoroughly before answering, giving all that she said due consideration. This made her far more careful in what she said. She racked her brains for the facts she had somewhere stored there so that she would not make a fool of herself. She found that she liked these conversations and had to admit a grudging respect for Shan and his ability.

Molly reminded her of Polly, an open book. Not a page of which could not be read by the expression on her face. Molly was sweet and kind. Things that would make life very difficult for her. Just as they had for Polly. She wondered how Polly was. Had Polly even been real? She did not know anymore but had to believe that Polly was real.

Polly had been her friend. That was too important to have been imagined. She made herself believe. Outside the Tower she had no friends. It had taken the Tower to show her that she was not so unlovable that no-one would like her. Here, she was one of a group. That meant more to her than all the fine crystal and silks she had to forego to come here. Would she be able to stay in the Tower if they went? Yes, she could choose to stay, but would she want to if they were no longer here? Deep inside, she hoped that they would not find a way out. That they would continue as they were, the three of them here, together in the Tower. As she was thinking, Molly turned around and urgently beckoned her to catchup.

Molly looked worried and said as Moira reached them, "Shan thinks something has changed."

Moira directed her attention to Shan who looked rather subdued. His eyes were darting around, obviously seeing things that she could not. His demeanour was so different to his normally confident exterior. "The lights are starting to swarm," he said, waving his arms above his head.

"What does that mean?" asked Moira.

"It's what they did before the light exploded," answered Molly.

"Before they were taken by the Tower," added Shan.

"Who was?" asked Moira.

"We don't know. But we think the Tower absorbed an unsuccessful one of us," Molly explained.

"But there aren't any Dark Ones here … are there?" Moira queried.

"No, not that I can see, but there weren't any last time, either," said Shan. "They didn't seem to be needed."

"But why? Why now?" asked Moira.

"How can we know?" said Shan. "Perhaps they do know and don't want me."

"Or it could be any of us," said Molly.

That last comment suddenly caught Moira's attention. "But we are successful," she said.

"Are we?" questioned Molly. "Who decides that? We certainly don't."

Now also starting to feel concerned, Moira looked about the corridor. "How can we find out?"

"When it happens, it happens, and then we will know," replied Shan.

"And until then?" Moira exclaimed.

"Until then we need to avoid staying in one place," Shan answered. "Let's move," he said. With that, he lifted the robes to his knees and started to run along the corridor. He was closely followed by Molly. Moira took a moment to look behind her. There in the distance, on the edge of her vision, she thought she saw a shape slightly darker than the surrounding gloom. Filled with a terror she had never felt before, she too turned and, hitching up her robes, raced after the others.

***

They kept up a fair pace. The initial run had only lasted less than half a league before all of them were too tired to run further. Shan confirmed the lights were no longer swirling. He indicated that they could stop for a rest before heading on. Molly collapsed on the floor and leant against the wall as she closed her eyes and steadied her breathing.

"We just can't keep on running," complained Moira. "We have to have some other plan."

"And what would that be?" asked Shan irritably. "Any ideas?"

Moira remained quiet.

"We can't see the lights, only Shan can. Who knows, it could all happen before we even know it," Molly exclaimed, terrified. "To be made a part of this place; what could be worse?"

Moira had to agree. To be ever made a part of this place without the power and authority was worse than … well, worse than being back in the estate, she thought. She felt confident that the lights would not be coming for her. Then again, she could not be absolutely sure. Perhaps this was her mother's final revenge. It would be just the type of thing she would do. She couldn't risk it. Not until she was sure. Until then she would just have to keep up with the others.

"There may have been a Dark One back there," she announced.

"A Watcher?" asked Molly.

"Couldn't tell," said Moira.

"Does it matter?" interrupted Shan. "But Moira is right, we can't just keep on running."

"A Watcher would suggest that this is a trial," said Molly crossly.

"And you want to wait and find out?" asked Shan, turning towards her impatiently.

Molly looked back at him. "No," she admitted quietly, "but what else can we do? Eventually they will catch up with us."

"If we can get back into the Tower, we might have the chance to find something," Shan said hopefully.

"That's not very specific," Moira said petulantly.

"No, it isn't," shot back Shan. "Perhaps you can come up with a better idea with all your study of the Tower?"

Moira glared at him as he glared back.

"This is not helping," Molly said crossly, looking from one to the other. "All we have in here is each other, so stop being such grouchy little toddlers and let's work together."

Shan looked at Molly with surprise. "She's right, you know." Looking at Moira he added, "I'm sorry. Any knowledge you have of the Tower could be vital."

Moira gave a haughty sniff but also conceded, "We will do better together if it is coming for us."

"Then let's try to work something out," suggested Molly.

"There are windows high up in the Tower. My mother escaped through one of them," said Shan. "She jumped and used Influence to soften her fall."

"So how is that going to help us?" asked Moira. "I can't jump out of a window and survive."

"No, neither can I," added Molly.

"Well, we need to get back to the great door then," said Shan.

"Even if we get there, they're not just going to leave it open for us," grumbled Moira.

"No, they're not. But once we're there, we can try and work that bit out."

"If we get there," added Moira.

"Is there an alternative?" said Shan as he turned his back on Moira. "The lights are starting to swarm again. We will have to move on soon."

"Ooooh, yuck! What's that?" cried Molly, jumping up quickly from the floor. She extended her hands so they could all see. A thick, oily substance was coating the palm of her hand. Sticky and sweet-smelling, it appeared to have a reddish tinge in the low light. Behind her, Molly saw that the same substance was now lightly coating the wall where she had been sitting. It was slowly oozing onto the floor. Turning back to the others, she saw Shan staring at the ooze with a horrified look on his face.

"We need to go," he said. "We need to go *now!*"

Without another word, he grabbed Molly's arm and started dragging her along the passage while yelling at Moira, "This is worse. The Tower's getting ready to take one of us." Not needing further explanation, Moira raced after the others.

***

Fear can fuel the muscles for only so long. They had already been walking for what must have been most of a day before the threat became real. But necessity kept them going, even if their pace had slowed dramatically. The last of the wine had been used at the last intersection while the remaining water had been rationed and drunk, with the empty bottles discarded. What had remained of the food had been eaten earlier but none of them felt the slightest twinge of hunger.

As they walked, they continually scanned the passage in front and behind them for any form, or shadow, that could indicate a Dark One. The walls now glistened in the silver light. It was as if they were coated in the sweat that clung to the three as they progressed. The air was still. There was no hint of a breeze.

It felt heavy, with a slightly sweet odour that just hung in the space, clogging the nostrils. Talk was scarce, each conserving what little strength they had.

As they moved, Shan watched the lights. There was now a greater concentration of them surrounding the three, although their movements were still erratic. They were not spiralling as he had seen before. The red and turquoise of Moira's and Molly's Influence glowed brightly, belying their exhaustion as they entered a new chamber.

This one was different. It was unlike any that Molly had seen before. It was massive. So large that she was unable to see the wall opposite nor the end of the walls to her left or right. The walls themselves were unlike any she had ever seen before in the Tower. These were of unfinished black rock. There were not smooth or regular and rose up further than the eye could see in the low light.

Moira stopped and gazed about, aware of how small a figure she was in such an enormous space. Shan broke the silence with a small voice, "It happened here. I'm sure of it." He looked at Molly and then at Moira. "It was here that the amber light was taken." In silence they stood. Paying a moment of respect to one of their own who had been lost to the Tower.

"It feels wrong," said Molly slowly. "I don't think we should be here." As she spoke there came a thud that was felt through the feet rather than heard. After a few moments came a second thud that was slightly stronger, and then a third. This one came a bit quicker than the last, and was slightly stronger again.

Shan grabbed an arm of each of the girls. "The Tower is getting ready," he said, looking upward at the many coloured lights that populated the space. "The lights are not swarming. Not yet, but they will," he added, turning to leave the chamber through the corridor behind them.

As they did, they met a dark form standing in the centre of the passage. Shan could see a blue light coming from it.

"A Watcher!" cried Molly.

"No, a Dark One," corrected Moira. This one was alive. She backed away from it, scanning the space about her for any others.

"There is only one," added Shan breathlessly. "I don't see any other lights," as the floor vibrated again under their feet.

"We can't go that way," whispered Molly, staring at the immobile figure.

"This way," called Shan, running off to the right. Molly and Moira followed closely behind. All were aware of the regular throbbing that now continued under their feet as they ran. Like a giant aroused, the Tower was waking from hibernation. It was hungry and looking for sustenance.

Chapter 34

Shan led the way down the cavern, keeping the wall to his right. He scanned the area ahead for any of the telltale blue lights. The colours were concentrated in the air above them, shadowing their progress as they ran. They were not yet swirling. Molly was beside him with Moira a pace behind. His aim was to get them out of the cavern. This was where it seemed to happen. It was where the Dark Ones wanted them. He was not going to lie down and just let it happen. He would fight. Right up until the time when there was no fight left in him.

The wall to his right remained unbroken as they ran. There was a vast expanse off to the left that continued into the gloom without end. At some point, they would have to find an exit. Desperation drove them forward, adrenaline alone providing them the energy to continue. Stopping was not an option. Eventually fatigue would set in. It would slow their progress until they could go no further.

He ran, continually checking that the other two were keeping up. Molly panted beside him. She gave him a slight smile as he looked. Moira was starting to lag behind. Indicating to Molly to slow their pace, they dropped back to Moira. No-one would be left. He nodded at Moira to provide some encouragement, and felt a tug from Molly on his arm, causing him to stop.

Barely having breath to speak, Molly pointed to the wall. "There," she puffed. Looking closely, he saw. There, nestled in the rough outline of the rock, was a narrow and irregular opening. Almost completely hidden from the direction that they had come by a protruding part of the wall, it was just discernible as a fissure in the rock. Not waiting for discussion, Shan made for the opening. Seeing no blue lights within, he entered it, beckoning the others to follow.

Rough-hewn stairs led upward. Without hesitation he started to climb. The prospect of stairs after an age of walking and running was something that would cause even the best to waiver in their determination. As he made his way up, Molly called out for him to stop. Turning, he saw Moira had collapsed on the bottom-most step, shielded and comforted by Molly.

Returning to the bottom he sat down beside them and scanned the area. "The lights are calm now," he stated and added, "I think that we could all do with a rest," as he patted Moira's arm. "We all need a break. This is as good a place as any."

Moira raised her face towards him, giving him a look of gratitude before hanging her head again in complete exhaustion.

Molly, looking at the stairs looming above them, simply said, "There's a lot of them," before also lowering her head. There they sat, silent, minds blank with exhaustion, catching their breath.

After a while Shan rose. He peered through the opening to the cavern. He could see the colours moving in erratic patterns high above him. They were not swarming, nor were there any Dark Ones discernible by their lights. Coming back to the others he gently suggested that they should start the climb. Each of them looked in despair at the steps rising above them. Together, with Shan between the two girls and each supporting the other, they began. One step after the other, resting a moment on each before tackling the next.

How many steps, none of them had the energy to count. All focus was directed at placing the next foot on the step ahead. Heads bowed, they concentrated only on the step before them. Keeping a hold of each other helped stabilise them. When a leg would fail, threatening a fall, it was Shan that held them up, willing them to keep going. Together, they were stronger than alone. They drew energy from each other and gave encouragement when they themselves had nothing left. All they had was each other and that was going to be enough. It had to be.

Time was in limbo as everything repeated itself over and over again. Step, pause, breathe, rest; step, pause, breathe, rest, when, unexpectedly, they found that there were no longer any steps ahead of them. Lifting their gazes, they discovered that they were standing in one of the alcoves that were scattered about the corridors of the Tower. The walls were once again smooth and finished. The space was filled with the silver-grey light. Cautiously moving into the hall, they turned back, only to be confronted by a solid wall behind them. No sign of the stairs they had just climbed. The wall was complete, solid and impenetrable.

Crumbling to the floor they rested with their backs against the wall. Safe was a word that came to mind, but they were still in the Tower. That was anything but safe. Tired, with throats parched, they collected what strength they had. Molly gave a small cry of disbelief. "I know this spot. I've been here before. On the first night I was here."

"How can you tell?" asked Shan, as Molly pointed to a small defect in the corner leading to the alcove.

"I did that. So I could find this spot again," she said.

"Why?" asked Moira.

Molly went quiet and blushed slightly without further explanation.

"Ooooh," said Moira, "I discovered that as well."

"What? What did you discover?" asked Shan, as both the girls looked at him.

"You didn't?" asked Molly in disbelief.

"Didn't what?" he asked, confused.

Moira looked at Molly and said, "Just anywhere? I knew boys were revolting," giving a slight giggle which Molly returned.

"Never mind, Shan. It's a girl thing," added Molly. "But it means that we must be back in the Tower. Now we just have to find the great door. I was coming from that direction." She climbed to her feet. "No time like the present, as Mama always says," she called, beginning to walk down the corridor.

"Wait!" cried Shan, "We need to look at the alcove."

"Why?" asked Moira. "You might find more than you were hoping for," giving another giggle that was echoed in a smile from Molly. Shan just looked at them and rolled his eyes.

"Because this has been changed by the illusion of perception, that's why. I need to look at the colours and see if there's something that shows that it has." Looking at Molly he asked, "Do you have the strength to probe it with Influence?"

Molly nodded and returned to stand before the alcove as Shan stood and examined the space about him. The erratic movements of the colours were unchanged, without a predominance of any one colour. He had hoped that there would be something obvious for him to see but nothing in the corridor alerted him to any difference at this spot.

Disappointed, he looked at Molly who was concentrating on the wall before her. As he waited, he paced the floor and stood on something irregular. Looking down, he saw the fragment of stone that Molly had broken off the wall. He picked it up, and it felt cool to the touch. He moved to the wall and placed the fragment into the corresponding defect. It looked different to the section from which it had come. The fragment was black – a deep, solid black – while the wall was black with a slight tinge of green. It was similar, but different, to the ooze that had been black with a tinge of red. The walls of the corridor outside the alcove were definitely a black-black, without the hint of any other colour. Excited, he waited for Molly to finish.

After a few minutes, Molly broke her concentration and looked at the others. "I can feel that there is something there, like a sheet covering it, but I can't seem to do anything else. I'm sorry."

"Don't be sorry. That's amazing that you can do anything. We're all so tired," said Shan, going on to explain what he saw. "If I can just see the difference, then we have a way to find them."

"Look!" cried Moira, pointing down the corridor. They saw a hooded figure, standing in the shadows, slowly raise one arm towards them.

As it did, Shan saw the lights started to coalesce above them. "It's making the lights swarm," he yelled. "Run!"

***

Reaching one of the larger chambers they slowed their pace. The figure had not followed them, and the lights had once again calmed. Shan took out the fragment and looked at it. He compared it to the walls about him. All were the same deep black colour without anything else. Disappointed, he put the fragment away.

"Now that we're back in the Tower, how do we find the entrance?" Moira asked.

"We go back to what we were doing originally," answered Shan, "alternate between the left and right passages. That should take us to the outer walls of the Tower. From there, I suppose we just have to keep looking."

"I don't expect that we will get any more sacks," pondered Molly.

"Not until the Tower is satisfied," Shan agreed.

"Well, we better be quick. We won't make it much further," observed Moira.

"I know," Shan said and then continued, "you wait here, I will quickly check the corridors for any Watchers."

Not having the energy to object, the girls sat on the floor in the middle of the chamber. They sat together, back to back, so that they could see all five entrances while Shan made his way into the first of the corridors. Each was engrossed in their own thoughts. Both were weary beyond measure and had started to drift off to sleep when they were abruptly roused by Shan racing back into the chamber, yelling at them to get up. As they did, they saw black-cloaked figures emerge from two of the three corridors on the right. Shan stared at the figures. They stopped at the entrance to the chamber.

"There's another one in that corridor!" he bellowed, pointing to the passage between the other two.

A third hooded figure appeared at the entrance to the chamber. It stood motionless between the others. Horrified, they watched as all three raised their right arms and pointed. Directly at Shan.

"It's me they want," he wailed as he pulled all his energy into himself, wishing and desiring his Influence to explode towards them. Concentrating and drawing on the essence of who he was, he formed a ball of air, making it denser and harder than steel before hurling it towards the nearest figure.

They all felt the air as it raced towards the hooded figure that stood, unmoving, directly in its path. As it was about to hit the air dissipated, all its force and power removed.

Shan slumped to the floor. The three hooded figures started to take slow and purposeful steps forward. Their arms remained pointed at Shan as they moved, deliberate and unhurried. Molly attempted to help Shan to rise without success. She stared at the figures, terrified. Not knowing what to do she tried to drag him away to the corridor on the left. Shan was too heavy for her and had yet to regain enough strength to help himself. Under their feet, the regular thumping of the Tower recommenced. Barely discernible at first, it quickly gained in strength, making the whole chamber vibrate with each beat. Behind the approaching figures, the walls glistened in the low light. They slowly converged on the centre of the chamber and Shan.

Beside them Moira stood rigidly erect in defiance of the impending threat. Molly called for her for help to support Shan. She ignored the plea. Instead, she stood unmoving, staring straight ahead at the central approaching figure.

Placing her body between Shan and the Dark Ones, Molly waited for the inevitable. She remembered the love of her family. If this was to be her final independent thought before being melded to the Tower, it had to be a good one. She waited. Her eyes were closed, cradling Shan. Together they waited. They had nothing left with which to fight.

They waited and nothing happened. Opening her eyes, Molly saw Moira slumped on the floor a few paces away from them. Turning her head, she saw that the central Dark One was also just a heap of robes on the floor. The other two stood silently, arms no longer pointing at Shan.

Shan, having now recovered a little strength, pushed Molly toward Moira. Racing to her side she found Moira breathing heavily but awake.

"Are you alright?" Molly cried.

"I told you I could do something," she responded breathlessly, "if they were a true Dark One." She paused. "There has to be three."

Shan slowly made his way over to Moira. "Can you walk?"

"I can try," she responded as the other two gave what support they could to help her rise. Once up, she said, "We might as well get going. We still have a bit more to do and," looking at the figure on the floor while giving a rueful smile, "there really is only a limited amount of time."

Each now was standing and holding onto another. Together, the three of them exited the chamber, trying to get a bit further away from imminent danger.

***

Slowly they made their way along the corridor. Gradually Shan and Moira gained back a little strength. Finally, they could walk unaided, allowing Molly a slight respite. Taking out the stone fragment, Shan constantly compared it to the walls around him. The lights above were once again erratic while the Tower remained silent and the walls dry.

Their progress was limited but they kept to the plan, taking the right- and then left-most passage at each intersection. Walking and resting in spurts, they saw no other figures but were now hungry, as well as thirsty. The physical discomfort was sapping their energy even further. Eventually, there were no more right-turning passages, giving hope that they had reached the outermost wall of the Tower.

Sitting against the wall in the corner of a small room that only had two entrances, they rested. The one on the left was the one by which they had come while the other went off at a right angle.

"We must be at the outer wall," Shan wished aloud. "It just must be a matter of time before we get to the great doors."

The others merely looked at him, having nothing to add. Taking out the stone fragment for the hundredth time, Shan peered at the walls opposite him. Black, just black, without any hint of green. Perhaps he had been mistaken in the alcove. Perhaps he had just imagined it. Rising once again to continue the journey, he looked at the wall behind him. There, to his great surprise, was a patch of wall that had an unmistakable tinge of green.

Whooping in delight he turned to the others. "There!" he pointed. "There it is. That wall. It's not real!" Grabbing Molly by the arm he pulled her to the wall, placing her directly in front of the patch he saw.

"What can you feel?" he asked expectantly.

"Ahh, what?" Molly exclaimed.

"And?" pressed Shan.

"Give me a moment," she complained. "It takes a bit."

Waiting impatiently Shan paced round the room. After a few moments Molly said, "I can definitely feel it there. There are edges to it that stop here and here," pointing to several places on the wall. "It's like a curtain covering something."

"Can you undo it?" Shan asked impatiently.

"Shan ..." admonished Moira. "Give her time. We all know that it takes a lot of effort."

Suitably chastised, Shan nodded and remained silent but continued to pace the room.

Molly stood transfixed by the wall, oblivious to Shan's frustration. Time passed and Molly remained as she was. Shan paced frequently, looking at Molly and obviously wanting to ask but holding his tongue. Moira sat listlessly off to the side, trying to be engaged in what was happening but too tired to care.

Eventually Molly boke her concentration and turned excitedly to the others. "There, just up there," she pointed. "I got the corner to start to peel back."

"What's behind it?" Shan pressed.

"Well, wall at present," Molly responded. "It's just the corner." Feeling his disappointment, she continued, "It's coming off, it is. It just takes time."

"We don't have time," Shan grumbled.

"Shan!" snapped Moira.

"I'm sorry, Molly," he said, turning to her. "That's amazing what you have done." Then, stopping, he added, "Do you think we should stay here and try, or move on?"

As he spoke, they felt the floor shudder with the all too familiar beat of the Tower. Looking up, Shan saw the colours start to circle above his head. Then to his horror he saw dark-hooded figures. There was one in each of the two corridors. Just standing. Still. Unmoving.

"Molly," he whispered pointing to the figures, "we're trapped."

"No!" she cried, turning to the wall and placing both hands on it. Summoning what little reserve was left, she focused her will, drawing on the strength she received from all those others in her life. From Mama and Father, Ester and Lucy, Shan, and Moira. Pulling them together she intensified their love by the love she had for them. Binding it all together, she aimed it all at the centre of the wall. She combined all her desires and wishes with the essence of who she was. She was ready to give it her all, regardless of the cost to herself, when the illusion dropped, revealing a curving set of stairs in front.

"Well done, Molly!" shrieked Shan as he helped Moira to cross onto the stairs, beckoning Molly to do the same. When she did the wall reappeared behind her, as solid and impenetrable as it had been before.

The thumping ceased as they sat, disbelieving, on the first few steps.

"Can they get through?" Moira asked.

"I don't know," Shan replied. "Molly, what do you think?"

Molly looked at them confused. "Umm, I don't know, but I didn't do that."

"Do what?" Shan asked.

"Open the stairs. I was about to try … when it just happened."

"You must have done it. Perhaps it started to undo when you peeled back the corner," Shan said. "It just took time."

Molly looked unconvinced but said nothing.

Looking around, Shan added, "More stairs!" while starting to rise.

As he did, Moira looked up at him and asked, "Are you really sure that they are wanting you?"

"Yes," he replied. "The lights swirl about me, not you or Molly. That means it must be me."

"Then you need to make sure you get out of here." A pause. "I can't climb any more stairs. I'll just slow you down. They might get you because of me."

"It's because of you that I'm still here," objected Shan. "We are stronger together. We can help you."

"No, be logical. If they don't want me then I am in no danger. I don't have the energy to do what I did again. So what use am I? All I am, is something that will pull you down." Looking at the floor, she said, "Don't put me in the position that I am the reason they got you. Please," she begged. "I've never been of any use to anyone before. It is good to know that I can be. Don't let them get you. Don't let me be the cause. If they do come through, I might be able to slow them."

Exchanging a look with Molly, all that Shan could do was nod. "I will come back for you, I promise."

Molly knelt down beside Moira and hugged her. "I will be back as soon as I can. Stay here so I can find you."

Moira nodded. "Don't forget me," she said as Shan and Molly turned to slowly make their way up the stairs.

***

The spiral stairs went on and on. Slow and steady, unable to rush, they continued. How high they climbed they couldn't tell. No window or landing broke the snake-like stairs. Without an immediate threat they could no longer rely on adrenaline to fuel their climb. They rested between short bursts of activity. Finally, they reached a landing, the first flat surface they had encountered since they began. Sitting on the top-most step they caught their breath, allowing their legs a bit of relief before moving on.

Behind them was an open door. A reddish light emanated from the door, but it was so different to the red that had coated the walls below. This one spoke of life and hope in the way that the other had evoked death and despair. Rising, they followed the light into a circular chamber. There they saw a single great window framing a glorious sunset over the Western Slopes. Transfixed by the view, they went to the window and stood there taking in the view and feeling a gentle breeze on their faces. Looking down, Molly pointed, "My house is down there."

"And mine is over there," said Shan pointing to the sunset in front of them.

In silence they thought of family and loved ones, wondering if they were well and what they were doing. Wiping a tear from her face, Molly said, "We made it. You can leave the Tower."

Gazing at the drop below, Shan looked worried. "I've never done this before. It's a long way down." Pausing, he added, "My mother barely survived it."

Molly looked at him with sympathy. "If there was another way…"

"But there isn't," Shan concluded.

"No," she said, shaking her head. Taking his hand she added, "You have to. Don't let the Tower win. At least one of us got out."

"Do you want me to give a message to your family?" he asked.

Molly smiled as another tear trickled down her cheek. "Say … say that I'm doing well. That I have friends here and … and that I love them and miss them very much.' Wiping away the tear she added, "Oh, and give Ester a huge hug for me."

"I will, I promise. I will find a way to get you out of here. Then you will be able to give Ester a hug yourself." Looking out the window again, Shan asked, "So, how should I do this?"

"I suppose you get ready and then … jump," she said.

"Sounds a lot easier than it is," he laughed. "Perhaps I might have a bit more of a rest first. Make sure I have enough energy."

"It's never going to be easy, no matter how long you wait," said Molly.

Turning to face her, Shan spoke softly. "Molly, you're the best friend I've ever had. I'm not going to forget you. Don't ever forget me. You promise?"

"How could I ever forget you?" she said, clasping him in a bearlike embrace that he returned with equal force.

As they separated the Tower shook. Looking about they saw a shadow within the doorway. It was quickly joined by a second. The Tower shook again. The first entered the chamber. Shan suddenly became aware that he saw no coloured lights here. There were none circling overhead, yet the beat of the Tower continued. The second hooded figure entered the room. It was quickly followed by a third. As Molly and Shan watched, each raised an arm and pointed it towards Shan. From the central figure came a voice, "They are not to be tolerated."

Molly turned to Shan and yelled, "Now … GO!" As she did, Shan leapt over the windowsill. He felt the cool evening air encompass him as a friend. Enfolded within the rushing wind, he began his fall.

The End

About the Author

Ian C Lawrance was born in Wollongong in NSW the youngest of three children. On finishing school he completed a Medical degree at Sydney University and went on to specialise in gastroenterology and complete a PhD in Molecular Medicine at the John Curtin School of Medical Research at the Australian National University. From there he undertook at Post-doctoral fellowship in the USA before returning to Australia and moving to Perth where he continued his basic Science and Clinical research as a Professor at the University of Western Australia. He is currently an Adjunct Professor and continues his research work having published over 120 peer-reviewed research papers and a number of book chapters.

He has four children and as yet no grandchildren. He is involved in the arts as an ambassador to STRUT Dance, plays the Alto Sax and learnt vocal technique for several years. He even considered pursuing a Musical Theatre career.

As an avid Fantasy and Science fiction reader as a teenager he loved the way new worlds could be created and populated by the imagination. He also loved the classics, particularly Jane Austen and the way she wrote in such beautiful melodic waves of prose. Having talked about writing a fantasy novel for over 30 years it has finally come to fruition. He wanted to try to write it in a way that was a little bit different to the standard fantasy novel and so here is the result, his debut novel the first of a three part series 'Blood Influence Vol 1'.